T0143823

Sir Gibbie

Sir Gibbie

George MacDonald

MINT EDITIONS

Sir Gibbie was first published in 1879.

This edition published by Mint Editions 2021.

ISBN 9781513272283 | E-ISBN 9781513277288

Published by Mint Editions®

 MINT
EDITIONS

minteditionbooks.com

Publishing Director: Jennifer Newens
Design & Production: Rachel Lopez Metzger
Project Manager: Micaela Clark
Typesetting: Westchester Publishing Services

Contents

I

The Earring

"Come oot o' the gutter, ye nickum!" cried, in harsh, half-masculine voice, a woman standing on the curbstone of a short, narrow, dirty lane, at right angles to an important thoroughfare, itself none of the widest or cleanest. She was dressed in dark petticoat and print wrapper. One of her shoes was down at the heel, and discovered a great hole in her stocking. Had her black hair been brushed and displayed, it would have revealed a thready glitter of grey, but all that was now visible of it was only two or three untidy tresses that dropped from under a cap of black net and green ribbons, which looked as if she had slept in it. Her face must have been handsome when it was young and fresh; but was now beginning to look tattooed, though whether the colour was from without or from within, it would have been hard to determine. Her black eyes looked resolute, almost fierce, above her straight, well-formed nose. Yet evidently circumstance clave fast to her. She had never risen above it, and was now plainly subjected to it.

About thirty yards from her, on the farther side of the main street, and just opposite the mouth of the lane, a child, apparently about six, but in reality about eight, was down on his knees raking with both hands in the grey dirt of the kennel. At the woman's cry he lifted his head, ceased his search, raised himself, but without getting up, and looked at her. They were notable eyes out of which he looked—of such a deep blue were they, and having such long lashes; but more notable far from their expression, the nature of which, although a certain witchery of confidence was at once discoverable, was not to be determined without the help of the whole face, whose diffused meaning seemed in them to deepen almost to speech. Whatever was at the heart of that expression, it was something that enticed question and might want investigation. The face as well as the eyes was lovely—not very clean, and not too regular for hope of a fine development, but chiefly remarkable from a general effect of something I can only call luminosity. The hair, which stuck out from his head in every direction, like a round fur cap, would have been of the red-gold kind, had it not been sunburned into a sort of human hay. An odd creature altogether the child appeared, as, shaking the gutter-drops from his little dirty hands, he gazed from his bare knees on the curbstone at the woman of rebuke. It was but for a moment. The next he was down, raking in the gutter again.

The woman looked angry, and took a step forward; but the sound of a sharp imperative little bell behind her, made her turn at once, and re-enter the shop from which she had just issued, following a man whose pushing the door wider had set the bell ringing. Above the door was a small board, nearly square, upon which was painted in lead-colour on a black ground the words, "Licensed to sell beer, spirits, and tobacco to be drunk on the premises." There was no other sign. "Them 'at likes my whusky 'ill no aye be speerin' my name," said Mistress Croale. As the day went on she would have more and more customers, and in the evening on to midnight, her parlour would be well filled. Then she would be always at hand, and the spring of the bell would be turned aside from the impact of the opening door. Now the bell was needful to recall her from house affairs.

"The likin' 'at craturs his for clean dirt! He's been at it this hale half-hoor!" she murmured to herself as she poured from a black bottle into a pewter measure a gill of whisky for the pale-faced toper who stood on the other side of the counter: far gone in consumption, he could not get through the forenoon without his morning. "I wad like," she went on, as she replaced the bottle without having spoken a word to her customer, whose departure was now announced with the same boisterous alacrity as his arrival by the shrill-toned bell—"I wad like, for's father's sake, honest man! to thraw Gibbie's lug. That likin' for dirt I canna fathom nor bide."

Meantime the boys attention seemed entirely absorbed in the gutter. Whatever vehicle passed before him, whatever footsteps behind, he never lifted his head, but went creeping slowly on his knees along the curb still searching down the flow of the sluggish, nearly motionless current.

It was a grey morning towards the close of autumn. The days began and ended with a fog, but often between, as golden a sunshine glorified the streets of the grey city as any that ripened purple grapes. To-day the mist had lasted longer than usual—had risen instead of dispersing; but now it was thinning, and at length, like a slow blossoming of the sky-flower, the sun came melting through the cloud. Between the gables of two houses, a ray fell upon the pavement and the gutter. It lay there a very type of purity, so pure that, rest where it might, it destroyed every shadow of defilement that sought to mingle with it. Suddenly the boy made a dart upon all fours, and pounced like a creature of prey upon something in the kennel. He had found what he had been looking for so long. He sprang to his feet and bounded with it into the sun, rubbing it as he ran upon what he had for trousers, of which there was nothing below the knees but a few streamers, and nothing above the knees but the body of the garment, which had been—I will not say made for, but last worn by a boy three times his size. His feet, of course, were bare as well as his knees and legs. But though they were dirty, red, and rough, they were nicely shaped little legs, and the feet were dainty.

The sunbeams he sought came down through the smoky air like a Jacob's ladder, and he stood at the foot of it like a little prodigal angel that wanted to go home again, but feared it was too much inclined for him to manage the ascent in the present condition of his wings. But all he did want was to see in the light of heaven what the gutter had yielded him. He held up his find in the radiance and regarded it admiringly. It was a little earring of amethyst-coloured glass, and in the sun looked lovely. The boy was in an ecstasy over it. He rubbed it on his sleeve, sucked it to clear it from the last of the gutter, and held it up once more in the sun, where, for a few blissful moments, he contemplated it speechless. He then caused it to disappear somewhere about his garments—I will not venture to say in a pocket—and ran off, his little bare feet sounding thud, thud, thud on the pavement, and the collar of his jacket sticking halfway up the back of his head, and threatening to rub it bare as he ran. Through street after street he sped— all built of granite, all with flagged footways, and all paved with granite blocks—a hard, severe city, not beautiful or stately with its thick, grey, sparkling walls, for the houses were not high, and the windows were small, yet in the better parts, nevertheless, handsome as well as massive and strong.

To the boy the great city was but a house of many rooms, all for his use, his sport, his life. He did not know much of what lay within the houses; but that only added the joy of mystery to possession: they were jewel-closets, treasure-caves, indeed, with secret fountains of life; and every street was a channel into which they overflowed.

It was in one of quite a third-rate sort that the urchin at length ceased his trot, and drew up at the door of a baker's shop—a divided door, opening in the middle by a latch of bright brass. But the child did not lift the latch—only raised himself on tiptoe by the help of its handle, to look through the upper half of the door, which was of glass, into the beautiful shop. The floor was of flags, fresh sanded; the counter was of deal, scrubbed as white almost as flour; on the shelves were heaped the loaves of the morning's baking, along with a large store of scones and rolls and baps—the last, the best bread in the world—biscuits hard and soft, and those brown discs of delicate flaky piecrust, known as buns. And the smell that came through the very glass, it seemed to the child, was as that of the tree of life in the Paradise of which he had never heard. But most enticing of all to the eyes of the little wanderer of the street were the penny-loaves, hot smoking from the oven—which fact is our first window into the ordered nature of the child. For the main point which made them more attractive than all the rest to him was, that sometimes he did have a penny, and that a penny loaf was the largest thing that could be had for a penny in the shop. So that, lawless as he looked, the desires of the child were moderate, and his imagination wrought within the bounds of reason. But no one who has never been blessed with only a penny to spend and a mighty hunger behind it, can understand the interest with which he stood there and through the glass watched the bread, having no penny and only the hunger. There is at least one powerful bond, though it may not always awake sympathy, between mudlark and monarch—that of hunger. No one has yet written the poetry of hunger—has built up in verse its stairs of grand ascent—from such hunger as Gibbie's for a penny-loaf up—no, no, not to an alderman's feast; that is the way down the mouldy cellar-stair—but up the white marble scale to the hunger after righteousness whose very longings are bliss.

Behind the counter sat the baker's wife, a stout, fresh-coloured woman, looking rather dull, but simple and honest. She was knitting, and if not dreaming, at least dozing over her work, for she never saw the forehead and eyes which, like a young ascending moon, gazed at her over the horizon of the opaque half of her door. There was no greed in those eyes—only much quiet interest. He did not want to get in; had to wait, and while waiting beguiled the time by beholding. He knew that Mysie, the baker's daughter, was at school, and that she would be home within half an hour. He had seen her with tear-filled eyes as she went, had learned from her the cause, and had in consequence unwittingly roused Mrs. Croale's anger, and braved it when aroused. But though he was waiting for her, such was the absorbing power of the spectacle before him that he never heard her approaching footsteps.

"Lat me in," said Mysie, with conscious dignity and a touch of indignation at being impeded on the very threshold of her father's shop.

The boy started and turned, but instead of moving out of the way, began searching in some mysterious receptacle hid in the recesses of his rags. A look of anxiety once appeared, but the same moment it vanished, and he held out in his hand the little drop of amethystine splendour. Mysie's face changed, and she clutched it eagerly.

"That's rale guid o' ye, wee Gibbie!" she cried. "Whaur did ye get it?"

He pointed to the kennel, and drew back from the door.

"I thank ye," she said heartily, and pressing down the thumbstall of the latch, went in.

"Wha's that ye're colloguin' wi', Mysie?" asked her mother, somewhat severely, but without lifting her eyes from her wires. "Ye maunna be speykin' to loons i' the street."

"It's only wee Gibbie, mither," answered the girl in a tone of confidence.

"Ou weel!" returned the mother, "he's no like the lave o' loons."

"But what had ye to say till him?" she resumed, as if afraid her leniency might be taken advantage of. "He's no fit company for the likes o' you, 'at his a father an' mither, an' a chop (shop). Ye maun hae little to say to sic rintheroot laddies."

"Gibbie has a father, though they say he never hid nae mither," said the child.

"Troth, a fine father!" rejoined the mother, with a small scornful laugh. "Na, but he's something to mak mention o'! Sic a father, lassie, as it wad be tellin' him he had nane! What said ye till 'im?"

"I bit thankit 'im, 'cause I tint my drop as I gaed to the schuil i' the mornin', an' he fan't till me, an' was at the chopdoor waitin' to gie me't back. They say he's aye fin'in' things."

"He's a guid-hertit cratur!" said the mother,—"for ane, that is, 'at's been sae ill broucht up."

She rose, took from the shelf a large piece of bread, composed of many adhering penny-loaves, detached one, and went to the door.

"Here, Gibbie!" she cried as she opened it; "here's a fine piece to ye."

But no Gibbie was there. Up and down the street not a child was to be seen. A sandboy with a donkey cart was the sole human arrangement in it. The baker's wife drew back, shut the door and resumed her knitting.

II

Sir George

The sun was hot for an hour or two in the middle of the day, but even then in the shadow dwelt a cold breath—of the winter, or of death—of something that humanity felt unfriendly. To Gibbie, however, bare-legged, bare-footed, almost bare-bodied as he was, sun or shadow made small difference, except as one of the musical intervals of life that make the melody of existence. His bare feet knew the difference on the flags, and his heart recognized unconsciously the secret as it were of a meaning and a symbol, in the change from the one to the other, but he was almost as happy in the dull as in the bright day. Hardy through hardship, he knew nothing better than a constant good-humoured sparring with nature and circumstance for the privilege of being, enjoyed what came to him thoroughly, never mourned over what he had not, and, like the animals, was at peace. For the bliss of the animals lies in this, that, on their lower level, they shadow the bliss of those—few at any moment on the earth—who do not "look before and after, and pine for what is not," but live in the holy carelessness of the eternal now. Gibbie by no means belonged to the higher order, was as yet, indeed, not much better than a very blessed little animal.

To him the city was all a show. He knew many of the people—some of them who thought no small things of themselves—better than they would have chosen he or any one else should know them. He knew all the peripatetic vendors, most of the bakers, most of the small grocers and tradespeople. Animal as he was, he was laying in a great stock for the time when he would be something more, for the time of reflection, whenever that might come. Chiefly, his experience was a wonderful provision for the future perception of character; for now he knew to a nicety how any one of his large acquaintance would behave to him in circumstances within the scope of that experience. If any such little vagabond rises in the scale of creation, he carries with him from the street an amount of material serving to the knowledge of human nature, human need, human aims, human relations in the business of life, such as hardly another can possess. Even the poet, greatly wise in virtue of his sympathy, will scarcely understand a given human condition so well as the man whose vital tentacles have been in contact with it for years.

When Gibbie was not looking in at a shop-window, or turning on one heel to take in all at a sweep, he was oftenest seen trotting. Seldom he walked. A gentle trot was one of his natural modes of being. And though this day he had been on the trot all the sunshine through, nevertheless, when the sun was going down there was wee Gibbie upon the trot in the chilling and darkening streets. He had not had much to eat. He had been very near having a penny loaf. Half a cookie, which a stormy child had thrown away to ease his temper, had done further and perhaps better service in easing Gibbie's hunger. The green-grocer woman at the entrance of the court where his father lived, a good way down the same street in which he had found the lost earring, had given him a small yellow turnip—to Gibbie nearly as welcome as an apple. A fishwife from Finstone with a creel on her back, had given him all his hands could hold of the sea-weed called dulse, presumably not from its sweetness, although it is good eating. She had added to the gift a small crab, but that he had carried to the seashore and set free, because it was alive. These, the half-cookie, the turnip, and the dulse, with the smell of the baker's bread, was all he had had. It had been rather one of his meagre days. But it is wonderful upon how little those rare natures capable of making the most of things will live and thrive. There is a great deal more to be got out of things than is generally got out of them, whether the thing be a chapter of the Bible or a yellow turnip, and the marvel is that those who use the most material should so often be those that show the least result in strength or character. A superstitious priest-ridden Catholic may, in the kingdom of heaven, be high beyond sight of one who counts himself the broadest of English churchmen. Truly Gibbie got no fat out of his food, but he got what was far better. What he carried—I can hardly say under or in, but along with those rags of his, was all muscle—small, but hard, and healthy, and knotting up like whipcord. There are all degrees of health in poverty as well as in riches, and Gibbie's health was splendid. His senses also were marvellously acute. I have already hinted at his gift for finding things. His eyes were sharp, quick, and roving, and then they went near the ground, he was such a little fellow. His success, however, not all these considerations could well account for, and he was regarded as born with a special luck in finding. I doubt if sufficient weight was given to the fact that, even when he was not so turning his mind it strayed in that direction, whence, if any object cast its reflected rays on his retina, those rays never failed to reach his mind also. On one occasion he picked up the pocket-book a gentleman had just dropped, and, in mingled fun and delight, was trying to put it in its owner's pocket unseen, when he collared him, and, had it not been for the testimony of a young woman who, coming behind, had seen the whole, would have handed him over to the police. After all, he remained in doubt, the thing seemed so incredible. He did give him a penny, however, which Gibbie at once spent upon a loaf.

It was not from any notions of honesty—he knew nothing about it—that he always did what he could to restore the things he found; the habit came from quite another cause. When he had no clue to the owner, he carried the thing found to his father, who generally let it lie a while, and at length, if it was of nature convertible, turned it into drink.

While Gibbie thus lived in the streets like a townsparrow—as like a human bird without storehouse or barn as boy could well be—the human father of him would all day be sitting in a certain dark court, as hard at work as an aching head and a bloodless system would afford. The said court was off the narrowest part of a long, poverty-stricken street, bearing a name of evil omen, for it was called the Widdiehill— the place of the gallows. It was entered by a low archway in the middle of an old house, around which yet clung a musty fame of departed grandeur and ancient note. In the court, against a wing of the same house, rose an outside stair, leading to the first floor; under the stair was a rickety wooden shed; and in the shed sat the father of Gibbie, and cobbled boots and shoes as long as, at this time of the year, the light lasted. Up that stair, and two more inside the house, he went to his lodging, for he slept in the garret. But when or how he got to bed, George Galbraith never knew, for then, invariably, he was drunk. In the morning, however, he always found himself in it—generally with an aching head, and always with a mingled disgust at and desire for drink. During the day, alas! the disgust departed, while the desire remained, and strengthened with the approach of evening. All day he worked with might and main, such might and main as he had—worked as if for his life, and all to procure the means of death. No one ever sought to treat him, and from no one would he accept drink. He was a man of such inborn honesty, that the usurping demon of a vile thirst had not even yet, at the age of forty, been able to cast it out. The last little glory-cloud of his origin was trailing behind him—but yet it trailed. Doubtless it needs but time to make of a drunkard a thief, but not yet, even when longing was at the highest, would he have stolen a forgotten glass of whisky; and still, often in spite of sickness and aches innumerable, George laboured that he might have wherewith to make himself drunk honestly. Strange honesty! Wee Gibbie was his only child, but about him or his well-being he gave himself almost as little trouble as Gibbie caused him! Not that he was hard-hearted; if he had seen the child in want, he would, at the drunkest, have shared his whisky with him; if he had fancied him cold, he would have put his last garment upon him; but to his whisky-dimmed eyes the child scarcely seemed to want anything, and the thought never entered his mind that, while Gibbie always looked smiling and contented, his father did so little to make him so. He had at the same time a very low opinion of himself and his deservings, and justly, for his consciousness had dwindled into little more than a live thirst. He did not do well for himself, neither did men praise him; and he shamefully neglected his child; but in one respect, and that a most important one, he did well by his neighbours: he gave the best of work, and made the lowest of charges. In no other way was he for much good. And yet I would rather be that drunken cobbler than many a "fair professor," as Bunyan calls him. A grasping merchant ranks infinitely lower than such a drunken cobbler. Thank God, the Son of Man is the judge, and to him will we plead the cause of such— yea, and of worse than they—for He will do right. It may be well for drunkards that they are social outcasts, but is there no intercession to be made for them—no excuse to be pleaded? Alas! the poor wretches would storm the kingdom of peace by the inspiration of the enemy. Let us try to understand George Galbraith. His very existence the sense of a sunless, dreary, cold-winded desert, he was evermore confronted, in all his resolves after betterment, by the knowledge that with the first eager mouthful of the strange element, a rosy dawn would begin to flush the sky, a mist of green to cover the arid waste, a wind of song to ripple the air, and at length the misery of the day would vanish utterly, and the night throb with dreams. For George was by nature no common man. At heart he was a poet—weak enough, but capable of endless delight. The time had been when now and then he read a good book and dreamed noble dreams. Even yet the stuff of which such dreams are made, fluttered in particoloured rags about his life; and colour is colour even on a scarecrow.

He had had a good mother, and his father was a man of some character, both intellectually and socially. Now and then, it is too true, he had terrible bouts of drinking; but all the time between he was perfectly sober. He had given his son more than a fair education; and George, for his part, had trotted through the curriculum of Elphinstone College not altogether without distinction. But beyond this his father had entirely neglected his future, not even revealing to him the fact—of which, indeed, he was himself but dimly aware—that from wilful oversight on his part and design on that of others, his property had all but entirely slipped from his possession.

While his father was yet alive, George married the daughter of a small laird in a neighbouring county—a woman of some education, and great natural refinement. He took her home to the ancient family house in the city—the same in which he now occupied a garret, and under whose outer stair he now cobbled shoes. There, during his father's life, they lived in peace and tolerable comfort, though in a poor enough way. It was all, even then, that the wife could do to make both ends meet; nor would her relations, whom she had grievously offended by her marriage, afford her the smallest assistance. Even then, too, her husband was on the slippery incline; but as long as she lived she managed to keep him within the bounds of what is called respectability. She died, however, soon after Gibbie was born; and then George began to lose himself altogether. The next year his father died, and creditors appeared who claimed everything. Mortgaged land and houses, with all upon and in them, were sold, and George left without a penny or any means of winning a livelihood, while already he had lost the reputation that might have introduced him to employment. For heavy work he was altogether unfit; and had it not been for a bottle companion—a merry, hard-drinking shoemaker—he would have died of starvation or sunk into beggary.

This man taught him his trade, and George was glad enough to work at it, both to deaden the stings of conscience and memory, and to procure the means of deadening them still further. But even here was something in the way of improvement, for hitherto he had applied himself to nothing, his being one of those dreamful natures capable of busy exertion for a time, but ready to collapse into disgust with every kind of effort.

How Gibbie had got thus far alive was a puzzle not a creature could have solved. It must have been by charity and ministration of more than one humble woman, but no one now claimed any particular interest in him—except Mrs. Croale, and hers was not very tender. It was a sad sight to some eyes to see him roving the streets, but an infinitely sadder sight was his father, even when bent over his work, with his hands and arms and knees going as if for very salvation. What thoughts might then be visiting his poor worn-out brain I cannot tell; but he looked the pale picture of misery. Doing his best to restore to service the nearly shapeless boots of carter or beggar, he was himself fast losing the very idea of his making, consumed heart and soul with a hellish thirst. For the thirst of the drunkard is even more of the soul than of the body. When the poor fellow sat with his drinking companions in Mistress Croale's parlour, seldom a flash broke from the reverie in which he seemed sunk, to show in what region of fancy his spirit wandered, or to lighten the dulness that would not unfrequently invade that forecourt of hell. For even the damned must at times become aware of what they are, and then surely a terrible though momentary hush must fall upon the forsaken region. Yet those drinking companions would have missed George Galbraith, silent as he was, and but poorly responsive to the wit and humour of the rest; for he was always courteous, always ready to share what he had, never looking beyond the present tumbler—altogether a genial, kindly, honest nature. Sometimes, when two or three of them happened to meet elsewhere, they would fall to wondering why the silent man sought their company, seeing he both contributed so little to the hilarity of the evening, and seemed to derive so little enjoyment from it. But I believe their company was necessary as well as the drink to enable him to elude his conscience and feast with his imagination. Was it that he knew they also fought misery by investments in her bonds—that they also were of those who by Beelzebub would cast out Beelzebub—therefore felt at home, and with his own?

III

MISTRESS CROALE

The house at which they met had yet not a little character remaining. Mistress Croale had come in for a derived worthiness, in the memory, yet lingering about the place, of a worthy aunt deceased, and always encouraged in herself a vague idea of obligation to live up to it. Hence she had made it a rule to supply drink only so long as her customers kept decent—that is, so long as they did not quarrel aloud, and put her in danger of a visit from the police; tell such tales as offended her modesty; utter oaths of any peculiarly atrocious quality; or defame the Sabbath Day, the Kirk, or the Bible. On these terms, and so long as they paid for what they had, they might get as drunk as they pleased, without the smallest offence to Mistress Croale. But if the least unquestionable infringement of her rules occurred, she would pounce upon the shameless one with sudden and sharp reproof. I doubt not that, so doing, she cherished a hope of recommending herself above, and making deposits in view of a coming balance-sheet. The result for this life so far was, that, by these claims to respectability, she had gathered a clientele of douce, well-disposed drunkards, who rarely gave her any trouble so long as they were in the house though sometimes she had reason to be anxious about the fate of individuals of them after they left it.

Another peculiarity in her government was that she would rarely give drink to a woman. "Na, na," she would say, "what has a wuman to dee wi' strong drink! Lat the men dee as they like, we canna help them." She made exception in behalf of her personal friends; and, for herself, was in the way of sipping—only sipping, privately, on account of her "trouble," she said—by which she meant some complaint, speaking of it as if it were generally known, although of the nature of it nobody had an idea. The truth was that, like her customers, she also was going down the hill, justifying to herself every step of her descent. Until lately, she had been in the way of going regularly to church, and she did go occasionally yet, and always took the yearly sacrament; but the only result seemed to be that she abounded the more in finding justifications, or, where they were not to be had, excuses, for all she did. Probably the stirring of her conscience made this the more necessary to her peace.

If the Lord were to appear in person amongst us, how much would the sight of him do for the sinners of our day? I am not sure that many like Mistress Croale would not go to him. She was not a bad woman, but slowly and surely growing worse.

That morning, as soon as the customer whose entrance had withdrawn her from her descent on Gibbie, had gulped down his dram, wiped his mouth with his blue cotton handkerchief, settled his face into the expression of a drink of water, gone demurely out, and crossed to the other side of the street, she would have returned to the charge, but was prevented by the immediately following entrance of the Rev. Clement Sclater—the minister of her parish, recently appointed. He was a man between young and middle-aged, an honest fellow, zealous to perform the duties of his office, but with notions of religion very beggarly. How could it be otherwise when he knew far more of what he called the Divine decrees than he did of his own heart, or the needs and miseries of human nature? At the moment, Mistress Croale was standing with her back to the door, reaching up to replace the black bottle on its shelf, and did not see the man she heard enter.

"What's yer wull?" she said indifferently.

Mr. Sclater made no answer, waiting for her to turn and face him, which she did the sooner for his silence. Then she saw a man unknown to her, evidently, from his white neckcloth and funereal garments, a minister, standing solemn, with wide-spread legs, and round eyes of displeasure, expecting her attention.

"What's yer wull, sir?" she repeated, with more respect, but less cordiality than at first.

"If you ask my will," he replied, with some pomposity, for who that has just gained an object of ambition can be humble?—"it is that you shut up this whisky shop, and betake yourself to a more decent way of life in my parish."

"My certie! but ye're no blate (over-modest) to craw sae lood i' my hoose, an' that's a nearer fit nor a perris!" she cried, flaring up in wrath both at the nature and rudeness of the address. "Alloo me to tell ye, sir, ye're the first 'at ever daured threep my hoose was no a dacent ane."

"I said nothing about your house. It was your shop I spoke of," said the minister, not guiltless of subterfuge.

"An' what's my chop but my hoose? Haith! my hoose wad be o' fell sma' consideration wantin' the chop. Tak ye heed o' beirin' fause witness, sir."

"I said nothing, and know nothing, against yours more than any other shop for the sale of drink in my parish."

"The Lord's my shepherd! Wad ye even (compare) my hoose to Jock Thamson's or Jeemie Deuk's, baith i' this perris?"

"My good woman,—"

"Naither better nor waur nor my neepers," interrupted Mistress Croale, forgetting what she had just implied: "a body maun live."

"There are limits even to that most generally accepted of all principles," returned Mr. Sclater; "and I give you fair warning that I mean to do what I can to shut up all such houses as yours in my parish. I tell you of it, not from the least hope that you will anticipate me by closing, but merely that no one may say I did anything in an underhand fashion."

The calmness with which he uttered the threat alarmed Mistress Croale. He might rouse unmerited suspicion, and cause her much trouble by vexatious complaint, even to the peril of her license. She must take heed, and not irritate her enemy. Instantly, therefore, she changed her tone to one of expostulation.

"It's a sair peety, doobtless," she said, "'at there sud be sae mony drouthie thrapples i' the kingdom, sir; but drouth maun drink, an' ye ken, sir, gien it war hauden frae them, they wad but see deils an' cut their throts."

"They're like to see deils ony gait er' lang," retorted the minister, relapsing into the vernacular for a moment.

"Ow, deed maybe, sir! but e'en the deils themsels war justifeed i' their objection to bein' committed to their ain company afore their time."

Mr. Sclater could not help smiling at the woman's readiness, and that was a point gained by her. An acquaintance with Scripture goes far with a Scotch ecclesiastic. Besides, the man had a redeeming sense of humour, though he did not know how to prize it, not believing it a gift of God.

"It's true, my woman," he answered. "Ay! it said something for them, deils 'at they war, 'at they preferred the swine. But even the swine cudna bide them!"

Encouraged by the condescension of the remark, but disinclined to follow the path of reflection it indicated, Mistress Croale ventured a little farther upon her own.

"Ye see, sir," she said, "as lang's there's whusky, it wull tak the throtro'd. It's the naitral w'y o' 't, ye see, to rin doon, an' it's no mainner o' use gangin' again natur. Sae, allooin' the thing maun be, ye'll hae till alloo likewise, an' it's a trouth I'm tellin' ye, sir, 'at it's o' nae sma' consequence to the toon 'at the drucken craturs sud fill themsels wi' dacency—an' that's what I see till. Gang na to the magistrate, sir; but as sune's ye hae gotten testimony—guid testimony though, sir—'at there's been disorder or immorawlity i' my hoose, come ye to me, an' I'll gie ye my han' to paper on't this meenute, 'at I'll gie up my chop, an' lea' yer perris—an' may ye sune get a better i' my place. Sir, I'm like a mither to the puir bodies! An' gin ye drive them to Jock Thamson's, or Jeemie Deuk's, it'll be just like—savin' the word, I dinna inten' 't for sweirin', guid kens!—I say it'll just be dammin' them afore their time, like the puir deils. Hech! but it'll come sune eneuch, an' they're muckle to be peetied!"

"And when those victims of your vile ministrations," said the clergyman, again mounting his wooden horse, and setting it rocking, "find themselves where there will be no whisky to refresh them, where do you think you will be, Mistress Croale?"

"Whaur the Lord wulls," answered the woman. "Whaur that may be, I confess I'm whiles laith to think. Only gien I was you, Maister Sclater, I wad think twise afore I made ill waur."

"But hear me, Mistress Croale: it's not your besotted customers only I have to care for. Your soul is as precious in my sight as any of which I shall have to render an account."

"As Mistress Bonniman's, for enstance?" suggested Mrs. Croale, interrogatively, and with just the least trace of pawkiness in the tone.

The city, large as it was, was yet not large enough to prevent a portion of the private affairs of individuals from coming to be treated as public property, and Mrs. Bonniman was a handsome and rich young widow, the rumour of whose acceptableness to Mr. Sclater had reached Mistress Croale's ear before ever she had seen the minister himself. An unmistakable shadow of confusion crossed his countenance; whereupon with consideration both for herself and him, the woman made haste to go on, as if she had but chosen her instance at merest random.

"Na, na, sir! what my sowl may be in the eyes o' my Maker, I hae ill tellin'," she said, "but dinna ye threip upo' me 'at it's o' the same vailue i' your eyes as the sowl o' sic a fine bonny, winsome leddy as yon. In trouth," she added, and shook her head mournfully, "I haena had sae mony preevileeges; an' maybe it'll be seen till, an' me passed ower a wheen easier nor some fowk."

"I wouldn't have you build too much upon that, Mistress Croale," said Mr. Sclater, glad to follow the talk down another turning, but considerably more afraid of rousing the woman than he had been before.

The remark drove her behind the categorical stockade of her religious merits.

"I pey my w'y," she said, with modest firmness. "I put my penny, and whiles my saxpence, intil the plate at the door when I gang to the kirk—an' I was jist thinkin' I wad win there the morn's nicht at farest, whan I turnt an' saw ye stan'in there, sir; an' little I thoucht—but that's neither here nor there, I'm thinkin'. I tell as feow lees as I can; I never sweir, nor tak the name o' the Lord in vain, anger me 'at likes; I sell naething but the best whusky; I never hae but broth to my denner upo' the Lord's day, an' broth canna brak the Sawbath, simmerin' awa' upo' the bar o' the grate, an' haudin' no lass frae the kirk; I confess, gien ye wull be speirin', 'at I dinna read my buik sae aften as maybe I sud; but, 'deed, sir, tho' I says't 'at sud haud my tongue, ye hae waur folk i' yer perris nor Benjie Croale's widow; an' gien ye wunna hae a drap to weet yer ain whustle for the holy wark ye hae afore ye the morn's mornin', I maun gang an' mak my bed, for the lass is laid up wi' a bealt thoom, an' I maunna lat a' thing gang to dirt an' green bree; though I'm sure it's rale kin' o' ye to come to luik efter me, an' that's mair nor Maister Rennie, honest gentleman, ever did me the fawvour o', a' the time he ministered the perris. I haena an ill name wi' them 'at kens me, sir; that I can say wi' a clean conscience; an' ye may ken me weel gien ye wull. An' there's jist ae thing mair, sir: I gie ye my Bible-word, 'at never, gien I saw sign o' repentance or turnin' upo' ane o' them 'at pits their legs 'aneth my table—Wad ye luik intil the parlour, sir? No!—as I was sayin', never did I, sin' I keepit hoose, an' never wad I set mysel' to quench the smokin' flax; I wad hae no man's deith, sowl or body, lie at my door."

"Well, well, Mistress Croale," said the minister, somewhat dazed by the cataract he had brought upon his brain, and rather perplexed what to say in reply with any hope of reaching her, "I don't doubt a word of what you tell me; but you know works cannot save us; our best righteousness is but as filthy rags."

"It's weel I ken that, Mr. Sclater. An' I'm sure I'll be glaid to see ye, sir, ony time ye wad dee me the fawvour to luik in as ye're passin' by. It'll be none to yer shame, sir, for mine's an honest hoose."

"I'll do that, Mistress Croale," answered the minister, glad to escape. "But mind," he added, "I don't give up my point for all that; and I hope you will think over what I have been saying to you—and that seriously."

With these words he left the shop rather hurriedly, in evident dread of a reply.

Mistress Croale turned to the shelves behind her, took again the bottle she had replaced, poured out a large half-glass of whisky, and tossed it off. She had been compelled to think and talk of things unpleasant, and it had put her, as she said, a' in a trim'le. She was but one of the many who get the fuel of their life in at the wrong door, their comfort from the world-side of the universe. I cannot tell whether Mr. Sclater or she was the farther from the central heat. The woman had the advantage in this, that she had to expend all her force on mere self-justification, and had no energy left for vain-glory. It was with a sad sigh she set about the work of the house. Nor would it have comforted her much to assure her that hers was a better defence than any distiller in the country could make. Even the whisky itself gave her little relief; it seemed to scald both stomach and conscience, and she vowed never to take it again. But alas! this time is never the time for self-denial; it is always the next time. Abstinence is so much more pleasant to contemplate upon the other side of indulgence! Yet the struggles after betterment that many a drunkard has made in vain, would, had his aim been high enough, have saved his soul from death, and turned the charnel of his life into a temple. Abject as he is, foiled and despised, such a one may not yet be half so contemptible as many a so-counted respectable member of society, who looks down on him from a height too lofty even for scorn. It is not the first and the last only, of whom many will have to change places; but those as well that come everywhere between.

IV

The Parlour

The day went on, and went out, its short autumnal brightness quenched in a chilly fog. All along the Widdiehill, the gas was alight in the low-browed dingy shops. To the well-to-do citizen hastening home to the topmost business of the day, his dinner, these looked the abodes of unlovely poverty and mean struggle. Even to those behind their counters, in their back parlours, and in their rooms above, everything about them looked common, to most of them, save the owners, wearisome. But to yon pale-faced student, gliding in the glow of his red gown, through the grey mist back to his lodging, and peeping in at every open door as he passes, they are so full of mystery, that gladly would he yield all he has gathered from books, for one genuine glance of insight into the vital movement of the hearts and households of which those open shops are the sole outward and visible signs. Each house is to him a nest of human birds, over which brood the eternal wings of love and purpose. Only such different birds are hatched from the same nest! And what a nest was then the city itself!—with its university, its schools, its churches, its hospitals, its missions; its homes, its lodging-houses, its hotels, its drinking shops, its houses viler still; its factories, its ships, its great steamers; and the same humanity busy in all!—here the sickly lady walking in the panoply of love unharmed through the horrors of vicious suffering; there the strong mother cursing her own child along half a street with an intensity and vileness of execration unheard elsewhere! The will of the brooding spirit must be a grand one, indeed, to enclose so much of what cannot be its will, and turn all to its purpose of eternal good! Our knowledge of humanity, how much more our knowledge of the Father of it, is moving as yet but in the first elements.

In his shed under the stair it had been dark for some time—too dark for work, that is, and George Galbraith had lighted a candle: he never felt at liberty to leave off so long as a man was recognizable in the street by daylight. But now at last, with a sigh of relief, he rose. The hour of his redemption was come, the moment of it at hand. Outwardly calm, he was within eager as a lover to reach Lucky Croale's back parlour. His hand trembled with expectation as he laid from it the awl, took

GEORGE MACDONALD

from between his knees the great boot on the toe of which he had been stitching a patch, lifted the yoke of his leather apron over his head, and threw it aside. With one hasty glance around, as if he feared some enemy lurking near to prevent his escape, he caught up a hat which looked as if it had been brushed with grease, pulled it on his head with both hands, stepped out quickly, closed the door behind him, turned the key, left it in the lock, and made straight for his earthly paradise—but with chastened step. All Mistress Croale's customers made a point of looking decent in the street—strove, in their very consciousness, to carry the expression of being on their way to their tea, not their toddy—or if their toddy, then not that they desired it, but merely that it was their custom always of an afternoon: man had no choice—he must fill space, he must occupy himself; and if so, why not Mistress Croale's the place, and the consumption of whisky the occupation? But alas for their would-be seeming indifference! Everybody in the lane, almost in the Widdiehill, knew every one of them, and knew him for what he was; knew that every drop of toddy he drank was to him as to a miser his counted sovereign; knew that, as the hart for the water-brooks, so thirsted his soul ever after another tumbler; that he made haste to swallow the last drops of the present, that he might behold the plenitude of the next steaming before him; that, like the miser, he always understated the amount of the treasure he had secured, because the less he acknowledged, the more he thought he could claim.

George was a tall man, of good figure, loosened and bowed. His face was well favoured, but not a little wronged by the beard and dirt of a week, through which it gloomed haggard and white. Beneath his projecting black brows, his eyes gleamed doubtful, as a wood-fire where white ash dims the glow. He looked neither to right nor left, but walked on with moveless dull gaze, noting nothing.

"Yon's his ain warst enemy," said the kindly grocer-wife, as he passed her door.

"Ay," responded her customer, who kept a shop near by for old furniture, or anything that had been already once possessed—"ay, I daursay. But eh! to see that puir negleckit bairn o' his rin scoorin' aboot the toon yon gait—wi' little o' a jacket but the collar, an' naething o' the breeks but the doup—eh, wuman! it maks a mither's hert sair to luik upo' 't. It's a providence 'at his mither's weel awa' an' canna see't; it wad gar her turn in her grave."

George was the first arrival at Mistress Croale's that night. He opened the door of the shop like a thief, and glided softly into the dim parlour, where the candles were not yet lit. There was light enough, however, from the busy little fire in the grate to show the clean sanded floor which it crossed with flickering shadows, the coloured prints and cases of stuffed birds on the walls, the full-rigged barque suspended from the centre of the ceiling, and, chief of all shows of heaven or earth, the black bottle on the table, with the tumblers, each holding its ladle, and its wine glass turned bottom upwards. Nor must I omit a part without which the rest could not have been a whole—the kettle of water that sat on the hob, softly crooning. Compared with the place where George had been at work all day, this was indeed an earthly paradise. Nor was the presence and appearance of Mistress Croale an insignificant element in the paradisial character of the place. She was now in a clean white cap with blue ribbons. Her hair was neatly divided, and drawn back from her forehead. Every trace of dirt and untidiness had disappeared from her person, which was one of importance both in size and in bearing. She wore a gown of some dark stuff with bright flowers on it, and a black silk apron. Her face was composed, almost to sadness, and throughout the evening, during which she waited in person upon her customers, she comported herself with such dignity, that her slow step and stately carriage seemed rather to belong to the assistant at some religious ceremony than to one who ministered at the orgies of a few drunken tradespeople.

She was seated on the horsehair sofa in the fire-twilight, waiting for customers, when the face of Galbraith came peering round the door-cheek.

"Come awa' ben," she said, hospitably, and rose. But as she did so, she added with a little change of tone, "But I'm thinkin' ye maun hae forgotten, Sir George. This is Setterday nicht, ye ken; an' gien it war to be Sunday mornin' afore ye wan to yer bed, it wadna be the first time, an' ye michtna be up ear eneuch to get yersel shaved afore kirk time."

She knew as well as George himself that never by any chance did he go to church; but it was her custom, as I fancy it is that of some other bulwarks of society and pillars of the church, "for the sake of example," I presume, to make not unfrequent allusion to certain observances, moral, religious, or sanatory as if they were laws that everybody kept.

Galbraith lifted his hand, black, and embossed with cobbler's wax, and rubbed it thoughtfully over his chin: he accepted the fiction offered him; it was but the well-known prologue to a hebdomadal passage between them. What if he did not intend going to church the next day? Was that any reason why he should not look a little tidier when his hard week's-work was over, and his nightly habit was turned into the comparatively harmless indulgence of a Saturday, in sure hope of the day of rest behind.

"Troth, I didna min' 'at it was Setterday," he answered. "I wuss I had pitten on a clean sark, an' washen my face. But I s' jist gang ower to the barber's an' get a scrape, an' maybe some o' them 'ill be here or I come back."

Mistress Croale knew perfectly that there was no clean shirt in George's garret. She knew also that the shirt he then wore, which probably, in consideration of her maid's festered hand, she would wash for him herself, was one of her late husband's which she had given him. But George's speech was one of those forms of sound words held fast by all who frequented Mistress Croale's parlour, and by herself estimated at more than their worth.

The woman had a genuine regard for Galbraith. Neither the character nor fate of one of the rest gave her a moment's trouble; but in her secret mind she deplored that George should drink so inordinately, and so utterly neglect his child as to let him spend his life in the streets. She comforted herself, however, with the reflection, that seeing he would drink, he drank with no bad companions—drank at all events where what natural wickedness might be in them, was suppressed by the sternness of her rule. Were he to leave her fold—for a fold in very truth, and not a sty, it appeared to her—and wander away to Jock Thamson's or Jeemie Deuk's, he would be drawn into loud and indecorous talk, probably into quarrel and uproar.

In a few minutes George returned, an odd contrast visible between the upper and lower halves of his face. Hearing his approach she met him at the door.

"Noo, Sir George," she said, "jist gang up to my room an' hae a wash, an' pit on the sark ye'll see lyin' upo' the bed; syne come doon an' hae yer tum'ler comfortable."

George's whole soul was bent upon his drink, but he obeyed as if she had been twice his mother. By the time he had finished his toilet, the usual company was assembled, and he appeared amongst them in all the respectability of a clean shirt and what purity besides the general adhesiveness of his trade-material would yield to a single ablution long delayed. They welcomed him all, with nod, or grin, or merry word, in individual fashion, as each sat measuring out his whisky, or pounding at the slow-dissolving sugar, or tasting the mixture with critical soul seated between tongue and palate.

The conversation was for some time very dull, with a strong tendency to the censorious. For in their circle, not only were the claims of respectability silently admitted, but the conduct of this and that man of their acquaintance, or of public note, was pronounced upon with understood reference to those claims—now with smile of incredulity or pity, now with headshake regretful or condemnatory—and this all the time that each was doing his best to reduce himself to a condition in which the word conduct could no longer have meaning in reference to him.

All of them, as did their hostess, addressed Galbraith as Sir George, and he accepted the title with a certain unassuming dignity. For, if it was not universally known in the city, it was known to the best lawyers in it, that he was a baronet by direct derivation from the hand of King James the Sixth.

The fire burned cheerfully, and the kettle making many journeys between it and the table, things gradually grew more lively. Stories were told, often without any point, but not therefore without effect; reminiscences, sorely pulpy and broken at the edges, were offered and accepted with a laughter in which sober ears might have detected a strangely alien sound; and adventures were related in which truth was no necessary element to reception. In the case of the postman, for instance, who had been dismissed for losing a bag of letters the week before, not one of those present believed a word he said; yet as he happened to be endowed with a small stock of genuine humour, his stories were regarded with much the same favour as if they had been authentic. But the revival scarcely reached Sir George. He said little or nothing, but, between his slow gulps of toddy, sat looking vacantly into his glass. It is true he smiled absently now and then when the others laughed, but that was only for manners. Doubtless he was seeing somewhere the saddest of all visions—the things that might have been. The wretched craving of the lower organs stilled, and something spared for his brain, I believe the chief joy his drink gave him lay in the power once more to feel himself a gentleman. The washed hands, the shaven face, the clean shirt, had something to do with it, no doubt, but the necromantic whisky had far more.

What faded ghosts of ancestral dignity and worth and story the evil potion called up in the mind of Sir George!—who himself hung ready to fall, the last, or all but the last, mildewed fruit of the tree of Galbraith! Ah! if this one and that of his ancestors had but lived to his conscience, and with some thought of those that were to come after him, he would not have transmitted to poor Sir George, in horrible addition to moral weakness, that physical proclivity which had now grown to such a hideous craving. To the miserable wretch himself it seemed that he could no more keep from drinking whisky than he could from breathing air.

V

Gibbie's Calling

I am not sure that his father's neglect was not on the whole better for Gibbie than would have been the kindness of such a father persistently embodying itself. But the picture of Sir George, by the help of whisky and the mild hatching oven of Mistress Croale's parlour, softly breaking from the shell of the cobbler, and floating a mild gentleman in the air of his lukewarm imagination, and poor wee Gibbie trotting outside in the frosty dark of the autumn night, through which the moon keeps staring down, vague and disconsolate, is hardly therefore the less pathetic. Under the window of the parlour where the light of revel shone radiant through a red curtain, he would stand listening for a moment, then, darting off a few yards suddenly and swiftly like a scared bird, fall at once into his own steady trot—up the lane and down, till he reached the window again, where again he would stand and listen. Whether he made this departure and return twenty or a hundred times in a night, he nor any one else could have told. Sometimes he would for a change extend his trot along the Widdiehill, sometimes along the parallel Vennel, but never far from Jink Lane and its glowing window. Never moth haunted lamp so persistently. Ever as he ran, up this pavement and down that, on the soft-sounding soles of his bare feet, the smile on the boy's face grew more and more sleepy, but still he smiled and still he trotted, still paused at the window, and still started afresh.

He was not so much to be pitied as my reader may think. Never in his life had he yet pitied himself. The thought of hardship or wrong had not occurred to him. It would have been difficult—impossible, I believe—to get the idea into his head that existence bore to him any other shape than it ought. Things were with him as they had always been, and whence was he to take a fresh start, and question what had been from the beginning? Had any authority interfered, with a decree that Gibbie should no more scour the midnight streets, no more pass and repass that far-shining splendour of red, then indeed would bitter, though inarticulate, complaint have burst from his bosom. But there was no evil power to issue such a command, and Gibbie's peace was not invaded.

GEORGE MACDONALD

It was now late, and those streets were empty; neither carriage nor cart, wheelbarrow nor truck, went any more bumping and clattering over their stones. They were well lighted with gas, but most of the bordering houses were dark. Now and then a single foot-farer passed with loud, hollow-sounding boots along the pavement; or two girls would come laughing along, their merriment echoing rude in the wide stillness. A cold wind, a small, forsaken, solitary wind, moist with a thin fog, seemed, as well as wee Gibbie, to be roaming the night, for it met him at various corners, and from all directions. But it had nothing to do, and nowhere to go, and there it was not like Gibbie, the business of whose life was even now upon him, the mightiest hope of whose conscious being was now awake.

All he expected, or ever desired to discover, by listening at the window, was simply whether there were yet signs of the company's breaking up; and his conclusions on that point were never mistaken: how he arrived at them it would be hard to say. Seldom had he there heard the voice of his father, still seldomer anything beyond its tone. This night, however, as the time drew near when they must go, lest the Sabbath should be broken in Mistress Croale's decent house, and Gibbie stood once more on tiptoe, with his head just on the level of the windowsill, he heard his father utter two words: "Up Daurside" came to him through the window, in the voice he loved, plain and distinct. The words conveyed to him nothing at all; the mere hearing of them made them memorable. For the time, however, he forgot them, for, by indications best known to himself, he perceived that the company was on the point of separating, and from that moment did not take his eyes off the door until he heard the first sounds of its opening. As, however, it was always hard for Gibbie to stand still, and especially hard on a midnight so cold that his feet threatened to grow indistinguishable from the slabs of the pavement, he was driven, in order not to lose sight of it, to practise the art, already cultivated by him to a crab-like perfection, of running first backwards, then forwards with scarcely superior speed. But it was not long ere the much expected sound of Mistress Croale's voice heralded the hour for patience to blossom into possession. The voice was neither loud nor harsh, but clear and firm; the noise that followed was both loud and strident. Voices had a part in it, but the movement of chairs and feet and the sudden contact of different portions of the body with walls and tables, had a larger. The guests were obeying the voice of their hostess all in one like a flock of sheep, but it was poor shepherd-work to turn them out of the fold at midnight. Gibbie bounded up and stood still as a statue at the very door-cheek, until he heard Mistress Croale's hand upon the lock, when he bolted, trembling with eagerness, into the entry of a court a few houses nearer to the Widdiehill.

One after one the pitiable company issued from its paradise, and each stumbled away, too far gone for leave-taking. Most of them passed Gibbie where he stood, but he took no heed; his father was always the last—and the least capable. But, often as he left her door, never did it close behind him until with her own eyes Mistress Croale had seen Gibbie dart like an imp out of the court—to take him in charge, and, all the weary way home, hover, not very like a guardian angel, but not the less one in truth, around the unstable equilibrium of his father's tall and swaying form. And thereupon commenced a series of marvellous gymnastics on the part of wee Gibbie. Imagine a small boy with a gigantic top, which, six times his own size, he keeps erect on its peg, not by whipping it round, but by running round it himself, unfailingly applying, at the very spot and at the very moment, the precise measure of impact necessary to counterbalance its perpetual tendency to fall in one direction or another, so that the two have all the air of a single invention—such an invention as one might meet with in an ancient clock, contrived when men had time to mingle play with earnest—and you will have in your mind's eye a real likeness of Sir George attended, any midnight in the week, by his son Gilbert. Home the big one staggered, reeled, gyrated, and tumbled; round and round him went the little one, now behind, now before, now on this side, now on that, his feet never more than touching the ground but dancing about like those of a prize-fighter, his little arms up and his hands well forward, like flying buttresses. And such indeed they were—buttresses which flew and flew all about a universally leaning tower. They propped it here, they propped it there; with wonderful judgment and skill and graduation of force they applied themselves, and with perfect success. Not once, for the last year and a half, during which time wee Gibbie had been the nightly guide of Sir George's homeward steps, had the self-disabled mass fallen prostrate in the gutter, there to snore out the night.

The first special difficulty, that of turning the corner of Jink Lane and the Widdiehill, successfully overcome, the twain went reeling and revolving along the street, much like a whirlwind that had half forgotten the laws of gyration, until at length it spun into the court, and up to the foot of the outside stair over the baronet's workshop. Then commenced the real struggle of the evening for Gibbie—and for his father too, though the latter was aware of it only in the momentary and evanescent flashes of such enlightenment as made him just capable of yielding to the pushes and pulls of the former. All up the outside and the two inside stairs, his waking and sleeping were as the alternate tictac of a pendulum; but Gibbie stuck to his business like a man, and his resolution and perseverance were at length, as always, crowned with victory.

The house in which lords and ladies had often reposed was now filled with very humble folk, who were all asleep when Gibbie and his father entered; but the noise they made in ascending caused no great disturbance of their rest; for, if any of them were roused for a moment, it was but to recognize at once the cause of the tumult, and with the remark, "It's only wee Gibbie luggin' hame Sir George," to turn on the other side and fall asleep again.

Arrived at last at the garret door, which stood wide open, Gibbie had small need of light in the nearly pitch darkness of the place, for there was positively nothing to stumble over or against between the door and the ancient four-post bed, which was all of his father's house that remained to Sir George. With heavy shuffling feet the drunkard lumbered laboriously bedward; and the bare posts and crazy frame groaned and creaked as he fell upon the oat-chaff that lay waiting him in place of the vanished luxury of feathers. Wee Gibbie flew at his legs, nor rested until, the one after the other, he had got them on the bed; if then they were not very comfortably deposited, he knew that, in his first turn, their owner would get them all right.

And now rose the culmen of Gibbie's day! its cycle, rounded through regions of banishment, returned to its nodus of bliss. In triumph he spread over his sleeping father his dead mother's old plaid of Gordon tartan, all the bedding they had, and without a moment's further delay—no shoes even to put off—crept under it, and nestled close upon the bosom of his unconscious parent. A victory more! another day ended with success! his father safe, and all his own! the canopy of the darkness and the plaid over them, as if they were the one only two in the universe! his father unable to leave him—his for whole dark hours to come! It was Gibbie's paradise now! His heaven was his father's bosom, to which he clung as no infant yet ever clung to his mother's. He never thought to pity himself that the embrace was all on his side, that no answering pressure came back from the prostrate form. He never said to himself, "My father is a drunkard, but I must make the best of it; he is all I have!" He clung to his one possession—only clung: this was his father—all in all to him. What must be the bliss of such a heart—of any heart, when it comes to know that there is a father of fathers, yea, a father of fatherhood! a father who never slumbers nor sleeps, but holds all the sleeping in his ever waking bosom—a bosom whose wakefulness is the sole fountain of their slumber!

The conscious bliss of the child was of short duration, for in a few minutes he was fast asleep; but for the gain of those few minutes only, the day had been well spent.

VI

A Sunday at Home

S uch were the events of every night, and such had they been since Gibbie first assumed this office of guardian—a time so long in proportion to his life that it seemed to him as one of the laws of existence that fathers got drunk and Gibbies took care of them. But Saturday night was always one of special bliss; for then the joy to come spread its arms beneath and around the present delight: all Sunday his father would be his. On that happiest day of all the week, he never set his foot out of doors, except to run twice to Mistress Croale's, once to fetch the dinner which she supplied from her own table, and for which Sir George regularly paid in advance on Saturday before commencing his potations.

But indeed the streets were not attractive to the child on Sundays: there were no shops open, and the people in their Sunday clothes, many of them with their faces studiously settled into masks intended to express righteousness, were far less interesting, because less alive, than the same people in their work-day attire, in their shops, or seated at their stalls, or driving their carts, and looking thoroughly human. As to going to church himself, such an idea had never entered his head. He had not once for a moment imagined that anybody would like him to go to church, that such as he ever went to church, that church was at all a place to which Gibbies with fathers to look after should have any desire to go. As to what church going meant, he had not the vaguest idea; it had not even waked the glimmer of a question in his mind. All he knew was that people went to church on Sundays. It was another of the laws of existence, the reason of which he knew no more than why his father went every night to Jink Lane and got drunk. George, however, although he had taught his son nothing, was not without religion, and had notions of duty in respect of the Sabbath. Not even with the prize of whisky in view, would he have consented to earn a sovereign on that day by the lightest of work.

Gibbie was awake some time before his father, and lay revelling in love's bliss of proximity. At length Sir George, the merest bubble of nature, awoke, and pushed him from him.

The child got up at once, but only to stand by the bed-side. He said no word, did not even think an impatient thought, yet his father seemed to feel that he was waiting for him. After two or three huge yawns, he spread out his arms, but, unable to stretch himself, yawned again, rolled himself off the bed, and crept feebly across the room to an empty chest that stood under the skylight. There he seated himself, and for half an hour sat motionless, a perfect type of dilapidation, moral and physical, while a little way off stood Gibbie, looking on, like one awaiting a resurrection. At length he seemed to come to himself—the expected sign of which was that he reached down his hand towards the meeting of roof and floor, and took up a tiny last with a half-made boot upon it. At sight of it in his father's hands, Gibbie clapped his with delight—an old delight, renewed every Sunday since he could remember. That boot was for him! and this being the second, the pair would be finished before night! By slow degrees of revival, with many pauses between, George got to work. He wanted no breakfast, and made no inquiry of Gibbie whether he had had any. But what cared Gibbie about breakfast! With his father all to himself, and that father working away at a new boot for him—for him who had never had a pair of any sort upon his feet since the woollen ones he wore in his mother's lap, breakfast or no breakfast was much the same to him. It could never have occurred to him that it was his father's part to provide him with breakfast. If he was to have none, it was Sunday that was to blame: there was no use in going to look for any when the shops were all shut, and everybody either at church, or closed in domestic penetralia, or out for a walk. More than contented, therefore, while busily his father wedded welt and sole with stitches infrangible, Gibbie sat on the floor, preparing waxed ends, carefully sticking in the hog's bristle, and rolling the combination, with quite professional aptitude, between the flat of his hand and what of trouser-leg he had left, gazing eagerly between at the advancing masterpiece. Occasionally the triumph of expectation would exceed his control, when he would spring from the floor, and caper and strut about like a pigeon—soft as a shadow, for he knew his father could not bear noise in the morning—or behind his back execute a pantomimic dumb show of delight, in which he seemed with difficulty to restrain himself from jumping upon him, and hugging him in his ecstasy. Oh, best of parents! working thus even on a Sunday for his Gibbie, when everybody else was at church enjoying himself! But Gibbie never dared hug his father except when he was drunk—why, he could hardly have told. Relieved by his dumb show, he would return, quite as an aged grimalkin, and again deposit himself on the floor near his father where he could see his busy hands.

All this time Sir George never spoke a word. Incredible as it may seem, however, he was continually, off and on, trying his hardest to think of some Sunday lesson to give his child. Many of those that knew the boy, regarded him as a sort of idiot, drawing the conclusion from Gibbie's practical honesty and his too evident love for his kind: it was incredible that a child should be poor, unselfish, loving, and not deficient in intellect! His father knew him better, yet he often quieted his conscience in regard to his education, with the reflection that not much could be done for him. Still, every now and then he would think perhaps he ought to do something: who could tell but the child might be damned for not understanding the plan of salvation? and brooding over the matter this morning, as well as his headache would permit, he came to the resolution, as he had often done before, to buy a Shorter Catechism; the boy could not learn it, but he would keep reading it to him, and something might stick. Even now perhaps he could begin the course by recalling some of the questions and answers that had been the plague of his life every Saturday at school. He set his recollection to work, therefore, in the lumber-room of his memory, and again and again sent it back to the task, but could find nothing belonging to the catechism except the first question with its answer, and a few incoherent fragments of others. Moreover, he found his mind so confused and incapable of continuous or concentrated effort, that he could not even keep "man's chief end" and the rosined end between his fingers from twisting up together in the most extraordinary manner. Yet if the child but "had the question," he might get some good of it. The hour might come when he would say, "My father taught me that!"—who could tell? And he knew he had the words correct, wherever he had dropped their meaning. For the sake of Gibbie's immortal part, therefore, he would repeat the answer to that first, most momentous of questions, over and over as he worked, in the hope of insinuating something—he could not say what—into the small mental pocket of the innocent. The first, therefore, and almost the only words which Gibbie heard from his father's lips that morning, were these, dozens of times repeated—"Man's chief end is to glorify God, and to enjoy Him for ever." But so far was Gibbie from perceiving in them any meaning, that even with his father's pronunciation of chief end as chifenn, they roused in his mind no sense or suspicion of obscurity. The word stuck there, notwithstanding; but Gibbie was years a man before he found out what a chifenn was. Where was the great matter? How many who have learned their catechism and deplore the ignorance of others, make the least effort to place their chief end even in the direction of that of their creation? Is it not the constant thwarting of their aims, the rendering of their desires futile, and their ends a mockery, that alone prevents them and their lives from proving an absolute failure? Sir George, with his inveterate, consuming thirst for whisky, was but the type of all who would gain their bliss after the scheme of their own fancies, instead of the scheme of their existence; who would build their house after their own childish wilfulness instead of the ground-plan of their being. How was Sir George to glorify the God whom he could honestly thank for nothing but whisky, the sole of his gifts that he prized? Over and over that day he repeated the words, "Man's chief end is to glorify God, and to enjoy Him for ever," and all the time his imagination, his desire, his hope, were centred on the bottle, which with his very back he felt where it stood behind him, away on the floor at the head of his bed. Nevertheless when he had gone over them a score of times or so, and Gibbie had begun, by a merry look and nodding of his head, to manifest that he knew what was coming next, the father felt more content with himself than for years past; and when he was satisfied that Gibbie knew all the words, though, indeed, they were hardly more than sounds to him, he sent him, with a great sense of relief, to fetch the broth and beef and potatoes from Mistress Croale's.

Eating a real dinner in his father's house, though without a table to set it upon, Gibbie felt himself a most privileged person. The only thing that troubled him was that his father ate so little. Not until the twilight began to show did Sir George really begin to revive, but the darker it grew without, the brighter his spirit burned. For, amongst not a few others, there was this strange remnant of righteousness in the man, that he never would taste drink before it was dark in winter, or in summer before the regular hour for ceasing work had arrived; and to this rule he kept, and that under far greater difficulties, on the Sunday as well. For Mistress Croale would not sell a drop of drink, not even on the sly, on the Sabbath-day: she would fain have some stake in the hidden kingdom; and George, who had not a Sunday stomach he could assume for the day any more than a Sunday coat, was thereby driven to provide his whisky and that day drink it at home; when, with the bottle so near him, and the sense that he had not to go out to find his relief, his resolution was indeed sorely tried; but he felt that to yield would be to cut his last cable and be swept on the lee-shore of utter ruin.

Breathless with eager interest, Gibbie watched his father's hands, and just as the darkness closed in, the boot was finished. His father rose, and Gibbie, glowing with delight, sprang upon the seat he had left, while his father knelt upon the floor to try upon the unaccustomed foot the result from which he had just drawn the last. Ah, pity! pity! But even Gibbie might by this time have learned to foresee it! three times already had the same thing happened: the boot would not go on the foot. The real cause of the failure it were useless to inquire. Sir George said that, Sunday being the only day he could give to the boots, before he could finish them, Gibbie's feet had always outgrown the measure. But it may be Sir George was not so good a maker as cobbler. That he meant honestly by the boy I am sure, and not the less sure for the confession I am forced to make, that on each occasion when he thus failed to fit him, he sold the boots the next day at a fair price to a ready-made shop, and drank the proceeds. A stranger thing still was, that, although Gibbie had never yet worn boot or shoe, his father's conscience was greatly relieved by the knowledge that he spent his Sundays in making boots for him. Had he been an ordinary child, and given him trouble, he would possibly have hated him; as it was, he had a great though sadly inoperative affection for the boy, which was an endless good to them both.

After many bootless trials, bootless the feet must remain, and George, laying the failure down in despair, rose from his knees, and left Gibbie seated on the chest more like a king discrowned, than a beggar unshod. And like a king the little beggar bore his pain. He heaved one sigh, and a slow moisture gathered in his eyes, but it did not overflow. One minute only he sat and hugged his desolation—then, missing his father, jumped off the box to find him.

He sat on the edge of the bed, looking infinitely more disconsolate than Gibbie felt, his head and hands hanging down, a picture of utter dejection. Gibbie bounded to him, climbed on the bed, and nearly strangled him in the sharp embrace of his little arms. Sir George took him on his knees and kissed him, and the tears rose in his dull eyes. He got up with him, carried him to the box, placed him on it once more, and fetched a piece of brown paper from under the bed. From this he tore carefully several slips, with which he then proceeded to take a most thoughtful measurement of the baffling foot. He was far more to be pitied than Gibbie, who would not have worn the boots an hour had they been the best fit in shoedom. The soles of his feet were very nearly equal in resistance to leather, and at least until the snow and hard frost came, he was better without boots.

But now the darkness had fallen, and his joy was at the door. But he was always too much ashamed to begin to drink before the child: he hated to uncork the bottle before him. What followed was in regular Sunday routine.

"Gang ower to Mistress Croale's, Gibbie," he said, "wi' my compliments."

Away ran Gibbie, nothing loath, and at his knock was admitted. Mistress Croale sat in the parlour, taking her tea, and expecting him. She was always kind to the child. She could not help feeling that no small part of what ought to be spent on him came to her; and on Sundays, therefore, partly for his sake, partly for her own, she always gave him his tea—nominally tea, really blue city-milk—with as much dry bread as he could eat, and a bit of buttered toast from her plate to finish off with. As he ate, he stood at the other side of the table; he looked so miserable in her eyes that, even before her servant, she was ashamed to have him sit with her; but Gibbie was quite content, never thought of sitting, and ate in gladness, every now and then looking up with loving, grateful eyes, which must have gone right to the woman's heart, had it not been for a vague sense she had of being all the time his enemy—and that although she spent much time in persuading herself that she did her best both for his father and him.

When he returned, greatly refreshed, and the boots all but forgotten, he found his father, as he knew he would, already started on the business of the evening. He had drawn the chest, the only seat in the room, to the side of the bed, against which he leaned his back. A penny candle was burning in a stone blacking bottle on the chimney piece, and on the floor beside the chest stood the bottle of whisky, a jug of water, a stoneware mug, and a wineglass.

There was no fire and no kettle, whence his drinking was sad, as became the Scotch Sabbath in distinction from the Jewish. There, however, was the drink, and thereby his soul could live—yea, expand her mouldy wings! Gibbie was far from shocked; it was all right, all in the order of things, and he went up to his father with radiant countenance. Sir George put forth his hands and took him between his knees. An evil wind now swelled his sails, but the cargo of the crazy human hull was not therefore evil.

"Gibbie," he said, solemnly, "never ye drink a drap o' whusky. Never ye rax oot the han' to the boatle. Never ye drink anything but watter, caller watter, my man."

As he said the words, he stretched out his own hand to the mug, lifted it to his lips, and swallowed a great gulp.

"Dinna do't, I tell ye, Gibbie," he repeated.

Gibbie shook his head with positive repudiation.

"That's richt, my man," responded his father with satisfaction. "Gien ever I see ye pree (taste) the boatle, I'll warstle frae my grave an' fleg ye oot o' the sma' wuts ye hae, my man."

Here followed another gulp from the mug.

The threat had conveyed nothing to Gibbie. Even had he understood, it would have carried anything but terror to his father-worshipping heart.

"Gibbie," resumed Sir George, after a brief pause, "div ye ken what fowk'll ca' ye whan I'm deid?"

Gibbie again shook his head—with expression this time of mere ignorance.

"They'll ca' ye Sir Gibbie Galbraith, my man," said his father, "an' richtly, for it'll be no nickname, though some may lauch 'cause yer father was a sutor, an' mair 'at, for a' that, ye haena a shee to yer fut yersel', puir fallow! Heedna ye what they say, Gibbie. Min' 'at ye're Sir Gibbie, an' hae the honour o' the faimily to haud up, my man—an' that ye can not dee an' drink. This cursit drink's been the ruin o' a' the Galbraiths as far back as I ken. 'Maist the only thing I can min' o' my gran'father—a big bonny man, wi' lang white hair—twise as big's me, Gibbie—is seein' him deid drunk i' the gutter o' the pump. He drank 'maist a' thing there was, Gibbie—lan's an' lordship, till there was hardly an accre left upo' haill Daurside to come to my father—'maist naething but a wheen sma' hooses. He was a guid man, my father; but his father learnt him to drink afore he was 'maist oot o' 's coaties, an' gae him nae schuilin'; an' gien he red himsel' o' a' 'at was left, it was sma' won'er—only, ye see, Gibbie, what was to come o' me? I pit it till ye, Gibbie—what was to come o' me?—Gien a kin' neiper, 'at kent what it was to drink, an' sae had a fallow-feelin', hadna ta'en an' learnt me my trade, the Lord kens what wad hae come o' you an' me, Gibbie, my man!—Gang to yer bed, noo, an' lea' me to my ain thouchts; no' 'at they're aye the best o' company, laddie.—But whiles they're no that ill," he concluded, with a weak smile, as some reflex of himself not quite unsatisfactory gloomed faintly in the besmeared mirror of his uncertain consciousness.

Gibbie obeyed, and getting under the Gordon tartan, lay and looked out, like a weasel from its hole, at his father's back. For half an hour or so Sir George went on drinking. All at once he started to his feet, and turning towards the bed a white face distorted with agony, kneeled down on the box and groaned out:

"O God, the pains o' hell hae gotten haud upo' me. O Lord, I'm i' the grup o' Sawtan. The deevil o' drink has me by the hause. I doobt, O Lord, ye're gauin' to damn me dreidfu'. What guid that'll do ye, O Lord, I dinna ken, but I doobtna ye'll dee what's richt, only I wuss I hed never crossed ye i' yer wull. I kenna what I'm to dee, or what's to be deene wi' me, or whaur ony help's to come frae. I hae tried an' tried to maister the drink, but I was aye whumled. For ye see, Lord, kennin' a' thing as ye dee, 'at until I hae a drap i' my skin, I canna even think; I canna min' the sangs I used to sing, or the prayers my mither learnt me sittin' upo' her lap. Till I hae swallowed a mou'fu' or twa, things luik sae awfu'-like 'at I'm fit to cut my thro't; an' syne ance I'm begun, there's nae mair thoucht o' endeevourin' to behaud (withhold) till I canna drink a drap mair. O God, what garred ye mak things 'at wad mak whusky, whan ye kenned it wad mak sic a beast o' me?"

He paused, stretched down his hand to the floor, lifted the mug, and drank a huge mouthful; then with a cough that sounded apologetic, set it down, and recommenced:

"O Lord, I doobt there's nae houp for me, for the verra river o' the watter o' life wadna be guid to me wantin' a drap frae the boatle intil 't. It's the w'y wi' a' hiz 'at drinks. It's no 'at we're drunkards, Lord—ow na! it's no that, Lord; it's only 'at we canna dee wantin' the drink. We're sair drinkers, I maun confess, but no jist drunkards, Lord. I'm no drunk the noo; I ken what I'm sayin', an' it's sair trowth, but I cudna hae prayt a word to yer lordship gien I hadna had a jooggy or twa first. O Lord, deliver me frae the pooer o' Sawtan.—O Lord! O Lord! I canna help mysel'. Dinna sen' me to the ill place. Ye loot the deils gang intil the swine, lat me tee."

With this frightful petition, his utterance began to grow indistinct. Then he fell forward upon the bed, groaning, and his voice died gradually away. Gibbie had listened to all he said, but the awe of hearing his father talk to one unseen, made his soul very still, and when he ceased he fell asleep.

Alas for the human soul inhabiting a drink-fouled brain! It is a human soul still, and wretched in the midst of all that whisky can do for it. From the pit of hell it cries out. So long as there is that which can sin, it is a man. And the prayer of misery carries its own justification, when the sober petitions of the self-righteous and the unkind are rejected. He who forgives not is not forgiven, and the prayer of the Pharisee is as the weary beating of the surf of hell, while the cry of a soul out of its fire sets the heart-strings of love trembling. There are sins which men must leave behind them, and sins which they must carry with them. Society scouts the drunkard because he is loathsome, and it matters nothing whether society be right or wrong, while it cherishes in its very bosom vices which are, to the God-born thing we call the soul, yet worse poisons. Drunkards and sinners, hard as it may be for them to enter into the kingdom of heaven, must yet be easier to save than the man whose position, reputation, money, engross his heart and his care, who seeks the praise of men and not the praise of God. When I am more of a Christian, I shall have learnt to be sorrier for the man whose end is money or social standing than for the drunkard. But now my heart, recoiling from the one, is sore for the other—for the agony, the helplessness, the degradation, the nightmare struggle, the wrongs and cruelties committed, the duties neglected, the sickening ruin of mind and heart. So often, too, the drunkard is originally a style of man immeasurably nobler than the money-maker! Compare a Coleridge, Samuel Taylor or Hartley, with—no; that man has not yet passed to his account. God has in his universe furnaces for the refining of gold, as well as for the burning of chaff and tares and fruitless branches; and, however they may have offended, it is the elder brother who is the judge of all the younger ones.

Gibbie slept some time. When he woke, it was pitch dark, and he was not lying on his father's bosom, He felt about with his hands till he found his father's head. Then he got up and tried to rouse him, and failing to get him on to the bed. But in that too he was sadly unsuccessful: what with the darkness and the weight of him, the result of the boy's best endeavour was, that Sir George half slipped, half rolled down upon the box, and from that to the floor. Assured then of his own helplessness, wee Gibbie dragged the miserable bolster from the bed, and got it under his father's head; then covered him with the plaid, and creeping under it, laid himself on his father's bosom, where soon he slept again.

He woke very cold, and getting up, turned heels-over-head several times to warm himself, but quietly, for his father was still asleep. The room was no longer dark, for the moon was shining through the skylight. When he had got himself a little warmer, he turned to have a look at his father. The pale light shone full upon his face, and it was that, Gibbie thought, which made him look so strange. He darted to him, and stared aghast: he had never seen him look like that before, even when most drunk! He threw himself upon him: his face was dreadfully cold. He pulled and shook him in fear—he could not have told of what, but he would not wake. He was gone to see what God could do for him there, for whom nothing more could be done here.

But Gibbie did not know anything about death, and went on trying to wake him. At last he observed that, although his mouth was wide open, the breath did not come from it. Thereupon his heart began to fail him. But when he lifted an eyelid, and saw what was under it, the house rang with the despairing shriek of the little orphan.

VII

The Town-Sparrow

This, too, will pass," is a Persian word: I should like it better if it were "This, too, shall pass."

Gibbie's agony passed, for God is not the God of the dead but of the living. Through the immortal essence in him, life became again life, and he ran about the streets as before. Some may think that wee Sir Gibbie—as many now called him, some knowing the truth, and others in kindly mockery—would get on all the better for the loss of such a father; but it was not so. In his father he had lost his Paradise, and was now a creature expelled. He was not so much to be pitied as many a child dismissed by sudden decree from a home to a school; but the streets and the people and the shops, the horses and the dogs, even the penny-loaves though he was hungry, had lost half their precious delight, when his father was no longer in the accessible background, the heart of the blissful city. As to food and clothing, he did neither much better nor any worse than before: people were kind as usual, and kindness was to Gibbie the very milk of mother Nature. Whose the hand that proffered it, or what the form it took, he cared no more than a stray kitten cares whether the milk set down to it be in a blue saucer or a white. But he always made the right return. The first thing a kindness deserves is acceptance, the next is transmission: Gibbie gave both, without thinking much about either. For he never had taken, and indeed never learned to take, a thought about what he should eat or what he should drink, or wherewithal he should be clothed—a fault rendering him, in the eyes of the economist of this world, utterly unworthy of a place in it. There is a world, however, and one pretty closely mixed up with this, though it never shows itself to one who has no place in it, the birds of whose air have neither storehouse nor barn, but are just such thoughtless cherubs—thoughtless for themselves, that is—as wee Sir Gibbie. It would be useless to attempt convincing the mere economist that this great city was a little better, a little happier, a little merrier, for the presence in it of the child, because he would not, even if convinced of the fact, recognize the gain; but I venture the assertion to him, that the conduct of not one of its inhabitants was the worse for the example of Gibbie's apparent idleness; and that not one of the poor women who now and then presented the small baronet with a penny, or a bit of bread, or a scrap of meat, or a pair of old trousers—shoes nobody gave him, and he neither desired nor needed any—ever felt the poorer for the gift, or complained that she should be so taxed.

Positively or negatively, then, everybody was good to him, and Gibbie felt it; but what could make up for the loss of his Paradise, the bosom of a father? Drunken father as he was, I know of nothing that can or ought to make up for such a loss, except that which can restore it—the bosom of the Father of fathers.

He roamed the streets, as all his life before, the whole of the day, and part of the night; he took what was given him, and picked up what he found. There were some who would gladly have brought him within the bounds of an ordered life; he soon drove them to despair, however, for the streets had been his nursery, and nothing could keep him out of them. But the sparrow and the rook are just as respectable in reality, though not in the eyes of the hen-wife, as the egg-laying fowl, or the dirt-gobbling duck; and, however Gibbie's habits might shock the ladies of Mr. Sclater's congregation who sought to civilize him, the boy was no more about mischief in the streets at midnight, than they were in their beds. They collected enough for his behoof to board him for a year with an old woman who kept a school, and they did get him to sleep one night in her house. But in the morning, when she would not let him run out, brought him into the school-room, her kitchen, and began to teach him to write, Gibbie failed to see the good of it. He must have space, change, adventure, air, or life was not worth the name to him. Above all he must see friendly faces, and that of the old dame was not such. But he desired to be friendly with her, and once, as she leaned over him, put up his hand—not a very clean one, I am bound to give her the advantage of my confessing—to stroke her cheek: she pushed him roughly away, rose in indignation upon her crutch, and lifted her cane to chastise him for the insult. A class of urchins, to Gibbie's eyes at least looking unhappy, were at the moment blundering through the twenty-third psalm. Ever after, even when now Sir Gilbert more than understood the great song, the words, "thy rod and thy staff," like the spell of a necromancer would still call up the figure of the dame irate, in her horn spectacles and her black-ribboned cap, leaning with one arm on her crutch, and with the other uplifting what was with her no mere symbol of authority. Like a shell from a mortar, he departed from the house. She hobbled to the door after him, but his diminutive figure many yards away, his little bare legs misty with swiftness as he ran, was the last she ever saw of him, and her pupils had a bad time of it the rest of the day. He never even entered the street again in which she lived. Thus, after one night's brief interval of respectability, he was again a rover of the city, a flitting insect that lighted here and there, and spread wings of departure the moment a fresh desire awoke.

It would be difficult to say where he slept. In summer anywhere; in winter where he could find warmth. Like animals better clad than he, yet like him able to endure cold, he revelled in mere heat when he could come by it. Sometimes he stood at the back of a baker's oven, for he knew all the haunts of heat about the city; sometimes he buried himself in the sids (husks of oats) lying ready to feed the kiln of a meal-mill; sometimes he lay by the furnace of the steam-engine of the water-works. One man employed there, when his time was at night, always made a bed for Gibbie: he had lost his own only child, and this one of nobody's was a comfort to him.

Even those who looked upon wandering as wicked, only scolded into the sweet upturned face, pouring gall into a cup of wine too full to receive a drop of it—and did not hand him over to the police. Useless verily that would have been, for the police would as soon have thought of taking up a town sparrow as Gibbie, and would only have laughed at the idea. They knew Gibbie's merits better than any of those good people imagined his faults. It requires either wisdom or large experience to know that a child is not necessarily wicked even if born and brought up in a far viler entourage than was Gibbie.

The merits the police recognized in him were mainly two—neither of small consequence in their eyes; the first, the negative, yet more important one, that of utter harmlessness; the second, and positive one—a passion and power for rendering help, taking notable shape chiefly in two ways, upon both of which I have already more than touched. The first was the peculiar faculty now pretty generally known—his great gift, some, his great luck, others called it—for finding things lost. It was no wonder the town crier had sought his acquaintance, and when secured, had cultivated it—neither a difficult task; for the boy, ever since he could remember, had been in the habit, as often as he saw the crier, or heard his tuck of drum in the distance, of joining him and following, until he had acquainted himself with all particulars concerning everything proclaimed as missing. The moment he had mastered the facts announced, he would dart away to search, and not unfrequently to return with the thing sought. But it was not by any means only things sought that he found. He continued to come upon things of which he had no simulacrum in his phantasy. These, having no longer a father to carry them to, he now, their owners unknown, took to the crier, who always pretended to receive them with a suspicion which Gibbie understood as little as the other really felt, and at once advertised them by drum and cry. What became of them after that, Gibbie never knew. If they did not find their owners, neither did they find their way back to Gibbie; if their owners were found, the crier never communicated with him on the subject. Plainly he regarded Gibbie as the favoured jackal, whose privilege it was to hunt for the crier, the royal lion of the city forest. But he spoke kindly to him, as well he might, and now and then gave him a penny.

The second of the positive merits by which Gibbie found acceptance in the eyes of the police, was a yet more peculiar one, growing out of his love for his father, and his experience in the exercise of that love. It was, however, unintelligible to them, and so remained, except on the theory commonly adopted with regard to Gibbie, namely, that he wasna a' there. Not the less was it to them a satisfactory whim of his, seeing it mitigated their trouble as guardians of the nightly peace and safety. It was indeed the main cause of his being, like themselves, so much in the street at night: seldom did Gibbie seek his lair—I cannot call it couch—before the lengthening hours of the morning. If the finding of things was a gift, this other peculiarity was a passion—and a right human passion—absolutely possessing the child: it was, to play the guardian angel to drunk folk. If such a distressed human craft hove in sight, he would instantly bear down upon and hover about him, until resolved as to his real condition. If he was in such distress as to require assistance, he never left him till he saw him safe within his own door. The police asserted that wee Sir Gibbie not only knew every drunkard in the city, and where he lived, but where he generally got drunk as well. That one was in no danger of taking the wrong turning, upon whom Gibbie was in attendance, to determine, by a shove on this side or that, the direction in which the hesitating, uncertain mass of stultified humanity was to go. He seemed a visible embodiment of that special providence which is said to watch over drunk people and children, only here a child was the guardian of the drunkard, and in this branch of his mission, was well known to all who, without qualifying themselves for coming under his cherubic cognizance, were in the habit of now and then returning home late. He was least known to those to whom he rendered most assistance. Rarely had he thanks for it, never halfpence, but not unfrequently blows and abuse. For the last he cared nothing; the former, owing to his great agility, seldom visited him with any directness. A certain reporter of humorous scandal, after his third tumbler, would occasionally give a graphic description of what, coming from a supper-party, he once saw about two o'clock in the morning. In the great street of the city, he overhauled a huge galleon, which proved, he declared, to be the provost himself, not exactly water-logged, and yet not very buoyant, but carrying a good deal of sail. He might possibly have escaped very particular notice, he said, but for the assiduous attendance upon him of an absurd little cock-boat, in the person of wee Gibbie—the two reminding him right ludicrously of the story of the Spanish Armada. Round and round the bulky provost gyrated the tiny baronet, like a little hero of the ring, pitching into him, only with open-handed pushes, not with blows, now on this side and now on that—not after such fashion of sustentation as might have sufficed with a man of ordinary size, but throwing all his force now against the provost's bulging bows, now against his over-leaning quarter, encountering him now as he lurched, now as he heeled, until at length he landed him high, though certainly not dry, on the top of his own steps. The moment the butler opened the door, and the heavy hulk rolled into dock, Gibbie darted off as if he had been the wicked one tormenting the righteous, and in danger of being caught by a pair of holy tongs. Whether the tale was true or not, I do not know: with after-dinner humourists there is reason for caution. Gibbie was not offered the post of henchman to the provost, and rarely could have had the chance of claiming salvage for so distinguished a vessel, seeing he generally cruised in waters where such craft seldom sailed. Though almost nothing could now have induced him to go down Jink Lane, yet about the time the company at Mistress Croale's would be breaking up, he would on most nights be lying in wait a short distance down the Widdiehill, ready to minister to that one of his father's old comrades who might prove most in need of his assistance; and if he showed him no gratitude, Gibbie had not been trained in a school where he was taught to expect or even to wish for any.

I could now give a whole chapter to the setting forth of the pleasures the summer brought him, city summer as it was, but I must content myself with saying that first of these, and not least, was the mere absence of the cold of the other seasons, bringing with it many privileges. He could lie down anywhere and sleep when he would; or spend, if he pleased, whole nights awake, in a churchyard, or on the deck of some vessel discharging her cargo at the quay, or running about the still, sleeping streets. Thus he got to know the shapes of some of the constellations, and not a few of the aspects of the heavens. But even then he never felt alone, for he gazed at the vista from the midst of a cityful of his fellows. Then there were the scents of the laylocks and the roses and the carnations and the sweet-peas, that came floating out from the gardens, contending sometimes with those of the grocers' and chemists' shops. Now and then too he came in for a small feed of strawberries, which were very plentiful in their season. Sitting then on a hospitable doorstep, with the feet and faces of friends passing him in both directions, and love embodied in the warmth of summer all about him, he would eat his strawberries, and inherit the earth.

VIII

SAMBO

No one was so sorry for the death of Sir George, or had so many kind words to say in memory of him, as Mistress Croale. Neither was her sorrow only because she had lost so good a customer, or even because she had liked the man: I believe it was much enhanced by a vague doubt that after all she was to blame for his death. In vain she said to herself, and said truly, that it would have been far worse for him, and Gibbie too, had he gone elsewhere for his drink; she could not get the account settled with her conscience. She tried to relieve herself by being kinder than before to the boy; but she was greatly hindered in this by the fact that, after his father's death, she could not get him inside her door. That his father was not there—would not be there at night, made the place dreadful to him. This addition to the trouble of mind she already had on account of the nature of her business, was the cause, I believe, why, after Sir George's death, she went down the hill with accelerated speed. She sipped more frequently from her own bottle, soon came to "tasting with" her customers, and after that her descent was rapid. She no longer refused drink to women, though for a time she always gave it under protest; she winked at card-playing; she grew generally more lax in her administration; and by degrees a mist of evil fame began to gather about her house. Thereupon her enemy, as she considered him, the Rev. Clement Sclater, felt himself justified in moving more energetically for the withdrawal of her license, which, with the support of outraged neighbours, he found no difficulty in effecting. She therefore flitted to another parish, and opened a worse house in a worse region of the city—on the river-bank, namely, some little distance above the quay, not too far to be within easy range of sailors, and the people employed about the vessels loading or discharging cargo. It pretended to be only a lodging-house, and had no license for the sale of strong drink, but nevertheless, one way and another, a great deal was drunk in the house, and, as always card-playing, and sometimes worse things were going on, getting more vigorous ever as the daylight waned, frequent quarrels and occasional bloodshed was the consequence. For some time, however, nothing very serious brought the place immediately within the conscious ken of the magistrates.

In the second winter after his father's death, Gibbie, wandering everywhere about the city, encountered Lucky Croale in the neighbourhood of her new abode; down there she was Mistress no longer, but, with a familiarity scarcely removed from contempt, was both mentioned and addressed as Lucky Croale. The repugnance which had hitherto kept Gibbie from her having been altogether to her place and not to herself, he at once accompanied her home, and after that went often to the house. He was considerably surprised when first he heard words from her mouth for using which she had formerly been in the habit of severely reproving her guests; but he always took things as he found them, and when ere long he had to hear such occasionally addressed to himself, when she happened to be more out of temper than usual, he never therefore questioned her friendship. What more than anything else attracted him to her house, however, was the jolly manners and open-hearted kindness of most of the sailors who frequented it, with almost all of whom he was a favourite; and it soon came about that, when his ministrations to the incapable were over, he would spend the rest of the night more frequently there than anywhere else; until at last he gave up, in a great measure, his guardianship of the drunk in the streets for that of those who were certainly in much more danger of mishap at Lucky Croale's. Scarcely a night passed when he was not present at one or more of the quarrels of which the place was a hot-bed; and as he never by any chance took a part, or favoured one side more than another, but confined himself to an impartial distribution of such peace-making blandishments as the ever-springing fountain of his affection took instinctive shape in, the wee baronet came to be regarded, by the better sort of the rough fellows, almost as the very identical sweet little cherub, sitting perched up aloft, whose department in the saving business of the universe it was, to take care of the life of poor Jack. I do not say that he was always successful in his endeavours at atonement, but beyond a doubt Lucky Croale's house was a good deal less of a hell through the haunting presence of the child. He was not shocked by the things he saw, even when he liked them least. He regarded the doing of them much as he had looked upon his father's drunkenness— as a pitiful necessity that overtook men—one from which there was no escape, and which caused a great need for Gibbies. Evil language and coarse behaviour alike passed over him, without leaving the smallest stain upon heart or conscience, desire or will. No one could doubt it who considered the clarity of his face and eyes, in which the occasional but not frequent expression of keenness and promptitude scarcely even ruffled the prevailing look of unclouded heavenly babyhood.

If any one thinks I am unfaithful to human fact, and overcharge the description of this child, I on my side doubt the extent of the experience of that man or woman. I admit the child a rarity, but a rarity in the right direction, and therefore a being with whom humanity has the greater need to be made acquainted. I admit that the best things are the commonest, but the highest types and the best combinations of them are the rarest. There is more love in the world than anything else, for instance; but the best love and the individual in whom love is supreme are the rarest of all things. That for which humanity has the strongest claim upon its workmen, is the representation of its own best; but the loudest demand of the present day is for the representation of that grade of humanity of which men see the most—that type of things which could never have been but that it might pass. The demand marks the commonness, narrowness, low-levelled satisfaction of the age. It loves its own—not that which might be, and ought to be its own—not its better self, infinitely higher than its present, for the sake of whose approach it exists. I do not think that the age is worse in this respect than those which have preceded it, but that vulgarity, and a certain vile contentment swelling to self-admiration, have become more vocal than hitherto; just as unbelief, which I think in reality less prevailing than in former ages, has become largely more articulate, and thereby more loud and peremptory. But whatever the demand of the age, I insist that that which ought to be presented to its beholding, is the common good uncommonly developed, and that not because of its rarity, but because it is truer to humanity. Shall I admit those conditions, those facts, to be true exponents of humanity, which, except they be changed, purified, or abandoned, must soon cause that humanity to cease from its very name, must destroy its very being? To make the admission would be to assert that a house may be divided against itself, and yet stand. It is the noble, not the failure from the noble, that is the true human; and if I must show the failure, let it ever be with an eye to the final possible, yea, imperative, success. But in our day, a man who will accept any oddity of idiosyncratic development in manners, tastes, or habits, will refuse, not only as improbable, but as inconsistent with human nature, the representation of a man trying to be merely as noble as is absolutely essential to his being—except, indeed, he be at the same time represented as failing utterly in the attempt, and compelled to fall back upon the imperfections of humanity, and acknowledge them as its laws. Its improbability, judged by the experience of most men I admit; its unreality in fact I deny; and its absolute unity with the true idea of humanity, I believe and assert.

It is hardly necessary for me now to remark, seeing my narrative must already have suggested it, that what kept Gibbie pure and honest was the rarely-developed, ever-active love of his kind. The human face was the one attraction to him in the universe. In deep fact, it is so to everyone; I state but the commonest reality in creation; only in Gibbie the fact had come to the surface; the common thing was his in uncommon degree and potency. Gibbie knew no music except the voice of man and woman; at least no other had as yet affected him. To be sure he had never heard much. Drunken sea-songs he heard every night almost; and now and then on Sundays he ran through a zone of psalm-singing; but neither of those could well be called music. There hung a caged bird here and there at a door in the poorer streets; but Gibbie's love embraced the lower creation also, and too tenderly for the enjoyment of its melody. The human bird loved liberty too dearly to gather anything but pain from the song of the little feathered brother who had lost it, and to whom he could not minister as to the drunkard. In general he ran from the presence of such a prisoner. But sometimes he would stop and try to comfort the naked little Freedom, disrobed of its space; and on one occasion was caught in the very act of delivering a canary that hung outside a little shop. Any other than wee Gibbie would have been heartily cuffed for the offence, but the owner of the bird only smiled at the would-be liberator, and hung the cage a couple of feet higher on the wall. With such a passion of affection, then, finding vent in constant action, is it any wonder Gibbie's heart and hands should be too full for evil to occupy them even a little?

One night in the spring, entering Lucky Croale's common room, he saw there for the first time a negro sailor, whom the rest called Sambo, and was at once taken with his big, dark, radiant eyes, and his white teeth continually uncovering themselves in good-humoured smiles. Sambo had left the vessel in which he had arrived, was waiting for another, and had taken up his quarters at Lucky Croale's. Gibbie's advances he met instantly, and in a few days a strong mutual affection had sprung up between them. To Gibbie Sambo speedily became absolutely loving and tender, and Gibbie made him full return of devotion.

The negro was a man of immense muscular power, like not a few of his race, and, like most of them, not easily provoked, inheriting not a little of their hard-learned long-suffering. He bore even with those who treated him with far worse than the ordinary superciliousness of white to black; and when the rudest of city boys mocked him, only showed his teeth by way of smile. The ill-conditioned among Lucky Croale's customers and lodgers were constantly taking advantage of his good nature, and presuming upon his forbearance; but so long as they confined themselves to mere insolence, or even bare-faced cheating, he endured with marvellous temper. It was possible, however, to go too far even with him.

One night Sambo was looking on at a game of cards, in which all the rest in the room were engaged. Happening to laugh at some turn it took, one of them, a Malay, who was losing, was offended, and abused him. Others objected to his having fun without risking money, and required him to join in the game. This for some reason or other he declined, and when the whole party at length insisted, positively refused. Thereupon they all took umbrage, nor did most of them make many steps of the ascent from displeasure to indignation, wrath, revenge; and then ensued a row. Gibbie had been sitting all the time on his friend's knee, every now and then stroking his black face, in which, as insult followed insult, the sunny blood kept slowly rising, making the balls of his eyes and his teeth look still whiter. At length a savage from Greenock threw a tumbler at him. Sambo, quick as a lizard, covered his face with his arm. The tumbler falling from it, struck Gibbie on the head—not severely, but hard enough to make him utter a little cry. At that sound, the latent fierceness came wide awake in Sambo. Gently as a nursing mother he set Gibbie down in a corner behind him, then with one rush sent every Jack of the company sprawling on the floor, with the table and bottles and glasses atop of them. At the vision of their plight his good humour instantly returned, he burst into a great hearty laugh, and proceeded at once to lift the table from off them. That effected, he caught up Gibbie in his arms, and carried him with him to bed.

In the middle of the night Gibbie half woke, and, finding himself alone, sought his father's bosom; then, in the confusion between sleeping and waking, imagined his father's death come again. Presently he remembered it was in Sambo's arms he fell asleep, but where he was now he could not tell: certainly he was not in bed. Groping, he pushed a door, and a glimmer of light came in. He was in a closet of the room in which Sambo slept—and something was to do about his bed. He rose softly and peeped out, There stood several men, and a struggle was going on—nearly noiseless. Gibbie was half-dazed, and could not understand; but he had little anxiety about Sambo, in whose prowess he had a triumphant confidence. Suddenly came the sound of a great gush, and the group parted from the bed and vanished. Gibbie darted towards it. The words, "O Lord Jesus!" came to his ears, and he heard no more: they were poor Sambo's last in this world. The light of a street lamp fell upon the bed: the blood was welling, in great thick throbs, out of his huge black throat. They had bent his head back, and the gash gaped wide.

For some moments Gibbie stood in ghastly terror. No sound except a low gurgle came to his ears, and the horror of the stillness overmastered him. He never could recall what came next. When he knew himself again, he was in the street, running like the wind, he knew not whither. It was not that he dreaded any hurt to himself; horror, not fear, was behind him.

His next recollection of himself was in the first of the morning, on the lofty chain-bridge over the river Daur. Before him lay he knew not what, only escape from what was behind. His faith in men seemed ruined. The city, his home, was frightful to him. Quarrels and curses and blows he had been used to, and amidst them life could be lived. If he did not consciously weave them into his theories, he unconsciously wrapped them up in his confidence, and was at peace. But the last night had revealed something unknown before. It was as if the darkness had been cloven, and through the cleft he saw into hell. A thing had been done that could not be undone, and he thought it must be what people called murder. And Sambo was such a good man! He was almost as good a man as Gibbie's father, and now he would not breathe any more! Was he gone where Gibbie's father was gone? Was it the good men that stopped breathing and grew cold? But it was those wicked men that had deaded Sambo! And with that his first vague perception of evil and wrong in the world began to dawn.

He lifted his head from gazing down on the dark river. A man was approaching the bridge. He came from the awful city! Perhaps he wanted him! He fled along the bridge like a low-flying water-bird. If another man had appeared at the other end, he would have got through between the rods, and thrown himself into the river. But there was no one to oppose his escape; and after following the road a little way up the river, he turned aside into a thicket of shrubs on the nearly precipitous bank, and sat down to recover the breath he had lost more from dismay than exertion.

The light grew. All at once he descried, far down the river, the steeples of the city. Alas! alas! there lay poor black Sambo, so dear to wee Sir Gibbie, motionless and covered with blood! He had two red mouths now, but was not able to speak a word with either! They would carry him to a churchyard and lay him in a hole to lie there for ever and ever. Would all the good people be laid into holes and leave Gibbie quite alone? Sitting and brooding thus, he fell into a dreamy state, in which, brokenly, from here and there, pictures of his former life grew out upon his memory. Suddenly, plainer than all the rest, came the last time he stood under Mistress Croale's window, waiting to help his father home. The same instant, back to the ear of his mind came his father's two words, as he had heard them through the window—"Up Daurside."

"Up Daurside!"—Here he was upon Daurside—a little way up too: he would go farther up. He rose and went on, while the great river kept flowing the other way, dark and terrible, down to the very door inside which lay Sambo with the huge gape in his big throat.

Meantime the murder came to the knowledge of the police, Mistress Croale herself giving the information, and all in the house were arrested. In the course of their examination, it came out that wee Sir Gibbie had gone to bed with the murdered man, and was now nowhere to be found. Either they had murdered him too, or carried him off. The news spread, and the whole city was in commotion about his fate. It was credible enough that persons capable of committing such a crime on such an inoffensive person as the testimony showed poor Sambo, would be capable also of throwing the life of a child after that of the man to protect their own. The city was searched from end to end, from side to side, and from cellar to garret. Not a trace of him was to be found—but indeed Gibbie had always been easier to find than to trace, for he had no belongings of any sort to betray him. No one dreamed of his having fled straight to the country, and search was confined to the city.

The murderers were at length discovered, tried, and executed. They protested their innocence with regard to the child, and therein nothing appeared against them beyond the fact that he was missing. The result, so far as concerned Gibbie, was, that the talk of the city, where almost everyone knew him, was turned, in his absence, upon his history; and from the confused mass of hearsay that reached him, Mr. Sclater set himself to discover and verify the facts. For this purpose he burrowed about in the neighbourhoods Gibbie had chiefly frequented, and was so far successful as to satisfy himself that Gibbie, if he was alive, was Sir Gilbert Galbraith, Baronet; but his own lawyer was able to assure him that not an inch of property remained anywhere attached to the title. There were indeed relations of the boy's mother, who were of some small consequence in a neighbouring county, also one in business in Glasgow, or its neighbourhood, reported wealthy; but these had entirely disowned her because of her marriage. All Mr. Sclater discovered besides was, in a lumber-room next the garret in which Sir George died, a box of papers—a glance at whose contents showed that they must at least prove a great deal of which he was already certain from other sources. A few of them had to do with the house in which they were found, still known as the Auld Hoose o' Galbraith; but most of them referred to property in land, and many were of ancient date. If the property were in the hands of descendants of the original stock, the papers would be of value in their eyes; and, in any case, it would be well to see to their safety. Mr. Sclater therefore had the chest removed to the garret of the manse, where it stood thereafter, little regarded, but able to answer for more than itself.

IX

ADRIFT

Gibbie was now without a home. He had had a whole city for his
dwelling, every street of which had been to him as another hall
in his own house, every lane as a passage from one set of rooms to
another, every court as a closet, every house as a safe, guarding the
only possessions he had, the only possessions he knew how to value—
his fellow-mortals, radiant with faces, and friendly with hands and
tongues. Great as was his delight in freedom, a delight he revelled
in from morning to night, and sometimes from night to morning, he
had never had a notion of it that reached beyond the city, he never
longed for larger space, for wider outlook. Space and outlook he had
skyward—and seaward when he would, but even into these regions
he had never yet desired to go. His world was the world of men; the
presence of many was his greater room; his people themselves were his
world. He had no idea of freedom in dissociation with human faces
and voices and eyes. But now he had left all these, and as he ran from
them a red pall seemed settling down behind him, wrapping up and
hiding away his country, his home. For the first time in his life, the
fatherless, motherless, brotherless, sisterless stray of the streets felt
himself alone. The sensation was an awful one. He had lost so many,
and had not one left! That gash in Sambo's black throat had slain "a
whole cityful." His loneliness grew upon him, until again he darted
aside from the road into the bush, this time to hide from the Spectre
of the Desert—the No Man. Deprived of human countenances, the
face of creation was a mask without eyes, and liberty a mere negation.
Not that Gibbie had ever thought about liberty; he had only enjoyed:
not that he had ever thought about human faces; he had only loved
them, and lived upon their smiles. "Gibbie wadna need to gang to
h'aven," said Mysie, the baker's daughter, to her mother, one night,
as they walked home from a merry-making. "What for that, lassie?"
returned her mother. "Cause he wad be meeserable whaur there was
nae drunk fowk," answered Mysie. And now it seemed to the poor,
shocked, heart-wounded creature, as if the human face were just the
one thing he could no more look upon. One haunted him, the black

one, with the white, staring eyes, the mouth in its throat, and the white grinning teeth.

It was a cold, fresh morning, cloudy and changeful, towards the end of April. It had rained, and would rain again; it might snow. Heavy undefined clouds, with saffron breaks and borders, hung about the east, but what was going to happen there—at least he did not think; he did not know east from west, and I doubt whether, although he had often seen the sun set, he had ever seen him rise. Yet even to him, city-creature as he was, it was plain something was going to happen there. And happen it did presently, and that with a splendour that for a moment blinded Gibbie. For just at the horizon there was a long horizontal slip of blue sky, and through that crack the topmost arc of the rising sun shot suddenly a thousand arrows of radiance into the brain of the boy. But the too-much light scorched there a blackness instantly; and to the soul of Gibbie it was the blackness of the room from which he had fled, and upon it out came the white eyeballs and the brilliant teeth of his dead Sambo, and the red burst from his throat that answered the knife of the Malay. He shrieked, and struck with his hands against the sun from which came the terrible vision. Had he been a common child, his reason would have given way; but one result of the overflow of his love was, that he had never yet known fear for himself. His sweet confident face, innocent eyes, and caressing ways, had almost always drawn a response more or less in kind; and that certain some should not repel him, was a fuller response from them than gifts from others. Except now and then, rarely, a street boy a little bigger than himself, no one had ever hurt him, and the hurt upon these occasions had not gone very deep, for the child was brave and hardy. So now it was not fear, but the loss of old confidence, a sickness coming over the heart and brain of his love, that unnerved him. It was not the horrid cruelty to his friend, and his own grievous loss thereby, but the recoil of his loving endeavour that, jarring him out of every groove of thought, every socket of habit, every joint of action, cast him from the city, and made of him a wanderer indeed, not a wanderer in a strange country, but a wanderer in a strange world.

To no traveller could one land well be so different from another, as to Gibbie the country was from the town. He had seen bushes and trees before, but only over garden walls, or in one or two of the churchyards. He had looked from the quay across to the bare shore on the other side, with its sandy hills, and its tall lighthouse on the top of the great rocks that bordered the sea; but, so looking, he had beheld space as one looking from this world into the face of the moon, as a child looks upon vastness and possible dangers from his nurse's arms where it cannot come near him; for houses backed the quay all along; the city was behind him, and spread forth her protecting arms. He had, once or twice, run out along the pier, which shot far into the immensity of the sea, like a causeway to another world—a stormy thread of granite, beaten upon both sides by the waves of the German Ocean; but it was with the sea and not the country he then made the small acquaintance—and that not without terror. The sea was as different from the city as the air into which he had looked up at night— too different to compare against it and feel the contrast; on neither could he set foot; in neither could he be required to live and act—as now in this waste of enterable and pervious extent.

Its own horror drove the vision away, and Gibbie saw the world again—saw, but did not love it. The sun seemed but to have looked up to mock him and go down again, for he had crossed the crack, and was behind a thick mass of cloud; a cold damp wind, spotted with sparkles of rain, blew fitfully from the east; the low bushes among which he sat, sent forth a chill sighing all about him, as they sifted the wind into sound; the smell of the damp earth was strange to him—he did not know the freshness, the new birth of which it breathed; below him the gloomy river, here deep, smooth, moody, sullen, there puckered with the grey ripples of a shallow laughter under the cold breeze, went flowing heedless to the city. There only was—or had been, friendliness, comfort, home! This was emptiness—the abode of things, not beings. Yet never once did Gibbie think of returning to the city. He rose and wandered up the wide road along the river bank, farther and farther from it—his only guide the words of his father, "Up Daurside;" his sole comfort the feeling of having once more to do with his father so long departed, some relation still with the paradise of his old world. Along cultivated fields and copses on the one side, and on the other a steep descent to the river, covered here and there with trees, but mostly with rough grass and bushes and stones, he followed the king's highway. There were buttercups and plenty of daisies within his sight—primroses, too, on the slope beneath; but he did not know flowers, and his was not now the mood for discovering what they were. The exercise revived him, and he began to be hungry. But how could there be anything to eat in the desert, inhospitable succession of trees and fields and hedges, through which the road wound endlessly along, like a dead street, having neither houses nor paving stones? Hunger, however, was far less enfeebling to Gibbie than to one accustomed to regular meals, and he was in no anxiety about either when or what he should eat.

The morning advanced, and by-and-by he began to meet a fellow-creature now and then upon the road; but at sight of everyone a feeling rose in him such as he had never had towards human being before: they seemed somehow of a different kind from those in the town, and they did not look friendly as they passed. He did not know that he presented to them a very different countenance from that which his fellow-citizens had always seen him wear; for the mingled and conflicting emotions of his spirit had sent out upon it an expression which, accompanied by the misery of his garments, might well, to the superficial or inexperienced observer, convey the idea that he was a fugitive and guilty. He was so uncomfortable at length from the way the people he met scrutinized him that, when he saw anyone coming, he would instantly turn aside and take the covert of thicket, or hedge, or stone wall, until the bearer of eyes had passed. His accustomed trot, which he kept up for several hours, made him look the more suspicious; but his feet, hardened from very infancy as they were, soon found the difference between the smooth flags and the sharp stones of the road, and before noon he was walking at quite a sober, although still active, pace. Doubtless it slackened the sooner that he knew no goal, no end to his wandering. Up Daurside was the one vague notion he had of his calling, his destiny, and with his short, quick step, his progress was considerable; he passed house after house, farm after farm; but, never in the way of asking for anything, though as little in the way of refusing, he went nearer none of them than the road led him. Besides, the houses were very unlike those in the city, and not at all attractive to him. He came at length to a field, sloping to the road, which was covered with leaves like some he had often seen in the market. They drew him; and as there was but a low and imperfect hedge between, he got over, and found it was a crop of small yellow turnips. He gathered as many as he could carry, and ate them as he went along. Happily no agricultural person encountered him for some distance, though Gibbie knew no special cause to congratulate himself upon that, having not the slightest conscience of offence in what he did. His notions of property were all associated with well-known visible or neighbouring owners, and in the city he would never have dreamed of touching anything that was not given him, except it lay plainly a lost thing. But here, where everything was so different, and he saw none of the signs of ownership to which he was accustomed, the idea of property did not come to him; here everything looked lost, or on the same category with the chips and parings and crusts that were thrown out in the city, and became common property. Besides, the love which had hitherto rendered covetousness impossible, had here no object whose presence might have suggested a doubt, to supply in a measure the lack of knowledge; hunger, instead, was busy in his world. I trust there were few farmers along the road who would have found fault with him for taking one or two; but none, I suspect, would have liked to see him with all the turnips he could carry, eating them like a very rabbit: they were too near a city to look upon such a spectacle with indifference. Gibbie made no attempt to hide his spoil; whatever could have given birth to the sense that caution would be necessary, would have prevented him from taking it. While yet busy he came upon a little girl feeding a cow by the roadside. She saw how he ate the turnips, and offered him a bit of oatmeal bannock. He received it gladly, and with beaming eyes offered her a turnip. She refused it with some indignation. Gibbie, disappointed, but not ungrateful, resumed his tramp, eating his bannock. He came soon after to a little stream that ran into the great river. For a few moments he eyed it very doubtfully, thinking it must, like the kennels along the sides of the streets, be far too dirty to drink of; but the way it sparkled and sang—most unscientific reasons—soon satisfied him, and he drank and was refreshed. He had still two turnips left, but, after the bannock, he did not seem to want them, and stowed them in the ends of the sleeves of his jacket, folded back into great cuffs.

All day the cold spring weather continued, with more of the past winter in it than of the coming summer. The sun would shine out for a few moments, with a grey, weary, old light, then retreat as if he had tried, but really could not. Once came a slight fall of snow, which, however, melted the moment it touched the earth. The wind kept blowing cheerlessly by fits, and the world seemed growing tired of the same thing over again so often. At length the air began to grow dusk: then, first, fears of the darkness, to Gibbie utterly unknown before, and only born of the preceding night, began to make him aware of their existence in the human world. They seemed to rise up from his lonely heart; they seemed to descend upon him out of the thickening air; they seemed to catch at his breath, and gather behind him as he went. But, happily, before it was quite dark, and while yet he could distinguish between objects, he came to the gate of a farmyard; it waked in him the hope of finding some place where he could sleep warmer than in the road, and he clambered over it. Nearest of the buildings to the gate, stood an open shed, and he could see the shafts of carts projecting from it: perhaps in one of those carts, or under it, he might find a place that would serve him to sleep in: he did not yet know what facilities for repose the country affords. But just as he entered the shed, he spied at the farther corner of it, outside, a wooden structure, like a small house, and through the arched door of it saw the floor covered with nice-looking straw. He suspected it to be a dog's kennel; and presently the chain lying beside it, with a collar at the end, satisfied him it was. The dog was absent, and it looked altogether enticing! He crept in, got under as much of the straw as he could heap over him, and fell fast asleep.

In a few minutes, as it seemed to him, he was roused by the great voice of a dog in conversation with a boy: the boy seemed, by the sound of the chain, to be fastening the collar on the dog's neck, and presently left him. The dog, which had been on the rampage the whole afternoon, immediately turned to creep in and rest till supper time, presenting to Gibbie, who had drawn himself up at the back of the kennel, the intelligent countenance of a large Newfoundland. Now Gibbie had been honoured with the acquaintance of many dogs, and the friendship of most of them, for a lover of humanity can hardly fail to be a lover of caninity. Even among dogs, however, there are ungracious individuals, and Gibbie had once or twice been bitten by quadrupedal worshippers of the respectable. Hence, with the sight of the owner of the dwelling, it dawned upon him that he must be startled to find a stranger in his house, and might, regarding him as an intruder rather than a guest, worry him before he had time to explain himself. He darted forward therefore to get out, but had scarcely reached the door, when the dog put in his nose, ready to follow with all he was and had. Gibbie, thereupon, began a loud barking, as much as to say—"Here I am: please do nothing without reflection." The dog started back in extreme astonishment, his ears erect, and a keen look of question on his sagacious visage: what strange animal, speaking like, and yet so unlike, an orthodox dog, could have got into his very chamber? Gibbie, amused at the dog's fright, and assured by his looks that he was both a good-natured and reasonable animal, burst into a fit of merry laughter as loud as his previous barking, and a good deal more musical. The dog evidently liked it better, and took it as a challenge to play: after a series of sharp bursts of barking, his eyes flashing straight in at the door, and his ears lifted up like two plumes on the top of them, he darted into the kennel, and began poking his nose into his visitor. Gibbie fell to patting and kissing and hugging him as if he had been a human—as who can tell but he was?—glad of any companion that belonged to the region of the light; and they were friends at once. Mankind had disappointed him, but here was a dog! Gibbie was not the one to refuse mercies which yet he would not have been content to pray for. Both were tired, however, for both had been active that day, and a few minutes of mingled wrestling and endearment, to which, perhaps, the narrowness of their play-ground gave a speedier conclusion, contented both, after which they lay side by side in peace, Gibbie with his head on the dog's back, and the dog every now and then turning his head over his shoulder to lick Gibbie's face.

Again he was waked by approaching steps, and the same moment the dog darted from under him, and with much rattle out of the kennel, in front of which he stood and whined expectant. It was not quite dark, for the clouds had drifted away, and the stars were shining, so that, when he put out his head, he was able to see the dim form of a woman setting down something before the dog—into which he instantly plunged his nose, and began gobbling. The sound stirred up all the latent hunger in Gibbie, and he leaped out, eager to have a share. A large wooden bowl was on the ground, and the half of its contents of porridge and milk was already gone; for the poor dog had not yet had experience enough to be perfect in hospitality, and had forgotten his guest's wants in his own: it was plain that, if Gibbie was to have any, he must lose no time in considering the means. Had he had a long nose and mouth all in one like him, he would have plunged them in beside the dog's; but the flatness of his mouth causing the necessity, in the case of such an attempt, of bringing the whole of his face into contact with the food, there was not room in the dish for the two to feed together after the same fashion, so that he was driven to the sole other possible expedient, that of making a spoon of his hand. The dog neither growled nor pushed away the spoon, but instantly began to gobble twice as fast as before, and presently was licking the bottom of the dish. Gibbie's hand, therefore, made but few journeys to his mouth, but what it carried him was good food—better than any he had had that day. When all was gone he crept again into the kennel; the dog followed, and soon they were both fast asleep in each other's arms and legs.

Gibbie woke at sunrise and went out. His host came after him, and stood wagging his tail and looking wistfully up in his face. Gibbie understood him, and, as the sole return he could make for his hospitality, undid his collar. Instantly he rushed off, his back going like a serpent, cleared the gate at a bound, and scouring madly across a field, vanished from his sight; whereupon Gibbie too set out to continue his journey up Daurside.

This day was warmer; the spring had come a step nearer; the dog had been a comforter to him, and the horror had begun to assuage; he began to grow aware of the things about him, and to open his eyes to them. Once he saw a primrose in a little dell, and left the road to look at it. But as he went, he set his foot in the water of a chalybeate spring, which was trickling through the grass, and dyeing the ground red about it: filled with horror he fled, and for some time dared never go near a primrose. And still upon his right hand was the great river, flowing down towards the home he had left; now through low meadows, now through upshouldered fields of wheat and oats, now through rocky heights covered with the graceful silver-barked birch, the mountain ash, and the fir. Every time Gibbie, having lost sight of it by some turn of the road or some interposing eminence, caught its gleam afresh, his first feeling was that it was hurrying to the city, where the dead man lay, to tell where Gibbie was. Why he, who had from infancy done just as he pleased, should now have begun to dread interference with his liberty, he could not himself have told. Perhaps the fear was but the shadow of his new-born aversion to the place where he had seen those best-loved countenances change so suddenly and terribly—cease to smile, but not cease to stare.

That second day he fared better, too, than the first; for he came on a family of mongrel gipsies, who fed him well out of their kettle, and, taken with his looks, thought to keep him for begging purposes. But now that Gibbie's confidence in human nature had been so rudely shaken, he had already begun, with analysis unconscious, to read the human countenance, questioning it; and he thought he saw something that would hurt, in the eyes of two of the men and one of the women. Therefore, in the middle of the night, he slipped silently out of the tent of rags, in which he had lain down with the gipsy children, and ere the mothers woke, was a mile up the river.

But I must not attempt the detail of this part of his journey. It is enough that he got through it. He met with some adventures, and suffered a good deal from hunger and cold. Had he not been hardy as well as fearless he must have died. But, now from this quarter, now from that, he got all that was needful for one of God's birds. Once he found in a hedge the nest of an errant and secretive hen, and recognizing the eggs as food authorized by the shop windows and market of the city, soon qualified himself to have an opinion of their worth. Another time he came upon a girl milking a cow in a shed, and his astonishment at the marvels of the process was such, that he forgot even the hunger that was rendering him faint. He had often seen cows in the city, but had never suspected what they were capable of. When the girl caught sight of him, staring with open mouth, she was taken with such a fit of laughter, that the cow, which was ill-tempered, kicked out, and overturned the pail. Now because of her troublesomeness this cow was not milked beside the rest, and the shed where she stood was used for farm-implements only. The floor of it was the earth, beaten hard, and worn into hollows. When the milk settled in one of these, Gibbie saw that it was lost to the girl, and found to him: undeterred by the astounding nature of the spring from which he had just seen it flow, he threw himself down, and drank like a calf. Her laughter ended, the girl was troubled: she would be scolded for her clumsiness in allowing Hawkie to kick over the pail, but the eagerness of the boy after the milk troubled her more. She told him to wait, and running to the house, returned with two large pieces of oatcake, which she gave him.

Thus, one way and another, food came to Gibbie. Drink was to be had in almost any hollow. Sleep was scattered everywhere over the world. For warmth, only motion and a seasoned skin were necessary: the latter Gibbie had; the former, already a habit learned in the streets, had now become almost a passion.

X

The Barn

By this time Gibbie had got well up towards the roots of the hills of Gormgarnet, and the river had dwindled greatly. He was no longer afraid of it, but would lie for hours listening to its murmurs over its pebbly bed, and sometimes even sleep in the hollows of its banks, or below the willows that overhung it. Every here and there, a brown rivulet from some peat-bog on a hill—brown and clear, like smoke-crystals molten together, flowed into it, and when he had lost it, guided him back to his guide. Farm after farm he passed, here one widely bordering a valley stream, there another stretching its skirts up the hillsides till they were lost in mere heather, where the sheep wandered about, cropping what stray grass-blades and other eatables they could find. Lower down he had passed through small towns and large villages: here farms and cottages, with an occasional country-seat and little village of low thatched houses, made up the abodes of men. By this time he had become greatly reconciled to the loneliness of Nature, and no more was afraid in her solitary presence.

At the same time his heart had begun to ache and long after the communion of his kind. For not once since he set out—and that seemed months where it was only weeks, had he had an opportunity of doing anything for anybody—except, indeed, unfastening the dog's collar; and not to be able to help was to Gibbie like being dead. Everybody, down to the dogs, had been doing for him, and what was to become of him! It was a state altogether of servitude into which he had fallen.

May had now set in, but up here among the hills she was May by courtesy only: or if she was May, she would never be Might. She was, indeed, only April, with her showers and sunshine, her tearful, childish laughter, and again the frown, and the despair irremediable. Nay, as if she still kept up a secret correspondence with her cousin March, banished for his rudeness, she would not very seldom shake from her skirts a snow storm, and oftener the dancing hail. Then out would come the sun behind her, and laugh, and say—"I could not help that; but here I am all the same, coming to you as fast as I can!" The green crops were growing darker, and the trees were all getting out their nets to catch carbon. The lambs were frolicking, and in sheltered places the flowers were turning the earth into a firmament. And now a mere daisy was enough to delight the heart of Gibbie. His joy in humanity so suddenly checked, and his thirst for it left unslaked, he had begun to see the human look in the face of the commonest flowers, to love the trusting stare of the daisy, that gold-hearted boy, and the gentle despondency of the girl harebell, dreaming of her mother, the azure. The wind, of which he had scarce thought as he met it roaming the streets like himself, was now a friend of his solitude, bringing him sweet odours, alive with the souls of bees, and cooling with bliss the heat of the long walk. Even when it blew cold along the waste moss, waving the heads of the cotton-grass, the only live thing visible, it was a lover, and kissed him on the forehead. Not that Gibbie knew what a kiss was, any more than he knew about the souls of bees. He did not remember ever having been kissed. In that granite city, the women were not much given to kissing children, even their own, but if they had been, who of them would have thought of kissing Gibbie! The baker's wife, kind as she always was to him, would have thought it defilement to press her lips to those of the beggar child. And how is any child to thrive without kisses! The first caresses Gibbie ever knew as such, were given him by Mother Nature herself. It was only, however, by degrees, though indeed rapid degrees, that he became capable of them. In the first part of his journey he was stunned, stupid, lost in change, distracted between a suddenly vanished past, and a future slow dawning in the present. He felt little beyond hunger, and that vague urging up Daurside, with occasional shoots of pleasure from kindness, mostly of woman and dog. He was less shy of the country people by this time, but he did not care to seek them. He thought them not nearly so friendly and good as the town-people, forgetting that these knew him and those did not. To Gibbie an introduction was the last thing necessary for any one who wore a face, and he could not understand why they looked at him so.

Whatever is capable of aspiring, must be troubled that it may wake and aspire—then troubled still, that it may hold fast, be itself, and aspire still.

One evening his path vanished between twilight and moonrise, and just as it became dark he found himself at a rough gate, through which he saw a field. There was a pretty tall hedge on each side of the gate, and he was now a sufficiently experienced traveller to conclude that he was not far from some human abode. He climbed the gate and found himself in a field of clover. It was a splendid big bed, and even had the night not been warm, he would not have hesitated to sleep in it. He had never had a cold, and had as little fear for his health as for his life. He was hungry, it is true; but although food was doubtless more delicious to such hunger as his—that of the whole body, than it can be to the mere palate and culinary imagination of an epicure, it was not so necessary to him that he could not go to sleep without it. So down he lay in the clover, and was at once unconscious.

When he woke, the moon was high in the heavens, and had melted the veil of the darkness from the scene of still, well-ordered comfort. A short distance from his couch, stood a little army of ricks, between twenty and thirty of them, constructed perfectly—smooth and upright and round and large, each with its conical top netted in with straw-rope, and finished off with what the herd-boy called a toupican—a neatly tied and trim tuft of the straw with which it was thatched, answering to the stone-ball on the top of a gable. Like triangles their summits stood out against the pale blue, moon-diluted air. They were treasure-caves, hollowed out of space, and stored with the best of ammunition against the armies of hunger and want; but Gibbie, though he had seen many of them, did not know what they were. He had seen straw used for the bedding of cattle and horses, and supposed that the chief end of such ricks. Nor had he any clear idea that the cattle themselves were kept for any other object than to make them comfortable and happy. He had stood behind their houses in the dark, and heard them munching and grinding away even in the night. Probably the country was for the cattle, as the towns for the men; and that would explain why the country-people were so inferior. While he stood gazing, a wind arose behind the hills, and came blowing down some glen that opened northwards; Gibbie felt it cold, and sought the shelter of the ricks.

Great and solemn they looked as he drew nigh—near each other, yet enough apart for plenty of air to flow and eddy between. Over a low wall of unmortared stones, he entered their ranks: above him, as he looked up from their broad base, they ascended huge as pyramids, and peopled the waste air with giant forms. How warm it was in the round-winding paths amongst the fruitful piles—tombs these, no cenotaphs! He wandered about them, now in a dusky yellow gloom, and now in the cold blue moonlight, which they seemed to warm. At length he discovered that the huge things were flanked on one side by a long low

GEORGE MACDONALD

house, in which there was a door, horizontally divided into two parts. Gibbie would fain have got in, to try whether the place was good for sleep; but he found both halves fast. In the lower half, however, he spied a hole, which, though not so large, reminded him of the entrance to the kennel of his dog host; but alas! it had a door too, shut from the inside. There might be some way of opening it. He felt about, and soon discovered that it was a sliding valve, which he could push to either side. It was, in fact, the cat's door, specially constructed for her convenience of entrance and exit. For the cat is the guardian of the barn; the grain which tempts the rats and mice is no temptation to her; the rats and mice themselves are; upon them she executes justice, and remains herself an incorruptible, because untempted, therefore a respectable member of the farm-community—only the dairy door must be kept shut; that has no cat-wicket in it.

The hole was a small one, but tempting to the wee baronet; he might perhaps be able to squeeze himself through. He tried and succeeded, though with some little difficulty. The moon was there before him, shining through a pane or two of glass over the door, and by her light on the hard brown clay floor, Gibbie saw where he was, though if he had been told he was in the barn, he would neither have felt nor been at all the wiser. It was a very old-fashioned barn. About a third of it was floored with wood—dark with age—almost as brown as the clay— for threshing upon with flails. At that labour two men had been busy during the most of the preceding day, and that was how, in the same end of the barn, rose a great heap of oat-straw, showing in the light of the moon like a mound of pale gold. Had Gibbie had any education in the marvellous, he might now, in the midnight and moonlight, have well imagined himself in some treasure-house of the gnomes. What he saw in the other corner was still liker gold, and was indeed greater than gold, for it was life—the heap, namely, of corn threshed from the straw: Gibbie recognized this as what he had seen given to horses. But now the temptation to sleep, with such facilities presented, was overpowering, and took from him all desire to examine further: he shot into the middle of the loose heap of straw, and vanished from the glimpses of the moon, burrowing like a mole. In the heart of the golden warmth, he lay so dry and comfortable that, notwithstanding his hunger had waked with him, he was presently in a faster sleep than before. And indeed what more luxurious bed, or what bed conducive to softer slumber was there in the world to find!

"The moving moon went down the sky," the cold wind softened and grew still; the stars swelled out larger; the rats came, and then came puss, and the rats went with a scuffle and patter; the pagan grey came in like a sleep-walker, and made the barn dreary as a dull dream; then the horses began to fidget with their big feet, the cattle to low with their great trombone throats, and the cocks to crow as if to give warning for the last time against the devil, the world, and the flesh; the men in the adjoining chamber woke, yawned, stretched themselves mightily, and rose; the god-like sun rose after them, and, entering the barn with them, drove out the grey; and through it all the orphan lay warm in God's keeping and his nest of straw, like the butterfly of a huge chrysalis.

When at length Gibbie became once more aware of existence, it was through a stormy invasion of the still realm of sleep; the blows of two flails fell persistent and quick-following, first on the thick head of the sheaf of oats untied and cast down before them, then grew louder and more deafening as the oats flew and the chaff fluttered, and the straw flattened and broke and thinned and spread—until at last they thundered in great hard blows on the wooden floor. It was the first of these last blows that shook Gibbie awake. What they were or indicated he could not tell. He wormed himself softly round in the straw to look out and see.

Now whether it was that sleep was yet heavy upon him, and bewildered his eyes, or that his imagination had in dreams been busy with foregone horrors, I cannot tell; but, as he peered through the meshes of the crossing and blinding straws, what he seemed to see was the body of an old man with dishevelled hair, whom, prostrate on the ground, they were beating to death with great sticks. His tongue clave to the roof of his mouth, not a sound could he utter, not a finger could he move; he had no choice but to lie still, and witness the fierce enormity. But it is good that we are compelled to see some things, life amongst the rest, to what we call the end of them. By degrees Gibbie's sight cleared; the old man faded away; and what was left of him he could see to be only an armful of straw. The next sheaf they threw down, he perceived, under their blows, the corn flying out of it, and began to understand a little. When it was finished, the corn that had flown dancing from its home, like hail from its cloud, was swept aside to the common heap, and the straw tossed up on the mound that harboured Gibbie. It was well that the man with the pitchfork did not spy his eyes peering out from the midst of the straw: he might have taken him for some wild creature, and driven the prongs into him. As it was, Gibbie did not altogether like the look of him, and lay still as a stone. Then another sheaf was unbound and cast on the floor, and the blows of the flails began again. It went on thus for an hour and a half, and Gibbie although he dropped asleep several times, was nearly stupid with the noise. The men at length, however, swept up the corn and tossed up the straw for the last time, and went out. Gibbie, judging by his own desires, thought they must have gone to eat, but did not follow them, having generally been ordered away the moment he was seen in a farmyard. He crept out, however, and began to look about him—first of all for something he could eat. The oats looked the most likely, and he took a mouthful for a trial. He ground at them severely, but, hungry as he was, he failed to find oats good for food. Their hard husks, their dryness, their instability, all slipping past each other at every attempt to crush them with his teeth, together foiled him utterly. He must search farther. Looking round him afresh, he saw an open loft, and climbing on the heap in which he had slept, managed to reach it. It was at the height of the walls, and the couples of the roof rose immediately from it. At the farther end was a heap of hay, which he took for another kind of straw. Then he spied something he knew; a row of cheeses lay on a shelf suspended from the rafters, ripening. Gibbie knew them well from the shop windows—knew they were cheeses, and good to eat, though whence and how they came he did not know, his impression being that they grew in the fields like the turnips. He had still the notion uncorrected, that things in the country belonged to nobody in particular, and were mostly for the use of animals, with which, since he became a wanderer, he had almost come to class himself. He was very hungry. He pounced upon a cheese and lifted it between his two hands; it smelled good, but felt very hard. That was no matter: what else were teeth made strong and sharp for? He tried them on one of the round edges, and, nibbling actively, soon got through to the softer body of the cheese. But he had not got much farther when he heard the men returning, and desisted, afraid of being discovered by the noise he made. The readiest way to conceal himself was to lie down flat on the loft, and he did so just where he could see the threshing-floor over the edge of it by lifting his head. This, however, he scarcely ventured to do; and all he could see as he lay was the tip of the swing-bar of one of the flails, ever as it reached the highest point of its ascent. But to watch for it very soon ceased to be interesting; and although he had eaten so little of the cheese, it had yet been enough to make him dreadfully thirsty, therefore he greatly desired to get away. But he dared not go down: with their sticks those men might knock him over in a moment! So he lay there thinking of the poor little hedgehog he had seen on the road as he came; how he stood watching it, and wishing he had a suit made all of great pins, which he could set up when he pleased; and how the driver of a cart, catching sight of him at the foot of the hedge, gave him a blow with his whip, and, poor fellow! notwithstanding his clothes of pins, that one blow of a whip was too much for him! There seemed nothing in the world but killing!

At length he could, unoccupied with something else, bear his thirst no longer, and, squirming round on the floor, crept softly towards the other end of the loft, to see what was to be seen there.

He found that the heap of hay was not in the loft at all. It filled a small chamber in the stable, in fact; and when Gibbie clambered upon it, what should he see below him on the other side, but a beautiful white horse, eating some of the same sort of stuff he was now lying upon! Beyond he could see the backs of more horses, but they were very different—big and clumsy, and not white. They were all eating, and this was their food on which he lay! He wished he too could eat it—and tried, but found it even less satisfactory than the oats, for it nearly choked him, and set him coughing so that he was in considerable danger of betraying his presence to the men in the barn. How did the horses manage to get such dry stuff down their throats? But the cheese was dry too, and he could eat that! No doubt the cheese, as well as the fine straw, was there for the horses! He would like to see the beautiful white creature down there eat a bit of it; but with all his big teeth he did not think he could manage a whole cheese, and how to get a piece broken off for him, with those men there, he could not devise. It would want a long-handled hammer like those with which he had seen men breaking stones on the road.

A door opened beyond, and a man came in and led two of the horses out, leaving the door open. Gibbie clambered down from the top of the hay into the stall beside the white horse, and ran out. He was almost in the fields, had not even a fence to cross.

He cast a glance around, and went straight for a neighbouring hollow, where, taught by experience, he hoped to find water.

XI

JANET

Once away, Gibbie had no thought of returning. Up Daurside was the sole propulsive force whose existence he recognized. But when he lifted his head from drinking at the stream, which was one of some size, and, greatly refreshed, looked up its channel, a longing seized him to know whence came the water of life which had thus restored him to bliss—how a burn first appears upon the earth. He thought it might come from the foot of a great conical mountain which seemed but a little way off. He would follow it up and see. So away he went, yielding at once, as was his wont, to the first desire that came. He had not trotted far along the bank, however, before, at a sharp turn it took, he saw that its course was a much longer one than he had imagined, for it turned from the mountain, and led up among the roots of other hills, while here in front of him, direct from the mountain, as it seemed, came down a smaller stream, and tumbled noisily into this. The larger burn would lead him too far from the Daur; he would follow the smaller one. He found a wide shallow place, crossed the larger, and went up the side of the smaller.

Doubly free after his imprisonment of the morning, Gibbie sped joyously along. Already nature, her largeness, her openness, her loveliness, her changefulness, her oneness in change, had begun to heal the child's heart, and comfort him in his disappointment with his kind. The stream he was now ascending ran along a claw of the mountain, which claw was covered with almost a forest of pine, protecting little colonies of less hardy timber. Its heavy green was varied with the pale delicate fringes of the fresh foliage of the larches, filling the air with aromatic breath. In the midst of their soft tufts, each tuft buttoned with a brown spot, hung the rich brown knobs and tassels of last year's cones. But the trees were all on the opposite side of the stream, and appeared to be mostly on the other side of a wall. Where Gibbie was, the mountain-root was chiefly of rock, interspersed with heather.

A little way up the stream, he came to a bridge over it, closed at the farther end by iron gates between pillars, each surmounted by a wolf's head in stone. Over the gate on each side leaned a rowan-tree, with trunk and branches aged and gnarled amidst their fresh foliage. He crossed the burn to look through the gate, and pressed his face between the bars to get a better sight of a tame rabbit that had got out of its hutch. It sat, like a Druid white with age, in the midst of a gravel drive, much overgrown with moss, that led through a young larch wood, with here and there an ancient tree, lonely amidst the youth of its companions. Suddenly from the wood a large spaniel came bounding upon the rabbit. Gibbie gave a shriek, and the rabbit made one white flash into the wood, with the dog after him. He turned away sad at heart.

"Ilka cratur 'at can," he said to himself, "ates ilka cratur 'at canna!"

It was his first generalization, but not many years passed before he supplemented it with a conclusion:

"But the man 'at wad be a man, he maunna."

Resuming his journey of investigation, he trotted along the bank of the burn, farther and farther up, until he could trot no more, but must go clambering over great stones, or sinking to the knees in bog, patches of it red with iron, from which he would turn away with a shudder. Sometimes he walked in the water, along the bed of the burn itself; sometimes he had to scramble up its steep side, to pass one of the many little cataracts of its descent. Here and there a small silver birch, or a mountain-ash, or a stunted fir-tree, looking like a wizard child, hung over the stream. Its banks were mainly of rock and heather, but now and then a small patch of cultivation intervened. Gibbie had no thought that he was gradually leaving the abodes of men behind him; he knew no reason why in ascending things should change, and be no longer as in plainer ways. For what he knew, there might be farm after farm, up and up for ever, to the gates of heaven. But it would no longer have troubled him greatly to leave all houses behind him for a season. A great purple foxglove could do much now—just at this phase of his story, to make him forget—not the human face divine, but the loss of it. A lark aloft in the blue, from whose heart, as from a fountain whose roots were lost in the air, its natural source, issued, not a stream, but an ever spreading lake of song, was now more to him than the memory of any human voice he had ever heard, except his father's and Sambo's. But he was not yet quite out and away from the dwellings of his kind.

I may as well now make the attempt to give some idea of Gibbie's appearance, as he showed after so long wandering. Of dress he had hardly enough left to carry the name. Shoes, of course, he had none.

Of the shape of trousers there remained nothing, except the division before and behind in the short petticoat to which they were reduced; and those rudimentary divisions were lost in the multitude of rents of equal apparent significance. He had never, so far as he knew, had a shirt upon his body; and his sole other garment was a jacket, so much too large for him, that to retain the use of his hands he had folded back the sleeves quite to his elbows. Thus reversed they became pockets, the only ones he had, and in them he stowed whatever provisions were given him of which he could not make immediate use—porridge and sowens and mashed potatoes included: they served him, in fact, like the first of the stomachs of those animals which have more than one—concerning which animals, by the way, I should much like to know what they were in "Pythagoras' time." His head had plentiful protection in his own natural crop—had never either had or required any other. That would have been of the gold order, had not a great part of its colour been sunburnt, rained, and frozen out of it. All ways it pointed, as if surcharged with electric fluid, crowning him with a wildness which was in amusing contrast with the placidity of his countenance. Perhaps the resulting queerness in the expression of the little vagrant, a look as if he had been hunted till his body and soul were nearly ruffled asunder, and had already parted company in aim and interest, might have been the first thing to strike a careless observer. But if the heart was not a careless one, the eye would look again and discover a stronger stillness than mere placidity—a sort of live peace abiding in that weather-beaten little face under its wild crown of human herbage. The features of it were well-shaped, and not smaller than proportioned to the small whole of his person. His eyes—partly, perhaps, because there was so little flesh upon his bones—were large, and in repose had much of a soft animal expression: there was not in them the look of You and I know. Frequently, too, when occasion roused the needful instinct, they had a sharp expression of outlook and readiness, which, without a trace of fierceness or greed, was yet equally animal. Only all the time there was present something else, beyond characterization: behind them something seemed to lie asleep. His hands and feet were small and childishly dainty, his whole body well-shaped and well put together—of which the style of his dress rather quashed the evidence.

Such was Gibbie to the eye, as he rose from Daurside to the last cultivated ground on the borders of the burn, and the highest dwelling on the mountain. It was the abode of a cottar, and was a dependency of the farm he had just left. The cottar was an old man of seventy; his wife was nearly sixty. They had reared stalwart sons and shapely daughters, now at service here and there in the valleys below—all ready to see God in nature, and recognize Him in providence. They belong to a class now, I fear, extinct, but once, if my love prejudice not my judgment too far, the glory and strength of Scotland: their little acres are now swallowed up in the larger farms.

It was a very humble dwelling, built of turf upon a foundation of stones, and roofed with turf and straw—warm, and nearly impervious to the searching airs of the mountain-side. One little window of a foot and a half square looked out on the universe. At one end stood a stack of peat, half as big as the cottage itself, All around it were huge rocks, some of them peaks whose masses went down to the very central fires, others only fragments that had rolled from above. Here and there a thin crop was growing in patches amongst them, the red grey stone lifting its baldness in spots numberless through the soft waving green. A few of the commonest flowers grew about the door, but there was no garden. The door-step was live rock, and a huge projecting rock behind formed the back and a portion of one of the end walls. This latter rock had been the attraction to the site, because of a hollow in it, which now served as a dairy. For up there with them lived the last cow of the valley—the cow that breathed the loftiest air on all Daurside—a good cow, and gifted in feeding well upon little. Facing the broad south, and leaning against the hill, as against the bosom of God, sheltering it from the north and east, the cottage looked so high-humble, so still, so confident, that it drew Gibbie with the spell of heart-likeness. He knocked at the old, weather-beaten, shrunk and rent, but well patched door. A voice, alive with the soft vibrations of thought and feeling, answered,

"Come yer wa's in, whae'er ye be."

Gibbie pulled the string that came through a hole in the door, so lifting the latch, and entered.

A woman sat on a creepie, her face turned over her shoulder to see who came. It was a grey face, with good simple features and clear grey eyes. The plentiful hair that grew low on her forehead, was half grey, mostly covered by a white cap with frills. A clean wrapper and apron, both of blue print, over a blue winsey petticoat, blue stockings, and strong shoes completed her dress. A book lay on her lap: always when she had finished her morning's work, and made her house tidy, she sat down to have her comfort, as she called it. The moment she saw Gibbie she rose. Had he been the angel Gabriel, come to tell her she was wanted at the throne, her attention could not have been more immediate or thorough. She was rather a little woman, and carried herself straight and light.

"Eh, ye puir ootcast!" she said, in the pitying voice of a mother, "hoo cam ye here sic a hicht? Cratur, ye hae left the warl' ahin' ye. What wad ye hae here? I hae naething."

Receiving no answer but one of the child's betwitching smiles, she stood for a moment regarding him, not in mere silence, but with a look of dumbness. She was a mother. One who is mother only to her own children is not a mother; she is only a woman who has borne children. But here was one of God's mothers.

Loneliness and silence, and constant homely familiarity with the vast simplicities of nature, assist much in the development of the deeper and more wonderful faculties of perception. The perceptions themselves may take this or that shape according to the education—may even embody themselves fantastically, yet be no less perceptions. Now the very moment before Gibbie entered, she had been reading the words of the Lord: "Inasmuch as ye have done it unto one of the least of these my brethren, ye have done it unto me"; and with her heart full of them, she lifted her eyes and saw Gibbie. For one moment, with the quick flashing response of the childlike imagination of the Celt, she fancied she saw the Lord himself. Another woman might have made a more serious mistake, and seen there only a child. Often had Janet pondered, as she sat alone on the great mountain, while Robert was with the sheep, or she lay awake by his side at night, with the wind howling about the cottage, whether the Lord might not sometimes take a lonely walk to look after such solitary sheep of his flock as they, and let them know he had not lost sight of them, for all the ups and downs of the hills. There stood the child, and whether he was the Lord or not, he was evidently hungry. Ah! who could tell but the Lord was actually hungry in every one of his hungering little ones!

In the mean time—only it was but thought-time, not clock-time— Gibbie stood motionless in the middle of the floor, smiling his innocent smile, asking for nothing, hinting at nothing, but resting his wild calm eyes, with a sense of safety and mother-presence, upon the grey thoughtful face of the gazing woman. Her awe deepened; it seemed to descend upon her and fold her in as with a mantle. Involuntarily she bowed her head, and stepping to him took him by the hand, and led him to the stool she had left. There she made him sit, while she brought forward her table, white with scrubbing, took from a hole in the wall and set upon it a platter of oatcakes, carried a wooden bowl to her dairy in the rock through a whitewashed door, and bringing it back filled, half with cream half with milk, set that also on the table. Then she placed a chair before it, and said—

"Sit ye doon, an' tak. Gin ye war the Lord himsel', my bonny man, an' ye may be for oucht I ken, for ye luik puir an' despised eneuch, I cud gie nae better, for it's a' I hae to offer ye—'cep it micht be an egg," she added, correcting herself, and turned and went out.

Presently she came back with a look of success, carrying two eggs, which, having raked out a quantity, she buried in the hot ashes of the peats, and left in front of the hearth to roast, while Gibbie went on eating the thick oatcake, sweet and substantial, and drinking such milk as the wildest imagination of town-boy could never suggest. It was indeed angels' food—food such as would have pleased the Lord himself after a hard day with axe and saw and plane, so good and simple and strong was it. Janet resumed her seat on the low three-legged stool, and took her knitting that he might feel neither that he was watched as he ate, nor that she was waiting for him to finish. Every other moment she gave a glance at the stranger she had taken in; but never a word he spoke, and the sense of mystery grew upon her.

Presently came a great bounce and scramble; the latch jumped up, the door flew open, and after a moment's pause, in came a sheep dog—a splendid thorough-bred collie, carrying in his mouth a tiny, long-legged lamb, which he dropped half dead in the woman's lap. It was a late lamb, born of a mother which had been sold from the hill, but had found her way back from a great distance, in order that her coming young one might have the privilege of being yeaned on the same spot where she had herself awaked to existence. Another moment, and her mba-a was heard approaching the door. She trotted in, and going up to Janet, stood contemplating the consequences of her maternal ambition. Her udder was full, but the lamb was too weak to suck. Janet rose, and going to the side of the room, opened the door of what might have seemed an old press, but was a bed. Folding back the counterpane, she laid the lamb in the bed, and covered it over. Then she got a caup, a wooden dish like a large saucer, and into it milked the ewe. Next she carried the caup to the bed; but what means she there used to enable the

GEORGE MACDONALD

lamb to drink, the boy could not see, though his busy eyes and loving heart would gladly have taken in all.

In the mean time the collie, having done his duty by the lamb, and perhaps forgotten it, sat on his tail, and stared with his two brave trusting eyes at the little beggar that sat in the master's chair, and ate of the fat of the land. Oscar was a gentleman, and had never gone to school, therefore neither fancied nor had been taught that rags make an essential distinction, and ought to be barked at. Gibbie was a stranger, and therefore as a stranger Oscar gave him welcome—now and then stooping to lick the little brown feet that had wandered so far.

Like all wild creatures, Gibbie ate fast, and had finished everything set before him ere the woman had done feeding the lamb. Without a notion of the rudeness of it, his heart full of gentle gratitude, he rose and left the cottage. When Janet turned from her shepherding, there sat Oscar looking up at the empty chair.

"What's come o' the laddie?" she said to the dog, who answered with a low whine, half-regretful, half-interrogative. It may be he was only asking, like Esau, if there was no residuum of blessing for him also; but perhaps he too was puzzled what to conclude about the boy. Janet hastened to the door, but already Gibbie's nimble feet refreshed to the point of every toe with the food he had just swallowed, had borne him far up the hill, behind the cottage, so that she could not get a glimpse of him. Thoughtfully she returned, and thoughtfully removed the remnants of the meal. She would then have resumed her Bible, but her hospitality had rendered it necessary that she should put on her girdle— not a cincture of leather upon her body, but a disc of iron on the fire, to bake thereon cakes ere her husband's return. It was a simple enough process, for the oat-meal wanted nothing but water and fire; but her joints had not yet got rid of the winter's rheumatism, and the labour of the baking was the hardest part of the sacrifice of her hospitality. To many it is easy to give what they have, but the offering of weariness and pain is never easy. They are indeed a true salt to salt sacrifices withal. That it was the last of her meal till her youngest boy should bring her a bag on his back from the mill the next Saturday, made no point in her trouble.

When at last she had done, and put the things away, and swept up the hearth, she milked the ewe, sent her out to nibble, took her Bible, and sat down once more to read. The lamb lay at her feet, with his little head projecting from the folds of her new flannel petticoat; and every time her eye fell from the book upon the lamb, she felt as if somehow the lamb was the boy that had eaten of her bread and drunk of her milk. After she had read a while, there came a change, and the lamb seemed the Lord himself, both lamb and shepherd, who had come to claim her hospitality. Then, divinely invaded with the dread lest in the fancy she should forget the reality, she kneeled down and prayed to the friend of Martha and Mary and Lazarus, to come as he had said, and sup with her indeed.

Not for years and years had Janet been to church; she had long been unable to walk so far; and having no book but the best, and no help to understand it but the highest, her faith was simple, strong, real, all-pervading. Day by day she pored over the great gospel—I mean just the good news according to Matthew and Mark and Luke and John—until she had grown to be one of the noble ladies of the kingdom of heaven—one of those who inherit the earth, and are ripening to see God. For the Master, and his mind in hers, was her teacher. She had little or no theology save what he taught her, or rather, what he is. And of any other than that, the less the better; for no theology, except the Theou logos, is worth the learning, no other being true. To know him is to know God. And he only who obeys him, does or can know him; he who obeys him cannot fail to know him. To Janet, Jesus Christ was no object of so-called theological speculation, but a living man, who somehow or other heard her when she called to him, and sent her the help she needed.

XII

Glashgar

Up and up the hill went Gibbie. The path ceased altogether; but when up is the word in one's mind—and up had grown almost a fixed idea with Gibbie—he can seldom be in doubt whether he is going right, even where there is no track. Indeed in all more arduous ways, men leave no track behind them, no finger-post—there is always but the steepness. He climbed and climbed. The mountain grew steeper and barer as he went, and he became absorbed in his climbing. All at once he discovered that he had lost the stream, where or when he could not tell. All below and around him was red granite rock, scattered over with the chips and splinters detached by air and wind, water and stream, light and heat and cold. Glashgar was only about three thousand feet in height, but it was the steepest of its group—a huge rock that, even in the midst of masses, suggested solidity.

Not once while he ascended had the idea come to him that by and by he should be able to climb no farther. For aught he knew there were oat-cakes and milk and sheep and collie dogs ever higher and higher still. Not until he actually stood upon the peak did he know that there was the earthly hitherto—the final obstacle of unobstancy, the everywhere which, from excess of perviousness, was to human foot impervious. The sun was about two hours towards the west, when Gibbie, his little legs almost as active as ever, surmounted the final slope. Running up like a child that would scale heaven he stood on the bare round, the head of the mountain, and saw, with an invading shock of amazement, and at first of disappointment, that there was no going higher: in every direction the slope was downward. He had never been on the top of anything before. He had always been in the hollows of things. Now the whole world lay beneath him. It was cold; in some of the shadows lay snow—weary exile from both the sky and the sea and the ways of them—captive in the fetters of the cold—prisoner to the mountain top; but Gibbie felt no cold. In a glow with the climb, which at the last had been hard, his lungs filled with the heavenly air, and his soul with the feeling that he was above everything that was, uplifted on the very crown of the earth, he stood in his rags, a fluttering scarecrow, the conqueror of height, the discoverer of immensity, the monarch of space. Nobody knew of such marvel but him! Gibbie had never even heard the word poetry, but none the less was he the very stuff out of which poems grow, and now all the latent poetry in him was set a swaying and heaving—an ocean inarticulate because unobstructed—a might that could make no music, no thunder of waves, because it had no shore, no rocks of thought against which to break in speech. He sat down on the topmost point; and slowly, in the silence and the loneliness, from the unknown fountains of the eternal consciousness, the heart of the child filled. Above him towered infinitude, immensity, potent on his mind through shape to his eye in a soaring dome of blue—the one visible symbol informed and insouled of the eternal, to reveal itself thereby. In it, centre and life, lorded the great sun, beginning to cast shadows to the south and east from the endless heaps of the world, that lifted themselves in all directions. Down their sides ran the streams, down busily, hasting away through every valley to the Daur, which bore them back to the ocean-heart—through woods and meadows, park and waste, rocks and willowy marsh. Behind the valleys rose mountains; and behind the mountains, other mountains, more and more, each swathed in its own mystery; and beyond all hung the curtain-depth of the sky-gulf. Gibbie sat and gazed, and dreamed and gazed. The mighty city that had been to him the universe, was dropped and lost, like a thing that was now nobody's, in far indistinguishable distance; and he who had lost it had climbed upon the throne of the world. The air was still; when a breath awoke, it but touched his cheek like the down of a feather, and the stillness was there again. The stillness grew great, and slowly descended upon him. It deepened and deepened. Surely it would deepen to a voice!—it was about to speak! It was as if a great single thought was the substance of the silence, and was all over and around him, and closer to him than his clothes, than his body, than his hands. I am describing the indescribable, and compelled to make it too definite for belief. In colder speech, an experience had come to the child; a link in the chain of his development glided over the windlass of his uplifting; a change passed upon him. In after years, when Gibbie had the idea of God, when he had learned to think about him, to desire his presence, to believe that a will of love enveloped his will, as the brooding hen spreads her wings over her eggs—as often as the thought of God came to him, it came in the shape of the silence on the top of Glashgar.

As he sat, with his eyes on the peak he had just chosen from the rest as the loftiest of all within his sight, he saw a cloud begin to grow upon it. The cloud grew, and gathered, and descended, covering its sides as it went, until the whole was hidden. Then swiftly, as he gazed, the cloud opened as it were a round window in the heart of it, and through that he saw the peak again. The next moment a flash of blue lightning darted across the opening, and whether Gibbie really saw what follows, he never could be sure, but always after, as often as the vision returned, in the flash he saw a rock rolling down the peak. The clouds swept together, and the window closed. The next thing which in after years he remembered was, that the earth, mountains, meadows, and streams, had vanished; everything was gone from his sight, except a few yards around him of the rock upon which he sat, and the cloud that hid world and heaven. Then again burst forth the lightning. He saw no flash, but an intense cloud-illumination, accompanied by the deafening crack, and followed by the appalling roar and roll of the thunder. Nor was it noise alone that surrounded him, for, as if he were in the heart and nest of the storm, the very wind-waves that made the thunder rushed in driven bellowing over him, and had nearly swept him away. He clung to the rock with hands and feet. The cloud writhed and wrought and billowed and eddied, with all the shapes of the wind, and seemed itself to be the furnace-womb in which the thunder was created. Was this then the voice into which the silence had been all the time deepening?—had the Presence thus taken form and declared itself? Gibbie had yet to learn that there is a deeper voice still into which such a silence may grow—and the silence not be broken. He was not dismayed. He had no conscience of wrong, and scarcely knew fear. It was an awful delight that filled his spirit. Mount Sinai was not to him a terror. To him there was no wrath in the thunder any more than in the greeting of the dog that found him in his kennel. To him there was no being in the sky so righteous as to be more displeased than pitiful over the wrongness of the children whom he had not yet got taught their childhood. Gibbie sat calm, awe-ful, but, I imagine, with a clear forehead and smile-haunted mouth, while the storm roared and beat and flashed and ran about him. It was the very fountain of tempest. From the bare crest of the mountain the water poured down its sides, as if its springs were in the rock itself, and not in the bosom of the cloud above. The tumult at last seized Gibbie like an intoxication; he jumped to his feet, and danced and flung his arms about, as if he himself were the storm. But the uproar did not last long. Almost suddenly it was gone, as if, like a bird that had been flapping the ground in agony, it had at last recovered itself, and taken to its great wings and flown. The sun shone out clear, and in all the blue abyss not a cloud was to be seen, except far away to leeward, where one was spread like a banner in the lonely air, fleeting away, the ensign of the charging storm—bearing for its device a segment of the many-coloured bow.

And now that its fierceness was over, the jubilation in the softer voices of the storm became audible. As the soul gives thanks for the sufferings that are overpast, offering the love and faith and hope which the pain has stung into fresh life, so from the sides of the mountain ascended the noise of the waters the cloud had left behind. The sun had kept on his journey; the storm had been no disaster to him; and now he was a long way down the west, and Twilight, in her grey cloak, would soon be tracking him from the east, like sorrow dogging delight. Gibbie, wet and cold, began to think of the cottage where he had been so kindly received, of the friendly face of its mistress, and her care of the lamb. It was not that he wanted to eat. He did not even imagine more eating, for never in his life had he eaten twice of the same charity in the same day. What he wanted was to find some dry hole in the mountain, and sleep as near the cottage as he could. So he rose and set out. But he lost his way; came upon one precipice after another, down which only a creeping thing could have gone; was repeatedly turned aside by torrents and swampy places; and when the twilight came, was still wandering upon the mountain. At length he found, as he thought, the burn along whose bank he had ascended in the morning, and followed it towards the valley, looking out for the friendly cottage. But the first indication of abode he saw, was the wall of the grounds of the house through whose gate he had looked in the morning. He was then a long way from the cottage, and not far from the farm; and the best thing he could do was to find again the barn where he had slept so well the night before. This was not very difficult even in the dusky night. He skirted the wall, came to his first guide, found and crossed the valley-stream, and descended it until he thought he recognized the slope of clover down which he had run in the morning. He ran up the brae, and there were the solemn cones of the corn-ricks between him and the sky! A minute more and he had crept through the cat-hole, and was feeling about in the dark barn. Happily the heap of straw was not yet removed. Gibbie shot into it like a mole, and burrowed to the very centre, there coiled himself up, and imagined himself lying in the heart of the rock on which he sat during the storm, and listening to the thunder winds over his head. The fancy enticed the sleep which before was ready enough to come, and he was soon far stiller than Ariel in the cloven pine of Sycorax.

XIII

The Ceiling

He might have slept longer the next morning, for there was no threshing to wake him, in spite of the cocks in the yard that made it their business to rouse sleepers to their work, had it not been for another kind of cock inside him, which bore the same relation to food that the others bore to light. He peeped first, then crept out. All was still except the voices of those same prophet cocks, crying in the wilderness of the yet sunless world; a moo now and then from the byres; and the occasional stamp of a great hoof in the stable. Gibbie clambered up into the loft, and turning the cheeses about until he came upon the one he had gnawed before, again attacked it, and enlarged considerably the hole he had already made in it. Rather dangerous food it was, perhaps, eaten in that unmitigated way, for it was made of skimmed milk, and was very dry and hard; but Gibbie was a powerful little animal, all bones and sinews, small hard muscle, and faultless digestion. The next idea naturally rising was the burn; he tumbled down over the straw heap to the floor of the barn, and made for the cat-hole. But the moment he put his head out, he saw the legs of a man: the farmer was walking through his ricks, speculating on the money they held. He drew back, and looked round to see where best he could betake himself should he come in. He spied thereupon a ladder leaning against the end-wall of the barn, opposite the loft and the stables, and near it in the wall a wooden shutter, like the door of a little cupboard. He got up the ladder, and opening the shutter, which was fastened only with a button, found a hole in the wall, through which popping his head too carelessly, he knocked from a shelf some piece of pottery, which fell with a great crash on a paved floor. Looking after it, Gibbie beheld below him a rich prospect of yellow-white pools ranged in order on shelves. They reminded him of milk, but were of a different colour. As he gazed, a door opened hastily, with sharp clicking latch, and a woman entered, exclaiming, "Care what set that cat!" Gibbie drew back, lest in her search for the cat she might find the culprit. She looked all round, muttering such truncated imprecations as befitted the mouth of a Scotchwoman; but as none of her milk was touched, her wrath gradually abated: she picked up the fragments and withdrew.

Thereupon Gibbie ventured to reconnoitre a little farther, and popping in his head again, saw that the dairy was open to the roof, but the door was in a partition which did not run so high. The place from which the woman entered, was ceiled, and the ceiling rested on the partition between it and the dairy; so that, from a shelf level with the hole, he could easily enough get on the top of the ceiling. This, urged by the instinct of the homeless to understand their surroundings, he presently effected, by creeping like a cat along the top shelf.

The ceiling was that of the kitchen, and was merely of boards, which, being old and shrunken, had here and there a considerable crack between two, and Gibbie, peeping through one after another of these cracks, soon saw several things he did not understand. Of such was a barrel-churn, which he took for a barrel-organ, and welcomed as a sign of civilization. The woman was sweeping the room towards the hearth, where the peat fire was already burning, with a great pot hanging over it, covered with a wooden lid. When the water in it was hot, she poured it into a large wooden dish, in which she began to wash other dishes, thus giving the observant Gibbie his first notion of housekeeping. Then she scoured the deal table, dusted the bench and the chairs, arranged the dishes on shelves and rack, except a few which she placed on the table, put more water on the fire, and disappeared in the dairy. Thence presently she returned, carrying a great jar, which, to Gibbie's astonishment, having lifted a lid in the top of the churn, she emptied into it; he was not, therefore, any farther astonished, when she began to turn the handle vigorously, that no music issued. As to what else might be expected, Gibbie had not even a mistaken idea. But the butter came quickly that morning, and then he did have another astonishment, for he saw a great mass of something half-solid tumbled out where he had seen a liquid poured in—nor that alone, for the liquid came out again too! But when at length he saw the mass, after being well washed, moulded into certain shapes, he recognized it as butter, such as he had seen in the shops, and had now and then tasted on the piece given him by some more than usually generous housekeeper. Surely he had wandered into a region of plenty! Only now, when he saw the woman busy and careful, the idea of things in the country being a sort of common property began to fade from his mind, and the perception to wake that they were as the things in the shops, which must not be touched without first paying money for them over a counter.

The butter-making, brought to a successful close, the woman proceeded to make porridge for the men's breakfast, and with hungry eyes Gibbie watched that process next. The water in the great pot boiling like a wild volcano, she took handful after handful of meal from a great wooden dish, called a bossie, and threw it into the pot, stirring as she threw, until the mess was presently so thick that she could no more move the spurtle in it; and scarcely had she emptied it into another great wooden bowl, called a bicker, when Gibbie heard the heavy tramp of the men crossing the yard to consume it.

For the last few minutes, Gibbie's nostrils—alas! not Gibbie—had been regaled with the delicious odour of the boiling meal; and now his eyes had their turn—but still, alas, not Gibbie! Prostrate on the ceiling he lay and watched the splendid spoonfuls tumble out of sight into the capacious throats of four men; all took their spoonfuls from the same dish, but each dipped his spoonful into his private caup of milk, ere he carried it to his mouth. A little apart sat a boy, whom the woman seemed to favour, having provided him with a plateful of porridge by himself, but the fact was, four were as many as could bicker comfortably, or with any chance of fair play. The boy's countenance greatly attracted Gibbie. It was a long, solemn face, but the eyes were bright-blue and sparkling; and when he smiled, which was not very often, it was a good and meaningful smile.

When the meal was over, and he saw the little that was left, with all the drops of milk from the caups, tumbled into a common receptacle, to be kept, he thought, for the next meal, poor Gibbie felt very empty and forsaken. He crawled away sad at heart, with nothing before him except a drink of water at the burn. He might have gone to the door of the house, in the hope of a bit of cake, but now that he had seen something of the doings in the house and of the people who lived in it—as soon, that is, as he had looked embodied ownership in the face—he began to be aware of its claims, and the cheese he had eaten to lie heavy upon his spiritual stomach; he had done that which he would not have done before leaving the city. Carefully he crept across the ceiling, his head hanging, like a dog scolded of his master, carefully along the shelf of the dairy, and through the opening in the wall, quickly down the ladder, and through the cat-hole in the barn door. There was no one in the corn-yard now, and he wandered about among the ricks looking, with little hope, for something to eat. Turning a corner he came upon a hen-house—and there was a crowd of hens and half-grown chickens about the very dish into which he had seen the

GEORGE MACDONALD

remnants of the breakfast thrown, all pecking billfuls out of it. As I may have said before, he always felt at liberty to share with the animals, partly, I suppose, because he saw they had no scrupulosity or ceremony amongst themselves; so he dipped his hand into the dish: why should not the bird of the air now and then peck with the more respectable of the barn-door, if only to learn his inferiority? Greatly refreshed, he got up from among the hens, scrambled over the dry stone-wall, and trotted away to the burn.

XIV

HORNIE

It was now time he should resume his journey up Daurside, and he set out to follow the burn that he might regain the river. It led him into a fine meadow, where a number of cattle were feeding. The meadow was not fenced—little more than marked off, indeed, upon one side, from a field of growing corn, by a low wall of earth, covered with moss and grass and flowers. The cattle were therefore herded by a boy, whom Gibbie recognized even in the distance as him by whose countenance he had been so much attracted when, like an old deity on a cloud, he lay spying through the crack in the ceiling. The boy was reading a book, from which every now and then he lifted his eyes to glance around him, and see whether any of the cows or heifers or stirks were wandering beyond their pasture of rye-grass and clover. Having them all before him, therefore no occasion to look behind, he did not see Gibbie approaching. But as soon as he seemed thoroughly occupied, a certain black cow, with short sharp horns and a wicked look, which had been gradually, as was her wont, edging nearer and nearer to the corn, turned suddenly and ran for it, jumped the dyke, and plunging into a mad revelry of greed, tore and devoured with all the haste not merely of one insecure, but of one that knew she was stealing. Now Gibbie had been observant enough during his travels to learn that this was against the law and custom of the country—that it was not permitted to a cow to go into a field where there were no others—and like a shot he was after the black marauder. The same instant the herd boy too, lifting his eyes from his book, saw her, and springing to his feet, caught up his great stick, and ran also: he had more than one reason to run, for he understood only too well the dangerous temper of the cow, and saw that Gibbie was a mere child, and unarmed—an object most provocative of attack to Hornie— so named, indeed, because of her readiness to use the weapons with which Nature had provided her. She was in fact a malicious cow, and but that she was a splendid milker, would have been long ago fatted up and sent to the butcher. The boy as he ran full speed to the rescue, kept shouting to warn Gibbie from his purpose, but Gibbie was too intent to understand the sounds he uttered, and supposed them addressed to the cow. With the fearless service that belonged to his very being, he ran straight at Hornie, and, having nothing to strike her with, flung himself against her with a great shove towards the dyke. Hornie, absorbed in her delicious robbery, neither heard nor saw before she felt him, and, startled by the sudden attack, turned tail. It was but for a moment. In turning, she caught sight of her ruler, sceptre in hand, at some little distance, and turned again, either to have another mouthful, or in the mere instinct to escape him. Then she caught sight of the insignificant object that had scared her, and in contemptuous indignation lowered her head between her forefeet, and was just making a rush at Gibbie, when a stone struck her on a horn, and the next moment the herd came up, and with a storm of fiercest blows, delivered with the full might of his arm, drove her in absolute rout back into the meadow. Drawing himself up in the unconscious majesty of success, Donal Grant looked down upon Gibbie, but with eyes of admiration.

"Haith, cratur!" he said, "ye're mair o' a man nor ye'll luik this saven year! What garred ye rin upo' the deevil's verra horns that gait?"

Gibbie stood smiling.

"Gien't hadna been for my club we wad baith be owre the mune 'gain this time. What ca' they ye, man?"

Still Gibbie only smiled.

"Whaur come ye frae?—Wha's yer fowk?—Whaur div ye bide?— Haena ye a tongue i' yer heid, ye rascal?"

Gibbie burst out laughing, and his eyes sparkled and shone: he was delighted with the herd-boy, and it was so long since he had heard human speech addressed to himself!

"The cratur's feel (foolish)!" concluded Donal to himself pityingly. "Puir thing! puir thing!" he added aloud, and laid his hand on Gibbie's head.

It was but the second touch of kindness Gibbie had received since he was the dog's guest: had he been acquainted with the bastard emotion of self-pity, he would have wept; as he was unaware of hardship in his lot, discontent in his heart, or discord in his feeling, his emotion was one of unmingled delight, and embodied itself in a perfect smile.

"Come, cratur, an' I'll gie ye a piece: ye'll aiblins un'erstan' that!" said Donal, as he turned to leave the corn for the grass, where Hornie was eating with the rest like the most innocent of hum'le (hornless) animals. Gibbie obeyed, and followed, as, with slow step and downbent face, Donal led the way. For he had tucked his club under his arm, and already his greedy eyes were fixed on the book he had carried all the time, nor did he take them from it until, followed in full and patient content by Gibbie, he had almost reached the middle of the field, some distance from Hornie and her companions, when, stopping abruptly short, he began without lifting his head to cast glances on this side and that.

"I houp nane o' them's swallowed my nepkin!" he said musingly. "I'm no sure whaur I was sittin'. I hae my place i' the beuk, but I doobt I hae tint my place i' the gerse."

Long before he had ended, for he spoke with utter deliberation, Gibbie was yards away, flitting hither and thither like a butterfly. A minute more and Donal saw him pounce upon his bundle, which he brought to him in triumph.

"Fegs! ye're no the gowk I took ye for," said Donal meditatively.

Whether Gibbie took the remark for a compliment, or merely was gratified that Donal was pleased, the result was a merry laugh.

The bundle had in it a piece of hard cheese, such as Gibbie had already made acquaintance with, and a few quarters of cakes. One of these Donal broke in two, gave Gibbie the half, replaced the other, and sat down again to his book—this time with his back against the fell-dyke dividing the grass from the corn. Gibbie seated himself, like a Turk, with his bare legs crossed under him, a few yards off, where, in silence and absolute content, he ate his piece, and gravely regarded him. His human soul had of late been starved, even more than his body—and that from no fastidiousness; and it was paradise again to be in such company. Never since his father's death had he looked on a face that drew him as Donal's. It was fair of complexion by nature, but the sun had burned it brown, and it was covered with freckles. Its forehead was high, with a mass of foxy hair over it, and under it two keen hazel eyes, in which the green predominated over the brown. Its nose was long and solemn, over his well-made mouth, which rarely smiled, but not unfrequently trembled with emotion—over his book. For age, Donal was getting towards fifteen, and was strongly built, and well grown. A general look of honesty, and an attractive expression of reposeful friendliness pervaded his whole appearance. Conscientious in regard to his work, he was yet in danger of forgetting his duty for minutes together in his book. The chief evil that resulted from it was such an occasional inroad on the corn as had that morning taken place; and many were Donal's self-reproaches ere he got to sleep when that had fallen out during the day. He knew his master would threaten him with dismissal if he came upon him reading in the field, but he knew also his master was well aware that he did read, and that it was possible to read and yet herd well. It was easy enough in this same meadow: on one side ran the Lorrie; on another was a stone wall; and on the third a ditch; only the cornfield lay virtually unprotected, and there he had to be himself the boundary. And now he sat leaning against the dyke, as if he held so a position of special defence; but he knew well enough that the dullest calf could outflank him, and invade, for a few moments at the least, the forbidden pleasure-ground. He had gained an ally, however, whose faculty and faithfulness he little knew yet. For Gibbie had begun to comprehend the situation. He could not comprehend why or how anyone should be absorbed in a book, for all he knew of books was from his one morning of dame-schooling; but he could comprehend that, if one's attention were so occupied, it must be a great vex to be interrupted continually by the ever-waking desires of his charge after dainties. Therefore, as Donal watched his book, Gibbie for Donal's sake watched the herd, and, as he did so, gently possessed himself of Donal's club. Nor had many minutes passed before Donal, raising his head to look, saw the curst cow again in the green corn, and Gibbie manfully encountering her with the club, hitting her hard upon head and horns, and deftly avoiding every rush she made at him.

"Gie her't upo' the nose," Donal shouted in terror, as he ran full speed to his aid, abusing Hornie in terms of fiercest vituperation.

But he needed not have been so apprehensive. Gibbie heard and obeyed, and the next moment Hornie had turned tail and was fleeing back to the safety of the lawful meadow.

"Hech, cratur! but ye maun be come o' fechtin' fowk!" said Donal, regarding him with fresh admiration.

Gibbie laughed; but he had been sorely put to it, and the big drops were coursing fast down his sweet face. Donal took the club from him, and rushing at Hornie, belaboured her well, and drove her quite to the other side of the field. He then returned and resumed his book, while Gibbie again sat down near by, and watched both Donal and his charge—the keeper of both herd and cattle. Surely Gibbie had at last found his vocation on Daurside, with both man and beast for his special care!

By and by Donal raised his head once more, but this time it was to regard Gibbie and not the nowt. It had gradually sunk into him that the appearance and character of the cratur were peculiar. He had regarded him as a little tramp, whose people were not far off, and who would soon get tired of herding and rejoin his companions; but while he read, a strange feeling of the presence of the boy had, in spite of the witchery of his book, been growing upon him. He seemed to feel his eyes without seeing them; and when Gibbie rose to look how the cattle were distributed, he became vaguely uneasy lest the boy should be going away. For already he had begun to feel him a humble kind of guardian angel. He had already that day, through him, enjoyed a longer spell of his book, than any day since he had been herd at the Mains of Glashruach. And now the desire had come to regard him more closely.

For a minute or two he sat and gazed at him. Gibbie gazed at him in return, and in his eyes the herd-boy looked the very type of power and gentleness. How he admired even his suit of small-ribbed, greenish-coloured corduroy, the ribs much rubbed and obliterated! Then his jacket had round brass buttons! his trousers had patches instead of holes at the knees! their short legs revealed warm woollen stockings! and his shoes had their soles full of great broad-headed iron tacks! while on his head he had a small round blue bonnet with a red tuft! The little outcast, on the other hand, with his loving face and pure clear eyes, bidding fair to be naked altogether before long, woke in Donal a divine pity, a tenderness like that nestling at the heart of womanhood. The neglected creature could surely have no mother to shield him from frost and wind and rain. But a strange thing was, that out of this pitiful tenderness seemed to grow, like its blossom, another unlike feeling—namely, that he was in the presence of a being of some order superior to his own, one to whom he would have to listen if he spoke, who knew more than he would tell. But then Donal was a Celt, and might be a poet, and the sweet stillness of the child's atmosphere made things bud in his imagination.

My reader must think how vastly, in all his poverty, Donal was Gibbie's superior in the social scale. He earned his own food and shelter, and nearly four pounds a year besides; lived as well as he could wish, dressed warm, was able for his work, and imagined it no hardship. Then he had a father and mother whom he went to see every Saturday, and of whom he was as proud as son could be—a father who was the priest of the family, and fed sheep; a mother who was the prophetess, and kept the house ever an open refuge for her children. Poor Gibbie earned nothing—never had earned more than a penny at a time in his life, and had never dreamed of having a claim to such penny. Nobody seemed to care for him, give him anything, do anything for him. Yet there he sat before Donal's eyes, full of service, of smiles, of contentment.

Donal took up his book, but laid it down again and gazed at Gibbie. Several times he tried to return to his reading, but as often resumed his contemplation of the boy. At length it struck him as something more than shyness would account for, that he had not yet heard a word from the lips of the child, even when running after the cows. He must watch him more closely.

By this it was his dinner time. Again he untied his handkerchief, and gave Gibbie what he judged a fair share for his bulk—namely about a third of the whole. Philosopher as he was, however, he could not help sighing a little when he got to the end of his diminished portion. But he was better than comforted when Gibbie offered him all that yet remained to him; and the smile with which he refused it made Gibbie as happy as a prince would like to be. What a day it had been for Gibbie! A whole human being, and some five and twenty four-legged creatures besides, to take care of!

After their dinner, Donal gravitated to his book, and Gibbie resumed the executive. Some time had passed when Donal, glancing up, saw Gibbie lying flat on his chest, staring at something in the grass. He slid himself quietly nearer, and discovered it was a daisy—one by itself alone; there were not many in the field. Like a mother leaning over her child, he was gazing at it. The daisy was not a cold white one, neither was it a red one; it was just a perfect daisy: it looked as if some gentle hand had taken it, while it slept and its star points were all folded together, and dipped them—just a tiny touchy dip, in a molten ruby, so that, when it opened again, there was its crown of silver pointed with rubies all about its golden sun-heart.

"He's been readin' Burns!" said Donal. He forgot that the daisies were before Burns, and that he himself had loved them before ever he heard of him. Now, he had not heard of Chaucer, who made love to the daisies four hundred years before Burns.—God only knows what gospellers they have been on his middle-earth. All its days his daisies have been coming and going, and they are not old yet, nor have worn out yet their lovely garments, though they patch and darn just as little as they toil and spin.

"Can ye read, cratur?" asked Donal.

Gibbie shook his head.

"Canna ye speyk, man?"

Again Gibbie shook his head.

"Can ye hear?"

Gibbie burst out laughing. He knew that he heard better than other people.

"Hearken till this than," said Donal.

He took his book from the grass, and read, in a chant, or rather in a lilt, the Danish ballad of Chyld Dyring, as translated by Sir Walter Scott. Gibbie's eyes grew wider and wider as he listened; their pupils dilated, and his lips parted: it seemed as if his soul were looking out of door and windows at once—but a puzzled soul that understood nothing of what it saw. Yet plainly, either the sounds, or the thought-matter vaguely operative beyond the line where intelligence begins, or, it may be, the sparkle of individual word or phrase islanded in a chaos of rhythmic motion, wrought somehow upon him, for his attention was fixed as by a spell. When Donal ceased, he remained open-mouthed and motionless for a time; then, drawing himself slidingly over the grass to Donal's feet, he raised his head and peeped above his knees at the book. A moment only he gazed, and drew back with a hungry sigh: he had seen nothing in the book like what Donal had been drawing from it—as if one should look into the well of which he had just drunk, and see there nothing but dry pebbles and sand! The wind blew gentle, the sun shone bright, all nature closed softly round the two, and the soul whose children they were was nearer than the one to the other, nearer than sun or wind or daisy or Chyld Dyring. To his amazement, Donal saw the tears gathering in Gibbie's eyes. He was as one who gazes into the abyss of God's will—sees only the abyss, cannot see the will, and weeps. The child in whom neither cold nor hunger nor nakedness nor loneliness could move a throb of self-pity, was moved to tears that a loveliness, to him strange and unintelligible, had passed away, and he had no power to call it back.

"Wad ye like to hear't again?" asked Donal, more than half understanding him instinctively.

Gibbie's face answered with a flash, and Donal read the poem again, and Gibbie's delight returned greater than before, for now something like a dawn began to appear among the cloudy words. Donal read it a third time, and closed the book, for it was almost the hour for driving the cattle home. He had never yet seen, and perhaps never again did see, such a look of thankful devotion on human countenance as met his lifted eyes.

How much Gibbie even then understood of the lovely eerie old ballad, it is impossible for me to say. Had he a glimmer of the return of the buried mother? Did he think of his own? I doubt if he had ever thought that he had a mother; but he may have associated the tale with his father, and the boots he was always making for him. Certainly it was the beginning of much. But the waking up of a human soul to know itself in the mirror of its thoughts and feelings, its loves and delights, oppresses me with so heavy a sense of marvel and inexplicable mystery, that when I imagine myself such as Gibbie then was, I cannot imagine myself coming awake. I can hardly believe that, from being such as Gibbie was the hour before he heard the ballad, I should ever have come awake. Yet here I am, capable of pleasure unspeakable from that and many another ballad, old and new! somehow, at one time or another, or at many times in one, I have at last come awake! When, by slow filmy unveilings, life grew clearer to Gibbie, and he not only knew, but knew that he knew, his thoughts always went back to that day in the meadow with Donal Grant as the beginning of his knowledge of beautiful things in the world of man. Then first he saw nature reflected, Narcissus-like, in the mirror of her humanity, her highest self. But when or how the change in him began, the turn of the balance, the first push towards life of the evermore invisible germ—of that he remained, much as he wondered, often as he searched his consciousness, as ignorant to the last as I am now. Sometimes he was inclined to think the glory of the new experience must have struck him dazed, and that was why he could not recall what went on in him at the time.

Donal rose and went driving the cattle home, and Gibbie lay where he had again thrown himself upon the grass. When he lifted his head, Donal and the cows had vanished.

Donal had looked all round as he left the meadow, and seeing the boy nowhere, had concluded he had gone to his people. The impression he had made upon him faded a little during the evening. For when he reached home, and had watered them, he had to tie up the animals, each in its stall, and make it comfortable for the night; next, eat his own supper; then learn a proposition of Euclid, and go to bed.

XV

Donal Grant

Hungering minds come of peasant people as often as of any, and have appeared in Scotland as often, I fancy, as in any nation; not every Scotsman, therefore, who may not himself have known one like Donal, will refuse to believe in such a herd-laddie. Besides, there are still those in Scotland, as well as in other nations, to whom the simple and noble, not the commonplace and selfish, is the true type of humanity. Of such as Donal, whether English or Scotch, is the class coming up to preserve the honour and truth of our Britain, to be the oil of the lamp of her life, when those who place her glory in knowledge, or in riches, shall have passed from her history as the smoke from her chimneys.

Cheap as education then was in Scotland, the parents of Donal Grant had never dreamed of sending a son to college. It was difficult for them to save even the few quarterly shillings that paid the fees of the parish schoolmaster: for Donal, indeed, they would have failed even in this, but for the help his brothers and sisters afforded. After he left school, however, and got a place as herd, he fared better than any of the rest, for at the Mains he found a friend and helper in Fergus Duff, his master's second son, who was then at home from college, which he had now attended two winters. Partly that he was delicate in health, partly that he was something of a fine gentleman, he took no share with his father and elder brother in the work of the farm, although he was at the Mains from the beginning of April to the end of October. He was a human kind of soul notwithstanding, and would have been much more of a man if he had thought less of being a gentleman. He had taken a liking to Donal, and having found in him a strong desire after every kind of knowledge of which he himself had any share, had sought to enliven the tedium of an existence rendered not a little flabby from want of sufficient work, by imparting to him of the treasures he had gathered. They were not great, and he could never have carried him far, for he was himself only a respectable student, not a little lacking in perseverance, and given to dreaming dreams of which he was himself the hero. Happily, however, Donal was of another sort, and from the first needed but to have the outermost shell of a thing broken for him, and that Fergus could do: by and by Donal would break a shell for himself.

But perhaps the best thing Fergus did for him was the lending him books. Donal had an altogether unappeasable hunger after every form of literature with which he had as yet made acquaintance, and this hunger Fergus fed with the books of the house, and many besides of such as he purchased or borrowed for his own reading—these last chiefly poetry. But Fergus Duff, while he revelled in the writings of certain of the poets of the age, was incapable of finding poetry for himself in the things around him: Donal Grant, on the other hand, while he seized on the poems Fergus lent him, with an avidity even greater than his, received from the nature around him influences similar to those which exhaled from the words of the poet. In some sense, then, Donal was original; that is, he received at first hand what Fergus required to have "put on" him, to quote Celia, in As you like it, "as pigeons feed their young." Therefore, fiercely as it would have harrowed the pride of Fergus to be informed of the fact, he was in the kingdom of art only as one who ate of what fell from the table, while his father's herd-boy was one of the family. This was as far from Donal's thought, however, as from that of Fergus, the condescension, therefore, of the latter did not impair the gratitude for which the former had such large reason; and Donal looked up to Fergus as to one of the lords of the world.

To find himself now in the reversed relation of superior and teacher to the little outcast, whose whole worldly having might be summed in the statement that he was not absolutely naked, woke in Donal an altogether new and strange feeling; yet gratitude to his master had but turned itself round, and become tenderness to his pupil.

After Donal left him in the field, and while he was ministering, first to his beasts and then to himself, Gibbie lay on the grass, as happy as child could well be. A loving hand laid on his feet or legs would have found them like ice; but where was the matter so long as he never thought of them? He could have supped a huge bicker of sowens, and eaten a dozen potatoes; but of what mighty consequence is hunger, so long as it neither absorbs the thought, nor causes faintness? The sun, however, was going down behind a great mountain, and its huge shadow, made of darkness, and haunted with cold, came sliding across the river, and over valley and field, nothing staying its silent wave, until it covered Gibbie with the blanket of the dark, under which he could not long forget that he was in a body to which cold is unfriendly. At the first breath of the night-wind that came after the shadow, he shivered, and starting to his feet, began to trot, increasing his speed until he was scudding up and down the field like a wild thing of the night, whose time was at hand, waiting until the world should lie open to him. Suddenly he perceived that the daisies, which all day long had been full-facing the sun, like true souls confessing to the father of them, had folded their petals together to points, and held them like spear-heads tipped with threatening crimson, against the onset of the night and her shadows, while within its white cone each folded in the golden heart of its life, until the great father should return, and, shaking the wicked out of the folds of the night, render the world once more safe with another glorious day. Gibbie gazed and wondered; and while he gazed—slowly, glidingly, back to his mind came the ghost-mother of the ballad, and in every daisy he saw her folding her neglected orphans to her bosom, while the darkness and the misery rolled by defeated. He wished he knew a ghost that would put her arms round him. He must have had a mother once, he supposed, but he could not remember her, and of course she must have forgotten him. He did not know that about him were folded the everlasting arms of the great, the one Ghost, which is the Death of death—the life and soul of all things and all thoughts. The Presence, indeed, was with him, and he felt it, but he knew it only as the wind and shadow, the sky and closed daisies: in all these things and the rest it took shape that it might come near him. Yea, the Presence was in his very soul, else he could never have rejoiced in friend, or desired ghost to mother him: still he knew not the Presence. But it was drawing nearer and nearer to his knowledge—even in sun and air and night and cloud, in beast and flower and herd-boy, until at last it would reveal itself to him, in him, as Life Himself. Then the man would know that in which the child had rejoiced. The stars came out, to Gibbie the heavenly herd, feeding at night, and gathering gold in the blue pastures. He saw them, looking up from the grass where he had thrown himself to gaze more closely at the daisies; and the sleep that pressed down his eyelids seemed to descend from the spaces between the stars. But it was too cold that night to sleep in the fields, when he knew where to find warmth. Like a fox into his hole, the child would creep into the corner where God had stored sleep for him: back he went to the barn, gently trotting, and wormed himself through the cat-hole.

The straw was gone! But he remembered the hay. And happily, for he was tired, there stood the ladder against the loft. Up he went, nor turned aside to the cheese; but sleep was common property still. He groped his way forward through the dark loft until he found the hay, when at once he burrowed into it like a sand-fish into the wet sand. All night the white horse, a glory vanished in the dark, would be close to him, behind the thin partition of boards. He could hear his very breath as he slept, and to the music of it, audible sign of companionship, he fell fast asleep, and slept until the waking horses woke him.

XVI

APPRENTICESHIP

He scrambled out on the top of the hay, and looked down on the beautiful creature below him, dawning radiant again with the morning, as it issued undimmed from the black bosom of the night. He was not, perhaps, just so well groomed as white steed might be; it was not a stable where they kept a blue-bag for their grey horses; but to Gibbie's eyes he was so pure, that he began, for the first time in his life, to doubt whether he was himself quite as clean as he ought to be. He did not know, but he would make an experiment for information when he got down to the burn. Meantime was there nothing he could do for the splendid creature? From above, leaning over, he filled his rack with hay; but he had eaten so much grass the night before, that he would not look at it, and Gibbie was disappointed. What should he do next? The thing he would like best would be to look through the ceiling again, and watch the woman at her work. Then, too, he would again smell the boiling porridge, and the burning of the little sprinkles of meal that fell into the fire. He dragged, therefore, the ladder to the opposite end of the barn, and gradually, with no little effort, raised it against the wall. Carefully he crept through the hole, and softly round the shelf, the dangerous part of the pass, and so on to the ceiling, whence he peeped once more down into the kitchen. His precautions had been so far unnecessary, for as yet it lay unvisited, as witnessed by its disorder. Suddenly came to Gibbie the thought that here was a chance for him— here a path back to the world. Rendered daring by the eagerness of his hope, he got again upon the shelf, and with every precaution lest he should even touch a milkpan, descended by the lower shelves to the floor. There finding the door only latched, he entered the kitchen, and proceeded to do everything he had seen the woman do, as nearly in her style as he could. He swept the floor, and dusted the seats, the window sill, the table, with an apron he found left on a chair, then arranged everything tidily, roused the rested fire, and had just concluded that the only way to get the great pot full of water upon it, would be to hang first the pot on the chain, and then fill it with the water, when his sharp ears caught sounds and then heard approaching feet. He darted into the dairy, and in a few seconds, for he was getting used to the thing now, had clambered upon the ceiling, and was lying flat across the joists, with his eyes to the most commanding crack he had discovered: he was anxious to know how his service would be received. When Jean Mavor—she was the farmer's half-sister—opened the door, she stopped short and stared; the kitchen was not as she had left it the night before! She concluded she must be mistaken, for who could have touched it? and entered. Then it became plain beyond dispute that the floor had been swept, the table wiped, the place redd up, and the fire roused.

"Hoot! I maun hae been walkin' i' my sleep!" said Jean to herself aloud. "Or maybe that guid laddie Donal Grant's been wullin' to gie me a helpin' han' for's mither's sake, honest wuman! The laddie's guid eneuch for onything!—ay, gien 'twar to mak' a minister o'!"

Eagerly, greedily, Gibbie now watched her every motion, and, bent upon learning, nothing escaped him: he would do much better next morning!—At length the men came in to breakfast, and he thought to enjoy the sight; but, alas! it wrought so with his hunger as to make him feel sick, and he crept away to the barn. He would gladly have lain down in the hay for a while, but that would require the ladder, and he did not now feel able to move it. On the floor of the barn he was not safe, and he got out of it into the cornyard, where he sought the henhouse. But there was no food there yet, and he must not linger near; for, if he were discovered, they would drive him away, and he would lose Donal Grant. He had not seen him at breakfast, for indeed he seldom, during the summer, had a meal except supper in the house. Gibbie, therefore, as he could not eat, ran to the burn and drank—but had no heart that morning for his projected inquiry into the state of his person. He must go to Donal. The sight of him would help him to bear his hunger.

The first indication Donal had of his proximity was the rush of Hornie past him in flight out of the corn. Gibbie was pursuing her with stones for lack of a stick. Thoroughly ashamed of himself, Donal threw his book from him, and ran to meet Gibbie.

"Ye maunna fling stanes, cratur," he said. "Haith! it's no for me to fin' fau't, though," he added, "sittin' readin' buiks like a gowk 'at I am, an' lattin' the beasts rin wull amo' the corn, 'at's weel peyed to haud them oot o' 't! I'm clean affrontit wi' mysel', cratur."

Gibbie's response was to set off at full speed for the place where Donal had been sitting. He was back in a moment with the book, which he pressed into Donal's hand, while from the other he withdrew his club. This he brandished aloft once or twice, then starting at a steady trot, speedily circled the herd, and returned to his adopted master—only to start again, however, and attack Hornie, whom he drove from the corn-side of the meadow right over to the other: she was already afraid of him. After watching him for a time, Donal came to the conclusion that he could not do more than the cratur if he had as many eyes as Argus, and gave not even one of them to his book. He therefore left all to Gibbie, and did not once look up for a whole hour. Everything went just as it should; and not once, all that day, did Hornie again get a mouthful of the grain. It was rather a heavy morning for Gibbie, though, who had eaten nothing, and every time he came near Donal, saw the handkerchief bulging in the grass, which a little girl had brought and left for him. But he was a rare one both at waiting and at going without.

At last, however, Donal either grew hungry of himself, or was moved by certain understood relations between the sun and the necessities of his mortal frame; for he laid down his book, called out to Gibbie, "Cratur, it's denner-time," and took his bundle. Gibbie drew near with sparkling eyes. There was no selfishness in his hunger, for, at the worst pass he had ever reached, he would have shared what he had with another, but he looked so eager, that Donal, who himself knew nothing of want, perceived that he was ravenous, and made haste to undo the knots of the handkerchief, which Mistress Jean appeared that day to have tied with more than ordinary vigour, ere she intrusted the bundle to the foreman's daughter. When the last knot yielded, he gazed with astonishment at the amount and variety of provision disclosed.

"Losh!" he exclaimed, "the mistress maun hae kenned there was two o' 's."

He little thought that what she had given him beyond the usual supply was an acknowledgment of services rendered by those same hands into which he now delivered a share, on the ground of other service altogether. It is not always, even where there is no mistake as to the person who has deserved it, that the reward reaches the doer so directly.

Before the day was over, Donal gave his helper more and other pay for his service. Choosing a fit time, when the cattle were well together and in good position, Hornie away at the stone dyke, he took from his pocket a somewhat wasted volume of ballads—ballants, he called them—and said, "Sit ye doon, cratur. Never min' the nowt. I'm gaein' to read till ye."

Gibbie dropped on his crossed legs like a lark to the ground, and sat motionless. Donal, after deliberate search, began to read, and Gibbie to listen; and it would be hard to determine which found the more pleasure in his part. For Donal had seldom had a listener—and never one so utterly absorbed.

When the hour came for the cattle to go home, Gibbie again remained behind, waiting until all should be still at the farm. He lay on the dyke, brooding over what he had heard, and wondering how it was that Donal got all those strange beautiful words and sounds and stories out of the book.

XVII

SECRET SERVICE

I must not linger over degrees and phases. Every morning, Gibbie got into the kitchen in good time; and not only did more and more of the work, but did it more and more to the satisfaction of Jean, until, short of the actual making of the porridge, he did everything antecedent to the men's breakfast. When Jean came in, she had but to take the lid from the pot, put in the salt, assume the spurtle, and, grasping the first handful of the meal, which stood ready waiting in the bossie on the stone cheek of the fire, throw it in, thus commencing the simple cookery of the best of all dishes to a true-hearted and healthy Scotsman. Without further question she attributed all the aid she received to the goodness, "enough for anything," of Donal Grant, and continued to make acknowledgment of the same in both sort and quantity of victuals, whence, as has been shown, the real labourer received his due reward.

Until he had thoroughly mastered his work, Gibbie persisted in regarding matters economic "from his loophole in the ceiling;" and having at length learned the art of making butter, soon arrived at some degree of perfection in it. But when at last one morning he not only churned, but washed and made it up entirely to Jean's satisfaction, she did begin to wonder how a mere boy could both have such perseverance, and be so clever at a woman's work. For now she entered the kitchen every morning without a question of finding the fire burning, the water boiling, the place clean and tidy, the supper dishes well washed and disposed on shelf and rack: her own part was merely to see that proper cloths were handy to so thorough a user of them. She took no one into her confidence on the matter: it was enough, she judged, that she and Donal understood each other.

And now if Gibbie had contented himself with rendering this house-service in return for the shelter of the barn and its hay, he might have enjoyed both longer; but from the position of his night-quarters, he came gradually to understand the work of the stable also; and before long, the men, who were quite ignorant of anything similar taking place in the house, began to observe, more to their wonder than satisfaction, that one or other of their horses was generally groomed before his man came to him; that often there was hay in their racks which they had not given them; and that the master's white horse every morning showed signs of having had some attention paid him that could not be accounted for. The result was much talk and speculation, suspicion and offence; for all were jealous of their rights, their duty, and their dignity, in relation to their horses: no man was at liberty to do a thing to or for any but his own pair. Even the brightening of the harness-brass, in which Gibbie sometimes indulged, was an offence; for did it not imply a reproach? Many were the useless traps laid for the offender, many the futile attempts to surprise him: as Gibbie never did anything except for half an hour or so while the men were sound asleep or at breakfast, he escaped discovery.

But he could not hold continued intercourse with the splendour of the white horse, and neglect carrying out the experiment on which he had resolved with regard to the effect of water upon his own skin; and having found the result a little surprising, he soon got into the habit of daily and thorough ablution. But many animals that never wash are yet cleaner than some that do; and, what with the scantiness of his clothing, his constant exposure to the atmosphere, and his generally lying in a fresh lair, Gibbie had always been comparatively clean. Besides, being nice in his mind, he was naturally nice in his body.

The new personal regard thus roused by the presence of Snowball, had its development greatly assisted by the scrupulosity with which most things in the kitchen, and chief of all in this respect, the churn, were kept. It required much effort to come up to the nicety considered by Jean indispensable in the churn; and the croucher on the ceiling, when he saw the long nose advance to prosecute inquiry into its condition, mentally trembled lest the next movement should condemn his endeavour as a failure. With his clothes he could do nothing, alas! but he bathed every night in the Lorrie as soon as Donal had gone home with the cattle. Once he got into a deep hole, but managed to get out again, and so learned that he could swim.

All day he was with Donal, and took from him by much the greater part of his labour: Donal had never had such time for reading. In return he gave him his dinner, and Gibbie could do very well upon one meal a day. He paid him also in poetry. It never came into his head, seeing he never spoke, to teach him to read. He soon gave up attempting to learn anything from him as to his place or people or history, for to all questions in that direction Gibbie only looked grave and shook his head. As often, on the other hand, as he tried to learn where he spent the night, he received for answer only one of his merriest laughs.

Nor was larger time for reading the sole benefit Gibbie conferred upon Donal. Such was the avidity and growing intelligence with which the little naked town-savage listened to what Donal read to him, that his presence was just so much added to Donal's own live soul of thought and feeling. From listening to his own lips through Gibbie's ears, he not only understood many things better, but, perceiving what things must puzzle Gibbie, came sometimes, rather to his astonishment, to see that in fact he did not understand them himself. Thus the bond between the boy and the child grew closer—far closer, indeed than Donal imagined; for, although still, now and then, he had a return of the fancy that Gibbie might be a creature of some speechless race other than human, of whom he was never to know whence he came or whither he went—a messenger, perhaps, come to unveil to him the depths of his own spirit, and make up for the human teaching denied him, this was only in his more poetic moods, and his ordinary mental position towards him was one of kind condescension.

It was not all fine weather up there among the mountains in the beginning of summer. In the first week of June even, there was sleet and snow in the wind—the tears of the vanquished Winter, blown, as he fled, across the sea, from Norway or Iceland. Then would Donal's heart be sore for Gibbie, when he saw his poor rags blown about like streamers in the wind, and the white spots melting on his bare skin. His own condition would then to many have appeared pitiful enough, but such an idea Donal would have laughed to scorn, and justly. Then most, perhaps then only, does the truly generous nature feel poverty, when he sees another in need and can do little or nothing to help him. Donal had neither greatcoat, plaid, nor umbrella, wherewith to shield Gibbie's looped and windowed raggedness. Once, in great pity, he pulled off his jacket, and threw it on Gibbie's shoulders. But the shout of laughter that burst from the boy, as he flung the jacket from him, and rushed away into the middle of the feeding herd, a shout that came from no cave of rudeness, but from the very depths of delight, stirred by the loving kindness of the act, startled Donal out of his pity into brief anger, and he rushed after him in indignation, with full purpose to teach him proper behaviour by a box on each ear. But Gibbie dived under the belly of a favourite cow, and peering out sideways from under her neck and between her forelegs, his arms grasping each a leg, while the cow went on twisting her long tongue round the grass and plucking it undisturbed, showed such an innocent countenance of holy merriment, that the pride of Donal's hurt benevolence melted away, and his laughter emulated Gibbie's. That sort of day was in truth drearier for Donal than for Gibbie, for the books he had were not his own, and he dared not expose them to the rain; some of them indeed came from Glashruach—the Muckle Hoose, they generally called it! When he left him, it was to wander disconsolately about the field; while Gibbie, sheltered under a whole cow, defied the chill and the sleet, and had no books of which to miss the use. He could not, it is true, shield his legs from the insidious attacks of such sneaking blasts as will always find out the undefended spots; but his great heart was so well-to-do in the inside of him, that, unlike Touchstone, his spirits not being weary, he cared not for his legs. The worst storm in the world could not have made that heart quail. For, think! there had just been the strong, the well-dressed, the learned, the wise, the altogether mighty and considerable Donal, the cowherd, actually desiring him, wee Sir Gibbie Galbraith, the cinder of the city furnace, the naked, and generally the hungry little tramp, to wear his jacket to cover him from the storm! The idea was one of eternal triumph; and Gibbie, exulting in the unheard-of devotion and condescension of the thing, kept on laughing like a blessed cherub under the cow's belly. Nor was there in his delight the smallest admixture of pride that he should have drawn forth such kindness; it was simple glorying in the beauteous fact. As to the cold and the sleet, so far as he knew they never hurt anybody. They were not altogether pleasant creatures, but they could not help themselves, and would soon give over their teasing. By to-morrow they would have wandered away into other fields, and left the sun free to come back to Donal and the cattle, when Gibbie, at present shielded like any lord by the friendliest of cows, would come in for a share of the light and the warmth. Gibbie was so confident with the animals, that they were already even more friendly with him than with Donal—all except Hornie, who, being of a low spirit, therefore incapable of obedience, was friendliest with the one who gave her the hardest blows.

XVIII

The Broonie

Things had gone on in this way for several weeks—if Gibbie had not been such a small creature, I hardly see how they could for so long—when one morning the men came in to breakfast all out of temper together, complaining loudly of the person unknown who would persist in interfering with their work. They were the louder that their suspicions fluttered about Fergus, who was rather overbearing with them, and therefore not a favourite. He was in reality not at all a likely person to bend back or defile hands over such labour, and their pitching upon him for the object of their suspicion, showed how much at a loss they were. Their only ground for suspecting him, beyond the fact that there was no other whom by any violence of imagination they could suspect, was, that, whatever else was done or left undone in the stable, Snowball, whom Fergus was fond of, and rode almost every day, was, as already mentioned, sure to have something done for him. Had he been in good odour with them, they would have thought no harm of most of the things they thought he did, especially as they eased their work; but he carried himself high, they said, doing nothing but ride over the farm and pick out every fault he could find—to show how sharp he was, and look as if he could do better than any of them; and they fancied that he carried their evil report to his father, and that this underhand work in the stable must be part of some sly scheme for bringing them into disgrace. And now at last had come the worst thing of all: Gibbie had discovered the corn-bin, and having no notion but that everything in the stable was for the delectation of the horses, had been feeding them largely with oats—a delicacy with which, in the plenty of other provisions, they were very sparingly supplied; and the consequences had begun to show themselves in the increased unruliness of the more wayward amongst them. Gibbie had long given up resorting to the ceiling, and remained in utter ignorance of the storm that was brewing because of him.

The same day brought things nearly to a crisis; for the overfed Snowball, proving too much for Fergus's horsemanship, came rushing home at a fierce gallop without him, having indeed left him in a ditch by the roadside. The remark thereupon made by the men in his hearing, that it was his own fault, led him to ask questions, when he came gradually to know what they attributed to him, and was indignant at the imputation of such an employment of his mornings to one who had his studies to attend to—scarcely a wise line of defence where the truth would have been more credible as well as convincing—namely, that at the time when those works of supererogation could alone be effected, he lay as lost a creature as ever sleep could make of a man.

In the evening, Jean sought a word with Donal, and expressed her surprise that he should be able to do everybody's work about the place, warning him it would be said he did it at the expense of his own. But what could he mean, she said, by wasting the good corn to put devilry into the horses? Donal stared in utter bewilderment. He knew perfectly that to the men suspicion of him was as impossible as of one of themselves. Did he not sleep in the same chamber with them? Could it be allusion to the way he spent his time when out with the cattle that Mistress Jean intended? He was so confused, looked so guilty as well as astray, and answered so far from any point in Jean's mind, that she at last became altogether bewildered also, out of which chaos of common void gradually dawned on her mind the conviction that she had been wasting both thanks and material recognition of service, where she was under no obligation. Her first feeling thereupon was, not unnaturally however unreasonably, one of resentment—as if Donal, in not doing her the kindness her fancy had been attributing to him, had all the time been doing her an injury; but the boy's honest bearing and her own good sense made her, almost at once, dismiss the absurdity.

Then came anew the question, utterly unanswerable now—who could it be that did not only all her morning work, but, with a passion for labour insatiable, part of that of the men also? She knew her nephew better than to imagine for a moment, with the men, it could be he. A good enough lad she judged him, but not good enough for that. He was too fond of his own comfort to dream of helping other people! But now, having betrayed herself to Donal, she wisely went farther, and secured herself by placing full confidence in him. She laid open the whole matter, confessing that she had imagined her ministering angel to be Donal himself: now she had not even a conjecture to throw at random after the person of her secret servant. Donal, being a Celt, and a poet, would have been a brute if he had failed of being a gentleman, and answered that he was ashamed it should be another and not himself who had been her servant and gained her commendation; but he feared, if he had made any such attempt, he would but have fared like the husband in the old ballad who insisted that his wife's work was much easier to do than his own. But as he spoke, he saw a sudden change come over Jean's countenance. Was it fear? or what was it? She gazed with big eyes fixed on his face, heeding neither him nor his words, and Donal, struck silent, gazed in return. At length, after a pause of strange import, her soul seemed to return into her deep-set grey eyes, and in a broken voice, low, and solemn, and fraught with mystery, she said,

"Donal, it's the broonie!"

Donal's mouth opened wide at the word, but the tenor of his thought it would have been hard for him to determine. Celtic in kindred and education, he had listened in his time to a multitude of strange tales, both indigenous and exotic, and, Celtic in blood, had been inclined to believe every one of them for which he could find the least *raison d'être*. But at school he had been taught that such stories deserved nothing better than mockery, that to believe them was contrary to religion, and a mark of such weakness as involved blame. Nevertheless, when he heard the word broonie issue from a face with such an expression as Jean's then wore, his heart seemed to give a gape in his bosom, and it rushed back upon his memory how he had heard certain old people talk of the brownie that used, when their mothers and grandmothers were young, to haunt the Mains of Glashruach. His mother did not believe such things, but she believed nothing but her New Testament!—and what if there should be something in them? The idea of service rendered by the hand of a being too clumsy, awkward, ugly, to consent to be seen by the more finished race of his fellow-creatures, whom yet he surpassed in strength and endurance and longevity, had at least in it for Donal the attraction of a certain grotesque yet homely poetic element. He remembered too the honour such a type of creature had had in being lapt around for ever in the airy folds of L'Allegro. And to think that Mistress Jean, for whom everybody had such a respect, should speak of the creature in such a tone!—it sent a thrill of horrific wonder and delight through the whole frame of the boy: might, could there be such creatures? And thereupon began to open to his imagination vista after vista into the realms of might-be possibility—where dwelt whole clans and kins of creatures, differing from us and our kin, yet occasionally, at the cross-roads of creation, coming into contact with us, and influencing us not greatly, perhaps, yet strangely and notably. Not once did the real brownie occur to him—the small, naked Gibbie, far more marvellous and admirable than any brownie of legendary fable or fact, whether celebrated in rude old Scots ballad for his taeless feet, or designated in noble English poem of perfect art, as lubber fiend of hairy length.

Jean Mavor came from a valley far withdrawn in the folds of the Gormgarnet mountains, where in her youth she had heard yet stranger tales than had ever come to Donal's ears, of which some had perhaps kept their hold the more firmly that she had never heard them even alluded to since she left her home. Her brother, a hard-headed highlander, as canny as any lowland Scot, would have laughed to scorn the most passing reference to such an existence; and Fergus, who had had a lowland mother—and nowhere is there less of so-called superstition than in most parts of the lowlands of Scotland—would have joined heartily in his mockery. For the cowherd, however, as I say, the idea had no small attraction, and his stare was the reflection of Mistress Jean's own—for the soul is a live mirror, at once receiving into its centre, and reflecting from its surface.

"Div ye railly think it, mem?" said Donal at last.

"Think what?" retorted Jean, sharply, jealous instantly of being compromised, and perhaps not certain that she had spoken aloud.

"Div ye railly think 'at there is sic craturs as broonies, Mistress Jean?" said Donal.

"Wha kens what there is an' what there isna?" returned Jean: she was not going to commit herself either way. Even had she imagined herself above believing such things, she would not have dared to say so; for there was a time still near in her memory, though unknown to any now upon the farm except her brother, when the Mains of Glashruach was the talk of Daurside because of certain inexplicable nightly disorders that fell out there; the slang rows, or the Scotch remishs (a form of the English romage), would perhaps come nearest to a designation of them, consisting as they did of confused noises, rumblings, exclamations; and the fact itself was a reason for silence, seeing a word might bring the place again into men's mouths in like fashion, and seriously affect the service of the farm; such a rumour would certainly be made in the market a ground for demanding more wages to fee to the Mains. "Ye haud yer tongue, laddie," she went on; "it's the least ye can efter a' 'at's come an' gane; an' least said's sunest mendit, Gang to yer wark."

But either Mistress Jean's influx of caution came too late, and someone had overheard her suggestion, or the idea was already abroad in the mind bucolic and georgic, for that very night it began to be reported upon the nearer farms, that the Mains of Glashruach was haunted by a brownie who did all the work for both men and maids—a circumstance productive of different opinions with regard to the desirableness of a situation there, some asserting they would not fee to it for any amount of wages, and others averring they could desire nothing better than a place where the work was all done for them.

Quick at disappearing as Gibbie was, a very little cunning on the part of Jean might soon have entrapped the brownie; but a considerable touch of fear was now added to her other motives for continuing to spend a couple of hours longer in bed than had formerly been her custom. So that for yet a few days things went on much as usual; Gibbie saw no sign that his presence was suspected, or that his doings were offensive; and life being to him a constant present, he never troubled himself about anything before it was there to answer for itself.

One morning the long thick mane of Snowball was found carefully plaited up in innumerable locks. This was properly elf-work, but no fairies had been heard of on Daurside for many a long year. The brownie, on the other hand, was already in every one's mouth—only a stray one, probably, that had wandered from some old valley away in the mountains, where they were still believed in—but not the less a brownie; and if it was not the brownie who plaited Snowball's mane, who or what was it? A phenomenon must be accounted for, and he who will not accept a theory offered, or even a word applied, is indebted in a full explanation. The rumour spread in long slow ripples, till at last one of them struck the membrana tympani of the laird, where he sat at luncheon in the House of Glashruach.

XIX

The Laird

Thomas Galbraith was by birth Thomas Durrant, but had married an heiress by whom he came into possession of Glashruach, and had, according to previous agreement, taken her name. When she died he mourned her loss as well as he could, but was consoled by feeling himself now first master of both position and possession, when the ladder by which he had attained them was removed. It was not that she had ever given him occasion to feel that marriage and not inheritance was the source of his distinction in the land, but that having a soul as keenly sensitive to small material rights as it was obtuse to great spiritual ones, he never felt the property quite his own until his wife was no longer within sight. Had he been a little more sensitive still, he would have felt that the property was then his daughter's, and his only through her; but this he failed to consider.

Mrs. Galbraith was a gentle sweet woman, who loved her husband, but was capable of loving a greater man better. Had she lived long enough to allow of their opinions confronting in the matter of their child's education, serious differences would probably have arisen between them; as it was, they had never quarrelled except about the name she should bear. The father, having for her sake—so he said to himself—sacrificed his patronymic, was anxious that in order to her retaining some rudimentary trace of himself in the ears of men, she should be overshadowed with his Christian name, and called Thomasina. But the mother was herein all the mother, and obdurate for her daughter's future; and, as was right between the two, she had her way, and her child a pretty name. Being more sentimental than artistic, however, she did not perceive how imperfectly the sweet Italian Ginevra concorded with the strong Scotch Galbraith. Her father hated the name, therefore invariably abbreviated it after such fashion as rendered it inoffensive to the most conservative of Scotish ears; and for his own part, at length, never said Ginny, without seeing and hearing and meaning Jenny. As Jenny, indeed, he addressed her in the one or two letters which were all he ever wrote to her; and thus he perpetuated the one matrimonial difference across the grave.

Having no natural bent to literature, but having in his youth studied for and practised at the Scotish bar, he had brought with him into the country a taste for certain kinds of dry reading, judged pre-eminently respectable, and for its indulgence had brought also a not insufficient store of such provender as his soul mildly hungered after, in the shape of books bound mostly in yellow-calf—books of law, history, and divinity. What the books of law were, I would not foolhardily add to my many risks of blundering by presuming to recall; the history was mostly Scotish, or connected with Scotish affairs; the theology was entirely of the New England type of corrupted Calvinism, with which in Scotland they saddle the memory of great-souled, hard-hearted Calvin himself. Thoroughly respectable, and a little devout, Mr. Galbraith was a good deal more of a Scotchman than a Christian; growth was a doctrine unembodied in his creed; he turned from everything new, no matter how harmonious with the old, in freezing disapprobation; he recognized no element in God or nature which could not be reasoned about after the forms of the Scotch philosophy. He would not have said an Episcopalian could not be saved, for at the bar he had known more than one good lawyer of the episcopal party; but to say a Roman Catholic would not necessarily be damned, would to his judgment have revealed at once the impending fate of the rash asserter. In religion he regarded everything not only as settled but as understood; but seemed aware of no call in relation to truth, but to bark at anyone who showed the least anxiety to discover it. What truth he held himself, he held as a sack holds corn—not even as a worm holds earth.

To his servants and tenants he was what he thought just—never condescending to talk over a thing with any of the former but the game-keeper, and never making any allowance to the latter for misfortune. In general expression he looked displeased, but meant to look dignified. No one had ever seen him wrathful; nor did he care enough for his fellow-mortals ever to be greatly vexed—at least he never manifested vexation otherwise than by a silence that showed more of contempt than suffering.

In person, he was very tall and very thin, with a head much too small for his height; a narrow forehead, above which the brown hair looked like a wig; pale-blue, ill-set eyes, that seemed too large for their sockets, consequently tumbled about a little, and were never at once brought to focus; a large, but soft-looking nose; a loose-lipped mouth, and very little chin. He always looked as if consciously trying to keep himself together. He wore his shirt-collar unusually high, yet out of it far shot his long neck, notwithstanding the smallness of which, his words always seemed to come from a throat much too big for them. He had greatly the look of a hen, proud of her maternal experiences, and silent from conceit of what she could say if she would. So much better would he have done as an underling than as a ruler—as a journeyman even, than a master, that to know him was almost to disbelieve in the good of what is generally called education. His learning seemed to have taken the wrong fermentation, and turned to folly instead of wisdom. But he did not do much harm, for he had a great respect for his respectability. Perhaps if he had been a craftsman, he might even have done more harm—making rickety wheelbarrows, asthmatic pumps, ill-fitting window-frames, or boots with a lurking divorce in each welt. He had no turn for farming, and therefore let all his land, yet liked to interfere, and as much as possible kept a personal jurisdiction.

There was one thing, however, which, if it did not throw the laird into a passion—nothing, as I have said, did that—brought him nearer to the outer verge of displeasure than any other, and that was, anything whatever to which he could affix the name of superstition. The indignation of better men than the laird with even a confessedly harmless superstition, is sometimes very amusing; and it was a point of Mr. Galbraith's poverty-stricken religion to denounce all superstitions, however diverse in character, with equal severity. To believe in the second sight, for instance, or in any form of life as having the slightest relation to this world, except that of men, that of animals, and that of vegetables, was with him wicked, antagonistic to the Church of Scotland, and inconsistent with her perfect doctrine. The very word ghost would bring upon his face an expression he meant for withering scorn, and indeed it withered his face, rendering it yet more unpleasant to behold. Coming to the benighted country, then, with all the gathered wisdom of Edinburgh in his gallinaceous cranium, and what he counted a vast experience of worldly affairs besides, he brought with him also the firm resolve to be the death of superstition, at least upon his own property. He was not only unaware, but incapable of becoming aware, that he professed to believe a number of things, any one of which was infinitely more hostile to the truth of the universe, than all the fancies and fables of a countryside, handed down from grandmother to grandchild. When, therefore, within a year of his settling at Glashruach, there arose a loud talk of the Mains, his best farm, as haunted by presences making all kinds of tumultuous noises, and even throwing utensils bodily about, he was nearer the borders of a rage, although he kept, as became a gentleman, a calm exterior, than ever he had been in his life. For were not ignorant clodhoppers asserting as facts what he knew never could take place! At once he set himself, with all his experience as a lawyer to aid him, to discover the buffooning authors of the mischief; where there were deeds there were doers, and where there were doers they were discoverable. But his endeavours, uninterrmitted for the space of three weeks, after which the disturbances ceased, proved so utterly without result, that he could never bear the smallest allusion to the hateful business. For he had not only been unhorsed, but by his dearest hobby.

He was seated with a game pie in front of him, over the top of which Ginevra was visible. The girl never sat nearer her father at meals than the whole length of the table, where she occupied her mother's place. She was a solemn-looking child, of eight or nine, dressed in a brown merino frock of the plainest description. Her hair, which was nearly of the same colour as her frock, was done up in two triple plaits, which hung down her back, and were tied at the tips with black ribbon. To the first glance she did not look a very interesting or attractive child; but looked at twice, she was sure to draw the eyes a third time. She was undeniably like her father, and that was much against her at first sight; but it required only a little acquaintance with her face to remove the prejudice; for in its composed, almost resigned expression, every feature of her father's seemed comparatively finished, and settled into harmony with the rest; its chaos was subdued, and not a little of the original underlying design brought out. The nose was firm, the mouth modelled, the chin larger, the eyes a little smaller, and full of life and feeling. The longer it was regarded by any seeing eye, the child's countenance showed fuller of promise, or at least of hope. Gradually the look would appear in it of a latent sensitive anxiety—then would dawn a glimmer of longing question; and then, all at once, it would slip back into the original ordinary look, which, without seeming attractive, had yet attracted. Her father was never harsh to her, yet she looked rather frightened at him; but then he was cold, very cold, and most children would rather be struck and kissed alternately than neither. And the bond cannot be very close between father and child, when the father has forsaken his childhood. The bond between any two is the one in the other; it is the father in the child, and the child in the father, that reach to each other eternal hands. It troubled Ginevra greatly that, when she

GEORGE MACDONALD

asked herself whether she loved her father better than anybody else, as she believed she ought, she became immediately doubtful whether she loved him at all.

She was eating porridge and milk: with spoon arrested in mid-passage, she stopped suddenly, and said:—

"Papa, what's a broonie?"

"I have told you, Jenny, that you are never to talk broad Scotch in my presence," returned her father. "I would lay severer commands upon you, were it not that I fear tempting you to disobey me, but I will have no vulgarity in the dining-room."

His words came out slowly, and sounded as if each was a bullet wrapped round with cotton wool to make it fit the barrel. Ginevra looked perplexed for a moment.

"Should I say brownie, papa?" she asked.

"How can I tell you what you should call a creature that has no existence?" rejoined her father.

"If it be a creature, papa, it must have a name!" retorted the little logician, with great solemnity.

Mr. Galbraith was not pleased, for although the logic was good, it was against him.

"What foolish person has been insinuating such contemptible superstition into your silly head?" he asked. "Tell me, child," he continued, "that I may put a stop to it at once."

He was rising to ring the bell, that he might give the orders consequent on the information he expected: he would have asked Mammon to dinner in black clothes and a white tie, but on Superstition in the loveliest garb would have loosed all the dogs of Glashruach, to hunt her from the property. Her next words, however, arrested him, and just as she ended, the butler came in with fresh toast.

"They say," said Ginevra, anxious to avoid the forbidden Scotch, therefore stumbling sadly in her utterance, "there's a broonie—brownie—at the Mains, who dis a'—does all the work."

"What is the meaning of this, Joseph?" said Mr. Galbraith, turning from her to the butler, with the air of rebuke, which was almost habitual to him, a good deal heightened.

"The meanin' o' what, sir?" returned Joseph, nowise abashed, for to him his master was not the greatest man in the world, or even in the highlands. "He's no a Galbraith," he used to say, when more than commonly provoked with him.

"I ask you, Joseph," answered the laird, "what this—this outbreak of superstition imports? You must be aware that nothing in the world could annoy me more than that Miss Galbraith should learn folly in her father's house. That staid servants, such as I had supposed mine to be, should use their tongues as if their heads had no more in them than so many bells hung in a steeple, is to me a mortifying reflection."

"Tongues as weel's clappers was made to wag, sir; an, wag they wull, sir, sae lang's the tow (string) hings oot at baith lugs," answered Joseph. The forms of speech he employed were not unfrequently obscure to his master, and in that obscurity lay more of Joseph's impunity than he knew. "Forby (besides), sir," he went on, "gien tongues didna wag, what w'y wad you, 'at has to set a' thing richt, come to ken what was wrang?"

"That is not a bad remark, Joseph," replied the laird, with woolly condescension. "Pray acquaint me with the whole matter."

"I hae naething till acquaint yer honour wi', sir, but the ting-a-ling o' tongues," replied Joseph; "an' ye'll hae till arreenge't like, till yer ain settisfaction."

Therewith he proceeded to report what he had heard reported, which was in the main the truth, considerably exaggerated—that the work of the house was done over night by invisible hands—and the work of the stables, too; but that in the latter, cantrips were played as well; that some of the men talked of leaving the place; and that Mr. Duff's own horse, Snowball, was nearly out of his mind with fear.

The laird clenched his teeth, and for a whole minute said nothing. Here were either his old enemies again, or some who had heard the old story, and in their turn were beating the drum of consternation in the ears of superstition.

"It is one of the men themselves," he said at last, with outward frigidity. "Or some ill-designed neighbour," he added. "But I shall soon be at the bottom of it. Go to the Mains at once, Joseph, and ask young Fergus Duff to be so good as step over, as soon as he conveniently can."

Fergus was pleased enough to be sent for by the laird, and soon told him all he knew from his aunt and the men, confessing that he had himself been too lazy of a morning to take any steps towards personal acquaintance with the facts, but adding that, as Mr. Galbraith took an interest in the matter, "he would be only too happy to carry out any suggestion he might think proper to make on the subject.

"Fergus," returned the laird, "do you imagine things inanimate can of themselves change their relations in space? In other words, are the utensils in your kitchen endowed with powers of locomotion? Can they take to themselves wings and fly? Or to use a figure more to the point, are they provided with members necessary to the washing of their own—persons, shall I say? Answer me those points, Fergus."

"Certainly not, sir," answered Fergus solemnly, for the laird's face was solemn, and his speech was very solemn.

"Then, Fergus, let me assure you, that to discover by what agency these apparent wonders are effected, you have merely to watch. If you fail, I will myself come to your assistance. Depend upon it, the thing when explained will prove simplicity itself."

Fergus at once undertook to watch, but went home not quite so comfortable as he had gone; for he did not altogether, notwithstanding his unbelief in the so-called supernatural, relish the approaching situation. Belief and unbelief are not always quite plainly distinguishable from each other, and Fear is not always certain which of them is his mother. He was not the less resolved, however, to carry out what he had undertaken—that was, to sit up all night, if necessary, in order to have an interview with the extravagant and erring—spirit, surely, whether embodied or not, that dared thus wrong "domestic awe, night-rest, and neighbourhood," by doing people's work for them unbidden. Not even to himself did he confess that he felt frightened, for he was a youth of nearly eighteen; but he could not quite hide from himself the fact that he anticipated no pleasure in the duty which lay before him.

XX

The Ambush

For more reasons than one, Fergus judged it prudent to tell not even auntie Jean of his intention; but, waiting until the house was quiet, stole softly from his room and repaired to the kitchen—at the other end of the long straggling house, where he sat down, and taking his book, an annual of the beginning of the century, began to read the story of Kathed and Eurelia. Having finished it, he read another. He read and read, but no brownie came. His candle burned into the socket. He lighted another, and read again. Still no brownie appeared, and, hard and straight as was the wooden chair on which he sat, he began to doze. Presently he started wide awake, fancying he heard a noise; but nothing was there. He raised his book once more, and read until he had finished the stories in it: for the verse he had no inclination that night. As soon as they were all consumed, he began to feel very eerie: his courage had been sheltering itself behind his thoughts, which the tales he had been reading had kept turned away from the object of dread. Still deeper and deeper grew the night around him, until the bare, soulless waste of it came at last, when a brave man might welcome any ghost for the life it would bring. And ever as it came, the tide of fear flowed more rapidly, until at last it rose over his heart, and threatened to stifle him. The direst foe of courage is the fear itself, not the object of it; and the man who can overcome his own terror is a hero and more. In this Fergus had not yet deserved to be successful. That kind of victory comes only of faith. Still, he did not fly the field; he was no coward. At the same time, prizing courage, scorning fear, and indeed disbelieving in every nocturnal object of terror except robbers, he came at last to such an all but abandonment of dread, that he dared not look over his shoulder, lest he should see the brownie standing at his back; he would rather be seized from behind and strangled in his hairy grasp, than turn and die of the seeing. The night was dark—no moon and many clouds. Not a sound came from the close. The cattle, the horses, the pigs, the cocks and hens, the very cats and rats seemed asleep. There was not a rustle in the thatch, a creak in the couples. It was well, for the slightest noise would have brought his heart into his mouth, and he would have been in great danger of scaring the household, and for ever disgracing himself, with a shriek. Yet he longed to hear something stir. Oh! for the stamp of a horse from the stable or the low of a cow from the byre! But they were all under the brownie's spell, and he was coming—toeless feet, and thumbed but fingerless hands! as if he was made with stockings, and hum'le mittens! Was it the want of toes that made him able to come and go so quietly?— Another hour crept by; when lo, a mighty sun-trumpet blew in the throat of the black cock! Fergus sprang to his feet with the start it gave him—but the next moment gladness rushed up in his heart: the morning was on its way! and, foe to superstition as he was, and much as he had mocked at Donal for what he counted some of his tendencies in that direction, he began instantly to comfort himself with the old belief that all things of the darkness flee from the crowing of the cock. The same moment his courage began to return, and the next he was laughing at his terrors, more foolish than when he felt them, seeing he was the same man of fear as before, and the same circumstances would wrap him in the same garment of dire apprehension. In his folly he imagined himself quite ready to watch the next night without even repugnance—for it was the morning, not the night, that came first!

When the grey of the dawn appeared, he said to himself he would lie down on the bench a while, he was so tired of sitting; he would not sleep. He lay down, and in a moment was asleep. The light grew and grew, and the brownie came—a different brownie indeed from the one he had pictured—with the daintiest-shaped hands and feet coming out of the midst of rags, and with no hair except roughly parted curls over the face of a cherub—for the combing of Snowball's mane and tail had taught Gibbie to use the same comb upon his own thatch. But as soon as he opened the door of the dairy, he was warned by the loud breathing of the sleeper, and looking about, espied him on the bench behind the table, and swiftly retreated. The same instant Fergus woke, stretched himself, saw it was broad daylight, and, with his brain muddled by fatigue and sleep combined, crawled shivering to bed. Then in came the brownie again; and when Jean Mavor entered, there was her work done as usual.

Fergus was hours late for breakfast, and when he went into the common room, found his aunt alone there.

"Weel, auntie." he said, "I think I fleggit yer broonie!"

"Did ye that, man? Ay!—An' syne ye set tee, an' did the wark yersel to save yer auntie Jean's auld banes?"

"Na, na! I was o'er tiret for that. Sae wad ye hae been yersel', gien ye had sitten up a' nicht."

"Wha did it, than?"

"Ow, jist yersel', I'm thinkin', auntie."

"Never a finger o' mine was laid till't, Fergus. Gien ye fleggit ae broonie, anither cam; for there's the wark done, the same's ever."

"Damn the cratur!" cried Fergus.

"Whisht, whisht, laddie! he's maybe hearin' ye this meenute. An' gien he binna, there's ane 'at is, an' likesna sweirin'."

"I beg yer pardon, auntie, but it's jist provokin'!" returned Fergus, and therewith recounted the tale of his night's watch, omitting mention only of his feelings throughout the vigil.

As soon as he had had his breakfast, he went to carry his report to Glashruach.

The laird was vexed, and told him he must sleep well before night, and watch to better purpose.

The next night, Fergus's terror returned in full force; but he watched thoroughly notwithstanding, and when his aunt entered, she found him there, and her kitchen in a mess. He had caught no brownie, it was true, but neither had a stroke of her work been done. The floor was unswept; not a dish had been washed; it was churning-day, but the cream stood in the jar in the dairy, not the butter in the pan on the kitchen-dresser. Jean could not quite see the good or the gain of it. She had begun to feel like a lady, she said to herself, and now she must tuck up her sleeves and set to work as before. It was a come-down in the world, and she did not like it. She conned her nephew little thanks, and not being in the habit of dissembling, let him feel the same. He crept to bed rather mortified. When he woke from a long sleep, he found no meal waiting him, and had to content himself with cakes[1] and milk before setting out for "the Muckle Hoose."

---

1. It amuses a Scotchman to find that the word cakes, as in "The Land of Cakes," is taken, not only by foreigners, but by some English people—as how, indeed, should it be otherwise?—to mean compositions of flour, more or less enriched, and generally appreciable; whereas, in fact, it stands for the dryest, simplest preparation in the world. The genuine cakes is—(My grammar follows usage: cakes is; broth are.)—literally nothing but oatmeal made into a dough with cold water and dried over the fire—sometimes then in front of it as well.

GEORGE MACDONALD

"You must add cunning to courage, my young friend," said Mr. Galbraith; and the result of their conference was that Fergus went home resolved on yet another attempt.

He felt much inclined to associate Donal with him in his watch this time, but was too desirous of proving his courage both to himself and to the world, to yield to the suggestion of his fear. He went to bed with a book immediately after the noon-day meal and rose in time for supper.

There was a large wooden press in the kitchen, standing out from the wall; this with the next wall made a little recess, in which there was just room for a chair; and in that recess Fergus seated himself, in the easiest chair he could get into it. He then opened wide the door of the press, and it covered him entirely.

This night would have been the dreariest of all for him, the laird having insisted that he should watch in the dark, had he not speedily fallen fast asleep, and slept all night—so well that he woke at the first noise Gibbie made.

It was broad clear morning, but his heart beat so loud and fast with apprehension and curiosity mingled, that for a few moments Fergus dare not stir, but sat listening breathless to the movement beside him, none the less appalling that it was so quiet. Recovering himself a little he cautiously moved the door of the press, and peeped out.

He saw nothing so frightful as he had, in spite of himself, anticipated, but was not therefore, perhaps, the less astonished. The dread brownie of his idea shrunk to a tiny ragged urchin, with a wonderful head of hair, azure eyes, and deft hands, noiselessly bustling about on bare feet. He watched him at his leisure, watched him keenly, assured that any moment he could spring upon him.

As he watched, his wonder sank, and he grew disappointed at the collapsing of the lubber-fiend into a poor half-naked child upon whom both his courage and his fear had been wasted. As he continued to watch, an evil cloud of anger at the presumption of the unknown minimus began to gather in his mental atmosphere, and was probably the cause of some movement by which his chair gave a loud creak. Without even looking round, Gibbie darted into the dairy, and shut the door. Instantly Fergus was after him, but only in time to see the vanishing of his last heel through the hole in the wall, and that way Fergus was much too large to follow him. He rushed from the house, and across the corner of the yard to the barn-door. Gibbie, who did not believe he had been seen, stood laughing on the floor, when suddenly he heard the key entering the lock. He bolted through the cat-hole—but again just one moment too late, leaving behind him on Fergus's retina the light from the soles of two bare feet. The key of the door to the rick-yard was inside, and Fergus was after him in a moment, but the ricks came close to the barn-door, and the next he saw of him was the fluttering of his rags in the wind, and the flashing of his white skin in the sun, as he fled across the clover field; and before Fergus was over the wall, Gibbie was a good way ahead towards the Lorrie. Gibbie was a better runner for his size than Fergus, and in better training too; but, alas! Fergus's legs were nearly twice as long as Gibbie's. The little one reached the Lorrie, first, and dashing across it, ran up the side of the Glashburn, with a vague idea of Glashgar in his head. Fergus behind him was growing more and more angry as he gained upon him but felt his breath failing him. Just at the bridge to the iron gate to Glashruach, he caught him at last, and sunk on the parapet exhausted. The smile with which Gibbie, too much out of breath to laugh, confessed himself vanquished, would have disarmed one harder-hearted than Fergus, had he not lost his temper in the dread of losing his labour; and the answer Gibbie received to his smile was a box on the ear that bewildered him. He looked pitifully in his captor's face, the smile not yet faded from his, only to receive a box on the other ear, which, though a contrary and similar both at once, was not a cure, and the water gathered in his eyes. Fergus, a little eased in his temper by the infliction, and in his breath by the wall of the bridge, began to ply him with questions; but no answer following, his wrath rose again, and again he boxed both his ears—without better result.

Then came the question what was he to do with the redoubted brownie, now that he had him. He was ashamed to show himself as the captor of such a miserable culprit, but the little rascal deserved punishment, and the laird would require him at his hands. He turned upon his prisoner and told him he was an impudent rascal. Gibbie had recovered again, and was able once more to smile a little. He had been guilty of burglary, said Fergus; and Gibbie smiled. He could be sent to prison for it, said Fergus; and Gibbie smiled—but this time a very grave smile. Fergus took him by the collar, which amounted to nearly a third part of the jacket, and shook him till he had half torn that third from the other two; then opened the gate, and, holding him by the back of the neck, walked him up the drive, every now and then giving him a fierce shake that jarred his teeth. Thus, over the old gravel, mossy and damp and grassy, and cool to his little bare feet, between rowan and birk and pine and larch, like a malefactor, and looking every inch the outcast he was, did Sir Gilbert Galbraith approach the house of his ancestors for the first time. Individually, wee Gibbie was anything but a prodigal; it had never been possible to him to be one; but none the less was he the type and result and representative of his prodigal race, in him now once more looking upon the house they had lost by their vices and weaknesses, and in him now beginning to reap the benefits of punishment. But of vice and loss, of house and fathers and punishment, Gibbie had no smallest cognition. His history was about him and in him, yet of it all he suspected nothing. It would have made little difference to him if he had known it all; he would none the less have accepted everything that came, just as part of the story in which he found himself.

XXI

THE PUNISHMENT

The house he was approaching, had a little the look of a prison. Of the more ancient portion the windows were very small, and every corner had a turret with a conical cap-roof. That part was all rough-cast, therefore grey, as if with age. The more modern part was built of all kinds of hard stone, roughly cloven or blasted from the mountain and its boulders. Granite red and grey, blue whinstone, yellow ironstone, were all mingled anyhow, fitness of size and shape alone regarded in their conjunctions; but the result as to colour was rather pleasing than otherwise, and Gibbie regarded it with some admiration. Nor, although he had received from Fergus such convincing proof that he was regarded as a culprit, had he any dread of evil awaiting him. The highest embodiment of the law with which he had acquaintance was the police, and from not one of them in all the city had he ever had a harsh word; his conscience was as void of offence as ever it had been, and the law consequently, notwithstanding the threats of Fergus, had for him no terrors.

The laird was an early riser, and therefore regarded the mere getting up early as a virtue, altogether irrespective of how the time, thus redeemed, as he called it, was spent. This morning, as it turned out, it would have been better spent in sleep. He was talking to his gamekeeper, a heavy-browed man, by the coach-house door, when Fergus appeared holding the dwindled brownie by the huge collar of his tatters. A more innocent-looking malefactor sure never appeared before awful Justice! Only he was in rags, and there are others besides dogs whose judgments go by appearance. Mr. Galbraith was one of them, and smiled a grim, an ugly smile.

"So this is your vaunted brownie, Mr. Duff!" he said, and stood looking down upon Gibbie, as if in his small person he saw superstition at the point of death, mocked thither by the arrows of his contemptuous wit.

"It's all the brownie I could lay hands on, sir," answered Fergus. "I took him in the act."

"Boy," said the laird, rolling his eyes, more unsteady than usual with indignation, in the direction of Gibbie, "what have you to say for yourself?"

Gibbie had no say—and nothing to say that his questioner could either have understood or believed; the truth from his lips would but have presented him a lying hypocrite to the wisdom of his judge. As it was, he smiled, looking up fearless in the face of the magistrate, so awful in his own esteem.

"What is your name?" asked the laird, speaking yet more sternly.

Gibbie still smiled and was silent, looking straight in his questioner's eyes. He dreaded nothing from the laird. Fergus had beaten him, but Fergus he classed with the bigger boys who had occasionally treated him roughly; this was a man, and men, except they were foreign sailors, or drunk, were never unkind. He had no idea of his silence causing annoyance. Everybody in the city had known he could not answer; and now when Fergus and the laird persisted in questioning him, he thought they were making kindly game of him, and smiled the more. Nor was there much about Mr. Galbraith to rouse a suspicion of the contrary; for he made a great virtue of keeping his temper when most he caused other people to lose theirs.

"I see the young vagabond is as impertinent as he is vicious," he said at last, finding that to no interrogation could he draw forth any other response than a smile. "Here Angus,"—and he turned to the gamekeeper—"take him into the coach-house, and teach him a little behaviour. A touch or two of the whip will find his tongue for him."

Angus seized the little gentleman by the neck, as if he had been a polecat, and at arm's length walked him unresistingly into the coach-house. There, with one vigorous tug, he tore the jacket from his back, and his only other garment, dependent thereupon by some device known only to Gibbie, fell from him, and he stood in helpless nakedness, smiling still: he had never done anything shameful, therefore had no acquaintance with shame. But when the scowling keeper, to whom poverty was first cousin to poaching, and who hated tramps as he hated vermin, approached him with a heavy cart whip in his hand, he cast his eyes down at his white sides, very white between his brown arms and brown legs, and then lifted them in a mute appeal, which somehow looked as if it were for somebody else, against what he could no longer fail to perceive the man's intent. But he had no notion of what the thing threatened amounted to. He had had few hard blows in his time, and had never felt a whip.

"Ye deil's glaur!" cried the fellow, clenching the cruel teeth of one who loved not his brother, "I s' lat ye ken what comes o' brakin' into honest hooses, an' takin' what's no yer ain!"

A vision of the gnawed cheese, which he had never touched since the idea of its being property awoke in him, rose before Gibbie's mental eyes, and inwardly he bowed to the punishment. But the look he had fixed on Angus was not without effect, for the man was a father, though a severe one, and was not all a brute: he turned and changed the cart whip for a gig one with a broken shaft, which lay near. It was well for himself that he did so, for the other would probably have killed Gibbie. When the blow fell the child shivered all over, his face turned white, and without uttering even a moan, he doubled up and dropped senseless. A swollen cincture, like a red snake, had risen all round his waist, and from one spot in it the blood was oozing. It looked as if the lash had cut him in two.

The blow had stung his heart and it had ceased to beat. But the gamekeeper understood vagrants! the young blackguard was only shamming!

"Up wi' ye, ye deevil! or I s' gar ye," he said from between his teeth, lifting the whip for a second blow.

Just as the stroke fell, marking him from the nape all down the spine, so that he now bore upon his back in red the sign the ass carries in black, a piercing shriek assailed Angus's ears, and his arm, which had mechanically raised itself for a third blow, hung arrested.

The same moment, in at the coach-house door shot Ginevra, as white as Gibbie. She darted to where he lay, and there stood over him, arms rigid and hands clenched hard, shivering as he had shivered, and sending from her body shriek after shriek, as if her very soul were the breath of which her cries were fashioned. It was as if the woman's heart in her felt its roots torn from their home in the bosom of God, and quivering in agony, and confronted by the stare of an eternal impossibility, shrieked against Satan.

"Gang awa, missie," cried Angus, who had respect to this child, though he had not yet learned to respect childhood; "he's a coorse cratur, an' maun hae's whups."

But Ginevra was deaf to his evil charming. She stopped her cries, however, to help Gibbie up, and took one of his hands to raise him. But his arm hung limp and motionless; she let it go; it dropped like a stick, and again she began to shriek. Angus laid his hand on her shoulder. She turned on him, and opening her mouth wide, screamed at him like a wild animal, with all the hatred of mingled love and fear; then threw herself on the boy, and covered his body with her own. Angus, stooping to remove her, saw Gibbie's face, and became uncomfortable.

"He's deid! he's deid! Ye've killt him, Angus! Ye're an ill man!" she cried fiercely. "I hate ye. I'll tell on ye. I'll tell my papa."

"Hoot! whisht, missie!" said Angus. "It was by yer papa's ain orders I gae him the whup, an' he weel deserved it forby. An' gien ye dinna gang awa, an' be a guid yoong leddy, I'll gie 'im mair yet."

"I'll tell God," shrieked Ginevra with fresh energy of defensive love and wrath.

Again he sought to remove her, but she clung so, with both legs and arms, to the insensible Gibbie, that he could but lift both together, and had to leave her alone.

"Gien ye daur to touch 'im again, Angus, I'll bite ye—bite ye—Bite Ye," she screamed, in a passage wildly crescendo.

The laird and Fergus had walked away together, perhaps neither of them quite comfortable at the orders given, but the one too self-sufficient to recall them, and the other too submissive to interfere. They heard the cries, nevertheless, and had they known them for Ginevra's, would have rushed to the spot; but fierce emotion had so utterly changed her voice—and indeed she had never in her life cried out before—that they took them for Gibbie's and supposed the whip had had the desired effect and loosed his tongue. As to the rest of the household, which would by this time have been all gathered in the coach-house, the laird had taken his stand where he could intercept them: he would not have the execution of the decrees of justice interfered with.

But Ginevra's shrieks brought Gibbie to himself. Faintly he opened his eyes, and stared, stupid with growing pain, at the tear-blurred face beside him. In the confusion of his thoughts he fancied the pain he felt was Ginevra's, not his, and sought to comfort her, stroking her cheek with feeble hand, and putting up his mouth to kiss her. But Angus, utterly scandalized at the proceeding, and restored to energy by seeing that the boy was alive, caught her up suddenly and carried her off—struggling, writhing, and scratching like a cat. Indeed she bit his arm, and that severely, but the man never even told his wife. Little Missie was a queen, and little Gibbie was a vermin, but he was ashamed to let the mother of his children know that the former had bitten him for the sake of the latter.

The moment she thus disappeared, Gibbie began to apprehend that she was suffering for him, not he for her. His whole body bore testimony to frightful abuse. This was some horrible place inhabited by men such as those that killed Sambo! He must fly. But would they hurt the little girl?

He thought not—she was at home. He started to spring to his feet, but fell back almost powerless; then tried more cautiously and got up wearily, for the pain and the terrible shock seemed to have taken the strength out of every limb. Once on his feet, he could scarcely stoop to pick up his remnant of trowsers without again falling, and the effort made him groan with distress. He was in the act of trying in vain to stand on one foot, so as to get the other into the garment, when he fancied he heard the step of his executioner, returning doubtless to resume his torture. He dropped the rag, and darted out of the door, forgetting aches and stiffness and agony. All naked as he was, he fled like the wind, unseen, or at least unrecognized, of any eye. Fergus did catch a glimpse of something white that flashed across a vista through the neighbouring wood, but he took it for a white peacock, of which there were two or three about the place. The three men were disgusted with the little wretch when they found that he had actually fled into the open day without his clothes. Poor Gibbie! it was such a small difference! It needed as little change to make a savage as an angel of him. All depended on the eyes that saw him.

He ran he knew not whither, feeling nothing but the desire first to get into some covert, and then to run farther. His first rush was for the shubbery, his next across the little park to the wood beyond. He did not feel the wind of his running on his bare skin. He did not feel the hunger that had made him so unable to bear the lash. On and on he ran, fancying ever he heard the cruel Angus behind him. If a dry twig snapped, he thought it was the crack of the whip; and a small wind that rose suddenly in the top of a pine, seemed the hiss with which it was about to descend upon him. He ran and ran, but still there seemed nothing between him and his persecutors. He felt no safety. At length he came where a high wall joining some water, formed a boundary. The water was a brook from the mountain, here widened and deepened into a still pool. He had been once out of his depth before: he threw himself in, and swam straight across: ever after that, swimming seemed to him as natural as walking.

Then first awoke a faint sense of safety; for on the other side he was knee deep in heather. He was on the wild hill, with miles on miles of cover! Here the unman could not catch him. It must be the same that Donal pointed out to him one day at a distance; he had a gun, and Donal said he had once shot a poacher and killed him. He did not know what a poacher was: perhaps he was one himself, and the man would shoot him. They could see him quite well from the other side! he must cross the knoll first, and then he might lie down and rest. He would get right into the heather, and lie with it all around and over him till the night came. Where he would go then, he did not know. But it was all one; he could go anywhere. Donal must mind his cows, and the men must mind the horses, and Mistress Jean must mind her kitchen, but Sir Gibbie could go where he pleased. He would go up Daurside; but he would not go just at once; that man might be on the outlook for him, and he wouldn't like to be shot. People who were shot lay still, and were put into holes in the earth, and covered up, and he would not like that.

Thus he communed with himself as he went over the knoll. On the other side he chose a tall patch of heather, and crept under. How nice and warm and kind the heather felt, though it did hurt the weals dreadfully sometimes. If he only had something to cover just them! There seemed to be one down his back as well as round his waist!

And now Sir Gibbie, though not much poorer than he had been, really possessed nothing separable, except his hair and his nails—nothing therefore that he could call his, as distinguished from him. His sole other possession was a negative quantity—his hunger, namely, for he had not even a meal in his body. He had eaten nothing since the preceding noon. I am wrong—he had one possession besides, though hardly a separable one—a ballad about a fair lady and her page, which Donal had taught him. That he now began to repeat to himself, but was disappointed to find it a good deal withered. He was not nearly reduced to extremity yet though—this little heir of the world: in his body he had splendid health, in his heart a great courage, and in his soul an ever-throbbing love. It was his love to the very image of man, that made the horror of the treatment he had received. Angus was and was not a man! After all, Gibbie was still one to be regarded with holy envy.

Poor Ginny was sent to bed for interfering with her father's orders; and what with rage and horror and pity, an inexplicable feeling of hopelessness took possession of her, while her affection for her father was greatly, perhaps for this world irretrievably, injured by that morning's experience; a something remained that never passed from her, and that something, as often as it stirred, rose between him and her.

Fergus told his aunt what had taken place, and made much game of her brownie. But the more Jean thought about the affair, the less she liked it. It was she upon whom it all came! What did it matter who or what her brownie was? And what had they whipped the creature for? What harm had he done? If indeed he was a little ragged urchin, the thing was only the more inexplicable! He had taken nothing! She had never missed so much as a barley scon! The cream had always brought her the right quantity of butter! Not even a bannock, so far as she knew, was ever gone from the press, or an egg from the bossie where they lay heaped! There was more in it than she could understand! Her nephew's mighty feat, so far from explaining anything, had only sealed up the mystery. She could not help cherishing a shadowy hope that, when things had grown quiet, he would again reveal his presence by his work, if not by his visible person. It was mortifying to think that he had gone as he came, and she had never set eyes upon him. But Fergus's account of his disappearance had also, in her judgment, a decided element of the marvellous in it. She was strongly inclined to believe that the brownie had cast a glamour over him and the laird and Angus, all three, and had been making game of them for his own amusement. Indeed Daurside generally refused the explanation of the brownie presented for its acceptance, and the laird scored nothing against the arch-enemy Superstition.

Donal Grant, missing his "cratur" that day for the first time, heard enough when he came home to satisfy him that he had been acting the brownie in the house and the stable as well as in the field, incredible as it might well appear that such a child should have had even mere strength for what he did. Then first also, after he had thus lost him, he began to understand his worth, and to see how much he owed him. While he had imagined himself kind to the urchin, the urchin had been laying him under endless obligation. For he left him with ever so much more in his brains than when he came. This book and that, through his aid, he had read thoroughly; and a score or so of propositions had been added to his stock in Euclid. His first feeling about the child revived as he pondered—namely, that he was not of this world. But even then Donal did not know the best Gibbie had done for him. He did not know of what far deeper and better things he had, through his gentleness, his trust, his loving service, his absolute unselfishness, sown the seeds in his mind. On the other hand, Donal had in return done more for Gibbie than he knew, though what he had done for him, namely, shared his dinners with him, had been less of a gift than he thought, and Donal had rather been sharing in Gibbie's dinner, than Gibbie in Donal's.

XXII

Refuge

It was a lovely Saturday evening on Glashgar. The few flowers about the small turf cottage scented the air in the hot western sun. The heather was not in bloom yet, and there were no trees; but there were rocks, and stones, and a brawling burn that half surrounded a little field of oats, one of potatoes, and a small spot with a few stocks of cabbage and kail, on the borders of which grew some bushes of double daisies, and primroses, and carnations. These Janet tended as part of her household, while her husband saw to the oats and potatoes. Robert had charge of the few sheep on the mountain which belonged to the farmer at the Mains, and for his trouble had the cottage and the land, most of which he had himself reclaimed. He had also a certain allowance of meal, which was paid in portions, as corn went from the farm to the mill. If they happened to fall short, the miller would always advance them as much as they needed, repaying himself—and not very strictly—the next time the corn was sent from the Mains. They were never in any want, and never had any money, except what their children brought them out of their small wages. But that was plenty for their every need, nor had they the faintest feeling that they were persons to be pitied. It was very cold up there in winter, to be sure, and they both suffered from rheumatism; but they had no debt, no fear, much love, and between them, this being mostly Janet's, a large hope for what lay on the other side of death: as to the rheumatism, that was necessary, Janet said, to teach them patience, for they had no other trouble. They were indeed growing old, but neither had begun to feel age a burden yet, and when it should prove such, they had a daughter prepared to give up service and go home to help them. Their thoughts about themselves were nearly lost in their thoughts about each other, their children, and their friends. Janet's main care was her old man, and Robert turned to Janet as the one stay of his life, next to the God in whom he trusted. He did not think so much about God as she: he was not able; nor did he read so much of his Bible; but she often read to him; and when any of his children were there of an evening, he always "took the book." While Janet prayed at home, his closet was the mountain-side, where he would kneel in the heather, and pray to Him who saw unseen, the King eternal, immortal, invisible, the only wise God. The sheep took no heed of him, but sometimes when he rose from his knees and saw Oscar gazing at him with deepest regard, he would feel a little as if he had not quite entered enough into his closet, and would wonder what the dog was thinking. All day, from the mountain and sky and preaching burns, from the sheep and his dog, from winter storms, spring sun and winds, or summer warmth and glow, but more than all, when he went home, from the presence and influence of his wife, came to him somehow—who can explain how!—spiritual nourishment and vital growth. One great thing in it was, that he kept growing wiser and better without knowing it. If St. Paul had to give up judging his own self, perhaps Robert Grant might get through without ever beginning it. He loved life, but if he had been asked why, he might not have found a ready answer. He loved his wife—just because she was Janet. Blithely he left his cottage in the morning, deep breathing the mountain air, as if it were his first in the blissful world; and all day the essential bliss of being was his; but the immediate hope of his heart was not the heavenly city; it was his home and his old woman, and her talk of what she had found in her Bible that day. Strangely mingled—mingled even to confusion with his faith in God, was his absolute trust in his wife—a confidence not very different in kind from the faith which so many Christians place in the mother of our Lord. To Robert, Janet was one who knew—one who was far ben??? with the Father of lights. She perceived his intentions, understood his words, did his will, dwelt in the secret place of the Most High. When Janet entered into the kingdom of her Father, she would see that he was not left outside. He was as sure of her love to himself, as he was of God's love to her, and was certain she could never be content without her old man. He was himself a dull soul, he thought, and could not expect the great God to take much notice of him, but he would allow Janet to look after him. He had a vague conviction that he would not be very hard to save, for he knew himself ready to do whatever was required of him. None of all this was plain to his consciousness, however, or I daresay he would have begun at once to combat the feeling.

His sole anxiety, on the other hand, was neither about life nor death, about this world nor the next, but that his children should be honest and honourable, fear God and keep his commandments. Around them, all and each, the thoughts of father and mother were constantly hovering—as if to watch them, and ward off evil.

Almost from the day, now many years ago, when, because of distance and difficulty, she ceased to go to church, Janet had taken to her New Testament in a new fashion.

She possessed an instinctive power of discriminating character, which had its root and growth in the simplicity of her own; she had always been a student of those phases of humanity that came within her ken; she had a large share of that interest in her fellows and their affairs which is the very bloom upon ripe humanity: with these qualifications, and the interpretative light afforded by her own calm practical way of living, she came to understand men and their actions, especially where the latter differed from what might ordinarily have been expected, in a marvellous way: her faculty amounted almost to sympathetic contact with the very humanity. When, therefore, she found herself in this remote spot, where she could see so little of her kind, she began, she hardly knew by what initiation, to turn her study upon the story of our Lord's life. Nor was it long before it possessed her utterly, so that she concentrated upon it all the light and power of vision she had gathered from her experience of humanity. It ought not therefore to be wonderful how much she now understood of the true humanity—with what simple directness she knew what many of the words of the Son of Man meant, and perceived many of the germs of his individual actions. Hence it followed naturally that the thought of him, and the hope of one day seeing him, became her one informing idea. She was now such another as those women who ministered to him on the earth.

A certain gentle indifference she allowed to things considered important, the neighbours attributed to weakness of character, and called softness; while the honesty, energy, and directness with which she acted upon insights they did not possess, they attributed to intellectual derangement. She was "ower easy," they said, when the talk had been of prudence or worldly prospect; she was "ower hard," they said, when the question had been of right and wrong.

The same afternoon, a neighbour, on her way over the shoulder of the hill to the next village, had called upon her and found her brushing the rafters of her cottage with a broom at the end of a long stick.

"Save 's a', Janet! what are ye efter? I never saw sic a thing!" she exclaimed.

"I kenna hoo I never thoucht o' sic a thing afore," answered Janet, leaning her broom against the wall, and dusting a chair for her visitor;

"but this mornin', whan my man an' me was sittin' at oor brakfast, there cam' sic a clap o' thunner, 'at it jist garred the bit hoosie trim'le; an' doon fell a snot o' soot intil the very spune 'at my man was cairryin' till's honest moo. That cudna be as things war inten'it, ye ken; sae what was to be said but set them richt?"

"Ow, weel! but ye micht hae waitit till Donal cam' hame; he wad hae dune 't in half the time, an' no raxed his jints."

"I cudna pit it aff," answered Janet. "Wha kenned whan the Lord micht come?—He canna come at cock-crawin' the day, but he may be here afore nicht."

"Weel, I's awa," said her visitor rising. "I'm gauin' ower to the toon to buy a feow hanks o' worset to weyve a pair o' stockins to my man. Guid day to ye, Janet.—What neist, I won'er?" she added to herself as she left the house. "The wuman's clean dementit!"

The moment she was gone, Janet caught up her broom again, and went spying about over the roof—ceiling there was none—after long tangles of agglomerated cobweb and smoke.

"Ay!" she said to herself, "wha kens whan he may be at the door? an' I wadna like to hear him say—'Janet, ye micht hae had yer hoose a bit cleaner, whan ye kenned I micht be at han'!'"

With all the cleaning she could give it, her cottage would have looked but a place of misery to many a benevolent woman, who, if she had lived there, would not have been so benevolent as Janet, or have kept the place half so clean. For her soul was alive and rich, and out of her soul, not education or habit, came the smallest of her virtues.—Having finished at last, she took her besom to the door, and beat it against a stone. That done, she stood looking along the path down the hill. It was that by which her sons and daughters, every Saturday, came climbing, one after the other, to her bosom, from their various labours in the valley below, through the sunset, through the long twilight, through the moonlight, each urged by a heart eager to look again upon father and mother.

The sun was now far down his western arc, and nearly on a level with her eyes; and as she gazed into the darkness of the too much light, suddenly emerged from it, rose upward, staggered towards her—was it an angel? was it a spectre? Did her old eyes deceive her? or was the second sight born in her now first in her old age?—It seemed a child—reeling, and spreading out hands that groped. She covered her eyes for a moment, for it might be a vision in the sun, not on the earth—and looked again. It was indeed a naked child! and—was she still so dazzled by the red sun as to see red where red was none?—or were those indeed blood-red streaks on his white skin? Straight now, though slow, he came towards her. It was the same child who had come and gone so strangely before! He held out his hands to her, and fell on his face at her feet like one dead. Then, with a horror of pitiful amazement, she saw a great cross marked in two cruel stripes on his back; and the thoughts that thereupon went coursing through her loving imagination, it would be hard to set forth. Could it be that the Lord was still, child and man, suffering for his race, to deliver his brothers and sisters from their sins?—wandering, enduring, beaten, blessing still? accepting the evil, slaying it, and returning none? his patience the one rock where the evil word finds no echo; his heart the one gulf into which the dead-sea wave rushes with no recoil—from which ever flows back only purest water, sweet and cool; the one abyss of destroying love, into which all wrong tumbles, and finding no reaction, is lost, ceases for evermore? there, in its own cradle, the primal order is still nursed, still restored; thence is still sent forth afresh, to leaven with new life the world ever ageing! Shadowy and vague they were—but vaguely shadowed were thoughts like these in Janet's mind, as she stood half-stunned, regarding for one moment motionless the prostrate child and his wrongs. The next she lifted him in her arms, and holding him tenderly to her mother-heart, carried him into the house, murmuring over him dove-like sounds of pity and endearment mingled with indignation. There she laid him on his side in her bed, covered him gently over, and hastened to the little byre at the end of the cottage, to get him some warm milk. When she returned, he had already lifted his heavy eyelids, and was looking wearily about the place. But when he saw her, did ever so bright a sun shine as that smile of his! Eyes and mouth and whole face flashed upon Janet! She set down the milk, and went to the bedside. Gibbie put up his arms, threw them round her neck, and clung to her as if she had been his mother. And from that moment she was his mother: her heart was big enough to mother all the children of humanity. She was like Charity herself, with her babes innumerable.

"What have they done to ye, my bairn?" she said, in tones pitiful with the pity of the Shepherd of the sheep himself.

No reply came back—only another heavenly smile, a smile of absolute content. For what were stripes and nakedness and hunger to Gibbie, now that he had a woman to love! Gibbie's necessity was to love;

but here was more; here was Love offering herself to him! Except in black Sambo he had scarcely caught a good sight of her before. He had never before been kissed by that might of God's grace, a true woman. She was an old woman who kissed him; but none who have drunk of the old wine of love, straightway desire the new, for they know that the old is better. Match such as hers with thy love, maiden of twenty, and where wilt thou find the man I say not worthy, but fit to mate with thee? For hers was love indeed—not the love of love—but the love of Life. Already Gibbie's faintness was gone—and all his ills with it. She raised him with one arm, and held the bowl to his mouth, and he drank; but all the time he drank, his eyes were fixed upon hers. When she laid him down again, he turned on his side, off his scored back, and in a moment was fast asleep. She stood gazing at him. So still was he, that she began to fear he was dead, and laid her hand on his heart. It was beating steadily, and she left him, to make some gruel for him against his waking. Her soul was glad, for she was ministering to her Master, not the less in his own self, that it was in the person of one of his little ones. Gruel, as such a one makes it, is no common fare, but delicate enough for a queen. She set it down by the fire, and proceeded to lay the supper for her expected children. The clean yellow-white table of soft smooth fir, needed no cloth—only horn spoons and wooden caups.

At length a hand came to the latch, and mother and daughter greeted as mother and daughter only can; then came a son, and mother and son greeted as mother and son only can. They kept on arriving singly to the number of six—two daughters and four sons, the youngest some little time after the rest. Each, as he or she came, Janet took to the bed, and showed her seventh child where he slept. Each time she showed him, to secure like pity with her own, she turned down the bedclothes, and revealed the little back, smitten with the eternal memorial of the divine perfection. The women wept. The young men were furious, each after his fashion.

"God damn the rascal 'at did it!" cried one of them, clenching his teeth, and forgetting himself quite in the rage of the moment.

"Laddie, tak back the word," said his mother calmly. "Gien ye dinna forgie yer enemies, ye'll no be forgi'en yersel'."

"That's some hard, mither," answered the offender, with an attempted smile.

"Hard!" she echoed; "it may weel be hard, for it canna be helpit. What wad be the use o' forgiein' ye, or hoo cud it win at ye, or what wad ye care for't, or mak o't, cairryin' a hell o' hate i' yer verra hert? For gien God be love, hell maun be hate. My bairn, them 'at winna forgie their enemies, cairries sic a nest o' deevilry i' their ain boasoms, 'at the verra speerit o' God himsel' canna win in till't for bein' scomfished wi' smell an' reik. Muckle guid wad ony pardon dee to sic! But ance lat them un'erstan' 'at he canna forgie them, an' maybe they'll be fleyt, an' turn again' the Sawtan 'at's i' them."

"Weel, but he's no my enemy," said the youth.

"No your enemy!" returned his mother; "—no your enemy, an' sair (serve) a bairn like that! My certy! but he's the enemy o' the haill race o' mankin'. He trespasses unco sair against me, I'm weel sure o' that! An' I'm glaid o' 't. I'm glaid 'at he has me for ane o' 's enemies, for I forgie him for ane; an' wuss him sae affrontit wi' himsel' er' a' be dune, 'at he wad fain hide his heid in a midden."

"Noo, noo, mither!" said the eldest son, who had not yet spoken, but whose countenance had been showing a mighty indignation, "that's surely as sair a bannin' as yon 'at Jock said."

"What, laddie! Wad ye hae a fellow-cratur live to a' eternity ohn been ashamed o' sic a thing 's that? Wad that be to wuss him weel? Kenna ye 'at the mair shame the mair grace? My word was the best beginnin' o' better 'at I cud wuss him. Na, na, laddie! frae my verra hert, I wuss he may be that affrontit wi' himsel' 'at he canna sae muckle as lift up's een to h'aven, but maun smite upo' 's breist an' say, 'God be mercifu' to me a sinner!' That's my curse upo' him, for I wadna hae 'im a deevil. Whan he comes to think that shame o' himsel', I'll tak him to my hert, as I tak the bairn he misguidit. Only I doobt I'll be lang awa afore that, for it taks time to fess a man like that till's holy senses."

The sixth of the family now entered, and his mother led him up to the bed.

"The Lord preserve's!" cried Donal Grant, "it's the cratur!—An' is that the gait they hae guidit him! The quaietest cratur an' the willin'est!"

Donal began to choke.

"Ye ken him than, laddie?" said his mother.

"Weel that," answered Donal. "He's been wi' me an' the nowt ilka day for weeks till the day."

With that he hurried into the story of his acquaintance with Gibbie; and the fable of the brownie would soon have disappeared from Daurside, had it not been that Janet desired them to say nothing about the boy, but let him be forgotten by his enemies, till he grew able to take care of himself. Besides, she said, their father might get into trouble with the master and the laird, if it were known they had him.

Donal vowed to himself, that, if Fergus had had a hand in the abuse, he would never speak civil word to him again.

He turned towards the bed, and there were Gibbie's azure eyes wide open and fixed upon him.

"Eh, ye cratur!" he cried; and darting to the bed, he took Gibbie's face between his hands, and said, in a voice to which pity and sympathy gave a tone like his mother's,

"Whaten a deevil was't 'at lickit ye like that? Eh! I wuss I had the trimmin' o' him!"

Gibbie smiled.

"Has the ill-guideship ta'en the tongue frae 'im, think ye?" asked the mother.

"Na, na," answered Donal; "he's been like that sin' ever I kenned him. I never h'ard word frae the moo' o' 'im."

"He'll be ane o' the deif an' dumb," said Janet.

"He's no deif, mither; that I ken weel; but dumb he maun be, I'm thinkin'.—Cratur," he continued, stooping over the boy, "gien ye hear what I'm sayin', tak haud o' my nose."

Thereupon, with a laugh like that of an amused infant, Gibbie raised his hand, and with thumb and forefinger gently pinched Donal's large nose, at which they all burst out laughing with joy. It was as if they had found an angel's baby in the bushes, and been afraid he was an idiot, but were now relieved. Away went Janet, and brought him his gruel. It was with no small difficulty and not without a moan or two, that Gibbie sat up in the bed to take it. There was something very pathetic in the full content with which he sat there in his nakedness, and looked smiling at them all. It was more than content—it was bliss that shone in his countenance. He took the wooden bowl, and began to eat; and the look he cast on Janet seemed to say he had never tasted such delicious food. Indeed he never had; and the poor cottage, where once more he was a stranger and taken in, appeared to Gibbie a place of wondrous wealth. And so it was—not only in the best treasures, those of loving kindness, but in all homely plenty as well for the needs of the body—a very temple of the God of simplicity and comfort—rich in warmth and rest and food.

Janet went to her kist, whence she brought out a garment of her own, and aired it at the fire. It had no lace at the neck or cuffs, no embroidery down the front; but when she put it on him, amid the tearful laughter of the women, and had tied it round his waist with a piece of list that had served as a garter, it made a dress most becoming in their eyes, and gave Gibbie indescribable pleasure from its whiteness, and its coolness to his inflamed skin.

They had just finished clothing him thus, when the goodman came home, and the mother's narration had to be given afresh, with Donal's notes explanatory and completive. As the latter reported the doings of the imagined brownie, and the commotion they had caused at the Mains and along Daurside, Gibbie's countenance flashed with pleasure and fun; and at last he broke into such a peal of laughter as had never, for pure merriment, been heard before so high on Glashgar. All joined involuntarily in the laugh—even the old man, who had been listening with his grey eyebrows knit, and hanging like bosky precipices over the tarns of his deepset eyes, taking in every word, but uttering not one. When at last his wife showed him the child's back, he lifted his two hands, and moved them slowly up and down, as in pitiful appeal for man against man to the sire of the race. But still he said not a word. As to utterance of what lay in the deep soul of him, the old man, except sometimes to his wife, was nearly as dumb as Gibbie himself.

They sat down to their homely meal. Simplest things will carry the result of honest attention as plainly as more elaborate dishes; and, which it might be well to consider, they will carry no more than they are worth: of Janet's supper it is enough to say that it was such as became her heart. In the judgment of all her guests, the porridge was such as none could make but mother, the milk such as none but mother's cow could yield, the cakes such as she only could bake.

Gibbie sat in the bed like a king on his throne, gazing on his kingdom. For he that loves has, as no one else has. It is the divine possession. Picture the delight of the child, in his passion for his kind, looking out upon this company of true hearts, honest faces, human forms—all strong and healthy, loving each other and generous to the taking in of the world's outcast! Gibbie could not, at that period of his history, have invented a heaven more to his mind, and as often as one of them turned eyes towards the bed, his face shone up with love and merry gratitude, like a better sun.

It was now almost time for the sons and daughters to go down the hill again, and leave the cottage and the blessed old parents and the harboured child to the night, the mountain-silence, and the living God.

The sun had long been down; but far away in the north, the faint thin fringe of his light-garment was still visible, moving with the unseen body of his glory softly eastward, dreaming along the horizon, growing fainter and fainter as it went, but at the faintest then beginning to revive and grow. Of the northern lands in summer, it may be said, as of the heaven of heavens, that there is no night there. And by and by the moon also would attend the steps of the returning children of labour.

"Noo, lads an' lasses, afore we hae worship, rin, ilk ane o' ye," said the mother, "an' pu' heather to mak a bed to the wee man—i' the neuk there, at the heid o' oors. He'll sleep there bonny, an' no ill 'ill come near 'im."

She was obeyed instantly. The heather was pulled, and set together upright as it grew, only much closer, so that the tops made a dense surface, and the many stalks, each weak, a strong upbearing whole. They boxed them in below with a board or two for the purpose, and bound them together above with a blanket over the top, and a white sheet over that—a linen sheet it was, and large enough to be doubled, and receive Gibbie between its folds. Then another blanket was added, and the bed, a perfect one, was ready. The eldest of the daughters took Gibbie in her arms, and, tenderly careful over his hurts, lifted him from the old folks' bed, and placed him in his own—one more luxurious, for heather makes a still better stratum for repose than oat-chaff—and Gibbie sank into it with a sigh that was but a smile grown vocal.

Then Donal, as the youngest, got down the big Bible, and having laid it before his father, lighted the rush-pith-wick projecting from the beak of the little iron lamp that hung against the wall, its shape descended from Roman times. The old man put on his spectacles, took the book, and found the passage that fell, in continuous process, to that evening.

Now he was not a very good reader, and, what with blindness and spectacles, and poor light, would sometimes lose his place. But it never troubled him, for he always knew the sense of what was coming, and being no idolater of the letter, used the word that first suggested itself, and so recovered his place without pausing. It reminded his sons and daughters of the time when he used to tell them Bible stories as they crowded about his knees; and sounding therefore merely like the substitution of a more familiar word to assist their comprehension, woke no surprise. And even now, the word supplied, being in the vernacular, was rather to the benefit than the disadvantage of his hearers. The word of Christ is spirit and life, and where the heart is aglow, the tongue will follow that spirit and life fearlessly, and will not err.

On this occasion he was reading of our Lord's cure of the leper; and having read, "put forth his hand," lost his place, and went straight on without it, from his memory of the facts.

"He put forth his han'—an' grippit him, and said, Aw wull—be clean."

After the reading followed a prayer, very solemn and devout. It was then only, when before God, with his wife by his side, and his family around him, that the old man became articulate. He would scarcely have been so then, and would have floundered greatly in the marshes of his mental chaos, but for the stepping-stones of certain theological forms and phrases, which were of endless service to him in that they helped him to utter what in him was far better, and so realise more to himself his own feelings. Those forms and phrases would have shocked any devout Christian who had not been brought up in the same school; but they did him little harm, for he saw only the good that was in them, and indeed did not understand them save in so far as they worded that lifting up of the heart after which he was ever striving.

By the time the prayer was over, Gibbie was fast asleep again. What it all meant he had not an idea; and the sound lulled him—a service often so rendered in lieu of that intended. When he woke next, from the aching of his stripes, the cottage was dark. The old people were fast asleep. A hairy thing lay by his side, which, without the least fear, he examined by palpation, and found to be a dog, whereupon he fell fast asleep again, if possible happier than ever. And while the cottage was thus quiet, the brothers and sisters were still tramping along the moonlight paths of Daurside. They had all set out together, but at one point after another there had been a parting, and now they were on six different roads, each drawing nearer to the labour of the new week.

XXIII

MORE SCHOOLING

The first opportunity Donal had, he questioned Fergus as to his share in the ill-usage of Gibbie. Fergus treated the inquiry as an impertinent interference, and mounted his high horse at once. What right had his father's herd-boy to question him as to his conduct? He put it so to him and in nearly just as many words. Thereupon answered Donal—

"It's this, ye see, Fergus: ye hae been unco guid to me, an' I'm mair obligatit till ye nor I can say. But it wad be a scunnerfu' thing to tak the len' o' buiks frae ye, an' spier quest'ons at ye 'at I canna mak oot mysel', an' syne gang awa despisin' ye i' my hert for cruelty an' wrang. What was the cratur punished for? Tell me that. Accordin' till yer aunt's ain accoont, he had taen naething, an' had dune naething but guid."

"Why didn't he speak up then, and defend himself, and not be so damned obstinate?" returned Fergus. "He wouldn't open his mouth to tell his name, or where he came from even. I couldn't get him to utter a single word. As for his punishment, it was by the laird's orders that Angus Mac Pholp took the whip to him. I had nothing to do with it.—" Fergus did not consider the punishment he had himself given him as worth mentioning—as indeed, except for honesty's sake, it was not, beside the other.

"Weel, I'll be a man some day, an' Angus 'll hae to sattle wi' me!" said Donal through his clenched teeth. "Man, Fergus! the cratur's as dumb's a worum. I dinna believe 'at ever he spak a word in's life."

This cut Fergus to the heart, for he was far from being without generosity or pity. How many things a man who is not awake to side strenuously with the good in him against the evil, who is not on his guard lest himself should mislead himself, may do, of which he will one day be bitterly ashamed!—a trite remark, it may be, but, reader, that will make the thing itself no easier to bear, should you ever come to know you have done a thing of the sort. I fear, however, from what I know of Fergus afterwards, that he now, instead of seeking about to make some amends, turned the strength that should have gone in that direction, to the justifying of himself to himself in what he had done.

Anyhow, he was far too proud to confess to Donal that he had done wrong—too much offended at being rebuked by one he counted so immeasurably his inferior, to do the right thing his rebuke set before him. What did the mighty business matter! The little rascal was nothing but a tramp; and if he didn't deserve his punishment this time, he had deserved it a hundred times without having it, and would ten thousand times again. So reasoned Fergus, while the feeling grew upon Donal that the cratur was of some superior race—came from some other and nobler world. I would remind my reader that Donal was a Celt, with a nature open to every fancy of love or awe—one of the same breed with the foolish Galatians, and like them ready to be bewitched; but bearing a heart that welcomed the light with glad rebound—loved the lovely, nor loved it only, but turned towards it with desire to become like it. Fergus too was a Celt in the main, but was spoiled by the paltry ambition of being distinguished. He was not in love with loveliness, but in love with praise. He saw not a little of what was good and noble, and would fain be such, but mainly that men might regard him for his goodness and nobility; hence his practical notion of the good was weak, and of the noble, paltry. His one desire in doing anything, was to be approved of or admired in the same—approved of in the opinions he held, in the plans he pursued, in the doctrines he taught; admired in the poems in which he went halting after Byron, and in the eloquence with which he meant one day to astonish great congregations. There was nothing original as yet discoverable in him; nothing to deliver him from the poor imitative apery in which he imagined himself a poet. He did possess one invaluable gift—that of perceiving and admiring more than a little, certain forms of the beautiful; but it was rendered merely ridiculous by being conjoined with the miserable ambition—poor as that of any mountebank emperor—to be himself admired for that admiration. He mistook also sensibility for faculty, nor perceived that it was at best but a probable sign that he might be able to do something or other with pleasure, perhaps with success. If any one judge it hard that men should be made with ambitions to whose objects they can never attain, I answer, ambition is but the evil shadow of aspiration; and no man ever followed the truth, which is the one path of aspiration, and in the end complained that he had been made this way or that. Man is made to be that which he is made most capable of desiring—but it goes without saying that he must desire the thing itself and not its shadow. Man is of the truth, and while he follows a lie, no indication his nature yields will hold, except the fear, the discontent, the sickness of soul, that tell him he is wrong. If he say, "I care not for what you call the substance—it is to me the shadow; I want what you call the shadow," the only answer is, that, to all eternity, he can never have it: a shadow can never be had.

Ginevra was hardly the same child after the experience of that terrible morning. At no time very much at home with her father, something had now come between them, to remove which all her struggles to love him as before were unavailing. The father was too stupid, too unsympathetic, to take note of the look of fear that crossed her face if ever he addressed her suddenly; and when she was absorbed in fighting the thoughts that would come, he took her constraint for sullenness.

With a cold spot in his heart where once had dwelt some genuine regard for Donal, Fergus went back to college. Donal went on herding the cattle, cudgeling Hornie, and reading what books he could lay his hands on: there was no supply through Fergus any more, alas! The year before, ere he took his leave, he had been careful to see Donal provided with at least books for study; but this time he left him to shift for himself. He was small because he was proud, spiteful because he was conceited. He would let Donal know what it was to have lost his favour! But Donal did not suffer much, except in the loss of the friendship itself. He managed to get the loan of a copy of Burns—better meat for a strong spirit than the poetry of Byron or even Scott. An innate cleanliness of soul rendered the occasional coarseness to him harmless, and the mighty torrent of the man's life, broken by occasional pools reflecting the stars; its headlong hatred of hypocrisy and false religion; its generosity, and struggling conscientiousness; its failures and its repentances, roused much in the heart of Donal. Happily the copy he had borrowed, had in it a tolerable biography; and that, read along with the man's work, enabled him, young as he was, to see something of where and how he had failed, and to shadow out to himself, not altogether vaguely, the perils to which the greatest must be exposed who cannot rule his own spirit, but, like a mere child, reels from one mood into another—at the will of—what?

From reading Burns, Donal learned also not a little of the capabilities of his own language; for, Celt as he was by birth and country and mental character, he could not speak the Gaelic: that language, soft as the speech of streams from rugged mountains, and wild as that of the wind in the tops of fir-trees, the language at once of bards and fighting men, had so far ebbed from the region, lingering only here and there in the hollow pools of old memories, that Donal had never learned it; and the lowland Scotch, an ancient branch of English, dry and gnarled, but still flourishing in its old age, had become instead, his mother-tongue; and the man who loves the antique speech, or even the mere patois, of his childhood, and knows how to use it, possesses therein a certain kind of power over the hearts of men, which the most refined and perfect of languages cannot give, inasmuch as it has travelled farther from the original sources of laughter and tears. But the old Scotish itself is, alas! rapidly vanishing before a poor, shabby imitation of modern English—itself a weaker language in sound, however enriched in words, since the days of Shakspere, when it was far more like Scotch in its utterance than it is now.

> *My mother-tongue, how sweet thy tone!*
> *How near to good allied!*
> *Were even my heart of steel or stone,*
> *Thou wouldst drive out the pride.*

So sings Klaus Groth, in and concerning his own Plattdeutsch—so nearly akin to the English.

To a poet especially is it an inestimable advantage to be able to employ such a language for his purposes. Not only was it the speech of his childhood, when he saw everything with fresh, true eyes, but it is itself a child-speech; and the child way of saying must always lie nearer the child way of seeing, which is the poetic way. Therefore, as the poetic faculty was now slowly asserting itself in Donal, it was of vast importance that he should know what the genius of Scotland had been able to do with his homely mother-tongue, for through that tongue alone, could what poetry he had in him have thoroughly fair play, and in turn do its best towards his development—which is the first and greatest use of poetry. It is a ruinous misjudgment—too contemptible to be asserted, but not too contemptible to be acted upon, that the end of poetry is publication. Its true end is to help first the man who makes it along the path to the truth: help for other people may or may not be in it; that, if it become a question at all, must be an after one. To the man who has it, the gift is invaluable; and, in proportion as it helps him to be a better man, it is of value to the whole world; but it may, in itself, be so nearly worthless, that the publishing of it would be more for harm than good. Ask any one who has had to perform the unenviable duty of editor to a magazine: he will corroborate what I say—that the quantity of verse good enough to be its own reward, but without the smallest claim to be uttered to the world, is enormous.

Not yet, however, had Donal written a single stanza. A line, or at most two, would now and then come into his head with a buzz, like a wandering honey-bee that had mistaken its hive—generally in the shape of a humorous malediction on Hornie—but that was all.

In the mean time Gibbie slept and waked and slept again, night after night—with the loveliest days between, at the cottage on Glashgar. The morning after his arrival, the first thing he was aware of was Janet's face beaming over him, with a look in its eyes more like worship then benevolence. Her husband was gone, and she was about to milk the cow, and was anxious lest, while she was away, he should disappear as before. But the light that rushed into his eyes was in full response to that which kindled the light in hers, and her misgiving vanished; he could not love her like that and leave her. She gave him his breakfast of porridge and milk, and went to her cow.

When she came back, she found everything tidy in the cottage, the floor swept, every dish washed and set aside; and Gibbie was examining an old shoe of Robert's, to see whether he could not mend it. Janet, having therefore leisure, proceeded at once with joy to the construction of a garment she had been devising for him. The design was simple, and its execution easy. Taking a blue winsey petticoat of her own, drawing it in round his waist, and tying it over the chemise which was his only garment, she found, as she had expected, that its hem reached his feet: she partly divided it up the middle, before and behind, and had but to backstitch two short seams, and there was a pair of sailor-like trousers, as tidy as comfortable! Gibbie was delighted with them. True, they had no pockets, but then he had nothing to put in pockets, and one might come to think of that as an advantage. Gibbie indeed had never had pockets, for the pockets of the garments he had had were always worn out before they reached him. Then Janet thought about a cap; but considering him a moment critically, and seeing how his hair stood out like thatch-eaves round his head, she concluded with herself "There maun be some men as weel's women fowk, I'm thinkin', whause hair's gien them for a coverin'," and betook herself instead to her New Testament.

Gibbie stood by as she read in silence, gazing with delight, for he thought it must be a book of ballads like Donal's that she was reading. But Janet found his presence, his unresting attitude, and his gaze, discomposing. To worship freely, one must be alone, or else with fellow-worshippers. And reading and worshipping were often so mingled with Janet, as to form but one mental consciousness. She looked up therefore from her book, and said—

"Can ye read, laddie?"

Gibbie shook his head.

"Sit ye doon than, an' I s' read till ye."

Gibbie obeyed more than willingly, expecting to hear some ancient Scots tale of love or chivalry. Instead, it was one of those love-awful, glory-sad chapters in the end of the Gospel of John, over which hangs the darkest cloud of human sorrow, shot through and through with the radiance of light eternal, essential, invincible. Whether it was the uncertain response to Janet's tone merely, or to truth too loud to be heard, save as a thrill, of some chord in his own spirit, having its one end indeed twisted around an earthly peg, but the other looped to a tail-piece far in the unknown—I cannot tell; it may have been that the name now and then recurring brought to his mind the last words of poor Sambo; anyhow, when Janet looked up, she saw the tears rolling down the child's face. At the same time, from the expression of his countenance, she judged that his understanding had grasped nothing. She turned therefore to the parable of the prodigal son, and read it. Even that had not a few words and phrases unknown to Gibbie, but he did not fail to catch the drift of the perfect story. For had not Gibbie himself had a father, to whose bosom he went home every night? Let but love be the interpreter, and what most wretched type will not serve the turn for the carriage of profoundest truth! The prodigal's lowest degradation, Gibbie did not understand; but Janet saw the expression of the boy's face alter with every tone of the tale, through all the gamut between the swine's trough and the arms of the father. Then at last he burst—not into tears—Gibbie was not much acquainted with weeping—but into a laugh of loud triumph. He clapped his hands, and in a shiver of ecstasy, stood like a stork upon one leg, as if so much of him was all that could be spared for this lower world, and screwed himself together.

Janet was well satisfied with her experiment. Most Scotch women, and more than most Scotch men, would have rebuked him for laughing, but Janet knew in herself a certain tension of delight which nothing served to relieve but a wild laughter of holiest gladness; and never in tears of deepest emotion did her heart appeal more directly to its God.

It is the heart that is not yet sure of its God, that is afraid to laugh in his presence.

Thus had Gibbie his first lesson in the only thing worth learning, in that which, to be learned at all, demands the united energy of heart and soul and strength and mind; and from that day he went on learning it. I cannot tell how, or what were the slow stages by which his mind budded and swelled until it burst into the flower of humanity, the knowledge of God. I cannot tell the shape of the door by which the Lord entered into that house, and took everlasting possession of it. I cannot even tell in what shape he appeared himself in Gibbie's thoughts—for the Lord can take any shape that is human. I only know it was not any unhuman shape of earthly theology that he bore to Gibbie, when he saw him with "that inward eye, which is the bliss of solitude." For happily Janet never suspected how utter was Gibbie's ignorance. She never dreamed that he did not know what was generally said about Jesus Christ. She thought he must know as well as she the outlines of his story, and the purpose of his life and death, as commonly taught, and therefore never attempted explanations for the sake of which she would probably have found herself driven to use terms and phrases which merely substitute that which is intelligible because it appeals to what in us is low, and is itself both low and false, for that which, if unintelligible, is so because of its grandeur and truth. Gibbie's ideas of God he got all from the mouth of Theology himself, the Word of God; and to the theologian who will not be content with his teaching, the disciple of Jesus must just turn his back, that his face may be to his Master.

So, teaching him only that which she loved, not that which she had been taught, Janet read to Gibbie of Jesus, talked to him of Jesus, dreamed to him about Jesus; until at length—Gibbie did not think to watch, and knew nothing of the process by which it came about—his whole soul was full of the man, of his doings, of his words, of his thoughts, of his life. Jesus Christ was in him—he was possessed by him. Almost before he knew, he was trying to fashion his life after that of his Master.

Between the two, it was a sweet teaching, a sweet learning. Under Janet, Gibbie was saved the thousand agonies that befall the conscientious disciple, from the forcing upon him, as the thoughts and will of the eternal Father of our spirits, of the ill expressed and worse understood experiences, the crude conjectures, the vulgar imaginations of would-be teachers of the multitude. Containing truth enough to save those of sufficiently low development to receive such teaching without disgust, it contains falsehood enough, but for the Spirit of God, to ruin all nobler—I mean all childlike natures, utterly; and many such it has gone far to ruin, driving them even to a madness in which they have died. Jesus alone knows the Father, and can reveal him. Janet studied only Jesus, and as a man knows his friend, so she, only infinitely better, knew her more than friend—her Lord and her God. Do I speak of a poor Scotch peasant woman too largely for the reader whose test of truth is the notion of probability he draws from his own experience? Let me put one question to make the real probability clearer. Should it be any wonder, if Christ be indeed the natural Lord of every man, woman, and child, that a simple, capable nature, laying itself entirely open to him and his influences, should understand him? How should he be the Lord of that nature if such a thing were not possible, or were at all improbable—nay, if such a thing did not necessarily follow? Among women, was it not always to peasant women that heavenly messages came? See revelation culminate in Elizabeth and Mary, the mothers of John the Baptist and Jesus. Think how much fitter that it should be so;—that they to whom the word of God comes should be women bred in the dignity of a natural life, and familiarity with the large ways of the earth; women of simple and few wants, without distraction, and with time for reflection—compelled to reflection, indeed, from the enduring presence of an unsullied consciousness: for wherever there is a humble, thoughtful nature, into that nature the divine consciousness, that is, the Spirit of God, presses as into its own place. Holy women are to be found everywhere, but the prophetess is not so likely to be found in the city as in the hill-country.

Whatever Janet, then, might, perhaps—I do not know—have imagined it her duty to say to Gibbie had she surmised his ignorance, having long ceased to trouble her own head, she had now no inclination to trouble Gibbie's heart with what men call the plan of salvation. It was enough to her to find that he followed her Master. Being in the light she understood the light, and had no need of system, either true or false, to explain it to her. She lived by the word proceeding out of the mouth of God. When life begins to speculate upon itself, I suspect it has begun to die. And seldom has there been a fitter soul, one clearer from evil, from folly, from human device—a purer cistern for such water of life as rose in the heart of Janet Grant to pour itself into, than the soul of Sir Gibbie. But I must not call any true soul a cistern: wherever the water of life is received, it sinks and softens and hollows, until it reaches, far down, the springs of life there also, that come straight from the eternal hills, and thenceforth there is in that soul a well of water springing up into everlasting life.

XXIV

The Slate

From that very next day, then, after he was received into the cottage on Glashgar, Gibbie, as a matter of course, took upon him the work his hand could find to do, and Janet averred to her husband that never had any of her daughters been more useful to her. At the same time, however, she insisted that Robert should take the boy out with him. She would not have him do woman's work, especially work for which she was herself perfectly able. She had not come to her years, she said, to learn idleset; and the boy would save Robert many a weary step among the hills.

"He canna speyk to the dog," objected Robert, giving utterance to the first difficulty that suggested itself.

"The dog canna speyk himsel'," returned Janet, "an' the won'er is he can un'erstan': wha kens but he may come full nigher ane 'at's speechless like himsel'! Ye gie the cratur the chance, an' I s' warran' he'll mak himsel' plain to the dog. Ye jist try 'im. Tell ye him to tell the dog sae and sae, an' see what 'll come o' 't."

Robert made the experiment, and it proved satisfactory. As soon as he had received Robert's orders, Gibbie claimed Oscar's attention. The dog looked up in his face, noted every glance and gesture, and, partly from sympathetic instinct, that gift lying so near the very essence of life, partly from observation of the state of affairs in respect of the sheep, divined with certainty what the duty required of him was, and was off like a shot.

"The twa dumb craturs un'erstan' ane anither better nor I un'erstan' aither o' them," said Robert to his wife when they came home.

And now indeed it was a blessed time for Gibbie. It had been pleasant down in the valley, with the cattle and Donal, and foul weather sometimes; but now it was the full glow of summer; the sweet keen air of the mountain bathed him as he ran, entered into him, filled him with life like the new wine of the kingdom of God, and the whole world rose in its glory around him. Surely it is not the outspread sea, however the sight of its storms and its labouring ships may enhance the sense of safety to the onlooker, but the outspread land of peace and plenty, with its nestling houses, its well-stocked yards, its cattle feeding in the meadows, and its men and horses at labour in the fields, that gives the deepest delight to the heart of the poet! Gibbie was one of the meek, and inherited the earth. Throned on the mountain, he beheld the multiform "goings on of life," and in love possessed the whole. He was of the poet-kind also, and now that he was a shepherd, saw everything with shepherd-eyes. One moment, to his fancy, the great sun above played the shepherd to the world, the winds were the dogs, and the men and women the sheep. The next, in higher mood, he would remember the good shepherd of whom Janet had read to him, and pat the head of the collie that lay beside him: Oscar too was a shepherd and no hireling; he fed the sheep; he turned them from danger and barrenness; and he barked well.

"I'm the dumb dog!" said Gibbie to himself, not knowing that he was really a copy in small of the good shepherd; "but maybe there may be mair nor ae gait o' barkin'."

Then what a joy it was to the heaven-born obedience of the child, to hearken to every word, watch every look, divine every wish of the old man! Child Hercules could not have waited on mighty old Saturn as Gibbie waited on Robert. For he was to him the embodiment of all that was reverend and worthy, a very gulf of wisdom, a mountain of rectitude. Gibbie was one of those few elect natures to whom obedience is a delight—a creature so different from the vulgar that they have but one tentacle they can reach such with—that of contempt.

"I jist lo'e the bairn as the verra aipple o' my ee." said Robert. "I can scarce consaive a wuss, but there's the cratur wi' a grip o' 't! He seems to ken what's risin' i' my min', an' in a moment he's up like the dog to be ready, an' luiks at me waitin'."

Nor was it long before the town-bred child grew to love the heavens almost as dearly as the earth. He would gaze and gaze at the clouds as they came and went, and watching them and the wind, weighing the heat and the cold, and marking many indications, known some of them perhaps only to himself, understood the signs of the earthly times at length nearly as well as an insect or a swallow, and far better than long-experienced old Robert. The mountain was Gibbie's very home; yet to see him far up on it, in the red glow of the setting sun, with his dog, as obedient as himself, hanging upon his every signal, one could have fancied him a shepherd boy come down from the plains of heaven to look after a lost lamb. Often, when the two old people were in bed

GEORGE MACDONALD

and asleep, Gibbie would be out watching the moon rise—seated, still as ruined god of Egypt, on a stone of the mountain-side, islanded in space, nothing alive and visible near him, perhaps not even a solitary night-wind blowing and ceasing like the breath of a man's life, and the awfully silent moon sliding up from the hollow of a valley below. If there be indeed a one spirit, ever awake and aware, should it be hard to believe that that spirit should then hold common thought with a little spirit of its own? If the nightly mountain was the prayer-closet of him who said he would be with his disciples to the end of the world, can it be folly to think he would hold talk with such a child, alone under the heaven, in the presence of the father of both? Gibbie never thought about himself, therefore was there wide room for the entrance of the spirit. Does the questioning thought arise to any reader: How could a man be conscious of bliss without the thought of himself? I answer the doubt: When a man turns to look at himself, that moment the glow of the loftiest bliss begins to fade; the pulsing fire-flies throb paler in the passionate night; an unseen vapour steams up from the marsh and dims the star-crowded sky and the azure sea; and the next moment the very bliss itself looks as if it had never been more than a phosphorescent gleam—the summer lightning of the brain. For then the man sees himself but in his own dim mirror, whereas ere he turned to look in that, he knew himself in the absolute clarity of God's present thought out-bodying him. The shoots of glad consciousness that come to the obedient man, surpass in bliss whole days and years of such ravined rapture as he gains whose weariness is ever spurring the sides of his intent towards the ever retreating goal of his desires. I am a traitor even to myself if I would live without my life.

But I withhold my pen; for vain were the fancy, by treatise or sermon or poem or tale, to persuade a man to forget himself. He cannot if he would. Sooner will he forget the presence of a raging tooth. There is no forgetting of ourselves but in the finding of our deeper, our true self— God's idea of us when he devised us—the Christ in us. Nothing but that self can displace the false, greedy, whining self, of which, most of us are so fond and proud. And that self no man can find for himself; seeing of himself he does not even know what to search for. "But as many as received him, to them gave he power to become the sons of God."

Then there was the delight, fresh every week, of the Saturday gathering of the brothers and sisters, whom Gibbie could hardly have loved more, had they been of his own immediate kin. Dearest of all was

Donal, whose greeting—"Weel, cratur," was heavenly in Gibbie's ears. Donal would have had him go down and spend a day, every now and then, with him and the nowt, as in old times—so soon the times grow old to the young!—but Janet would not hear of it, until the foolish tale of the brownie should have quite blown over.

"Eh, but I wuss," she added, as she said so, "I cud win at something aboot his fowk, or aiven whaur he cam frae, or what they ca'd him! Never ae word has the cratur spoken!"

"Ye sud learn him to read, mither," said Donal.

"Hoo wad I du that, laddie? I wad hae to learn him to speyk first," returned Janet.

"Lat him come doon to me, an' I'll try my han'," said Donal.

Janet, notwithstanding, persisted in her refusal—for the present. By Donal's words set thinking of the matter, however, she now pondered the question day after day, how she might teach him to read; and at last the idea dawned upon her to substitute writing for speech.

She took the Shorter Catechism, which, in those days, had always an alphabet as janitor to the gates of its mysteries—who, with the catechism as a consequence even dimly foreboded, would even have learned it?—and showed Gibbie the letters, naming each several times, and going over them repeatedly. Then she gave him Donal's school-slate, with a sklet-pike, and said, "Noo, mak a muckle A, cratur."

Gibbie did so, and well too: she found that already he knew about half the letters.

"He's no fule!" she said to herself in triumph.

The other half soon followed; and she then began to show him words—not in the Catechism, but in the New Testament. Having told him what any word was, and led him to consider the letters composing it, she would desire him to make it on the slate, and he would do so with tolerable accuracy: she was not very severe about the spelling, if only it was plain he knew the word. Ere long he began to devise short ways of making the letters, and soon wrote with remarkable facility in a character modified from the printed letters. When at length Janet saw him take the book by himself, and sit pondering over it, she had not a doubt he was understanding it, and her heart leapt for joy. He had to ask her a good many words at first, and often the meaning of one and another; but he seldom asked a question twice; and as his understanding was far ahead of his reading, he was able to test a conjectured meaning by the sense or nonsense it made of the passage.

One day she turned him to the paraphrases.[2] At once, to his astonishment, he found there, all silent, yet still the same delight which Donal used to divide to him from the book of ballants. His joy was unbounded. He jumped from his seat; he danced, and laughed, and finally stood upon one leg: no other mode of expression but this, the expression of utter failure to express, was of avail to the relief of his feeling.

One day, a few weeks after Gibbie had begun to read by himself, Janet became aware that he was sitting on his stool, in what had come to be called the cratur's corner, more than usually absorbed in some attempt with slate and pencil—now ceasing, lost in thought, and now commencing anew. She went near and peeped over his shoulder. At the top of the slate he had written the word give, then the word giving, and below them, gib, then gibing; upon these followed gib again, and he was now plainly meditating something further. Suddenly he seemed to find what he wanted, for in haste, almost as if he feared it might escape him, he added a y, making the word giby—then first lifted his head, and looked round, evidently seeking her. She laid her hand on his head. He jumped up with one of his most radiant smiles, and holding out the slate to her, pointed with his pencil to the word he had just completed. She did not know it for a word, but sounded it as it seemed to stand, making the g soft, as I daresay some of my readers, not recognizing in Gibbie the diminutive of Gilbert, may have treated its more accurate form. He shook his head sharply, and laid the point of his pencil upon the g of the give written above. Janet had been his teacher too long not to see what he meant, and immediately pronounced the word as he would have it. Upon this he began a wild dance, but sobering suddenly, sat down, and was instantly again absorbed in further attempt. It lasted so long that Janet resumed her previous household occupation. At length he rose, and with thoughtful, doubtful contemplation of what he had done, brought her the slate. There, under the fore-gone success, he had written the words galatians and breath, and under them, galbreath. She read them all, and at the last, which, witnessing to his success, she pronounced to his satisfaction, he began another dance, which again he ended abruptly, to draw her attention once more to the slate. He pointed to the giby first, and the galbreath next, and she read them

---

2. Metrical paraphrases of passages of Scripture, always to be found at the end of the Bibles printed for Scotland.

together. This time he did not dance, but seemed waiting some result. Upon Janet the idea was dawning that he meant himself, but she was thrown out by the cognomen's correspondence with that of the laird, which suggested that the boy had been merely attempting the name of the great man of the district. With this in her mind, and doubtfully feeling her way, she essayed the tentative of setting him right in the Christian name, and said: "Thomas—Thomas Galbraith." Gibbie shook his head as before, and again resumed his seat. Presently he brought her the slate, with all the rest rubbed out, and these words standing alone— sir giby galbreath. Janet read them aloud, whereupon Gibbie began stabbing his forehead with the point of his slate-pencil, and dancing once more in triumph: he had, he hoped, for the first time in his life, conveyed a fact through words.

"That's what they ca' ye, is't?" said Janet, looking motherly at him: "—Sir Gibbie Galbraith?"

Gibbie nodded vehemently.

"It'll be some nickname the bairns hae gien him," said Janet to herself, but continued to gaze at him, in questioning doubt of her own solution. She could not recall having ever heard of a Sir in the family; but ghosts of things forgotten kept rising formless and thin in the sky of her memory: had she never heard of a Sir Somebody Galbraith somewhere? And still she stared at the child, trying to grasp what she could not even see. By this time Gibbie was standing quite still, staring at her in return: he could not think what made her stare so at him.

"Wha ca'd ye that?" said Janet at length, pointing to the slate.

Gibbie took the slate, dropped upon his seat, and after considerable cogitation and effort, brought her the words, gibyse fapher. Janet for a moment was puzzled, but when she thought of correcting the p with a t, Gibbie entirely approved.

"What was yer father, cratur?" she asked.

Gibbie, after a longer pause, and more evident labour than hitherto, brought her the enigmatical word, asootr, which, the Sir running about in her head, quite defeated Janet. Perceiving his failure, he jumped upon a chair, and reaching after one of Robert's Sunday shoes on the crap o' the wa', the natural shelf running all round the cottage, formed by the top of the wall where the rafters rested, caught hold of it, tumbled with it upon his creepie, took it between his knees, and began a pantomime of the making or mending of the same with such verisimilitude of imitation, that it was clear to Janet he must have been familiar with the processes collectively called shoemaking; and therewith she recognized the word on the slate—a sutor. She smiled to herself at the association of name and trade, and concluded that the Sir at least was a nickname. And yet—and yet—whether from the presence of some rudiment of an old memory, or from something about the boy that belonged to a higher style than his present showing, her mind kept swaying in an uncertainty whose very object eluded her.

"What is 't yer wull 'at we ca' ye, than, cratur?" she asked, anxious to meet the child's own idea of himself.

He pointed to the giby.

"Weel, Gibbie," responded Janet,—and at the word, now for the first time addressed by her to himself, he began dancing more wildly than ever, and ended with standing motionless on one leg: now first and at last he was fully recognized for what he was!—"Weel, Gibbic, I s' ca' ye what ye think fit," said Janet. "An' noo gang yer wa's, Gibbie, an' see 'at Crummie's no ower far oot o' sicht."

From that hour Gibbie had his name from the whole family—his Christian name only, however, Robert and Janet having agreed it would be wise to avoid whatever might possibly bring the boy again under the notice of the laird. The latter half of his name they laid aside for him, as parents do a dangerous or over-valuable gift to a child.

XXV

Rumours

Almost from the first moment of his being domiciled on Glashgar, what with the good food, the fine exercise, the exquisite air, and his great happiness, Gibbie began to grow; and he took to growing so fast that his legs soon shot far out of his winsey garment. But, of all places, that was a small matter in Gormgarnet, where the kilt was as common as trowsers. His wiry limbs grew larger without losing their firmness or elasticity; his chest, the effort in running up hill constantly alternated with the relief of running, down, rapidly expanded, and his lungs grew hardy as well as powerful; till he became at length such in wind and muscle, that he could run down a wayward sheep almost as well as Oscar. And his nerve grew also with his body and strength, till his coolness and courage were splendid. Never, when the tide of his affairs ran most in the shallows, had Gibbie had much acquaintance with fears, but now he had forgotten the taste of them, and would have encountered a wild highland bull alone on the mountain, as readily as tie Crummie up in her byre.

One afternoon, Donal, having got a half-holiday, by the help of a friend and the favour of Mistress Jean, came home to see his mother, and having greeted her, set out to find Gibbie. He had gone a long way, looking and calling without success, and had come in sight of a certain tiny loch, or tarn, that filled a hollow of the mountain. It was called the Deid Pot; and the old awe, amounting nearly to terror, with which in his childhood he had regarded it, returned upon him, the moment he saw the dark gleam of it, nearly as strong as ever—an awe indescribable, arising from mingled feelings of depth, and darkness, and lateral recesses, and unknown serpent-like fishes. The pot, though small in surface, was truly of unknown depth, and had elements of dread about it telling upon far less active imaginations than Donal's. While he stood gazing at it, almost afraid to go nearer, a great splash that echoed from the steep rocks surrounding it, brought his heart into his mouth, and immediately followed a loud barking, in which he recognized the voice of Oscar. Before he had well begun to think what it could mean, Gibbie appeared on the opposite side of the loch, high above its level, on the top of the rocks forming its basin. He began instantly a rapid descent towards the water, where the rocks were so steep, and the footing so precarious, that Oscar wisely remained at the top, nor attempted to follow him. Presently the dog caught sight of Donal, where he stood on a lower level, whence the water was comparatively easy of access, and starting off at full speed, joined him, with much demonstration of welcome. But he received little notice from Donal, whose gaze was fixed, with much wonder and more fear, on the descending Gibbie. Some twenty feet from the surface of the loch, he reached a point whence clearly, in Donal's judgment, there was no possibility of farther descent. But Donal was never more mistaken; for that instant Gibbie flashed from the face of the rock head foremost, like a fishing bird, into the lake. Donal gave a cry, and ran to the edge of the water, accompanied by Oscar, who, all the time, had showed no anxiety, but had stood wagging his tail, and uttering now and then a little half-disappointed whine; neither now were his motions as he ran other than those of frolic and expectancy. When they reached the loch, there was Gibbie already but a few yards from the only possible landing-place, swimming with one hand, while in the other arm he held a baby lamb, its head lying quite still on his shoulder: it had been stunned by the fall, but might come round again. Then first Donal began to perceive that the cratur was growing an athlete. When he landed, he gave Donal a merry laugh of welcome, but without stopping flew up the hill to take the lamb to its mother. Fresh from the icy water, he ran so fast that it was all Donal could do to keep up with him.

The Deid Pot, then, taught Gibbie what swimming it could, which was not much, and what diving it could, which was more; but the nights of the following summer, when everybody on mountain and valley were asleep, and the moon shone, he would often go down to the Daur, and throwing himself into its deepest reaches, spend hours in lonely sport with water and wind and moon. He had by that time learned things knowing which a man can never be lonesome.

The few goats on the mountain were for a time very inimical to him. So often did they butt him over, causing him sometimes severe bruises, that at last he resolved to try conclusions with them; and when next a goat made a rush at him, he seized him by the horns and wrestled with him mightily. This exercise once begun, he provoked engagements, until his strength and aptitude were such and so well known, that not a billy-goat on Glashgar would have to do with him. But when he saw that every one of them ran at his approach, Gibbie, who could not bear to be in discord with any creature, changed his behaviour towards them, and took equal pains to reconcile them to him—nor rested before he had entirely succeeded.

Every time Donal came home, he would bring some book of verse with him, and, leading Gibbie to some hollow, shady or sheltered as the time required, would there read to him ballads, or songs, or verse more stately, as mood or provision might suggest. The music, the melody and the cadence and the harmony, the tone and the rhythm and the time and the rhyme, instead of growing common to him, rejoiced Gibbie more and more every feast, and with ever-growing reverence he looked up to Donal as a mighty master-magician. But if Donal could have looked down into Gibbie's bosom, he would have seen something there beyond his comprehension. For Gibbie was already in the kingdom of heaven, and Donal would have to suffer, before he would begin even to look about for the door by which a man may enter into it.

I wonder how much Gibbie was indebted to his constrained silence during all these years. That he lost by it, no one will doubt; that he gained also, a few will admit: though I should find it hard to say what and how great, I cannot doubt it bore an important part in the fostering of such thoughts and feelings and actions as were beyond the vision of Donal, poet as he was growing to be. While Donal read, rejoicing in the music both of sound and sense, Gibbie was doing something besides: he was listening with the same ears, and trying to see with the same eyes, which he brought to bear upon the things Janet taught him out of the book. Already those first weekly issues, lately commenced, of a popular literature had penetrated into the mountains of Gormgarnet; but whether Donal read Blind Harry from a thumbed old modern edition, or some new tale or neat poem from the Edinburgh press, Gibbie was always placing what he heard by the side, as it were, of what he knew; asking himself, in this case and that, what Jesus Christ would have done, or what he would require of a disciple. There must be one right way, he argued. Sometimes his innocence failed to see that no disciple of the Son of Man could, save by fearful failure, be in such circumstances as the tale or ballad represented. But, whether successful or not in the individual inquiry, the boy's mind and heart and spirit, in this silent, unembarrassed brooding, as energetic as it was peaceful, expanded upwards when it failed to widen, and the widening would

GEORGE MACDONALD

come after. Gifted, from the first of his being, with such a rare drawing to his kind, he saw his utmost affection dwarfed by the words and deeds of Jesus—beheld more and more grand the requirements made of a man who would love his fellows as Christ loved them. When he sank foiled from any endeavour to understand how a man was to behave in certain circumstances, these or those, he always took refuge in doing something—and doing it better than before; leaped the more eagerly if Robert called him, spoke the more gently to Oscar, turned the sheep more careful not to scare them—as if by instinct he perceived that the only hope of understanding lies in doing. He would cleave to the skirt when the hand seemed withdrawn; he would run to do the thing he had learned yesterday, when as yet he could find no answer to the question of to-day. Thus, as the weeks of solitude and love and thought and obedience glided by, the reality of Christ grew upon him, till he saw the very rocks and heather and the faces of the sheep like him, and felt his presence everywhere, and ever coming nearer. Nor did his imagination aid only a little in the growth of his being. He would dream waking dreams about Jesus, gloriously childlike. He fancied he came down every now and then to see how things were going in the lower part of his kingdom; and that when he did so, he made use of Glashgar and its rocks for his stair, coming down its granite scale in the morning, and again, when he had ended his visit, going up in the evening by the same steps. Then high and fast would his heart beat at the thought that some day he might come upon his path just when he had passed, see the heather lifting its head from the trail of his garment, or more slowly out of the prints left by his feet, as he walked up the stairs of heaven, going back to his Father. Sometimes, when a sheep stopped feeding and looked up suddenly, he would fancy that Jesus had laid his hand on its head, and was now telling it that it must not mind being killed; for he had been killed, and it was all right.

Although he could read the New Testament for himself now, he always preferred making acquaintance with any new portion of it first from the mouth of Janet. Her voice made the word more of a word to him. But the next time he read, it was sure to be what she had then read. She was his priestess; the opening of her Bible was the opening of a window in heaven; her cottage was the porter's lodge to the temple; his very sheep were feeding on the temple-stairs. Smile at such fancies if you will, but think also whether they may not be within sight of the greatest of facts. Of all teachings that which presents a far distant God is the nearest to absurdity. Either there is none, or he is nearer to every one of us than our nearest consciousness of self. An unapproachable divinity is the veriest of monsters, the most horrible of human imaginations.

When the winter came, with its frost and snow, Gibbie saved Robert much suffering. At first Robert was unwilling to let him go out alone in stormy weather; but Janet believed that the child doing the old man's work would be specially protected. All through the hard time, therefore, Gibbie went and came, and no evil befell him. Neither did he suffer from the cold; for, a sheep having died towards the end of the first autumn, Robert, in view of Gibbie's coming necessity, had begged of his master the skin, and dressed it with the wool upon it; and of this, between the three of them, they made a coat for him; so that he roamed the hill like a savage, in a garment of skin.

It became, of course, before very long, well known about the country that Mr. Duff's crofters upon Glashgar had taken in and were bringing up a foundling—some said an innocent, some said a wild boy—who helped Robert with his sheep, and Janet with her cow, but could not speak a word of either Gaelic or English. By and by, strange stories came to be told of his exploits, representing him as gifted with bodily powers as much surpassing the common, as his mental faculties were assumed to be under the ordinary standard. The rumour concerning him swelled as well as spread, mainly from the love of the marvellous common in the region, I suppose, until, towards the end of his second year on Glashgar, the notion of Gibbie in the imaginations of the children of Daurside, was that of an almost supernatural being, who had dwelt upon, or rather who had haunted, Glashgar from time immemorial, and of whom they had been hearing all their lives; and, although they had never heard anything bad of him—that he was wild, that he wore a hairy skin, that he could do more than any other boy dared attempt, that he was dumb, and that yet (for this also was said) sheep and dogs and cattle, and even the wild creatures of the mountain, could understand him perfectly— these statements were more than enough, acting on the suspicion and fear belonging to the savage in their own bosoms, to envelope the idea of him in a mist of dread, deepening to such horror in the case of the more timid and imaginative of them, that when the twilight began to gather about the cottages and farmhouses, the very mention of "the beast-loon o' Glashgar" was enough, and that for miles up and down the river, to send many of the children scouring like startled hares into the house. Gibbie, in his atmosphere of human grace and tenderness, little thought what clouds of foolish fancies, rising from the valleys below, had, by their distorting vapours, made of him an object of terror to those whom at the very first sight he would have loved and served. Amongst these, perhaps the most afraid of him were the children of the gamekeeper, for they lived on the very foot of the haunted hill, near the bridge and gate of Glashruach; and the laird himself happened one day to be witness of their fear. He inquired the cause, and yet again was his enlightened soul vexed by the persistency with which the shadows of superstition still hung about his lands. Had he been half as philosophical as he fancied himself, he might have seen that there was not necessarily a single film of superstition involved in the belief that a savage roamed a mountain—which was all that Mistress Mac Pholp, depriving the rumour of its richer colouring, ventured to impart as the cause of her children's perturbation; but anything a hair's-breadth out of the common, was a thing hated of Thomas Galbraith's soul, and whatever another believed which he did not choose to believe, he set down at once as superstition. He held therefore immediate communication with his gamekeeper on the subject, who in his turn was scandalized that his children should have thus proved themselves unworthy of the privileges of their position, and given annoyance to the liberal soul of their master, and took care that both they and his wife should suffer in consequence. The expression of the man's face as he listened to the laird's complaint, would not have been a pleasant sight to any lover of Gibbie; but it had not occurred either to master or man that the offensive being whose doubtful existence caused the scandal, was the same towards whom they had once been guilty of such brutality; nor would their knowledge of the fact have been favourable to Gibbie. The same afternoon, the laird questioned his tenant of the Mains concerning his cottars; and was assured that better or more respectable people were not in all the region of Gormgarnet.

When Robert became aware, chiefly through the representations of his wife and Donal, of Gibbie's gifts of other kinds than those revealed to himself by his good shepherding, he began to turn it over in his mind, and by and by referred the question to his wife whether they ought not to send the boy to school, that he might learn the things he was so much more than ordinarily capable of learning. Janet would give no immediate opinion. She must think, she said; and she took three days to turn the matter over in her mind. Her questioning cogitation was to this effect: "What need has a man to know anything but what the New Testament teaches him? Life was little to me before I began to understand its good news; now it is more than good—it is grand. But then, man is to live by every word that proceedeth out of the mouth of God; and everything came out of his mouth, when he said, Let there be this, and Let there be that. Whatever is true is his making, and the more we know of it the better. Besides, how much less of the New Testament would I understand now, if it were not for things I had gone through and learned before!"

"Ay, Robert," she answered, without preface, the third day, "I'm thinkin' there's a heap o' things, gien I hed them, 'at wad help me to ken what the Maister spak till. It wad be a sin no to lat the laddie learn. But wha'll tak the trible needfu' to the learnin' o' a puir dummie?"

"Lat him gang doon to the Mains, an' herd wi' Donal," answered Robert. "He kens a hantle mair nor you or me or Gibbie aither; an' whan he's learnt a' 'at Donal can shaw him it'll be time to think what neist."

"Weel," answered Janet, "nane can say but that's sense, Robert; an' though I'm laith, for your sake mair nor my ain, to lat the laddie gang, let him gang to Donal. I houp, atween the twa, they winna lat the nowt amo' the corn."

"The corn's 'maist cuttit noo," replied Robert; "an' for the maitter o' that, twa guid consciences winna blaw ane anither oot.—But he needna gang ilka day. He can gie ae day to the learnin', an' the neist to thinkin' aboot it amo' the sheep. An' ony day 'at ye want to keep him, ye can keep him; for it winna be as gien he gaed to the schuil."

Gibbie was delighted with the proposal.

"Only," said Robert, in final warning, "dinna ye lat them tak ye, Gibbie, an' score yer back again, my cratur; an' dinna ye answer naebody, whan they speir what ye're ca'd, onything mair nor jist Gibbie."

The boy laughed and nodded, and, as Janet said, the bairn's nick was guid 's the best man's word.

Now came a happy time for the two boys. Donal began at once to teach Gibbie Euclid and arithmetic. When they had had enough of that for a day, he read Scotish history to him; and when they had done what seemed their duty by that, then came the best of the feast— whatever tales or poetry Donal had laid his hands upon.

Somewhere about this time it was that he first got hold of a copy of the Paradise Lost. He found that he could not make much of it. But he found also that, as before with the ballads, when he read from it aloud to Gibbie, his mere listening presence sent back a spiritual echo that helped him to the meaning; and when neither of them understood it, the grand organ roll of it, losing nothing in the Scotch voweling, delighted them both.

Once they were startled by seeing the gamekeeper enter the field. The moment he saw him, Gibbie laid himself flat on the ground, but ready to spring to his feet and run. The man, however, did not come near them.

XXVI

The Gamekeeper

The second winter came, and with the first frost Gibbie resumed his sheepskin coat and the brogues and leggings which he had made for himself of deer-hide tanned with the hair. It pleased the two old people to see him so warmly clad. It pleased them also that, thus dressed, he always reminded them of some sacred personage undetermined—Jacob, or John the Baptist, or the man who went to meet the lion and be killed by him—in Robert's big Bible, that is, in one or other of the woodcuts of the same. Very soon the stories about him were all stirred up afresh, and new rumours added. This one and that of the children declared they had caught sight of the beast-loon, running about the rocks like a goat; and one day a boy of Angus's own, who had been a good way up the mountain, came home nearly dead with terror, saying the beast-loon had chased him a long way. He did not add that he had been throwing stones at the sheep, not perceiving any one in charge of them. So, one fine morning in December, having nothing particular to attend to, Angus shouldered his double-barrelled gun, and set out for a walk over Glashgar, in the hope of coming upon the savage that terrified the children. He must be off. That was settled. Where Angus was in authority, the outlandish was not to be suffered. The sun shone bright, and a keen wind was blowing.

About noon he came in sight of a few sheep, in a sheltered spot, where were little patches of coarse grass among the heather. On a stone, a few yards above them, sat Gibbie, not reading, as he would be half the time now, but busied with a Pan's-pipes—which, under Donal's direction, he had made for himself—drawing from them experimental sounds, and feeling after the possibility of a melody. He was so much occupied that he did not see Angus approach, who now stood for a moment or two regarding him. He was hirsute as Esau, his head crowned with its own plentiful crop—even in winter he wore no cap—his body covered with the wool of the sheep, and his legs and feet with the hide of the deer—the hair, as in nature, outward. The deer-skin Angus knew for what it was from afar, and concluding it the spoil of the only crime of which he recognized the enormity, whereas it was in truth part of a skin he had himself sold to a saddler in the next village, to make sporrans of, boiled over with wrath, and strode nearer, grinding his teeth. Gibbie looked up, knew him, and starting to his feet, turned to the hill. Angus, levelling his gun, shouted to him to stop, but Gibbie only ran the harder, nor once looked round. Idiotic with rage, Angus fired. One of his barrels was loaded with shot, the other with ball: meaning to use the shot barrel, he pulled the wrong trigger, and liberated the bullet. It went through the calf of Gibbie's right leg, and he fell. It had, however, passed between two muscles without injuring either greatly, and had severed no artery. The next moment he was on his feet again and running, nor did he yet feel pain. Happily he was not very far from home, and he made for it as fast as he could—preceded by Oscar, who, having once by accident been shot himself, had a mortal terror of guns. Maimed as Gibbie was, he could yet run a good deal faster up hill than the rascal who followed him. But long before he reached the cottage, the pain had arrived, and the nearer he got to it the worse it grew. In spite of the anguish, however, he held on with determination; to be seized by Angus and dragged down to Glashruach, would be far worse.

Robert Grant was at home that day, suffering from rheumatism. He was seated in the ingle-neuk, with his pipe in his mouth, and Janet was just taking the potatoes for their dinner off the fire, when the door flew open, and in stumbled Gibbie, and fell on the floor. The old man threw his pipe from him, and rose trembling, but Janet was before him. She dropt down on her knees beside the boy, and put her arm under his head. He was white and motionless.

"Eh, Robert Grant!" she cried, "he's bleedin'."

The same moment they heard quick yet heavy steps approaching. At once Robert divined the truth, and a great wrath banished rheumatism and age together. Like a boy he sprang to the crap o' the wa', whence his yet powerful hand came back armed with a huge rusty old broadsword that had seen service in its day. Two or three fierce tugs at the hilt proving the blade immovable in the sheath, and the steps being now almost at the door, he clubbed the weapon, grasping it by the sheathed blade, and holding it with the edge downward, so that the blow he meant to deal should fall from the round of the basket hilt. As he heaved it aloft, the gray old shepherd seemed inspired by the god of battles; the rage of a hundred ancestors was welling up in his peaceful breast. His red eye flashed, and the few hairs that were left him stood erect on his head like the mane of a roused lion. Ere Angus had his second foot over the threshold, down came the helmet-like hilt with a dull crash on his head, and he staggered against the wall.

"Tak ye that, Angus Mac Pholp!" panted Robert through his clenched teeth, following the blow with another from his fist, that prostrated the enemy. Again he heaved his weapon, and standing over him where he lay, more than half-stunned, said in a hoarse voice,

"By the great God my maker, Angus Mac Pholp, gien ye seek to rise, I'll come doon on ye again as ye lie!—Here, Oscar!—He's no ane to haud ony fair play wi', mair nor a brute beast.—Watch him, Oscar, and tak him by the thro't gien he muv a finger."

The gun had dropped from Angus's hand, and Robert, keeping his eye on him, secured it.

"She's lodd," muttered Angus.

"Lie still than," returned Robert, pointing the weapon at his head.

"It'll be murder," said Angus, and made a movement to lay hold of the barrel.

"Haud him doon, Oscar," cried Robert. The dog's paws were instantly on his chest, and his teeth grinning within an inch of his face. Angus vowed in his heart he would kill the beast on the first chance. "It wad be but blude for blude, Angus Mac Pholp," he went on. "Yer hoor's come, my man. That bairn's is no the first blude o' man ye hae shed, an' it's time the Scripture was fulfillt, an' the han' o' man shed yours."

"Ye're no gauin to kill me, Rob Grant?" growled the fellow in growing fright.

"I'm gauin to see whether the shirra winna be perswaudit to hang ye," answered the shepherd. "This maun be putten a stap till.—Quaiet! or I'll brain ye, an' save him the trouble.—Here, Janet, fess yer pot o' pitawtas. I'm gauin to toom the man's gun. Gien he daur to muv, jist gie him the haill bilin', bree an a', i' the ill face o' 'm; gien ye lat him up he'll kill's a'; only tak care an' haud aff o' the dog, puir fallow!—I wad lay the stock o' yer murderin' gun i' the fire gien 'twarna 'at I reckon it's the laird's an' no yours. Ye're no fit to be trustit wi' a gun. Ye're waur nor a weyver."

So saying he carried the weapon to the door, and, in terror lest he might, through wrath or the pressure of dire necessity, use it against his foe, emptied its second barrel into the earth, and leaned it up against the wall outside.

Janet obeyed her husband so far as to stand over Angus with the potato-pot: how far she would have carried her obedience had he attempted to rise may remain a question. Doubtless a brave man doing his duty would have scorned to yield himself thus; but right and wrong had met face to face, and the wrong had a righteous traitor in his citadel.

When Robert returned and relieved her guard, Janet went back to Gibbie, whom she had drawn towards the fire. He lay almost insensible, but in vain Janet attempted to get a teaspoonful of whisky between his lips. For as he grew older, his horror of it increased; and now, even when he was faint and but half conscious, his physical nature seemed to recoil from contact with it. It was with signs of disgust, rubbing his mouth with the back of each hand alternately, that he first showed returning vitality. In a minute or two more he was able to crawl to his bed in the corner, and then Janet proceeded to examine his wound.

By this time his leg was much swollen, but the wound had almost stopped bleeding, and it was plain there was no bullet in it, for there were the two orifices. She washed it carefully and bound it up. Then Gibbie raised his head and looked somewhat anxiously round the room.

"Ye're luikin' efter Angus?" said Janet; "he's yon'er upo' the flure, a twa yairds frae ye. Dinna be fleyt; yer father an' Oscar has him safe eneuch, I s' warran'."

"Here, Janet!" cried her husband; "gien ye be throu' wi' the bairn, I maun be gauin'."

"Hoot, Robert! ye're no surely gauin' to lea' me an' puir Gibbie, 'at maunna stir, i' the hoose oor lanes wi' the murderin' man!" returned Janet.

"'Deed am I, lass! Jist rin and fess the bit tow 'at ye hing yer duds upo' at the washin', an' we'll bin' the feet an' the han's o' 'im."

Janet obeyed and went. Angus, who had been quiet enough for the last ten minutes, meditating and watching, began to swear furiously, but Robert paid no more heed than if he had not heard him—stood calm and grim at his head, with the clubbed sword heaved over his shoulder. When she came back, by her husband's directions, she passed the rope repeatedly round the keeper's ankles, then several times between them, drawing the bouts tightly together, so that, instead of the two sharing one ring, each ankle had now, as it were, a close-fitting one for itself. Again and again, as she tied it, did Angus meditate a sudden spring, but the determined look of Robert, and his feeling memory of the blows he had so unsparingly delivered upon him, as well as the weakening effect of that he had received on his head, caused him to hesitate until it was altogether too late. When they began to bind his hands, however, he turned desperate, and struck at both, cursing and raging.

"Gien ye binna quaiet, ye s' taste the dog's teeth," said Robert.— Angus reflected that he would have a better chance when he was left alone with Janet, and yielded.—"Troth!" Robert went on, as he continued his task, "I hae no pity left for ye, Angus Mac Pholp; an' gien ye tyauve ony mair, I'll lat at ye. I wad care no more to caw oot yer harns nor I wad to kill a tod (fox). To be hangt for't, I wad be but prood. It's a fine thing to be hangt for a guid cause, but ye'll be hangt for an ill ane.— Noo, Janet, fess a bun'le o' brackens frae the byre, an' lay aneth's heid. We maunna be sairer upo' him, nor the needcessity laid upo' hiz. I s' jist trail him aff o' the door, an' a bit on to the fire, for he'll be cauld whan he's quaitet doon, an' syne I'll awa' an' get word o' the shirra'. Scotlan's come till a pretty pass, whan they shot men wi' guns, as gien they war wull craturs to be peelt an' aiten. Care what set him! He may weel be a keeper o' ghem, for he's as ill a keeper o' 's brither as auld Cain himsel'. But," he concluded, tying the last knot hard, "we'll e'en dee what we can to keep the keeper."

It was seldom Robert spoke at such length, but the provocation, the wrath, the conflict, and the victory, had sent the blood rushing through his brain, and loosed his tongue like strong drink.

"Ye'll tak yer denner afore ye gang, Robert," said his wife.

"Na, I can ait naething; I'll tak a bannock i' my pooch. Ye can gie my denner to Angus: he'll want hertenin' for the wuddie (gallows)."

So saying he put the bannock in his pocket, flung his broad blue bonnet upon his head, took his stick, and ordering Oscar to remain at home and watch the prisoner, set out for a walk of five miles, as if he had never known such a thing as rheumatism. He must find another magistrate than the laird; he would not trust him where his own gamekeeper, Angus Mac Pholp, was concerned.

"Keep yer ee upon him, Janet," he said, turning in the doorway. "Dinna lowse sicht o' him afore I come back wi' the constable. Dinna lippen. I s' be back in three hoors like."

With these words he turned finally, and disappeared.

The mortification of Angus as he lay thus trapped in the den of the beast-loon, at being taken and bound by an old man, a woman, and a collie dog, was extreme. He went over the whole affair again and again in his mind, ever with a fresh burst of fury. It was in vain he excused himself on the ground that the attack had been so sudden and treacherous, and the precautions taken so complete. He had proved himself an ass, and the whole country would ring with mockery of him! He had sense enough, too, to know that he was in a serious as well as ludicrous predicament: he had scarcely courage enough to contemplate the possible result. If he could but get his hands free, it would be easy to kill Oscar and disable Janet. For the idiot, he counted him nothing. He had better wait, however, until there should be no boiling liquid ready to her hand.

Janet set out the dinner, peeled some potatoes, and approaching Angus, would have fed him. In place of accepting her ministration, he fell to abusing her with the worst language he could find. She withdrew without a word, and sat down to her own dinner; but, finding the torrent of vituperation kept flowing, rose again, and going to the door, fetched a great jug of cold water from the pail that always stood there, and coming behind her prisoner, emptied it over his face. He gave a horrid yell taking the douche for a boiling one.

"Ye needna cry oot like that at guid cauld watter," said Janet. "But ye'll jist absteen frae ony mair sic words i' my hearin', or ye s' get the like ilka time ye brak oot." As she spoke, she knelt, and wiped his face and head with her apron.

A fresh oath rushed to Angus's lips, but the fear of a second jugful made him suppress it, and Janet sat down again to her dinner. She could scarcely eat a mouthful, however, for pity of the rascal beside her, at whom she kept looking wistfully without daring again to offer him anything.

While she sat thus, she caught a swift investigating look he cast on the cords that bound his hands, and then at the fire. She perceived at once what was passing in his mind. Rising, she went quickly to the byre, and returned immediately with a chain they used for tethering the cow. The end of it she slipt deftly round his neck, and made it fast, putting the little bar through a link.

"Ir ye gauin' to hang me, ye she-deevil?" he cried, making a futile attempt to grasp the chain with his bound hands.

"Ye'll be wantin' a drappy mair cauld watter, I'm thinkin'," said Janet.

She stretched the chain to its length, and with a great stone drove the sharp iron stake at the other end of it, into the clay-floor. Fearing next that, bound as his hands were, he might get a hold of the chain and drag out the stake, or might even contrive to remove the rope from his feet with them, or that he might indeed with his teeth undo the knot that confined his hands themselves—she got a piece of rope, and made a loop at the end of it, then watching her opportunity passed the loop between his hands, noosed the other end through it, and drew the noose tight. The free end of the rope she put through the staple that received the bolt of the cottage-door, and gradually, as he grew weary in pulling against her, tightened the rope until she had his arms at their stretch beyond his head. Not quite satisfied yet, she lastly contrived, in part by setting Oscar to occupy his attention, to do the same with his feet, securing them to a heavy chest in the corner opposite the door, upon which chest she heaped a pile of stones. If it pleased the Lord to deliver them from this man, she would have her honest part in the salvation! And now at last she believed she had him safe.

Gibbie had fallen asleep, but he now woke and she gave him his dinner; then redd up, and took her Bible. Gibbie had lain down again, and she thought he was asleep.

Angus grew more and more uncomfortable, both in body and in mind. He knew he was hated throughout the country, and had hitherto rather enjoyed the knowledge; but now he judged that the popular feeling, by no means a mere prejudice, would tell against him committed for trial. He knew also that the magistrate to whom Robert had betaken himself, was not over friendly with his master, and certainly would not listen to any intercession from him. At length, what with pain, hunger, and fear, his pride began to yield, and, after an hour had passed in utter silence, he condescended to parley.

"Janet Grant," he said, "lat me gang, an' I'll trouble you or yours no more."

"Wadna ye think me some fule to hearken till ye?" suggested Janet.

"I'll sweir ony lawfu' aith 'at ye like to lay upo' me," protested Angus, "'at I'll dee whatever ye please to require o' me."

"I dinna doobt ye wad sweir; but what neist?" said Janet.

"What neist but ye'll lowse my han's?" rejoined Angus.

"It's no mainner o' use mentionin' 't," replied Janet; "for, as ye ken, I'm un'er authority, an' yersel' h'ard my man tell me to tak unco percaution no to lat ye gang; for verily, Angus, ye hae conduckit yersel' this day more like ane possessed wi' a legion, than the douce faimily man 'at ye're supposit by the laird, yer maister, to be."

"Was ever man," protested Angus "made sic a fule o', an' sae misguidit, by a pair o' auld cottars like you an' Robert Grant!"

"Wi' the help o' the Lord, by means o' the dog," supplemented Janet. "I wuss frae my hert I hed the great reid draigon i' yer place, an' I wad watch him bonny, I can tell ye, Angus Mac Pholp. I wadna be clear aboot giein him his denner, Angus."

"Let me gang, wuman, wi' yer reid draigons! I'll hairm naebody. The puir idiot's no muckle the waur, an' I'll tak mair tent when I fire anither time."

"Wiser fowk nor me maun see to that," answered Janet.

"Hoots, wuman! it was naething but an accident."

"I kenna; but it'll be seen what Gibbie says."

"Awva! his word's guid for naething."

"For a penny, or a thoosan' poun'."

"My wife 'll be oot o' her wuts," pleaded Angus.

"Wad ye like a drink o' milk?" asked Janet, rising.

"I wad that," he answered.

She filled her little teapot with milk, and he drank it from the spout, hoping she was on the point of giving way.

"Noo," she said, when he had finished his draught, "ye maun jist mak the best o' it, Angus. Ony gait, it's a guid lesson in patience to ye, an' that ye haena had ower aften, I'm thinkin'—Robert'll be here er lang."

With these words she set down the teapot, and went out: it was time to milk her cow.

In a little while Gibbie rose, tried to walk, but failed, and getting down on his hands and knees, crawled out after her. Angus caught a glimpse of his face as he crept past him, and then first recognized the boy he had lashed. Not compunction, but an occasional pang of dread lest he should have been the cause of his death, and might come upon his body in one of his walks, had served so to fix his face in his memory, that, now he had a near view of him, pale with suffering and loss of blood and therefore more like his former self, he knew him beyond a doubt. With a great shoot of terror he concluded that the idiot had been lying there silently gloating over his revenge, waiting only till Janet should be out of sight, and was now gone after some instrument wherewith to take it. He pulled and tugged at his bonds, but only to find escape absolutely hopeless. In gathering horror, he lay moveless at last, but strained his hearing towards every sound.

Not only did Janet often pray with Gibbie, but sometimes as she read, her heart would grow so full, her soul be so pervaded with the conviction, perhaps the consciousness, of the presence of the man who had said he would be always with his friends, that, sitting there on her stool, she would begin talking to him out of the very depth of her life, just as if she saw him in Robert's chair in the ingle-neuk, at home in her cottage as in the house where Mary sat at his feet and heard his word. Then would Gibbie listen indeed, awed by very gladness. He never doubted that Jesus was there, or that Janet saw him all the time although he could not.

This custom of praying aloud, she had grown into so long before Gibbie came to her, and he was so much and such a child, that his presence was no check upon the habit. It came in part from the intense reality of her belief, and was in part a willed fostering of its intensity. She never imagined that words were necessary; she believed that God knew her every thought, and that the moment she lifted up her heart, it entered into communion with him; but the very sound of the words she spoke seemed to make her feel nearer to the man who, being the eternal Son of the Father, yet had ears to hear and lips to speak, like herself. To talk to him aloud, also kept her thoughts together, helped her to feel the fact of the things she contemplated, as well as the reality of his presence.

Now the byre was just on the other side of the turf wall against which was the head of Gibbie's bed, and through the wall Gibbie had heard her voice, with that something in the tone of it which let him understand she was not talking to Crummie, but to Crummie's maker; and it was therefore he had got up and gone after her. For there was no reason, so far as he knew or imagined, why he should not hear, as so many times before, what she was saying to the Master. He supposed that as she could not well speak to him in the presence of a man like Angus, she had gone out to the byre to have her talk with him there. He crawled to the end of the cottage so silently that she heard no sound of his approach. He would not go into the byre, for that might disturb her, for she would have to look up to know that it was only Gibbie; he would listen at the door. He found it wide open, and peeping in, saw Crummie chewing away, and Janet on her knees with her forehead leaning against the cow and her hands thrown up over her shoulder. She spoke in such a voice of troubled entreaty as he had never heard from her before, but which yet woke a strange vibration of memory in his deepest heart.—Yes, it was his father's voice it reminded him of! So had he cried in prayer the last time he ever heard him speak. What she said was nearly this:

GEORGE MACDONALD

"O Lord, gin ye wad but say what ye wad hae deen! Whan a body disna ken yer wull, she's jist driven to distraction. Thoo knows, my Maister, as weel's I can tell ye, 'at gien ye said till me, 'That man's gauin' to cut yer thro't: tak the tows frae him, an' lat him up,' I wad rin to dee't. It's no revenge, Lord; it's jist 'at I dinna ken. The man's dune me no ill, 'cep' as he's sair hurtit yer bonnie Gibbie. It's Gibbie 'at has to forgie 'im an' syne me. But my man tellt me no to lat him up, an' hoo am I to be a wife sic as ye wad hae, O Lord, gien I dinna dee as my man tellt me! It wad ill befit me to lat my auld Robert gang sae far wantin' his denner, a' for naething. What wad he think whan he cam hame! Of coorse, Lord, gien ye tellt me, that wad mak a' the differ, for ye're Robert's maister as weel's mine, an' your wull wad saitisfee him jist as weel's me. I wad fain lat him gang, puir chiel! but I daurna. Lord, convert him to the trowth. Lord, lat him ken what hate is.—But eh, Lord! I wuss ye wad tell me what to du. Thy wull's the beginnin' an' mids an' en' o' a' thing to me. I'm wullin' eneuch to lat him gang, but he's Robert's pris'ner an' Gibbie's enemy; he's no my pris'ner an' no my enemy, an' I dinna think I hae the richt. An' wha kens but he micht gang shottin' mair fowk yet, 'cause I loot him gang!—But he canna shot a hare wantin' thy wull, O Jesus, the Saviour o' man an' beast; an' ill wad I like to hae a han' i' the hangin' o' 'm. He may deserve 't, Lord, I dinna ken; but I'm thinkin' ye made him no sae weel tempered—as my Robert, for enstance."

Here her voice ceased, and she fell a moaning.

Her trouble was echoed in dim pain from Gibbie's soul. That the prophetess who knew everything, the priestess who was at home in the very treasure-house of the great king, should be thus abandoned to dire perplexity, was a dreadful, a bewildering fact. But now first he understood the real state of the affair in the purport of the old man's absence; also how he was himself potently concerned in the business: if the offence had been committed against Gibbie, then with Gibbie lay the power, therefore the duty of forgiveness. But verily Gibbie's merit and his grace were in inverse ratio. Few things were easier to him than to love his enemies, and his merit in obeying the commandment was small indeed. No enemy had as yet done him, in his immediate person, the wrong he could even imagine it hard to forgive. No sooner had Janet ceased than he was on his way back to the cottage: on its floor lay one who had to be waited upon with forgiveness.

Wearied with futile struggles, Angus found himself compelled to abide his fate, and was lying quite still when Gibbie re-entered. The boy thought he was asleep, but on the contrary he was watching his every motion, full of dread. Gibbie went hopping upon one foot to the hole in the wall where Janet kept the only knife she had. It was not there. He glanced round, but could not see it. There was no time to lose. Robert's returning steps might be heard any moment, and poor Angus might be hanged—only for shooting Gibbie! He hopped up to him and examined the knots that tied his hands: they were drawn so tight—in great measure by his own struggles—and so difficult to reach from their position, that he saw it would take him a long time to undo them. Angus thought, with fresh horror, he was examining them to make sure they would hold, and was so absorbed in watching his movements that he even forgot to curse, which was the only thing left him. Gibbie looked round again for a moment, as if in doubt, then darted upon the tongs—there was no poker—and thrust them into the fire, caught up the asthmatic old bellows, and began to blow the peats. Angus saw the first action, heard the second, and a hideous dismay clutched his very heart: the savage fool was about to take his revenge in pinches with the red hot tongs! He looked for no mercy—perhaps felt that he deserved none. Manhood held him silent until he saw him take the implement of torture from the fire, glowing, not red but white hot, when he uttered such a terrific yell, that Gibbie dropped the tongs—happily not the hot ends—on his own bare foot, but caught them up again instantly, and made a great hop to Angus: if Janet had heard that yell and came in, all would be spoilt. But the faithless keeper began to struggle so fiercely, writhing with every contortion, and kicking with every inch, left possible to him, that Gibbie hardly dared attempt anything for dread of burning him, while he sent yell after yell "as fast as mill-wheels strike." With a sudden thought Gibbie sprang to the door and locked it, so that Janet should not get in, and Angus, hearing the bolt, was the more convinced that his purpose was cruel, and struggled and yelled, with his eyes fixed on the glowing tongs, now fast cooling in Gibbie's hand. If instead of glowering at the tongs, he had but lent one steadfast regard to the face of the boy whom he took for a demoniacal idiot, he would have seen his supposed devil smile the sweetest of human, troubled, pitiful smiles. Even then, I suspect, however, his eye being evil, he would have beheld in the smile only the joy of malice in the near prospect of a glut of revenge.

In the mean time Janet, in her perplexity, had, quite forgetful of the poor cow's necessities, abandoned Crummie, and wandered down the path as far as the shoulder her husband must cross ascending from the other side: thither, a great rock intervening, so little of Angus's cries reached, that she heard nothing through the deafness of her absorbing appeal for direction to her shepherd, the master of men.

Gibbie thrust the tongs again into the fire, and while blowing it, bethought him that it might give Angus confidence if he removed the chain from his neck. He laid down the bellows, and did so. But to Angus the action seemed only preparatory to taking him by the throat with the horrible implement. In his agony and wild endeavour to frustrate the supposed intent, he struggled harder than ever. But now Gibbie was undoing the rope fastened round the chest. This Angus did not perceive, and when it came suddenly loose in the midst of one of his fierce straining contortions, the result was that he threw his body right over his head, and lay on his face for a moment confused. Gibbie saw his advantage. He snatched his clumsy tool out of the fire, seated himself on the corresponding part of Angus's person, and seizing with the tongs the rope between his feet, held on to both, in spite of his heaves and kicks. In the few moments that passed while Gibbie burned through a round of the rope, Angus imagined a considerable number of pangs; but when Gibbie rose and hopped away, he discovered that his feet were at liberty, and scrambled up, his head dizzy, and his body reeling. But such was then the sunshine of delight in Gibbie's countenance that even Angus stared at him for a moment—only, however, with a vague reflection on the inconsequentiality of idiots, to which succeeded the impulse to take vengeance upon him for his sufferings. But Gibbie still had the tongs, and Angus's hands were still tied. He held them out to him. Gibbie pounced upon the knots with hands and teeth. They occupied him some little time, during which Angus was almost compelled to take better cognizance of the face of the savage; and dull as he was to the good things of human nature, he was yet in a measure subdued by what he there looked upon rather than perceive; while he could scarcely mistake the hearty ministration of his teeth and nails! The moment his hands were free, Gibbie looked up at him with a smile, and Angus did not even box his ears. Holding by the wall, Gibbie limped to the door and opened it. With a nod meant for thanks, the gamekeeper stepped out, took up his gun from where it leaned against the wall, and hurried away down the hill. A moment sooner and he would have met Janet; but she had just entered the byre again to milk poor Crummie.

When she came into the cottage, she stared with astonishment to see no Angus on the floor. Gibbie, who had lain down again in much pain, made signs that he had let him go: whereupon such a look of relief came over her countenance that he was filled with fresh gladness, and was if possible more satisfied still with what he had done.

It was late before Robert returned—alone, weary, and disappointed. The magistrate was from home; he had waited for him as long as he dared; but at length, both because of his wife's unpleasant position, and the danger to himself if he longer delayed his journey across the mountain, seeing it threatened a storm, and there was no moon, he set out. That he too was relieved to find no Angus there, he did not attempt to conceal. The next day he went to see him, and told him that, to please Gibbie, he had consented to say nothing more about the affair. Angus could not help being sullen, but he judged it wise to behave as well as he could, kept his temper therefore, and said he was sorry he had been so hasty, but that Robert had punished him pretty well, for it would be weeks before he recovered the blow on the head he had given him. So they parted on tolerable terms, and there was no further persecution of Gibbie from that quarter.

It was some time before he was able to be out again, but no hour spent with Janet was lost.

XXVII

A Voice

That winter the old people were greatly tried with rheumatism; for not only were the frosts severe, but there was much rain between. Their children did all in their power to minister to their wants, and Gibbie was nurse as well as shepherd. He who when a child had sought his place in the live universe by attending on drunk people and helping them home through the midnight streets, might have felt himself promoted considerably in having the necessities of such as Robert and Janet to minister to, but he never thought of that. It made him a little mournful sometimes to think that he could not read to them. Janet, however, was generally able to read aloud. Robert, being also asthmatic, suffered more than she, and was at times a little impatient.

Gibbie still occupied his heather-bed on the floor, and it was part of his business, as nurse, to keep up a good fire on the hearth: peats, happily, were plentiful. Awake for this cause, he heard in the middle of one night, the following dialogue between the husband and wife.

"I'm growin' terrible auld, Janet," said Robert. "It's a sair thing this auld age, an' I canna bring mysel' content wi' 't. Ye see I haena been used till't."

"That's true, Robert," answered Janet. "Gien we had been born auld, we micht by this time hae been at hame wi't. But syne what wad hae come o' the gran' delicht o' seein' auld age rin hirplin awa' frae the face o' the Auncient o' Days?"

"I wad fain be contentit wi' my lot, thouch," persisted Robert; "but whan I fin' mysel' sae helpless like, I canna get it oot o' my heid 'at the Lord has forsaken me, an' left me to mak an ill best o' 't wantin' him."

"I wadna lat sic a thoucht come intil my heid, Robert, sae lang as I kenned I cudna draw breath nor wag tongue wantin' him, for in him we leeve an' muv an' hae oor bein'. Gien he be the life o' me, what for sud I trible mysel' aboot that life?"

"Ay, lass! but gien ye hed this ashmy, makin' a' yer breist as gien 'twar lined wi' the san' paper 'at they hed been lichtin' a thoosan' or twa lucifer spunks upo'—ye micht be driven to forget 'at the Lord was yer life—for I can tell ye it's no like haein' his breith i' yer nostrils."

"Eh, my bonny laad!" returned Janet with infinite tenderness, "I micht weel forget it! I doobt I wadna be half sae patient as yersel'; but jist to help to haud ye up, I s' tell ye what I think I wad ettle efter. I wad say to mysel' Gien he be the life o' me, I hae no business wi' ony mair o' 't nor he gies me. I hae but to tak ae breath, be 't hard, be 't easy, ane at a time, an' lat him see to the neist himsel'. Here I am, an' here's him; an' 'at he winna lat's ain wark come to ill, that I'm weel sure o'. An' ye micht jist think to yersel', Robert, 'at as ye are born intil the warl', an' here ye are auld intil't—ye may jist think, I say, 'at hoo ye're jist new-born an auld man, an' beginnin' to grow yoong, an' 'at that's yer business. For naither you nor me can be that far frae hame, Robert, an' whan we win there we'll be yoong eneuch, I'm thinkin'; an' no ower yoong, for we'll hae what they say ye canna get doon here—a pair o' auld heids upo' yoong shoothers."

"Eh! but I wuss I may hae ye there, Janet, for I kenna what I wad do wantin' ye. I wad be unco stray up yon'er, gien I had to gang my lane, an' no you to refar till, 'at kens the w'ys o' the place."

"I ken no more about the w'ys o' the place nor yersel', Robert, though I'm thinkin' they'll be unco quaiet an' sensible, seein' 'at a' there maun be gentle fowk. It's eneuch to me 'at I'll be i' the hoose o' my Maister's father; an' my Maister was weel content to gang to that hoose; an' it maun be something by ordinar' 'at was fit for him. But puir simple fowk like oorsel's 'ill hae no need to hing down the heid an' luik like gowks 'at disna ken mainners. Bairns are no expeckit to ken a' the w'ys o' a muckle hoose 'at they hae never been intil i' their lives afore."

"It's no that a'thegither 'at tribles me, Janet; it's mair 'at I'll be expeckit to sing an' luik pleased-like, an' I div not ken hoo it'll be poassible, an' you naegait 'ithin my sicht or my cry, or the hearin' o' my ears."

"Div ye believe this, Robert'—at we're a' ane, jist ane, in Christ Jesus?"

"I canna weel say. I'm no denyin' naething 'at the buik tells me; ye ken me better nor that, Janet; but there's mony a thing it says 'at I dinna ken whether I believe't 'at my ain han', or whether it be only at a' thing 'at ye believe, Janet, 's jist to me as gien I believet it mysel'; an' that's a sair thought, for a man canna be savet e'en by the proxy o' 's ain wife."

"Weel, ye're just muckle whaur I fin' mysel' whiles, Robert; an' I comfort mysel' wi' the houp 'at we'll ken the thing there, 'at maybe we're but tryin' to believe here. But ony gait ye hae pruv't weel 'at you an' me's ane, Robert. Noo we ken frae Scriptur' 'at the Maister cam to mak aye ane o' them 'at was at twa; an' we ken also 'at he conquered Deith; sae he wad never lat Deith mak the ane 'at he had made ane, intil twa again: it's no rizon to think it. For oucht I ken, what luiks like a gangin' awa may be a comin' nearer. An' there may be w'ys o' comin' nearer till ane anither up yon'er 'at we ken naething aboot doon here. There's that laddie, Gibbie: I canna but think 'at gien he hed the tongue to speyk, or aiven gien he cud mak' ony soon' wi' sense intil't, like singin', say, he wad fin' himsel' nearer till's nor he can i' the noo. Wha kens but them 'at's singin' up there afore the throne, may sing so bonny, 'at, i' the pooer o' their braw thouchts, their verra sangs may be like laidders for them to come doon upo', an' hing aboot them 'at they hae left ahin' them, till the time comes for them to gang an' jine them i' the green pasturs aboot the tree o' life."

More of like talk followed, but these words concerning appropinquation in song, although their meaning was not very clear, took such a hold of Gibbie that he heard nothing after, but fell asleep thinking about them.

In the middle of the following night, Janet woke her husband.

"Robert! Robert!" she whispered in his ear, "hearken. I'm thinkin' yon maun be some wee angel come doon to say, 'I ken ye, puir fowk.'"

Robert, scarce daring to draw his breath listened with his heart in his mouth. From somewhere, apparently within the four walls of the cottage, came a low lovely sweet song—something like the piping of a big bird, something like a small human voice.

"It canna be an angel," said Robert at length, "for it's singin' 'My Nannie's Awa'.'"

"An' what for no an angel?" returned Janet. "Isna that jist what ye micht be singin' yersel', efter what ye was sayin' last nicht? I'm thinkin' there maun be a heap o' yoong angels up there, new deid, singin', 'My Nannie's Awa'.'"

"Hoot, Janet! ye ken there's naither merryin' nor giein' in merriage there."

"Wha was sayin' onything aboot merryin' or giein' in merriage, Robert? Is that to say 'at you an' me's to be no more to ane anither nor ither fowk? Nor it's no to say 'at, 'cause merriage is no the w'y o' the country, 'at there's to be naething better i' the place o' 't."

"What garred the Maister say onything aboot it than?"

"Jist 'cause they plaguit him wi' speirin'. He wad never hae opened his moo' anent it—it wasna ane o' his subjec's—gien it hadna been 'at a wheen pride-prankit beuk-fowk 'at didna believe there was ony angels, or speerits o' ony kin', but said 'at a man ance deid was aye an' a'thegither deid, an' yet preten'it to believe in God himsel' for a' that, thoucht to bleck (nonplus) the Maister wi' speirin' whilk o' saiven a puir body 'at had been garred merry them a', wad be the wife o' whan they gat up again."

"A body micht think it wad be left to hersel' to say," suggested Robert. "She had come throu' eneuch to hae some claim to be considert."

"She maun hae been a richt guid ane," said Janet, "gien ilk ane o' the saiven wad be wantin' her again. But I s' warran' she kenned weel eneuch whilk o' them was her ain. But, Robert, man, this is jokin'— no 'at it's your wyte (blame)—an' it's no becomin', I doobt, upo' sic a sarious subjec'. An' I'm feart—ay! there!—I thoucht as muckle!—the wee sangie's drappit itsel' a'thegither, jist as gien the laverock had fa'ntit intil 'ts nest. I doobt we'll hear nae mair o' 't."

As soon as he could hear what they were saying, Gibbie had stopped to listen; and now they had stopped also, and there was an end.

For weeks he had been picking out tunes on his Pan's-pipes, also, he had lately discovered that, although he could not articulate, he could produce tones, and had taught himself to imitate the pipes. Now, to his delight, he had found that the noises he made were recognized as song by his father and mother. From that time he was often heard crooning to himself. Before long he began to look about the heavens for airs—to suit this or that song he came upon, or heard from Donal.

XXVIII

THE WISDOM OF THE WISE

C hange, meantime, was in progress elsewhere, and as well upon the foot as high on the side of Glashgar—change which seemed all important to those who felt the grind of the glacier as it slipped. Thomas Galbraith, of Glashruach, Esquire, whom no more than any other could negation save, was not enfranchised from folly, or lifted above belief in a lie, by his hatred to what he called superstition: he had long fallen into what will ultimately prove the most degrading superstition of all—the worship of Mammon, and was rapidly sinking from deep to lower deep. First of all, this was the superstition of placing hope and trust in that which, from age to age, and on the testimony of all sorts of persons who have tried it, has been proved to fail utterly; next, such was the folly of the man whose wisdom was indignant with the harmless imagination of simple people for daring flutter its wings upon his land, that he risked what he loved best in the world, even better than Mammon, the approbation of fellow worshippers, by investing in Welsh gold mines.

The property of Glashruach was a good one, but not nearly so large as it had been, and he was anxious to restore it to its former dimensions. The rents were low, and it could but tardily widen its own borders, while of money he had little and no will to mortgage. To increase his money, that he might increase his property, he took to speculation, but had never had much success until that same year, when he disposed of certain shares at a large profit—nothing troubled by the conviction that the man who bought them—in ignorance of many a fact which the laird knew—must in all probability be ruined by them. He counted this success, and it gave him confidence to speculate further. In the mean time, with what he had thus secured, he reannexed to the property a small farm which had been for some time in the market, but whose sale he had managed to delay. The purchase gave him particular pleasure, because the farm not only marched with his home-grounds, but filled up a great notch in the map of the property between Glashruach and the Mains, with which also it marched. It was good land, and he let it at once, on his own terms, to Mr. Duff.

In the spring, affairs looked rather bad for him, and in the month of May, he considered himself compelled to go to London: he had a faith in his own business-faculty quite as foolish as any superstition in Gormgarnet. There he fell into the hands of a certain man, whose true place would have been in the swell mob, and not in the House of Commons—a fellow who used his influence and facilities as member of Parliament in promoting bubble companies. He was intimate with an elder brother of the laird, himself member for a not unimportant borough—a man, likewise, of principles that love the shade; and between them they had no difficulty in making a tool of Thomas Galbraith, as chairman of a certain aggregate of iniquity, whose designation will not, in some families, be forgotten for a century or so. During the summer, therefore, the laird was from home, working up the company, hoping much from it, and trying hard to believe in it— whipping up its cream, and perhaps himself taking the froth, certainly doing his best to make others take it, for an increase of genuine substance. He devoted the chamber of his imagination to the service of Mammon, and the brownie he kept there played him fine pranks.

A smaller change, though of really greater importance in the end, was, that in the course of the winter, one of Donal's sisters was engaged by the housekeeper at Glashruach, chiefly to wait upon Miss Galbraith. Ginevra was still a silent, simple, unconsciously retiring, and therewith dignified girl, in whom childhood and womanhood had begun to interchange hues, as it were with the play of colours in a dove's neck. Happy they in whom neither has a final victory! Happy also all who have such women to love! At one moment Ginevra would draw herself up—bridle her grandmother would have called it—with involuntary recoil from doubtful approach; the next, Ginny would burst out in a merry laugh at something in which only a child could have perceived the mirth-causing element; then again the woman would seem suddenly to re-enter and rebuke the child, for the sparkle would fade from her eyes, and she would look solemn, and even a little sad. The people about the place loved her, but from the stillness on the general surface of her behaviour, the far away feeling she gave them, and the impossibility of divining how she was thinking except she chose to unbosom herself, they were all a little afraid of her as well. They did not acknowledge, even to themselves, that her evident conscientiousness bore no small part in causing that slight uneasiness of which they were aware in her presence. Possibly it roused in some

GEORGE MACDONALD

of them such a dissatisfaction with themselves as gave the initiative to dislike of her.

In the mind of her new maid, however, there was no strife, therefore no tendency to dislike. She was thoroughly well-meaning, like the rest of her family, and finding her little mistress dwell in the same atmosphere, the desire to be acceptable to her awoke at once, and grew rapidly in her heart. She was the youngest of Janet's girls, about four years older than Donal, not clever, but as sweet as honest, and full of divine service. Always ready to think others better than herself, the moment she saw the still face of Ginevra, she took her for a little saint, and accepted her as a queen, whose will to her should be law. Ginevra, on her part, was taken with the healthy hue and honest eyes of the girl, and neither felt any dislike to her touching her hair, nor lost her temper when she was awkward and pulled it. Before the winter was over, the bond between them was strong.

One principal duty required of Nicie—her parents had named her after the mother of St. Paul's Timothy—was to accompany her mistress every fine day to the manse, a mile and a half from Glashruach. For some time Ginevra had been under the care of Miss Machar, the daughter of the parish clergyman, an old gentleman of sober aspirations, to whom the last century was the Augustan age of English literature. He was genial, gentle, and a lover of his race, with much reverence for, and some faith in, a Scotch God, whose nature was summed up in a series of words beginning with omni. Partly that the living was a poor one, and her father old and infirm, Miss Marchar, herself middle-aged, had undertaken the instruction of the little heiress, never doubting herself mistress of all it was necessary a lady should know. By nature she was romantic, but her romance had faded a good deal. Possibly had she read the new poets of her age, the vital flame of wonder and hope might have kept not a little of its original brightness in her heart; but under her father's guidance, she had never got beyond the Night Thoughts, and the Course of Time. Both intellectually and emotionally, therefore, Miss Machar had withered instead of ripening. As to her spiritual carriage, she thought too much about being a lady to be thoroughly one. The utter graciousness of the ideal lady would blush to regard itself. She was both gentle and dignified; but would have done a nature inferior to Ginevra's injury by the way she talked of things right and wrong as becoming or not becoming in a lady of position such as Ginevra would one day find herself. What lessons she taught her she taught her well. Her music was old-fashioned, of course; but I have a fancy that perhaps the older the music one learns first, the better; for the deeper is thereby the rooting of that which will have the atmosphere of the age to blossom in. But then to every lover of the truth, a true thing is dearer because it is old-fashioned, and dearer because it is new-fashioned: and true music, like true love, like all truth, laughs at the god Fashion, because it knows him to be but an ape.

Every day, then, except Saturday and Sunday, Miss Machar had for two years been in the habit of walking or driving to Glashruach, and there spending the morning hours; but of late her father had been ailing, and as he was so old that she could not without anxiety leave him when suffering from the smallest indisposition, she had found herself compelled either to give up teaching Ginevra, or to ask Mr. Galbraith to allow her to go, when such occasion should render it necessary, to the manse. She did the latter; the laird had consented; and thence arose the duty required of Nicie. Mr. Machar's health did not improve as the spring advanced, and by the time Mr. Galbraith left for London, he was confined to his room, and Ginevra's walk to the manse for lessons had settled into a custom.

XXIX

The Beast-Boy

One morning they found, on reaching the manse, that the minister was very unwell, and that in consequence Miss Machar could not attend to Ginevra; they turned, therefore, to walk home again. Now the manse, upon another root of Glashgar, was nearer than Glashruach to Nicie's home, and many a time as she went and came, did she lift longing eyes to the ridge that hid it from her view. This morning, Ginevra observed that, every other moment, Nicie was looking up the side of the mountain, as if she saw something unusual upon it—occasionally, indeed, when the winding of the road turned their backs to it, stopping and turning round to gaze.

"What is the matter with you, Nicie?" she asked. "What are you looking at up there?"

"I'm won'erin' what my mother'll be decin'," answered Nicie. "she's up there."

"Up there!" exclaimed Ginny, and, turning, stared at the mountain too, expecting to perceive Nicie's mother somewhere upon the face of it.

"Na, na, missie! ye canna see her," said the girl; "she's no in sicht. She's ower ayont there. Only gien we war up whaur ye see yon twa three sheep again' the lift (sky), we cud see the bit hoosie whaur her an' my father bides."

"How I should like to see your father and mother, Nicie!" exclaimed Ginevra.

"Weel, I'm sure they wad be richt glaid to see yersel', missie, ony time 'at ye likit to gang an' see them."

"Why shouldn't we go now, Nicie? It's not a dangerous place, is it?"

"No, missie. Glashgar's as quaiet an' weel-behaved a hill as ony in a' the cweentry," answered Nicie, laughing. "She's some puir, like the lave o' 's, an' hasna muckle to spare, but the sheep get a feow nibbles upon her, here an' there; an' my mither manages to keep a coo, an' get plenty o' milk frae her tee."

"Come, then, Nicie. We have plenty of time. Nobody wants either you or me, and we shall get home before any one misses us."

Nicie was glad enough to consent; they turned at once to the hill, and began climbing. But Nicie did not know this part of it nearly so well as that which lay between Glashruach and the cottage, and after they had climbed some distance, often stopping and turning to look down on the valley below, the prospect of which, with its streams and river, kept still widening and changing as they ascended, they arrived at a place where the path grew very doubtful, and she could not tell in which of two directions they ought to go.

"I'll take this way, and you take that, Nicie," said Ginevra, "and if I find there is no path my way, I will come back to yours; and if you find there is no path your way, you will come back to mine."

It was a childish proposal, and one to which Nicie should not have consented, but she was little more than a child herself. Advancing a short distance in doubt, and the path re-appearing quite plainly, she sat down, expecting her little mistress to return directly. No thought of anxiety crossed her mind: how should one, in broad sunlight, on a mountain-side, in the first of summer, and with the long day before them? So, there sitting in peace, Nicie fell into a maidenly reverie, and so there Nicie sat for a long time, half dreaming in the great light, without once really thinking about anything. All at once she came to herself: some latent fear had exploded in her heart: yes! what could have become of her little mistress? She jumped to her feet, and shouted "Missie! Missie Galbraith! Ginny!" but no answer came back. The mountain was as still as at midnight. She ran to the spot where they had parted, and along the other path: it was plainer than that where she had been so idly forgetting herself. She hurried on, wildly calling as she ran.

In the mean time Ginevra, having found the path indubitable, and imagining it led straight to the door of Nicie's mother's cottage, and that Nicie would be after her in a moment, thinking also to have a bit of fun with her, set off dancing and running so fast, that by the time Nicie came to herself, she was a good mile from her. What a delight it was to be thus alone upon the grand mountain! with the earth banished so far below, and the great rocky heap climbing and leading and climbing up and up towards the sky!

Ginny was not in the way of thinking much about God. Little had been taught her concerning him, and nothing almost that was pleasant to meditate upon—nothing that she could hide in her heart, and be dreadfully glad about when she lay alone in her little bed, listening to the sound of the burn that ran under her window. But there was in her soul a large wilderness ready for the voice that should come crying to prepare the way of the king.

The path was after all a mere sheep-track, and led her at length into a lonely hollow in the hill-side, with a swampy peat-bog at the bottom of it. She stopped. The place looked unpleasant, reminding her of how she always felt when she came unexpectedly upon Angus Mac Pholp. She would go no further alone; she would wait till Nicie overtook her. It must have been just in such places that the people possessed with devils—only Miss Machar always made her read the word, demons—ran about! As she thought thus, a lone-hearted bird uttered a single, wailing cry, strange to her ear. The cry remained solitary, unanswered, and then first suddenly she felt that there was nobody there but herself, and the feeling had in it a pang of uneasiness. But she was a brave child; nothing frightened her much except her father; she turned and went slowly back to the edge of the hollow: Nicie must by this time be visible.

In her haste and anxiety, however, Nicie had struck into another sheep-track, and was now higher up the hill; so that Ginny could see no living thing nearer than in the valley below: far down there—and it was some comfort, in the desolation that now began to invade her—she saw upon the road, so distant that it seemed motionless, a cart with a man in it, drawn by a white horse. Never in her life before had she felt that she was alone. She had often felt lonely, but she had always known where to find the bodily presence of somebody. Now she might cry and scream the whole day, and nobody answer! Her heart swelled into her throat, then sank away, leaving a wide hollow. It was so eerie! But Nicie would soon come, and then all would be well.

She sat down on a stone, where she could see the path she had come a long way back. But "never and never" did any Nicie appear. At last she began to cry. This process with Ginny was a very slow one, and never brought her much relief. The tears would mount into her eyes, and remain there, little pools of Baca, a long time before the crying went any further. But with time the pools would grow deeper, and swell larger, and at last, when they had become two huge little lakes, the larger from the slowness of their gathering, two mighty tears would tumble over the edges of their embankments, and roll down her white mournful cheeks. This time many more followed, and her eyes were fast becoming fountains, when all at once a verse she had heard the Sunday before at church seemed to come of itself into her head: "Call upon me in the time of trouble and I will answer thee." It must mean that she was to ask God to help her: was that the same as saying prayers? But she wasn't good, and he wouldn't hear anybody that wasn't good. Then, if he was only the God of the good people, what was to become of the rest when they were lost on mountains? She had better try; it could not do much harm. Even if he would not hear her, he would not surely be angry with her for calling upon him when she was in such trouble. So thinking, she began to pray to what dim distorted reflection of God there was in her mind. They alone pray to the real God, the maker of the heart that prays, who know his son Jesus. If our prayers were heard only in accordance with the idea of God to which we seem to ourselves to pray, how miserably would our infinite wants be met! But every honest cry, even if sent into the deaf ear of an idol, passes on to the ears of the unknown God, the heart of the unknown Father.

"O God, help me home again," cried Ginevra, and stood up in her great loneliness to return.

The same instant she spied, seated upon a stone, a little way off, but close to her path, the beast-boy. There could be no mistake. He was just as she had heard him described by the children at the gamekeeper's cottage. That was his hair sticking all out from his head, though the sun in it made it look like a crown of gold or a shining mist. Those were his bare arms, and that was dreadful indeed! Bare legs and feet she was used to; but bare arms! Worst of all, making it absolutely certain he was the beast-boy, he was playing upon a curious kind of whistling thing, making dreadfully sweet music to entice her nearer that he might catch her and tear her to pieces! Was this the answer God sent to the prayer she had offered in her sore need—the beast-boy? She asked him for protection and deliverance, and here was the beast-boy! She asked him to help her home, and there, right in the middle of her path, sat the beast-boy, waiting for her! Well, it was just like what they said about him on Sundays in the churches, and in the books Miss Machar made her read! But the horrid creature's music should not have any power over her! She would rather run down to the black water, glooming in those holes, and be drowned, than the beast-boy should have her to eat!

Most girls would have screamed, but such was not Ginny's natural mode of meeting a difficulty. With fear, she was far more likely to choke than to cry out. So she sat down again and stared at him. Perhaps he would go away when he found he could not entice her. He did not move, but kept playing on his curious instrument. Perhaps, by returning into the hollow, she could make a circuit, and so pass him, lower down the hill. She rose at once and ran.

Now Gibbie had seen her long before she saw him, but, from experience, was afraid of frightening her. He had therefore drawn gradually near, and sat as if unaware of her presence. Treating her as he would a bird with which he wanted to make better acquaintance, he would have her get accustomed to the look of him before he made advances. But when he saw her run in the direction of the swamp, knowing what a dangerous place it was, he was terrified, sprung to his feet, and darted off to get between her and the danger. She heard him coming like the wind at her back, and, whether from bewilderment, or that she did intend throwing herself into the water to escape him, instead of pursuing her former design, she made straight for the swamp. But was the beast-boy ubiquitous? As she approached the place, there he was, on the edge of a great hole half full of water, as if he had been sitting there for an hour! Was he going to drown her in that hole? She turned again, and ran towards the descent of the mountain. But there Gibbie feared a certain precipitous spot; and, besides, there was no path in that direction. So Ginevra had not run far before again she saw him right in her way. She threw herself on the ground in despair, and hid her face. After thus hunting her as a cat might a mouse, or a lion a man, what could she look for but that he would pounce upon her, and tear her to pieces? Fearfully expectant of the horrible grasp, she lay breathless. But nothing came. Still she lay, and still nothing came. Could it be that she was dreaming? In dreams generally the hideous thing never arrived. But she dared not look up. She lay and lay, weary and still, with the terror slowly ebbing away out of her. At length to her ears came a strange sweet voice of singing—such a sound as she had never heard before. It seemed to come from far away: what if it should be an angel God was sending, in answer after all to her prayer, to deliver her from the beast-boy! He would of course want some time to come, and certainly no harm had happened to her yet. The sound grew and grew, and came nearer and nearer. But although it was song, she could distinguish no vowel-melody in it, nothing but a tone-melody, a crooning, as it were, ever upon one vowel in a minor key. It came quite near at length, and yet even then had something of the far away sound left in it. It was like the wind of a summer night inside a great church bell in a deserted tower. It came close, and ceased suddenly, as if, like a lark, the angel ceased to sing the moment he lighted. She opened her eyes and looked up. Over her stood the beast-boy, gazing down upon her! Could it really be the beast-boy? If so, then he was fascinating her, to devour her the more easily, as she had read of snakes doing to birds; but she could not believe it. Still—she could not take her eyes off him—that was certain. But no marvel! From under a great crown of reddish gold, looked out two eyes of heaven's own blue, and through the eyes looked out something that dwells behind the sky and every blue thing. What if the angel, to try her, had taken to himself the form of the beast-boy? No beast-boy could sing like what she had heard, or look like what she now saw! She lay motionless, flat on the ground, her face turned sideways upon her hands, and her eyes fixed on the heavenly vision. Then a curious feeling began to wake in her of having seen him before—somewhere, ever so long ago—and that sight of him as well as this had to do with misery—with something that made a stain that would not come out. Yes—it was the very face, only larger, and still sweeter, of the little naked child whom Angus had so cruelly lashed! That was ages ago, but she had not forgotten, and never could forget either the child's back, or the lovely innocent white face that he turned round upon her. If it was indeed he, perhaps he would remember her. In any case, she was now certain he would not hurt her.

While she looked at him thus, Gibbie's face grew grave: seldom was his grave when fronting the face of a fellow-creature, but now he too was remembering, and trying to recollect; as through a dream of sickness and pain he saw a face like the one before him, yet not the same.

Ginevra recollected first, and a sweet slow diffident smile crept like a dawn up from the depth of her under-world to the sky of her face, but settled in her eyes, and made two stars of them. Then rose the very sun himself in Gibbie's, and flashed a full response of daylight—a smile that no woman, girl, or matron, could mistrust.

From brow to chin his face was radiant. The sun of this world had made his nest in his hair, but the smile below it seemed to dim the aureole he wore. Timidly yet trustingly Ginevra took one hand from under her cheek, and stretched it up to him. He clasped it gently. She moved, and he helped her to rise.

"I've lost Nicie," she said.

Gibbie nodded, but did not look concerned,

"Nicie is my maid," said Ginevra.

Gibbie nodded several times. He knew who Nicie was rather better than her mistress.

"I left her away back there, a long, long time ago, and she has never come to me," she said.

Gibbie gave a shrill loud whistle that startled her. In a few seconds, from somewhere unseen, a dog came bounding to him over stones and heather. How he spoke to the dog, or what he told him to do, she had not an idea; but the next instant Oscar was rushing along the path she had come, and was presently out of sight. So full of life was Gibbie, so quick and decided was his every motion, so full of expression his every glance and smile, that she had not yet begun to wonder he had not spoken; indeed she was hardly yet aware of the fact. She knew him now for a mortal, but, just as it had been with Donal and his mother, he continued to affect her as a creature of some higher world, come down on a mission of good-will to men. At the same time she had, oddly enough, a feeling as if the beast-boy were still somewhere not far off, held aloof only by the presence of the angel who had assumed his shape.

Gibbie took her hand, and led her towards the path she had left; she yielded without a movement of question. But he did not lead her far in that direction; he turned to the left up the mountain. It grew wilder as they ascended. But the air was so thin and invigorating, the changes so curious and interesting, as now they skirted the edge of a precipitous rock, now scrambled up the steepest of paths by the help of the heather that nearly closed over it, and the reaction of relief from the terror she had suffered so exciting, that she never for a moment felt tired. Then they went down the side of a little burn—a torrent when the snow was dissolving, and even now a good stream, whose dance and song delighted her: it was the same, as she learned afterwards, to whose song under her window she listened every night in bed, trying in vain to make out the melted tune. Ever after she knew this, it seemed, as she listened, to come straight from the mountain to her window, with news of the stars and the heather and the sheep. They crossed the burn and climbed the opposite bank. Then Gibbie pointed, and there was the cottage, and there was Nicie coming up the path to it, with Oscar bounding before her! The dog was merry, but Nicie was weeping bitterly. They were a good way off, with another larger burn between; but Gibbie whistled, and Oscar came flying to him. Nicie looked up, gave a cry, and like a sheep to her lost lamb came running.

"Oh, missie!" she said, breathless, as she reached the opposite bank of the burn, and her tone had more than a touch of sorrowful reproach in it, "what garred ye rin awa'?"

"There was a road, Nicie, and I thought you would come after me."

"I was a muckle geese, missie; but eh! I'm glaid I hae gotten ye. Come awa' an' see my mother."

"Yes, Nicie. We'll tell her all about it. You see I haven't got a mother to tell, so I will tell yours."

From that hour Nicie's mother was a mother to Ginny as well.

"Anither o' 's lambs to feed!" she said to herself.

If a woman be a mother she may have plenty of children.

Never before had Ginny spent such a happy day, drunk such milk as Crummie's, or eaten such cakes as Janet's. She saw no more of Gibbie: the moment she was safe, he and Oscar were off again to the sheep, for Robert was busy cutting peats that day, and Gibbie was in sole charge. Eager to know about him, Ginevra gathered all that Janet could tell of his story, and in return told the little she had seen of it, which was the one dreadful point.

"Is he a good boy, Mistress Grant?" she asked.

"The best boy ever I kenned—better nor my ain Donal, an' he was the best afore him," answered Janet.

Ginny gave a little sigh, and wished she were good.

"Whan saw ye Donal?" asked Janet of Nicie.

"No this lang time—no sin' I was here last," answered Nicie, who did not now get home so often as the rest.

"I was thinkin'," returned her mother, "ye sud 'maist see him noo frae the back o' the muckle hoose; for he was tellin' me he was wi' the nowt' i' the new meadow upo' the Lorrie bank, 'at missie's papa boucht frae Jeames Glass."

"Ow, is he there?" said Nicie. "I'll maybe get sicht, gien I dinna get word o' him. He cam ance to the kitchen-door to see me, but Mistress Mac Farlane wadna lat him in. She wad hae nae loons comin' aboot the place she said. I said 'at hoo he was my brither. She said, says she, that was naething to her, an' she wad hae no brithers. My sister micht come whiles, she said, gien she camna ower aften; but lasses had naething to dee wi' brithers. Wha was to tell wha was or wha wasna my brither? I tellt her 'at a' my brithers was weel kenned for douce laads; an' she tellt me to haud my tongue, an' no speyk up; an' I cud hae jist gien her a guid cloot o' the lug—I was that angert wi' her."

"She'll be soary for't some day," said Janet, with a quiet smile; "an' what a body's sure to be soary for, ye may as weel forgie them at ance."

"Hoo ken ye, mither, she'll be soary for't?" asked Nicie, not very willing to forgive Mistress Mac Farlane.

"'Cause the Maister says 'at we'll hae to pey the uttermost fardin'. There's naebody 'ill be latten aff. We maun dee oor neiper richt."

"But michtna the Maister himsel' forgie her?" suggested Nicie, a little puzzled.

"Lassie," said her mother solemnly, "ye dinna surely think 'at the Lord's forgifness is to lat fowk aff ohn repentit? That wad be a strange fawvour to grant them! He winna hurt mair nor he can help; but the grue (horror) maun mak w'y for the grace. I'm sure it was sae whan I gied you yer whups, lass. I'll no say aboot some o' the first o' ye, for at that time I didna ken sae weel what I was aboot, an' was mair angert whiles nor there was ony occasion for—tuik my beam to dang their motes. I hae been sair tribled aboot it, mony's the time."

"Eh, mither!" said Nicie, shocked at the idea of her reproaching herself about anything concerning her children, "I'm weel sure there's no ane o' them wad think, no to say say, sic a thing."

"I daursay ye're richt there, lass. I think whiles a woman's bairns are like the God they cam frae—aye ready to forgie her onything."

Ginevra went home with a good many things to think about.

XXX

The Lorrie Meadow

I t was high time, according to agricultural economics, that Donal Grant should be promoted a step in the ranks of labour. A youth like him was fit for horses and their work, and looked idle in a field with cattle. But Donal was not ambitious, at least in that direction. He was more and more in love with books, and learning and the music of thought and word; and he knew well that no one doing a man's work upon a farm could have much time left for study—certainly not a quarter of what the herd-boy could command. Therefore, with his parents approval, he continued to fill the humbler office, and receive the scantier wages belonging to it.

The day following their adventure on Glashgar, in the afternoon, Nicie being in the grounds with her little mistress, proposed that they should look whether they could see her brother down in the meadow of which her mother had spoken. Ginevra willingly agreed, and they took their way through the shrubbery to a certain tall hedge which divided the grounds from a little grove of larches on the slope of a steep bank descending to the Lorrie, on the other side of which lay the meadow. It was a hawthorn hedge, very old, and near the ground very thin, so that they easily found a place to creep through. But they were no better on the other side, for the larches hid the meadow. They went down through them, therefore, to the bank of the little river— the largest tributary of the Daur from the roots of Glashgar.

"There he is!" cried Nicie.

"I see him," responded Ginny, "—with his cows all about the meadow." Donal sat a little way from the river, reading.

"He's aye at 's buik!" said Nicie.

"I wonder what book it is," said Ginny.

"That wad be ill to say," answered Nicie. "Donal reads a hantle o' buiks—mair, his mither says, nor she doobts he can weel get the guid o'."

"Do you think it's Latin, Nicie?"

"Ow! I daursay. But no; it canna be Laitin—for, leuk! he's lauchin', an' he cudna dee that gien 'twar Laitin. I'm thinkin' it'll be a story: there's a heap o' them prentit noo, they tell me. Or 'deed maybe it may be a sang.

He thinks a heap o' sangs. I h'ard my mither ance say she was some feared Donal micht hae ta'en to makin' sangs himsel'; no 'at there was ony ill i' that, she said, gien there wasna ony ill i' the sangs themsel's; but it was jist some trifflin' like, she said, an' they luikit for better frae Donal, wi' a' his buik lear, an' his Euclid—or what ca' they't?—nor makin' sangs."

"What's Euclid, Nicie?"

"Ye may weel speir, missie! but I hae ill tellin' ye. It's a keerious name till a buik, an' min's me o' naething but whan the lid o' yer e'e yeuks (itches); an' as to what lies atween the twa brods o' 't, I ken no more nor the man i' the meen."

"I should like to ask Donal what book he has got," said Ginny.

"I'll cry till 'im, an' ye can speir," said Nicie.—"Donal!—Donal!"

Donal looked up, and seeing his sister, came running to the bank of the stream.

"Canna ye come ower, Donal?" said Nicie. "Here's Miss Galbraith wants to spier ye a question."

Donal was across in a moment, for here the water was nowhere over a foot or two in depth.

"Oh, Donal! you've wet your feet!" cried Ginevra.

Donal laughed.

"What ill 'ill that dee me, mem?"

"None, I hope," said Ginny; "but it might, you know."

"I micht hae been droont," said Donal.

"Nicie," said Ginny, with dignity, "your brother is laughing at me."

"Na, na, mem," said Donal, apologetically. "I was only so glaid to see you an' Nicie 'at I forgot my mainners."

"Then," returned Ginny, quite satisfied, "would you mind telling me what book you were reading?"

"It's a buik o' ballants," answered Donal. "I'll read ane o' them till ye, gien ye like, mem."

"I should like very much," responded Ginny. "I've read all my own books till I'm tired of them, and I don't like papa's books.—And, do you know, Donal!"—Here the child-woman's voice grew solemn sad— "—I'm very sorry, and I'm frightened to say it; and if you weren't Nicie's brother, I couldn't say it to you;—but I am very tired of the Bible too."

"That's a peety, mem," replied Donal. "I wad hae ye no tell onybody that; for them 'at likes 't no a hair better themsel's, 'ill tak ye for waur nor a haithen for sayin' 't. Jist gang ye up to my mither, an' tell her a' aboot it. She's aye fair to a' body, an' never thinks ill o' onybody 'at says the trowth—whan it's no for contrariness. She says 'at a heap o' ill comes o' fowk no speykin' oot what they ken, or what they're thinkin', but aye guissin' at what they dinna ken, an' what ither fowk's thinkin'."

"Ay!" said Nicie, "it wad be a gey cheenged warl' gien fowk gaed to my mither, an' did as she wad hae them. She says fowk sud never tell but the ill they ken o' themsel's, an' the guid they ken o' ither fowk; an' that's jist the contrar', ye ken, missie, to what fowk maistly dis dee."

A pause naturally followed, which Ginny broke.

"I don't think you told me the name of the book you were reading, Donal," she said.

"Gien ye wad sit doon a meenute, mem," returned Donal, "—here's a bonnie gowany spot—I wad read a bit till ye, an' see gien ye likit it, afore I tellt ye the name o' 't."

She dropped at once on the little gowany bed, gathered her frock about her ankles, and said,

"Sit down, Nicie. It's so kind of Donal to read something to us! I wonder what it's going to be."

She uttered everything in a deliberate, old-fashioned way, with precise articulation, and a certain manner that an English mother would have called priggish, but which was only the outcome of Scotch stiffness, her father's rebukes, and her own sense of propriety.

Donal read the ballad of Kemp Owen.

"I think—I think—I don't think I understand it," said Ginevra. "It is very dreadful, and—and—I don't know what to think. Tell me about it, Donal.—Do you know what it means, Nicie?"

"No ae glimp, missie," answered Nicie.

Donal proceeded at once to an exposition. He told them that the serpent was a lady, enchanted by a wicked witch, who, after she had changed her, twisted her three times round the tree, so that she could not undo herself, and laid the spell upon her that she should never have the shape of a woman, until a knight kissed her as often as she was twisted round the tree. Then, when the knight did come, at every kiss a coil of her body unwound itself, until, at the last kiss, she stood before him the beautiful lady she really was.

"What a good, kind, brave knight!" said Ginevra.

"But it's no true, ye ken, missie," said Nicie, anxious that she should not be misled. "It's naething but Donal's nonsense."

"Nonsense here, nonsense there!" said Donal, "I see a heap o' sense intil 't. But nonsense or no, Nicie, its nane o' my nonsense: I wuss it war. It's hun'ers o' years auld, that ballant, I s' warran'."

"It's beautiful," said Ginevra, with decision and dignity. "I hope he married the lady, and they lived happy ever after."

"I dinna ken, mem. The man 'at made the ballant, I daursay, thoucht him weel payed gien the bonny leddy said thank ye till him."

"Oh! but, Donal, that wouldn't be enough!—Would it, Nicie?"

"Weel, ye see, missie," answered Nicie, "he but gae her three kisses— that wasna sae muckle to wur (lay out) upon a body."

"But a serpent!—a serpent's mouth, Nicie!"

Here, unhappily, Donal had to rush through the burn without leave-taking, for Hornie was attempting a trespass; and the two girls, thinking it was time to go home, rose, and climbed to the house at their leisure.

The rest of the day Ginevra talked of little else than the serpent lady and the brave knight, saying now and then what a nice boy that Donal of Nicie's was. Nor was more than the gentlest hint necessary to make Nicie remark, the next morning, that perhaps, if they went down again to the Lorrie, Donal might come, and bring the book. But when they reached the bank and looked across, they saw him occupied with Gibbie. They had their heads close together over a slate, upon which now the one, now the other, seemed to be drawing. This went on and on, and they never looked up. Ginny would have gone home, and come again in the afternoon, but Nicie instantly called Donal. He sprang to his feet and came to them, followed by Gibbie. Donal crossed the burn, but Gibbie remained on the other side, and when presently Donal took his "buik o' ballants" from his pocket, and the little company seated themselves, stood with his back to them, and his eyes on the nowt. That morning they were not interrupted.

Donal read to them for a whole hour, concerning which reading, and Ginevra's reception of it, Nicie declared she could not see what for they made sic a wark aboot a wheen auld ballants, ane efter anither.— "They're no half sae bonnie as the paraphrases, Donal," she said.

After this, Ginevra went frequently with Nicie to see her mother, and learned much of the best from her. Often also they went down to the Lorrie, and had an interview with Donal, which was longer or shorter as Gibbie was there or not to release him.

Ginny's life was now far happier than it had ever been. New channels of thought and feeling were opened, new questions were started, new interests awaked; so that, instead of losing by Miss Machar's continued inability to teach her, she was learning far more than she could give her, learning it, too, with the pleasure which invariably accompanies true learning.

Little more than child as she was, Donal felt from the first the charm of her society; and she by no means received without giving, for his mental development was greatly expedited thereby. Few weeks passed before he was her humble squire, devoted to her with all the chivalry of a youth for a girl whom he supposes as much his superior in kind as she is in worldly position; his sole advantage, in his own judgment, and that which alone procured him the privilege of her society, being, that he was older, and therefore knew a little more. So potent and genial was her influence on his imagination, that, without once thinking of her as their object, he now first found himself capable of making verses—such as they were; and one day, with his book before him—it was Burns, and he had been reading the Gowan poem to Ginevra and his sister—he ventured to repeat, as if he read them from the book, the following: they halted a little, no doubt, in rhythm, neither were perfectly rimed, but for a beginning, they had promise. Gibbie, who had thrown himself down on the other bank, and lay listening, at once detected the change in the tone of his utterance, and before he ceased had concluded that he was not reading them, and that they were his own.

> *Rin, burnie! clatter;*
> *To the sea win:*
> *Gien I was a watter,*
> *Sae wad I rin.*

> *Blaw, win', caller, clean!*
> *Here an' hyne awa':*
> *Gien I was a win',*
> *Wadna I blaw!*

> *Shine, auld sun,*
> *Shine strang an' fine:*
> *Gien I was the sun's son,*
> *Herty I wad shine.*

Hardly had he ended, when Gibbie's pipes began from the opposite side of the water, and, true to time and cadence and feeling, followed with just the one air to suit the song—from which Donal, to his no small comfort, understood that one at least of his audience had received his lilt. If the poorest nature in the world responds with the tune to the mightiest master's song, he knows, if not another echo should come back, that he has uttered a true cry. But Ginevra had not received it, and being therefore of her own mind, and not of the song's, was critical. It is of the true things it does not, perhaps cannot receive, that human nature is most critical.

"That one is nonsense, Donal," she said. "Isn't it now? How could a man be a burn, or a wind, or the sun? But poets are silly. Papa says so."

In his mind Donal did not know which way to look; physically, he regarded the ground. Happily at that very moment Hornie caused a diversion, and Gibbie understood what Donal was feeling too well to make even a pretence of going after her. I must, to his praise, record the fact that, instead of wreaking his mortification upon the cow, Donal spared her several blows out of gratitude for the deliverance her misbehaviour had wrought him. He was in no haste to return to his audience. To have his first poem thus rejected was killing. She was but a child who had so unkindly criticized it, but she was the child he wanted to please; and for a few moments life itself seemed scarcely worth having. He called himself a fool, and resolved never to read another poem to a girl so long as he lived. By the time he had again walked through the burn, however, he was calm and comparatively wise, and knew what to say.

"Div ye hear yon burn efter ye gang to yer bed, mem?" he asked Genevra, as he climbed the bank, pointing a little lower down the stream to the mountain brook which there joined it.

"Always," she answered. "It runs right under my window."

"What kin' o' a din dis't mak'?" he asked again.

"It is different at different times," she answered. "It sings and chatters in summer, and growls and cries and grumbles in winter, or after rain up in Glashgar."

"Div ye think the burn's ony happier i' the summer, mem?"

"No, Donal; the burn has no life in it, and therefore can't be happier one time than another."

"Weel, mem, I wad jist like to speir what waur it is to fancy yersel' a burn, than to fancy the burn a body, ae time singin' an' chatterin', an' the neist growlin' an' grum'lin'."

"Well, but, Donal, can a man be a burn?"

"Weel, mem, no—at least no i' this warl', an' at 'is ain wull. But whan ye're lyin' hearkenin' to the burn, did ye never imagine yersel' rinnin' doon wi' 't—doon to the sea?"

"No, Donal; I always fancy myself going up the mountain where it comes from, and running about wild there in the wind, when all the time I know I'm safe and warm in bed."

"Weel, maybe that's better yet—I wadna say," answered Donal; "but jist the nicht, for a cheenge like, ye turn an' gang doon wi' 't—i' yer thouchts, I mean. Lie an' hearken he'rty till 't the nicht, whan ye're i' yer bed; hearken an' hearken till the soon' rins awa' wi' ye like, an' ye forget a' aboot yersel', an' think yersel' awa' wi' the burn, rinnin', rinnin', throu' this an' throu' that, throu' stanes an' birks an' bracken, throu' heather, an' plooed lan' an' corn, an' wuds an' gairdens, aye singin', an' aye cheengin' yer tune accordin', till it wins to the muckle roarin' sea, an' 's a' tint. An' the first nicht 'at the win' 's up an' awa', dee the same, mem, wi' the win'. Get up upo' the back o' 't, like, as gien it was yer muckle horse, an' jist ride him to the deith; an' efter that, gien ye dinna maybe jist wuss 'at ye was a burn or a blawin' win'—aither wad be a sair loss to the universe—ye wunna, I'm thinkin', be sae ready to fin' fau't wi' the chield 'at made yon bit sangy."

"Are you vexed with me, Donal?—I'm so sorry!" said Ginevra, taking the earnestness of his tone for displeasure.

"Na, na, mem. Ye're ower guid an' ower bonny," answered Donal, "to be a vex to onybody; but it wad be a vex to hear sic a cratur as you speykin' like ane o' the fules o' the warl', 'at believe i' naething but what comes in at the holes i' their heid."

Ginevra was silent. She could not quite understand Donal, but she felt she must be wrong somehow; and of this she was the more convinced when she saw the beautiful eyes of Gibbie fixed in admiration, and brimful of love, upon Donal.

The way Donal kept his vow never to read another poem of his own to a girl, was to proceed that very night to make another for the express purpose, as he lay awake in the darkness.

The last one he ever read to her in that meadow was this:

What gars ye sing, said the herd laddie,
What gars ye sing sae lood?
To tice them oot o' the yerd, laddie,
The worms, for my daily food.

An' aye he sang, an' better he sang,
An' the worms creepit in an' oot;
An' ane he tuik, an' twa he loot gang,
But still he carolled stoot.

It's no for the worms, sir, said the herd,
They comena for yer sang.
Think ye sae, sir? answered the bird,
Maybe ye're no i' the wrang.
But aye &c.

Sing ye yoong sorrow to beguile
Or to gie auld fear the flegs?
Na, quo' the mavis; it's but to wile
My wee things oot o' her eggs.
An' aye &c.

The mistress is plenty for that same gear,
Though ye sangna ear' nor late.
It's to draw the deid frae the moul' sae drear,
An' open the kirkyard gate.
An' aye &c.

Na, na; it's a better sang nor yer ain,
Though ye hae o' notes a feck,
'At wad mak auld Barebanes there sae fain
As to lift the muckle sneck!
But aye &c.

Better ye sing nor a burn i' the mune,
Nor a wave ower san' that flows,
Nor a win' wi' the glintin' stars abune,
An' aneth the roses in rows;
An' aye &c.

But I'll speir ye nae mair, sir, said the herd.
I fear what ye micht say neist.
Ye wad but won'er the mair, said the bird,
To see the thouchts i' my breist.

And aye he sang, an' better he sang,
An' the worms creepit in an' oot;
An' ane he tuik, an' twa he loot gang,
But still he carolled stoot.

I doubt whether Ginevra understood this song better than the first, but she was now more careful of criticizing; and when by degrees it dawned upon her that he was the maker of these and other verses he read, she grew half afraid of Donal, and began to regard him with big eyes; he became, from a herd-boy, an unintelligible person, therefore a wonder. For, brought thus face to face with the maker of verses, she could not help trying to think how he did the thing; and as she felt no possibility of making verses herself, it remained a mystery and an astonishment, causing a great respect for the poet to mingle with the kindness she felt towards Nicie's brother.

GEORGE MACDONALD

XXXI

Their Reward

By degrees Gibbie had come to be well known about the Mains and Glashruach. Angus's only recognition of him was a scowl in return for his smile; but, as I have said, he gave him no farther annoyance, and the tales about the beast-loon were dying out from Daurside. Jean Mavor was a special friend to him: for she knew now well enough who had been her brownie, and made him welcome as often as he showed himself with Donal. Fergus was sometimes at home; sometimes away; but he was now quite a fine gentleman, a student of theology, and only condescendingly cognizant of the existence of Donal Grant. All he said to him when he came home a master of arts, was, that he had expected better of him: he ought to be something more than herd by this time. Donal smiled and said nothing. He had just finished a little song that pleased him, and could afford to be patronized. I am afraid, however, he was not contented with that, but in his mind's eye measured Fergus from top to toe.

In the autumn, Mr. Galbraith returned to Glashruach, but did not remain long. His schemes were promising well, and his self-importance was screwed yet a little higher in consequence. But he was kinder than usual to Ginevra. Before he went he said to her that, as Mr. Machar had sunk into a condition requiring his daughter's constant attention, he would find her an English governess as soon as he reached London; meantime she must keep up her studies by herself as well as she could. Probably he forgot all about it, for the governess was not heard of at Glashruach, and things fell into their old way. There was no spiritual traffic between the father and daughter, consequently Ginevra never said anything about Donal or Gibbie, or her friendship for Nicie. He had himself to blame altogether; he had made it impossible for her to talk to him. But it was well he remained in ignorance, and so did not put a stop to the best education she could at this time of her life have been having—such as neither he nor any friend of his could have given her.

It was interrupted, however, by the arrival of the winter—a wild time in that region, fierce storm alternating with the calm of death.

After howling nights, in which it seemed as if all the polter-geister of the universe must be out on a disembodied lark, the mountains stood there in the morning solemn still, each with his white turban of snow unrumpled on his head, in the profoundest silence of blue air, as if he had never in his life passed a more thoughtful, peaceful time than the very last night of all. To such feet as Ginevra's the cottage on Glashgar was for months almost as inaccessible as if it had been in Sirius. More than once the Daur was frozen thick; for weeks every beast was an absolute prisoner to the byre, and for months was fed with straw and turnips and potatoes and oilcake. Then was the time for stories; and often in the long dark, while yet it was hours too early for bed, would Ginevra go with Nicie, who was not much of a raconteuse, to the kitchen, to get one of the other servants to tell her an old tale. For even in his own daughter and his own kitchen, the great laird could not extinguish the accursed superstition. Not a glimpse did Ginevra get all this time of Donal or of Gibbie.

At last, like one of its own flowers in its own bosom, the spring began again to wake in God's thought of his world; and the snow, like all other deaths, had to melt and run, leaving room for hope; then the summer woke smiling, as if she knew she had been asleep; and the two youths and the two maidens met yet again on Lorrie bank, with the brown water falling over the stones, the gold nuggets of the broom hanging over the water, and the young larch-wood scenting the air all up the brae side between them and the house, which the tall hedge hid from their view. The four were a year older, a year nearer trouble, and a year nearer getting out of it. Ginevra was more of a woman, Donal more of a poet, Nicie as nice and much the same, and Gibbie, if possible, more a foundling of the universe than ever. He was growing steadily, and showed such freedom and ease, and his motions were all so rapid and direct, that it was plain at a glance the beauty of his countenance was in no manner or measure associated with weakness. The mountain was a grand nursery for him, and the result, both physical and spiritual, corresponded. Janet, who, better than anyone else, knew what was in the mind of the boy, revered him as much as he revered her; the first impression he made upon her had never worn off—had only changed its colour a little. More even than a knowledge of the truth, is a readiness to receive it; and Janet saw from the first that Gibbie's ignorance at its worst was but room vacant for the truth: when it came it found bolt nor bar on door or window, but had immediate entrance. The secret of this power of reception was, that to see a truth and to do it was one and the same thing with Gibbie. To know and not do would have seemed to him an impossibility, as it is in vital idea a monstrosity.

This unity of vision and action was the main cause also of a certain daring simplicity in the exercise of the imagination, which so far from misleading him reacted only in obedience—which is the truth of the will—the truth, therefore, of the whole being. He did not do the less well for his sheep, that he fancied they knew when Jesus Christ was on the mountain, and always at such times both fed better and were more frolicsome. He thought Oscar knew it also, and interpreted a certain look of the dog by the supposition that he had caught a sign of the bodily presence of his Maker. The direction in which his imagination ran forward, was always that in which his reason pointed; and so long as Gibbie's fancies were bud-blooms upon his obedience, his imagination could not be otherwise than in harmony with his reason. Imagination is a poor root, but a worthy blossom, and in a nature like Gibbie's its flowers cannot fail to be lovely. For no outcome of a man's nature is so like himself as his imaginations, except it be his fancies, indeed. Perhaps his imaginations show what he is meant to be, his fancies what he is making of himself.

In the summer, Mr. Galbraith, all unannounced, reappeared at Glashruach, but so changed that, startled at the sight of him, Ginevra stopped midway in her advance to greet him. The long thin man was now haggard and worn; he looked sourer too, and more suspicious—either that experience had made him so, or that he was less equal to the veiling of his feelings in dignified indifference. He was annoyed that his daughter should recognize an alteration in him, and, turning away, leaned his head on the hand whose arm was already supported by the mantelpiece, and took no further notice of her presence; but perhaps conscience also had something to do with this behaviour. Ginevra knew from experience that the sight of tears would enrage him, and with all her might repressed those she felt beginning to rise. She went up to him timidly, and took the hand that hung by his side. He did not repel her—that is, he did not push her away, or even withdraw his hand, but he left it hanging lifeless, and returned with it no pressure upon hers—which was much worse.

"Is anything the matter, papa?" she asked with trembling voice.

"I am not aware that I have been in the habit of communicating with you on the subject of my affairs," he answered; "nor am I likely to begin to do so, where my return after so long an absence seems to give so little satisfaction."

"Oh, papa! I was frightened to see you looking so ill."

"Such a remark upon my personal appearance is but a poor recognition of my labours for your benefit, I venture to think, Jenny," he said.

He was at the moment contemplating, as a necessity, the sale of every foot of the property her mother had brought him. Nothing less would serve to keep up his credit, and gain time to disguise more than one failing scheme. Everything had of late been going so badly, that he had lost a good deal of his confidence and self-satisfaction; but he had gained no humility instead. It had not dawned upon him yet that he was not unfortunate, but unworthy. The gain of such a conviction is to a man enough to outweigh infinitely any loss that even his unworthiness can have caused him; for it involves some perception of the worthiness of the truth, and makes way for the utter consolation which the birth of that truth in himself will bring. As yet Mr. Galbraith was but overwhelmed with care for a self which, so far as he had to do with the making of it, was of small value indeed, although in the possibility, which is the birthright of every creature, it was, not less than that of the wretchedest of dog-licked Lazaruses, of a value by himself unsuspected and inappreciable. That he should behave so cruelly to his one child, was not unnatural to that self with which he was so much occupied: failure had weakened that command of behaviour which so frequently gains the credit belonging only to justice and kindness, and a temper which never was good, but always feeling the chain, was ready at once to show its ugly teeth. He was a proud man, whose pride was always catching cold from his heart. He might have lived a hundred years in the same house with a child that was not his own, without feeling for her a single movement of affection.

The servants found more change in him than Ginevra did; his relations with them, if not better conceived than his paternal ones, had been less evidently defective. Now he found fault with every one, so that even Joseph dared hardly open his mouth, and said he must give warning. The day after his arrival, having spent the morning with Angus walking over certain fields, much desired, he knew, of a neighbouring proprietor, inwardly calculating the utmost he could venture to ask for them with a chance of selling, he scolded Ginevra severely on his return because she had not had lunch, but had waited for him; whereas a little reflection might have shown him she dared not take it without him. Naturally, therefore, she could not now eat, because of a certain sensation in her throat. The instant he saw she was not eating, he ordered her out of the room: he would have no such airs in his family! By the end of the week—he arrived on the Tuesday—such a sense of estrangement possessed Ginevra, that she would turn on the stair and run up again, if she heard her father's voice below. Her aversion to meeting him, he became aware of, and felt relieved in regard to the wrong he was doing his wife, by reflecting upon her daughter's behaviour towards him; for he had a strong constitutional sense of what was fair, and a conscience disobeyed becomes a cancer.

In this evil mood he received from some one—all his life Donal believed it was Fergus—a hint concerning the relations between his daughter and his tenant's herd-boy. To describe his feelings at the bare fact that such a hint was possible, would be more labour than the result would repay.—What! his own flesh and blood, the heiress of Glashruach, derive pleasure from the boorish talk of such a companion! It could not be true, when the mere thought, without the belief of it, filled him with such indignation! He was overwhelmed with a righteous disgust. He did himself the justice of making himself certain before he took measures; but he never thought of doing them the justice of acquainting himself first with the nature of the intercourse they held. But it mattered little; for he would have found nothing in that to give him satisfaction, even if the thing itself had not been outrageous. He watched and waited, and more than once pretended to go from home: at last one morning, from the larch-wood, he saw the unnatural girl seated with her maid on the bank of the river, the cow-herd reading to them, and on the other side the dumb idiot lying listening. He was almost beside himself—with what, I can hardly define. In a loud voice of bare command he called to her to come to him. With a glance of terror at Nicie she rose, and they went up through the larches together.

I will not spend my labour upon a reproduction of the verbal torrent of wrath, wounded dignity, disgust, and contempt, with which the father assailed his shrinking, delicate, honest-minded woman-child. For Nicie, he dismissed her on the spot. Not another night would he endure her in the house, after her abominable breach of confidence! She had to depart without even a good-bye from Ginevra, and went home weeping in great dread of what her mother would say.

"Lassie," said Janet, when she heard her story, "gien onybody be to blame it's mysel'; for ye loot me ken ye gaed whiles wi' yer bonnie missie to hae a news wi' Donal, an' I saw an' see noucht 'at's wrang intill't. But the fowk o' this warl' has ither w'ys o' jeedgin' o' things, an' I maun bethink mysel' what lesson o' the serpent's wisdom I hae to learn frae 't. Ye're walcome hame, my bonnie lass. Ye ken I aye keep the wee closet ready for ony o' ye 'at micht come ohn expeckit."

Nicie, however, had not long to occupy the closet, for those of her breed were in demand in the country.

XXXII

Prologue

Ever since he became a dweller in the air of Glashgar, Gibbie, mindful of his first visit thereto, and of his grand experience on that occasion, had been in the habit, as often as he saw reason to expect a thunder-storm, and his duties would permit, of ascending the mountain, and there on the crest of the granite peak, awaiting the arrival of the tumult. Everything antagonistic in the boy, everything that could naturally find relief, or pleasure, or simple outcome, in resistance or contention, debarred as it was by the exuberance of his loving kindness from obtaining satisfaction or alleviation in strife with his fellows, found it wherever he could encounter the forces of Nature, in personal wrestle with them where possible, and always in wildest sympathy with any uproar of the elements. The absence of personality in them allowed the co-existence of sympathy and antagonism in respect of them. Except those truths awaking delight at once calm and profound, of which so few know the power, and the direct influence of human relation, Gibbie's emotional joy was more stirred by storm than by anything else; and with all forms of it he was so familiar that, young as he was, he had unconsciously begun to generalize on its phases.

Towards the evening of a wondrously fine day in the beginning of August—a perfect day of summer in her matronly beauty, it began to rain. All the next day the slopes and stairs of Glashgar were alternately glowing in sunshine, and swept with heavy showers, driven slanting in strong gusts of wind from the northwest. How often he was wet through and dried again that day, Gibbie could not have told. He wore so little that either took but a few moments, and he was always ready for a change. The wind and the rain together were cold, but that only served to let the sunshine deeper into him when it returned.

In the afternoon there was less sun, more rain, and more wind; and at last the sun seemed to give it up; the wind grew to a hurricane, and the rain strove with it which should inhabit the space. The whole upper region was like a huge mortar, in which the wind was the pestle, and, with innumerable gyres, vainly ground at the rain. Gibbie drove his sheep to the refuge of a pen on the lower slope of a valley that ran at right angles to the wind, where they were sheltered by a rock behind, forming one side of the enclosure, and dykes of loose stones, forming the others, at a height there was no tradition of any flood having reached. He then went home, and having told Robert what he had done, and had his supper, set out in the early-failing light, to ascend the mountain. A great thunder-storm was at hand, and was calling him. It was almost dark before he reached the top, but he knew the surface of Glashgar nearly as well as the floor of the cottage. Just as he had fought his way to the crest of the peak in the face of one of the fiercest of the blasts abroad that night, a sudden rush of fire made the heavens like the smoke-filled vault of an oven, and at once the thunder followed, in a succession of single sharp explosions without any roll between. The mountain shook with the windy shocks, but the first of the thunder-storm was the worst, and it soon passed. The wind and the rain continued, and the darkness was filled with the rush of the water everywhere wildly tearing down the sides of the mountain. Thus heaven and earth held communication in torrents all the night. Down the steeps of the limpid air they ran to the hard sides of the hills, where at once, as if they were no longer at home, and did not like the change, they began to work mischief. To the ears and heart of Gibbie their noises were a mass of broken music. Every spring and autumn the floods came, and he knew them, and they were welcome to him in their seasons.

It required some care to find his way down through the darkness and the waters to the cottage, but as he was neither in fear nor in haste, he was in little danger, and his hands and feet could pick out the path where his eyes were useless. When at length he reached his bed, it was not for a long time to sleep, but to lie awake and listen to the raging of the wind all about and above and below the cottage, and the rushing of the streams down past it on every side. To his imagination it was as if he lay in the very bed of the channel by which the waters of heaven were shooting to the valleys of the earth; and when he fell asleep at last, his dream was of the rush of the river of the water of life from under the throne of God; and he saw men drink thereof, and everyone as he drank straightway knew that he was one with the Father, and one with every child of his throughout the infinite universe.

He woke, and what remained of his dream was love in his heart, and in his ears the sound of many waters. It was morning. He rose, and, dressing hastily, opened the door. What a picture of grey storm rose outspread before him! The wind fiercely invaded the cottage, thick charged with water-drops, and stepping out he shut the door in haste, lest it should blow upon the old people in bed and wake them. He could not see far on any side, for the rain that fell, and the mist and steam that rose, upon which the wind seemed to have no power; but wherever he did see, there water was running down. Up the mountain he went—he could hardly have told why. Once, for a moment, as he ascended, the veil of the vapour either rose, or was torn asunder, and he saw the great wet gleam of the world below. By the time he reached the top, it was as light as it was all the day; but it was with a dull yellow glare, as if the sun were obscured by the smoke and vaporous fumes of a burning world which the rain had been sent to quench. It was a wild, hopeless scene—as if God had turned his face away from the world, and all Nature was therefore drowned in tears—no Rachel weeping for her children, but the whole creation crying for the Father, and refusing to be comforted. Gibbie stood gazing and thinking. Did God like to look at the storm he made? If Jesus did, would he have left it all and gone to sleep, when the wind and waves were howling, and flinging the boat about like a toy between them? He must have been tired, surely! With what? Then first Gibbie saw that perhaps it tired Jesus to heal people; that every time what cured man or woman was life that went out of him, and that he missed it, perhaps—not from his heart, but from his body; and if it were so, then it was no wonder if he slept in the midst of a right splendid storm. And upon that Gibbie remembered what St. Matthew says just before he tells about the storm—that "he cast out the spirits with his word, and healed all that were sick, that it might be fulfilled which was spoken by Esaias the prophet, saying, Himself took our infirmities, and bare our sicknesses."

That moment it seemed as if he must be himself in some wave-tossed boat, and not upon a mountain of stone, for Glashgar gave a great heave under him, then rocked and shook from side to side a little, and settled down so still and steady, that motion and the mountain seemed again two ideas that never could be present together in any mind. The next instant came an explosion, followed by a frightful roaring and hurling, as of mingled water and stones; and on the side of the mountain beneath him he saw what, through the mist, looked like a cloud of smoke or dust rising to a height. He darted towards it. As he drew nearer, the cloud seemed to condense, and presently he saw plainly enough that it was a great column of water shooting up and out from the face of the mountain. It sank and rose again, with the alternation of a huge pulse:

the mountain was cracked, and through the crack, with every throb of its heart, the life-blood of the great hull of the world seemed beating out. Already it had scattered masses of gravel on all sides, and down the hill a river was shooting in sheer cataract, raving and tearing, and carrying stones and rocks with it like foam. Still and still it pulsed and rushed and ran, born, like another Xanthus, a river full-grown, from the heart of the mountain.

Suddenly Gibbie, in the midst of his astonishment and awful delight, noted the path of the new stream, and from his knowledge of the face of the mountain, perceived that its course was direct for the cottage. Down the hill he shot after it, as if it were a wild beast that his fault had freed from its cage. He was not terrified. One believing like him in the perfect Love and perfect Will of a Father of men, as the fact of facts, fears nothing. Fear is faithlessness. But there is so little that is worthy the name of faith, that such a confidence will appear to most not merely incredible but heartless. The Lord himself seems not to have been very hopeful about us, for he said, When the Son of man cometh, shall he find faith on the earth? A perfect faith would lift us absolutely above fear. It is in the cracks, crannies, and gulfy faults of our belief, the gaps that are not faith, that the snow of apprehension settles, and the ice of unkindness forms.

The torrent had already worn for itself a channel: what earth there was, it had swept clean away to the rock, and the loose stones it had thrown up aside, or hurled with it in its headlong course. But as Gibbie bounded along, following it with a speed almost equal to its own, he was checked in the midst of his hearty haste by the sight, a few yards away, of another like terror—another torrent issuing from the side of the hill, and rushing to swell the valley stream. Another and another he saw, with growing wonder, as he ran; before he reached home he passed some six or eight, and had begun to think whether a second deluge of the whole world might not be at hand, commencing this time with Scotland. Two of them joined the one he was following, and he had to cross them as he could; the others he saw near and farther off—one foaming deliverance after another, issuing from the entrails of the mountain, like imprisoned demons, that, broken from their bonds, ran to ravage the world with the accumulated hate of dreariest centuries. Now and then a huge boulder, loosened from its bed by the trail of this or that watery serpent, would go rolling, leaping, bounding down the hill before him, and just in time he escaped one that came springing after him as if it were a living thing that wanted to devour him. Nor was Glashgar the only torrent-bearing mountain of Gormgarnet that day, though the rain prevented Gibbie from seeing anything of what the rest of them were doing. The fountains of the great deep were broken up, and seemed rushing together to drown the world. And still the wind was raging, and the rain tumbling to the earth, rather in sheets than in streams.

Gibbie at length forsook the bank of the new torrent to take the nearest way home, and soon reached the point whence first, returning in that direction, he always looked to see the cottage. For a moment he was utterly bewildered: no cottage was to be seen. From the top of the rock against which it was built, shot the whole mass of the water he had been pursuing, now dark with stones and gravel, now grey with foam, or glassy in the lurid light.

"O Jesus Christ!" he cried, and darted to the place. When he came near, to his amazement there stood the little house unharmed, the very centre of the cataract! For a few yards on the top of the rock, the torrent had a nearly horizontal channel, along which it rushed with unabated speed to the edge, and thence shot clean over the cottage, dropping only a dribble of rain on the roof from the underside of its half-arch. The garden ground was gone, swept clean from the bare rock, which made a fine smooth shoot for the water a long distance in front. He darted through the drizzle and spray, reached the door, and lifted the hatch. The same moment he heard Janet's voice in joyful greeting.

"Noo, noo! come awa', laddie," she said. "Wha wad hae thoucht we wad hae to lea' the rock to win oot o' the water? We're but waitin' you to gang.—Come, Robert, we'll awa' doon the hill."

She stood in the middle of the room in her best gown, as if she had been going to church, her Bible, a good-sized octavo, under her arm, with a white handkerchief folded round it, and her umbrella in her hand.

"He that believeth shall not make haste," she said, "but he maunna tempt the Lord, aither. Drink that milk, Gibbie, an' pit a bannock i' yer pooch, an' come awa'."

Robert rose from the edge of the bed, staff in hand, ready too. He also was in his Sunday clothes. Oscar, who could make no change of attire, but was always ready, and had been standing looking up in his face for the last ten minutes, wagged his tail when he saw him rise, and got out of his way. On the table were the remains of their breakfast of oat-cake and milk—the fire Janet had left on the hearth was a spongy mass of peat, as wet as the winter before it was dug from the bog, so they had had no porridge. The water kept coming in splashes down the lum, the hillocks of the floor were slimy, and in the hollows little lakes were gathering: the lowest film of the torrent-water ran down the rock behind, and making its way between rock and roof, threatened soon to render the place uninhabitable.

"What's the eese o' lo'denin' yersel' wi' the umbrell?" said Robert. "Ye'll get it a' drookit (drenched)."

"Ow, I'll jist tak it," replied Janet, with a laugh in acknowledgment of her husband's fun; "it'll haud the rain ohn blin't me."

"That's gien ye be able to haud it up. I doobt the win' 'll be ower sair upo' 't. I'm thinkin', though, it'll be mair to haud yer beuk dry!"

Janet smiled and made no denial.

"Noo, Gibbie," she said, "ye gang an' lowse Crummie. But ye'll hae to lead her. She winna be to caw in sic a win' 's this, an' no plain ro'd afore her."

"Whaur div ye think o' gauin'?" asked Robert, who, satisfied as usual with whatever might be in his wife's mind, had not till this moment thought of asking her where she meant to take refuge.

"Ow, we'll jist mak for the Mains, gien ye be agreeable, Robert," she answered. "It's there we belang till, an' in wather like this naebody wad refeese bield till a beggar, no to say Mistress Jean till her ain fowk."

With that she led the way to the door and opened it.

"His v'ice was like the soon' o' mony watters," she said to herself softly, as the liquid thunder of the torrent came in the louder.

Gibbie shot round the corner to the byre, whence through all the roar, every now and then they had heard the cavernous mooing of Crummie, piteous and low. He found a stream a foot deep running between her fore and hind legs, and did not wonder that she wanted to be on the move. Speedily he loosed her, and fastening the chain-tether to her halter, led her out. She was terrified at sight of the falling water, and they had some trouble in getting her through behind it, but presently after, she was making the descent as carefully and successfully as any of them.

It was a heavy undertaking for the two old folk to walk all the way to the Mains, and in such a state of the elements; but where there is no choice, we do well to make no difficulty. Janet was half troubled that her mountain, and her foundation on the rock, should have failed

GEORGE MACDONALD

her; but consoled herself that they were but shadows of heavenly things and figures of the true; and that a mountain or a rock was in itself no more to be trusted than a horse or a prince or the legs of a man. Robert plodded on in contented silence, and Gibbie was in great glee, singing, after his fashion, all the way, though now and then half-choked by the fierceness of the wind round some corner of rock, filled with rain-drops that stung like hailstones.

By and by Janet stopped and began looking about her. This naturally seemed to her husband rather odd in the circumstances.

"What are ye efter, Janet?" he said, shouting through the wind from a few yards off, by no means sorry to stand for a moment, although any recovering of his breath seemed almost hopeless in such a tempest.

"I want to lay my umbrell in safity," answered Janet, "—gien I cud but perceive a shuitable spot. Ye was richt, Robert, it's mair w'alth nor I can get the guid o'."

"Hoots! fling't frae ye, than, lass," he returned. "Is this a day to be thinkin' o' warl' 's gear?"

"What for no, Robert?" she rejoined. "Ae day's as guid's anither for thinkin' aboot onything the richt gait."

"What!" retorted Robert, "—whan we hae ta'en oor lives in oor han', an' can no more than houp we may cairry them throu' safe!"

"What's that 'at ye ca' oor lives, Robert? The Maister never made muckle o' the savin' o' sic like's them. It seems to me they're naething but a kin' o' warl' 's gear themsel's."

"An' yet," argued Robert, "ye'll tak thoucht aboot an auld umbrell? Whaur's yer consistency, lass?"

"Gien I war tribled aboot my life," said Janet, "I cud ill spare thoucht for an auld umbrell. But they baith trible me sae little, 'at I may jist as weel luik efter them baith. It's auld an' casten an' bow-ribbit, it's true, but it wad ill become me to drap it wi'oot a thoucht, whan him 'at could mak haill loaves, said, 'Gether up the fragments 'at naething be lost.'— Na," she continued, still looking about her, "I maun jist dee my duty by the auld umbrell; syne come o' 't 'at likes, I carena."

So saying she walked to the lee side of a rock, and laid the umbrella close under it, then a few large stones upon it to keep it down.

I may add, that the same umbrella, recovered, and with two new ribs, served Janet to the day of her death.

XXXIII

The Mains

They reached at length the valley road. The water that ran in the bottom was the Lorrie. Three days ago it was a lively little stream, winding and changing within its grassy banks—here resting silent in a deep pool, there running and singing over its pebbles. Now it had filled and far overflowed its banks, and was a swift river. It had not yet, so far up the valley, encroached on the road; but the torrents on the mountain had already in places much injured it, and with considerable difficulty they crossed some of the new-made gullies. When they approached the bridge, however, by which they must cross the Lorrie to reach the Mains, their worst trouble lay before them. For the enemy, with whose reinforcements they had all the time been descending, showed himself ever in greater strength the farther they advanced; and here the road was flooded for a long way on both sides of the bridge. There was therefore a good deal of wading to be done; but the road was an embankment, there was little current, and in safety at last they ascended the rising ground on which the farm-building stood. When they reached the yard, they sent Gibbie to find shelter for Crummie, and themselves went up to the house.

"The Lord preserve 's!" cried Jean Mavor, with uplifted hands, when she saw them enter the kitchen.

"He'll dee that, mem," returned Janet, with a smile.

"But what can he dee? Gien ye be droont oot o' the hills, what's to come o' hiz i' the how? I wad ken that!" said Jean.

"The watter's no up to yer door yet," remarked Janet.

"God forbid!" retorted Jean, as if the very mention of such a state of things was too dreadful to be polite. "—But, eh, ye're weet!"

"Weet's no the word," said Robert, trying to laugh, but failing from sheer exhaustion, and the beginnings of an asthmatic attack.

The farmer, hearing their voices, came into the kitchen—a middle-sized and middle-aged, rather coarse-looking man, with keen eyes, who took snuff amazingly. His manner was free, with a touch of satire. He was proud of driving a hard bargain, but was thoroughly hospitable. He had little respect for person or thing, but showed an occasional touch of tenderness.

"Hoot, Rob!" he said roughly as he entered, "I thoucht ye had mair sense! What's broucht ye here at sic a time?"

But as he spoke he held out his snuff-box to the old man.

"Fell needcessity, sir," answered Robert, taking a good pinch.

"Necessity!" retorted the farmer. "Was ye oot o' meal?"

"Oot o' dry meal, I doobt, by this time, sir," replied Robert.

"Hoots! I wuss we war a' in like necessity—weel up upo' the hill i'stead o' doon here upo' the haugh (river-meadow). It's jist clean ridic'lous. Ye sud hae kenned better at your age, Rob. Ye sud hae thoucht twise, man."

"'Deed, sir," answered Robert, quietly finishing his pinch of snuff, "there was sma' need, an' less time to think, an' Glashgar bursten, an' the watter comin' ower the tap o' the bit hoosie as gien 'twar a muckle owershot wheel, an' no a place for fowk to bide in. Ye dinna think Janet an' me wad be twa sic auld fules as pit on oor Sunday claes to sweem in, gien we thoucht to see things as we left them whan we gaed back! Ye see, sir, though the hoose be fun't upo' a rock, it's maist biggit o' fells, an' the foundation's a' I luik even to see o' 't again. Whan the force o' the watter grows less, it'll come down upo' the riggin' wi' the haill weicht o' 't."

"Ay!" said Janet, in a low voice, "the live stanes maun come to the live rock to bigg the hoose 'at'll stan."

"What think ye, Maister Fergus, you 'at's gauin' to be a minister?" said Robert, referring to his wife's words, as the young man looked in at the door of the kitchen.

"Lat him be," interposed his father, blowing his nose with unnecessary violence; "setna him preachin' afore's time. Fess the whusky, Fergus, an' gie auld Robert a dram. Haith! gien the watter be rinnin' ower the tap o' yer hoose, man, it was time to flit. Fess twa or three glaisses, Fergus; we hae a' need o' something 'at's no watter. It's perfeckly ridic'lous!"

Having taken a little of the whisky, the old people went to change their clothes for some Jean had provided, and in the mean time she made up her fire, and prepared some breakfast for them.

"An' whaur's yer dummie?" she asked, as they re-entered the kitchen.

"He had puir Crummie to luik efter," answered Janet; "but he micht hae been in or this time."

"He'll be wi' Donal i' the byre, nae doobt," said Jean: "he's aye some shy o' comin' in wantin' an inveet." She went to the door, and called with a loud voice across the yard, through the wind and the clashing torrents, "Donal, sen' Dummie in till's brakfast."

"He's awa' till's sheep," cried Donal in reply.

"Preserve's!—the cratur 'll be lost!" said Jean.

"Less likly nor ony man aboot the place," bawled Donal, half angry with his mistress for calling his friend dummie. "Gibbie kens better what he's aboot nor ony twa 'at thinks him a fule 'cause he canna lat oot sic stuff an' nonsense as they canna haud in."

Jean went back to the kitchen, only half reassured concerning her brownie, and far from contented with his absence. But she was glad to find that neither Janet nor Robert appeared alarmed at the news.

"I wuss the cratur had had some brakfast," she said.

"He has a piece in 's pooch," answered Janet. "He's no oonprovidit wi' what can be made mair o'."

"I dinna richtly un'erstan' ye there," said Jean.

"Ye canna hae failt to remark, mem," answered Janet, "'at whan the Maister set himsel' to feed the hungerin' thoosan's, he teuk intil's han' what there was, an' vroucht upo' that to mak mair o' 't. I hae wussed sometimes 'at the laddie wi' the five barley loaves an' the twa sma' fishes, hadna been there that day. I wad fain ken hoo the Maister wad hae managed wantin' onything to begin upo'. As it was, he aye hang what he did upo' something his Father had dune afore him."

"Hoots!" returned Jean, who looked upon Janet as a lover of conundrums, "ye're aye warstlin' wi' run k-nots an' teuch moo'fu's."

"Ow na, no aye," answered Janet; "—only whiles, whan the speerit o' speirin' gets the upper han' o' me for a sizon."

"I doobt that same speerit 'll lead ye far frae the still watters some day, Janet," said Jean, stirring the porridge vehemently.

"Ow, I think not," answered Janet very calmly. "Whan the Maister says—what's that to thee?—I tak care he hasna to say't twise, but jist get up an' follow him."

This was beyond Jean, but she held her peace, for, though she feared for Janet's orthodoxy, and had a strong opinion of the superiority of her own common sense—in which, as in the case of all who pride themselves in the same, there was a good deal more of the common than of the sense—she had the deepest conviction of Janet's goodness, and regarded her as a sort of heaven-favoured idiot, whose utterances were somewhat privileged. Janet, for her part, looked upon Jean as "an honest wuman, wha 'll get a heap o' licht some day."

When they had eaten their breakfast, Robert took his pipe to the barn, saying there was not much danger of fire that day; Janet washed up the dishes, and sat down to her Book; and Jean went out and in, attending to many things.

Mean time the rain fell, the wind blew, the water rose. Little could be done beyond feeding the animals, threshing a little corn in the barn, and twisting straw ropes for the thatch of the ricks of the coming harvest—if indeed there was a harvest on the road, for, as the day went on, it seemed almost to grow doubtful whether any ropes would be wanted; while already not a few of last year's ricks, from farther up the country, were floating past the Mains, down the Daur to the sea. The sight was a dreadful one—had an air of the day of judgment about it to farmers' eyes. From the Mains, to right and left beyond the rising ground on which the farm buildings stood, everywhere as far as the bases of the hills, instead of fields was water, yellow brown, here in still expanse or slow progress, there sweeping along in fierce current. The quieter parts of it were dotted with trees, divided by hedges, shaded with ears of corn; upon the swifter parts floated objects of all kinds.

Mr. Duff went wandering restlessly from one spot to another, finding nothing to do. In the gloaming, which fell the sooner that a rain-blanket miles thick wrapt the earth up from the sun, he came across from the barn, and, entering the kitchen, dropped, weary with hopelessness, on a chair.

"I can weel un'erstan'," he said, "what for the Lord sud set doon Bony an' set up Louy, but what for he sud gar corn grow, an' syne sen' a spate to sweem awa' wi' 't, that's mair nor mortal man can see the sense o'.—Haud yer tongue, Janet. I'm no sayin' there's onything wrang; I'm sayin' naething but the sair trowth, 'at I canna see the what-for o' 't. I canna see the guid o' 't till onybody. A'thing's on the ro'd to the German Ocean. The lan''s jist miltin' awa' intill the sea!"

Janet sat silent, knitting hard at a stocking she had got hold of, that Jean had begun for her brother. She knew argument concerning the uses of adversity was vain with a man who knew of no life but that which consisted in eating and drinking, sleeping and rising, working and getting on in the world: as to such things existing only that they may subserve a real life, he was almost as ignorant, notwithstanding he was an elder of the church, as any heathen.

From being nearly in the centre of its own land, the farm-steading of the Mains was at a considerable distance from any other; but there were two or three cottages upon the land, and as the evening drew on, another aged pair, who lived in one only a few hundred yards from the house, made their appearance, and were soon followed by the wife of the foreman with her children, who lived farther off. Quickly the night closed in, and Gibbie was not come. Robert was growing very uneasy; Janet kept comforting and reassuring him.

"There's ae thing," said the old man: "Oscar's wi' 'im."

"Ay," responded Janet, unwilling, in the hearing of others, to say a word that might seem to savour of rebuke to her husband, yet pained that he should go to the dog for comfort—"Ay; he's a well-made animal, Oscar! There's been a fowth o' sheep-care pitten intil 'im. Ye see him 'at made 'im, bein' a shepherd himsel', kens what's wantit o' the dog."— None but her husband understood what lay behind the words.

"Oscar's no wi' im," said Donal. "The dog cam to me i' the byre, lang efter Gibbie was awa', greitin' like, an' luikin' for 'im."

Robert gave a great sigh, but said nothing.

Janet did not sleep a wink that night: she had so many to pray for. Not Gibbie only, but every one of her family was in perils of waters, all being employed along the valley of the Daur. It was not, she said, confessing to her husband her sleeplessness, that she was afraid. She was only "keepin' them company, an' haudin' the yett open," she said. The latter phrase was her picture-periphrase for praying. She never said she prayed; she held the gate open. The wonder is but small that Donal should have turned out a poet.

The dawn appeared—but the farm had vanished. Not even heads of growing corn were anywhere more to be seen. The loss would be severe, and John Duff's heart sank within him. The sheep which had been in the mown clover-field that sloped to the burn, were now all in the corn-yard, and the water was there with them. If the rise did not soon cease, every rick would be afloat. There was little current, however, and not half the danger there would have been had the houses stood a few hundred yards in any direction from where they were.

"Tak yer brakfast, John," said his sister.

"Lat them tak 'at hungers," he answered.

"Tak, or ye'll no hae the wut to save," said Jean.

Thereupon he fell to, and ate, if not with appetite, then with a will that was wondrous.

The flood still grew, and still the rain poured, and Gibbie did not come. Indeed no one any longer expected him, whatever might have become of him: except by boat the Mains was inaccessible now, they thought. Soon after breakfast, notwithstanding, a strange woman came to the door.

Jean, who opened it to her knock, stood and stared speechless. It was a greyhaired woman, with a more disreputable look than her weather-flouted condition would account for.

"Gran' wither for the deuks!" she said.

"Whaur come ye frae?" returned Jean, who did not relish the freedom of her address.

"Frae ower by," she answered.

"An' hoo wan ye here?"

"Upo' my twa legs."

Jean looked this way and that over the watery waste, and again stared at the woman in growing bewilderment.—They came afterwards to the conclusion that she had arrived, probably half-drunk, the night before, and passed it in one of the outhouses.

"Yer legs maun be langer nor they luik than, wuman," said Jean, glancing at the lower part of the stranger's person.

The woman only laughed—a laugh without any laughter in it.

"What's yer wull, noo 'at ye are here?" continued Jean with severity. "Ye camna to the Mains to tell them there what kin' o' wather it wis!"

"I cam whaur I cud win," answered the woman; "an' for my wull, that's naething to naebody noo—it's no as it was ance—though, gien I cud get it, there micht be mair nor me the better for't. An' sae as ye wad gang the len'th o' a glaiss o' whusky—"

"Ye s' get nae whusky here," interrupted Jean, with determination.

The woman gave a sigh, and half turned away as if she would depart. But however she might have come, it was plainly impossible she should depart and live.

"Wuman," said Jean, "ken an' I care naething aboot ye, an' mair, I dinna like ye, nor the luik o' ye; and gien 't war a fine simmer nicht 'at a body cud lie thereoot, or gang the farther, I wad steek the door i' yer face; but that I daurna dee the day again' my neebour's soo; sae ye can come in an' sit doon' an', my min' spoken, ye s' get what'll haud the life i' ye, an' a puckle strae i' the barn. Only ye maun jist hae a quaiet sough, for the gudeman disna like tramps."

"Tramps here, tramps there!" exclaimed the woman, starting into high displeasure; "I wad hae ye ken I'm an honest wuman, an' no tramp!"

"Ye sudna luik sae like ane than," said Jean coolly. "But come yer wa's in, an' I s' say naething sae lang as ye behave."

The woman followed her, took the seat pointed out to her by the fire, and sullenly ate, without a word of thanks, the cakes and milk handed her, but seemed to grow better tempered as she ate, though her black eyes glowed at the food with something of disgust and more of contempt: she would rather have had a gill of whisky than all the milk on the Mains. On the other side of the fire sat Janet, knitting away busily, with a look of ease and leisure. She said nothing, but now and then cast a kindly glance out of her grey eyes at the woman: there was an air of the lost sheep about the stranger, which, in whomsoever she might see it, always drew her affection. "She maun be ane o' them the Maister cam' to ca'," she said to herself. But she was careful to suggest no approach, for she knew the sheep that has left the flock has grown wild, and is more suspicious and easily startled than one in the midst of its brethren.

With the first of the light, some of the men on the farm had set out to look for Gibbie, well knowing it would be a hard matter to touch Glashgar. About nine they returned, having found it impossible. One of them, caught in a current and swept into a hole, had barely escaped with his life. But they were unanimous that the dummie was better off in any cave on Glashgar than he would be in the best bed-room at the Mains, if things went on as they threatened.

Robert had kept on going to the barn, and back again to the kitchen, all the morning, consumed with anxiety about the son of his old age; but the barn began to be flooded, and he had to limit his prayer-walk to the space between the door of the house and the chair where Janet sat—knitting busily, and praying with countenance untroubled, amidst the rush of the seaward torrents, the mad howling and screeching of the wind, and the lowing of the imprisoned cattle.

"O Lord," she said in her great trusting heart, "gien my bonny man be droonin' i' the watter, or deein' o' cauld on the hill-side, haud 's han'. Binna far frae him, O Lord; dinna lat him be fleyt."

To Janet, what we call life and death were comparatively small matters, but she was very tender over suffering and fear. She did not pray half so much for Gibbie's life as for the presence with him of him who is at the deathbed of every sparrow. She went on waiting, and refused to be troubled. True, she was not his bodily mother, but she loved him far better than the mother who, in such a dread for her child, would have been mad with terror. The difference was, that Janet loved up as well as down, loved down so widely, so intensely, because the Lord of life, who gives his own to us, was more to her than any child can be to any mother, and she knew he could not forsake her Gibbie, and that his presence was

more and better than life. She was unnatural, was she?—inhuman?—
Yes, if there be no such heart and source of humanity as she believed
in; if there be, then such calmness and courage and content as hers are
the mere human and natural condition to be hungered after by every
aspiring soul. Not until such condition is mine shall I be able to regard
life as a godlike gift, except in the hope that it is drawing nigh. Let him
who understands, understand better; let him not say the good is less
than perfect, or excuse his supineness and spiritual sloth by saying to
himself that a man can go too far in his search after the divine, can sell
too much of what he has to buy the field of the treasure. Either there is
no Christ of God, or my all is his.

Robert seemed at length to have ceased his caged wandering. For a
quarter of an hour he had been sitting with his face buried in his hands.
Janet rose, went softly to him, and said in a whisper:

"Is Gibbie waur aff, Robert, i' this watter upo' Glashgar, nor the
dissiples i' the boat upo' yon loch o' Galilee, an' the Maister no come to
them? Robert, my ain man! dinna gar the Maister say to you, O ye o' little
faith! Wharfor did ye doobt? Tak hert, man; the Maister wadna hae his
men be cooards."

"Ye're richt, Janet; ye're aye richt," answered Robert, and rose.

She followed him into the passage.

"Whaur are ye gauin', Robert?" she said.

"I wuss I cud tell ye," he answered. "I'm jist hungerin' to be my lane.
I wuss I had never left Glashgar. There's aye room there. Or gien I cud
win oot amo' the rigs! There's nane o' them left, but there's the rucks—
they're no soomin' yet! I want to gang to the Lord, but I maunna weet
Willie Mackay's claes."

"It's a sair peety," said Janet, "at the men fowk disna learn to weyve
stockin's, or dee something or ither wi' their han's. Mony's the time my
stockin''s been maist as guid's a cloaset to me, though I cudna jist gang
intil't. But what maitters 't! A prayer i' the hert 's sure to fin' the ro'd
oot. The hert's the last place 'at can haud ane in. A prayin' hert has nae
reef (roof) till't."

She turned and left him. Comforted by her words, he followed her
back into the kitchen, and sat down beside her.

"Gibbie 'ill be here mayhap whan least ye luik for him," said Janet.

Neither of them caught the wild eager gleam that lighted the face
of the strange woman at those last words of Janet. She looked up at
her with the sharpest of glances, but the same instant compelled her

countenance to resume its former expression of fierce indifference, and under that became watchful of everything said and done.

Still the rain fell and the wind blew; the torrents came tearing down from the hills, and shot madly into the rivers; the rivers ran into the valleys, and deepened the lakes that filled them. On every side of the Mains, from the foot of Glashgar to Gormdhu, all was one yellow and red sea, with roaring currents and vortices numberless. It burrowed holes, it opened long-deserted channels and water-courses; here it deposited inches of rich mould, there yards of sand and gravel; here it was carrying away fertile ground, leaving behind only bare rock or shingle where the corn had been waving; there it was scooping out the bed of a new lake. Many a thick soft lawn, of loveliest grass, dotted with fragrant shrubs and rare trees, vanished, and nothing was there when the waters subsided but a stony waste, or a gravelly precipice. Woods and copses were undermined, and trees and soil together swept into the wash: sometimes the very place was hardly there to say it knew its children no more. Houses were torn to pieces, and their contents, as from broken boxes, sent wandering on the brown waste, through the grey air, to the discoloured sea, whose saltness for a long way out had vanished with its hue. Haymows were buried to the very top in sand; others went sailing bodily down the mighty stream—some of them followed or surrounded, like big ducks, by a great brood of ricks for their ducklings. Huge trees went past as if shot down an Alpine slide, cottages, and bridges of stone, giving way before them. Wooden mills, thatched roofs, great mill-wheels, went dipping and swaying and hobbling down. From the upper windows of the Mains, looking towards the chief current, they saw a drift of everything belonging to farms and dwelling-houses that would float. Chairs and tables, chests, carts, saddles, chests of drawers, tubs of linen, beds and blankets, workbenches, harrows, girnels, planes, cheeses, churns, spinning-wheels, cradles, iron pots, wheel-barrows—all these and many other things hurried past as they gazed. Everybody was looking, and for a time all had been silent.

"Lord save us!" cried Mr. Duff, with a great start, and ran for his telescope.

A four-post bed came rocking down the river, now shooting straight for a short distance, now slowly wheeling, now shivering, struck by some swifter thing, now whirling giddily round in some vortex. The soaked curtains were flacking and flying in the great wind—and—yes, the telescope revealed it!—there was a figure in it! dead or alive the farmer could not tell, but it lay still!—A cry burst from them all; but on swept the strange boat, bound for the world beyond the flood, and none could stay its course.

The water was now in the stable and cow-houses and barn. A few minutes more and it would be creeping into the kitchen. The Daur and its tributary the Lorrie were about to merge their last difference on the floor of Jean's parlour. Worst of all, a rapid current had set in across the farther end of the stable, which no one had as yet observed.

Jean bustled about her work as usual, nor, although it was so much augmented, would accept help from any of her guests until it came to preparing dinner, when she allowed Janet and the foreman's wife to lend her a hand. "The tramp-wife" she would not permit to touch plate or spoon, knife or potato. The woman rose in anger at her exclusion, and leaving the house waded to the barn. There she went up the ladder to the loft where she had slept, and threw herself on her straw-bed.

As there was no doing any work, Donal was out with two of the men, wading here and there where the water was not too deep, enjoying the wonder of the strange looks and curious conjunctions of things. None of them felt much of dismay at the havoc around them: beyond their chests with their Sunday clothes and at most two clean shirts, neither of the men had anything to lose worth mentioning; and for Donal, he would gladly have given even his books for such a ploy.

"There's ae thing, mither," he said, entering the kitchen, covered with mud, a rabbit in one hand and a large salmon in the other, "we're no like to sterve, wi' sawmon i' the hedges, an' mappies i' the trees!"

His master questioned him with no little incredulity. It was easy to believe in salmon anywhere, but rabbits in trees!

"I catched it i' the brainches o' a lairick (larch)," Donal answered, "easy eneuch, for it cudna rin far, an' was mair fleyt at the watter nor at me; but for the sawmon, haith I was ower an' ower wi' hit i' the watter, efter I gruppit it, er' I cud ca' 't my ain."

Before the flood subsided, not a few rabbits were caught in trees, mostly spruce-firs and larches. For salmon, they were taken everywhere—among grass, corn, and potatoes, in bushes, and hedges, and cottages. One was caught on a lawn with an umbrella; one was reported to have been found in a press-bed; another, coiled round in a pot hanging from the crook—ready to be boiled, only that he was alive and undressed.

Donal was still being cross-questioned by his master when the strange woman re-entered. Lying upon her straw, she had seen, through the fanlight over the stable door, the swiftness of the current there passing, and understood the danger.

"I doobt," she said, addressing no one in particular, "the ga'le o' the stable winna stan' abune anither half-hoor."

"It maun fa' than," said the farmer, taking a pinch of snuff in hopeless serenity, and turning away.

"Hoots!" said the woman, "dinna speyk that gait, sir. It's no wice-like. Tak a dram, an' tak hert, an' dinna fling the calf efter the coo. Whaur's yer boatle, sir?"

John paid no heed to her suggestion, but Jean took it up.

"The boatle's whaur ye s' no lay han' upo' 't," she said.

"Weel, gien ye hae nae mercy upo' yer whusky, ye sud hae some upo' yer horse-beasts, ony gait," said the woman indignantly.

"What mean ye by that?" returned Jean, with hard voice, and eye of blame.

"Ye might at the leest gie the puir things a chance," the woman rejoined.

"Hoo wad ye dee that?" said Jean. "Gien ye lowsed them they wad but tak to the watter wi' fear, an' droon the seener."

"Na, na, Jean," interposed the farmer, "they wad tak care o' themsel's to the last, an' aye haud to the dryest, jist as ye wad yersel'."

"Allooin'," said the stranger, replying to Jean, yet speaking rather as if to herself, while she thought about something else, "I wad raither droon soomin' nor tied by the heid.—But what's the guid o' doctrine whaur there's onything to be dune?—Ye hae whaur to put them.—What kin' 's the fleers (floors) up the stair, sir?" she asked abruptly, turning full on her host, with a flash in her deep-set black eyes.

"Ow, guid dale fleers—what ither?" answered the farmer. "—It's the wa's, wuman, no the fleers we hae to be concernt aboot i' this wather."

"Gien the j'ists be strang, an' weel set intil the wa's, what for sudna ye tak the horse up the stair intil yer bedrooms? It'll be a' to the guid o' the wa's, for the weicht o' the beasts 'll be upo' them to haud them doon, an' the haill hoose again' the watter. An' gien I was you, I wad pit the best o' the kye an' the nowt intil the parlour an' the kitchen here. I'm thinkin' we'll lowse them a' else; for the byre wa's 'ill gang afore the hoose."

Mr. Duff broke into a strange laughter.

"Wad ye no tak up the carpets first, wuman?" he said.

"I wad," she answered; "that gangs ohn speirt—gien there was time; but I tell ye there's nane; an' ye'll buy twa or three carpets for the price o' ae horse."

"Haith! the wuman's i' the richt," he cried, suddenly waking up to the sense of the proposal, and shot from the house.

All the women, Jean making no exception to any help now, rushed to carry the beds and blankets to the garret.

Just as Mr. Duff entered the stable from the nearer end, the opposite gable fell out with a great splash, letting in the wide level vision of turbidly raging waters, fading into the obscurity of the wind-driven rain. While he stared aghast, a great tree struck the wall like a battering-ram, so that the stable shook. The horses, which had been for some time moving uneasily, were now quite scared. There was not a moment to be lost. Duff shouted for his men; one or two came running; and in less than a minute more those in the house heard the iron-shod feet splashing and stamping through the water, as, one after another, the horses were brought across the yard to the door of the house. Mr. Duff led by the halter his favourite Snowball, who was a good deal excited, plunging and rearing so that it was all he could do to hold him. He had ordered the men to take the others first, thinking he would follow more quietly. But the moment Snowball heard the first thundering of hoofs on the stair, he went out of his senses with terror, broke from his master, and went plunging back to the stable. Duff darted after him, but was only in time to see him rush from the further end into the swift current, where he was at once out of his depth, and was instantly caught and hurried, rolling over and over, from his master's sight. He ran back into the house, and up to the highest window. From that he caught sight of him a long way down, swimming. Once or twice he saw him turned heels over head—only to get his neck up again presently, and swim as well as before. But alas! it was in the direction of the Daur, which would soon, his master did not doubt, sweep his carcase into the North Sea. With troubled heart he strained his sight after him as long as he could distinguish his lessening head, but it got amongst some wreck, and unable to tell any more whether he saw it or not, he returned to his men with his eyes full of tears.

XXXIV

Glashruach

As soon as Gibbie had found a stall for Crummie, and thrown a great dinner before her, he turned and sped back the way he had come: there was no time to lose if he would have the bridge to cross the Lorrie by; and his was indeed the last foot that ever touched it. Guiding himself by well-known points yet salient, for he knew the country perhaps better than any man born and bred in it, he made straight for Glashgar, itself hid in the rain. Now wading, now swimming, now walking along the top of a wall, now caught and baffled in a hedge, Gibbie held stoutly on. Again and again he got into a current, and was swept from his direction, but he soon made his lee way good, and at length clear of the level water, and with only the torrents to mind, seated himself on a stone under a rock a little way up the mountain. There he drew from his pocket the putty-like mass to which the water had reduced the cakes with which it was filled, and ate it gladly, eyeing from his shelter the slanting lines of the rain, and the rushing sea from which he had just emerged. So lost was the land beneath the water, that he had to think to be certain under which of the roofs, looking like so many foundered Noah's arks, he had left his father and mother. Ah! yonder were cattle!—a score of heads, listlessly drifting down, all the swim out of them, their long horns, like bits of dry branches, knocking together! There was a pig, and there another! And, alas! yonder floated half a dozen helpless sponges of sheep!

At sight of these last he started to his feet, and set off up the hill. It was not so hard a struggle as to cross the water, but he had still to get to the other side of several torrents far more dangerous than any current he had been in. Again and again he had to ascend a long distance before he found a possible place to cross at; but he reached the fold at last.

It was in a little valley opening on that where lay the tarn. Swollen to a lake, the waters of it were now at the very gate of the pen. For a moment he regretted he had not brought Oscar, but the next he saw that not much could with any help have been done for the sheep, beyond what they could, if at liberty, do for themselves. Left where they were they would probably be drowned; if not they would be starved; but if he let them go, they would keep out of the water, and find for themselves what food and shelter were to be had. He opened the gate, drove them out, and a little way up the hill and left them.

By this time it was about two o'clock, and Gibbie was very hungry. He had had enough of the water for one day, however, and was not inclined to return to the Mains. Where could he get something to eat? If the cottage were still standing—and it might be—he would find plenty there. He turned towards it. Great was his pleasure when, after another long struggle, he perceived that not only was the cottage there, but the torrent gone: either the flow from the mountain had ceased, or the course of the water had been diverted. When he reached the Glashburn, which lay between him and the cottage, he saw that the torrent had found its way into it, probably along with others of the same brood, for it was frightfully swollen, and went shooting down to Glashruach like one long cataract. He had to go a great way up before he could cross it.

When at length he reached home, he discovered that the overshooting stream must have turned aside very soon after they left, for the place was not much worse than then. He swept out the water that lay on the floor, took the dryest peats he could find, succeeded with the tinder-box and sulphur-match at the first attempt, lighted a large fire, and made himself some water-brose—which is not only the most easily cooked of dishes, but is as good as any for a youth of capacity for strong food.

His hunger appeased, he sat resting in Robert's chair, gradually drying; and falling asleep, slept for an hour or so. When he woke, he took his New Testament from the crap o' the wa', and began to read.

Of late he had made a few attempts upon one and another of the Epistles, but, not understanding what he read, had not found profit, and was on the point of turning finally from them for the present, when his eye falling on some of the words of St. John, his attention was at once caught, and he had soon satisfied himself, to his wonder and gladness, that his First Epistle was no sealed book any more than his Gospel. To the third chapter of that Epistle he now turned, and read until he came to these words: "Hereby perceive we the love of God, because he laid down his life for us, and we ought to lay down our lives for the brethren."

"What learned him that?" said Gibbie to himself; Janet had taught him to search the teaching of the apostles for what the Master had taught them. He thought and thought, and at last remembered "This is my commandment, that ye love one another as I have loved you."

"And here am I," said Gibbie to himself, "sittin' here in idleseat, wi' my fire, an' my brose, an' my Bible, and a' the warl' aneath Glashgar lyin' in a speat (flood)! I canna lay doon my life to save their sowls; I maun save for them what I can—it may be but a hen or a calf. I maun dee the warks o' him 'at sent me—he's aye savin' at men."

The Bible was back in its place, and Gibbie out of the door the same moment. He had not an idea what he was going to do. All he yet understood was, that he must go down the hill, to be where things might have to be done—and that before the darkness fell. He must go where there were people. As he went his heart was full of joy, as if he had already achieved some deliverance. Down the hill he went singing and dancing. If mere battle with storm was a delight to the boy, what would not a mortal tussle with the elements for the love of men be? The thought itself was a heavenly felicity, and made him "happy as a lover."

His first definitely directive thought was, that his nearest neighbours were likely enough to be in trouble—"the fowk at the muckle hoose." He would go thither straight.

Glashruach, as I have already said, stood on one of the roots of Glashgar, where the mountain settles down into the valley of the Daur. Immediately outside its principal gate ran the Glashburn; on the other side of the house, within the grounds, ran a smaller hill-stream, already mentioned as passing close under Ginevra's window. Both these fell into the Lorrie. Between them the mountain sloped gently up for some little distance, clothed with forest. On the side of the smaller burn, however, the side opposite the house, the ground rose abruptly. There also grew firs, but the soil was shallow, with rock immediately below, and they had not come to much. Straight from the mountain, between the two streams, Gibbie approached the house, through larches and pines, raving and roaring in the wind. As he drew nearer, and saw how high the house stood above the valley and its waters, he began to think he had been foolish in coming there to find work; but when he reached a certain point whence the approach from the gate was visible, he started, stopped and stared. He rubbed his eyes. No; he was not asleep and dreaming by the cottage fire; the wind was about him, and the firs were howling and hissing; there was the cloudy mountain, with the Glashburn, fifty times its usual size, darting like brown lightning from it; but where was the iron gate with its two stone pillars, crested with wolf's-heads? where was the bridge? where was the wall, and the gravelled road to the house? Had he mistaken his bearings? was he looking in a wrong direction? Below him was a wide, swift, fiercely rushing river, where water was none before! No; he made no mistake: there was the rest of the road, the end of it next the house! That was a great piece of it that fell frothing into the river and vanished! Bridge and gate and wall were gone utterly. The burn had swallowed them, and now, foaming with madness, was roaring along, a great way within the grounds, and rapidly drawing nearer to the house, tearing to pieces and devouring all that defended it. There! what a mouthful of the shrubbery it gobbled up! Slowly, graciously, the tall trees bowed their heads and sank into the torrent, but the moment they touched it, shot away like arrows. Would the foundations of the house outstand it? Were they as strong as the walls of Babylon, yet if the water undermined them, down they must! Did the laird know that the enemy was within his gates? Not with all he had that day seen and gone through, had Gibbie until now gathered any notion of the force of rushing water.

Rousing himself from his bewildered amazement, he darted down the hill. If the other burn was behaving in like fashion, then indeed the fate of the house was sealed. But no; huge and wild as that was also, it was not able to tear down its banks of rock. From that side the house did not seem in danger.

Mr. Galbraith had gone again, leaving Ginevra to the care of Mistress Mac Farlane, with a strict order to both, and full authority to the latter to enforce it, that she should not set foot across the threshold on any pretext, or on the smallest expedition, without the housekeeper's attendance. He must take Joseph with him, he said, as he was going to the Duke's, but she could send for Angus upon any emergency.

The laird had of late been so little at home, that the establishment had been much reduced; Mistress Mac Farlane did most of the cooking herself; had quarrelled with the housemaid and not yet got another; and, Nicie dismissed, and the kitchen maid gone to visit her mother, was left alone in the house with her Mistress, if such we can call her who was really her prisoner. At this moment, however, she was not alone, for on the other side of the fire sat Angus, not thither attracted by any friendship for the housekeeper, but by the glass of whisky of which he sipped as he talked. Many a flood had Angus seen, and some that had done frightful damage, but never one that had caused him anxiety; and although this was worse than any of the rest, he had not yet a notion how bad it really was. For, as there was nothing to be done out of doors, and he was not fond of being idle, he had been busy all the morning in the woodhouse, sawing and splitting for the winter-store, and working the better that he knew what honorarium awaited his appearance in the kitchen. In the woodhouse he only heard the wind and the rain and the roar, he saw nothing of the flood; when he entered the kitchen, it was by the back door, and he sat there without the smallest suspicion of what was going on in front.

Ginevra had had no companion since Nicie left her, and her days had been very dreary, but this day had been the dreariest in her life. Mistress Mac Farlane made herself so disagreeable that she kept away from her as much as she could, spending most of her time in her own room, with her needlework and some books of poetry she had found in the library. But the poetry had turned out very dull—not at all like what Donal read, and throwing one of them aside for the tenth time that day, she wandered listlessly to the window, and stood there gazing out on the wild confusion—the burn roaring below, the trees opposite ready to be torn to pieces by the wind, and the valley beneath covered with stormy water. The tumult was so loud, that she did not hear a gentle knock at her door: as she turned away, weary of everything, she saw it softly open—and there to her astonishment stood Gibbie—come, she imagined, to seek shelter, because their cottage had been blown down.—Calculating the position of her room from what he knew of its windows, he had, with the experienced judgment of a mountaineer, gone to it almost direct.

"You mustn't come here, Gibbie," she said, advancing. "Go down to the kitchen, to Mistress Mac Farlane. She will see to what you want."

Gibbie made eager signs to her to go with him. She concluded that he wanted her to accompany him to the kitchen and speak for him; but knowing that would only enrage her keeper with them both, she shook her head, and went back to the window. She thought, as she approached it, there seemed a lull in the storm, but the moment she looked out, she gave a cry of astonishment, and stood staring. Gibbie had followed her as softly as swiftly, and looking out also, saw good cause indeed for her astonishment: the channel of the raging burn was all but dry! Instantly he understood what it meant. In his impotence to persuade, he caught the girl in his arms, and rushed with her from the room. She had faith enough in him by this time not to struggle or scream. He shot down the stair with her, and out of the front door. Her weight was nothing to his excited strength. The moment they issued, and she saw the Glashburn raving along through the lawn, with little more than the breadth of the drive between it and the house, she saw the necessity of escape, though she did not perceive half the dire necessity for haste. Every few moments, a great gush would dash out twelve or fifteen yards over the gravel and sink again, carrying many feet of the bank with it, and widening by so much the raging channel.

"Put me down, Gibbie," she said; "I will run as fast as you like."

He obeyed at once.

"Oh!" she cried, "Mistress Mac Farlane!—I wonder if she knows. Run and knock at the kitchen window."

Gibbie darted off, gave three loud hurried taps on the window, came flying back, took Ginevra's hand in his, drew her on till she was at her full speed, turned sharp to the left round the corner of the house, and shot down to the empty channel of the burn. As they crossed it, even to the inexperienced eyes of the girl it was plain what had caused the phenomenon. A short distance up the stream, the whole facing of its lofty right bank had slipped down into its channel. Not a tree, not a shrub, not a bed of moss was to be seen; all was bare wet roots. A confused heap of mould, with branches and roots sticking out of it in all directions, lay at its foot, closing the view upward. The other side of the heap was beaten by the raging burn. They could hear, though they could not see it. Any moment the barrier might give way, and the water resume its course. They made haste, therefore, to climb the opposite bank. In places it was very steep, and the soil slipped so that often it seemed on its way with them to the bottom, while the wind threatened to uproot the trees to which they clung, and carry them off through the air. It was with a fierce scramble they gained the top. Then the sight was a grand one. The arrested water swirled and beat and foamed against the landslip, then rushed to the left, through the wood, over bushes and stones, a ragging river, the wind tearing off the tops of its waves, to the Glashburn, into which it plunged, swelling yet higher its huge volume. Rapidly it cut for itself a new channel. Every moment a tree fell and shot with it like a rocket. Looking up its course, they saw it come down the hillside a white streak, and burst into boiling brown and roar at their feet. The wind nearly swept them from their place; but they clung to the great stones, and saw the airy torrent, as if emulating that below it, fill itself with branches and leaves and lumps of foam. Then first Ginevra became fully aware of the danger in which the house was, and from which Gibbie had rescued her. Augmented in volume and rapidity by the junction of its neighbour, the Glashburn was now within a yard—so it seemed from that height at least—of the door. But they must not linger. The nearest accessible shelter was the cottage, and Gibbie knew it would need all Ginevra's strength to reach it. Again he took her by the hand.

"But where's Mistress Mac Farlane?" she said. "Oh, Gibbie! we mustn't leave her."

He replied by pointing down to the bed of the stream: there were she and Angus crossing. Ginevra, was satisfied when she saw the gamekeeper with her, and they set out, as fast as they could go, ascending the mountain, Gibbie eager to have her in warmth and safety before it was dark.

Both burns were now between them and the cottage, which greatly added to their difficulties. The smaller burn came from the tarn, and round that they must go, else Ginevra would never get to the other side of it; and then there was the Glashburn to cross. It was an undertaking hard for any girl, especially such for one unaccustomed to exertion; and what made it far worse was that she had only house-shoes, which were continually coming off as she climbed. But the excitement of battling with the storm, the joy of adventure, and the pleasure of feeling her own strength, sustained her well for a long time; and in such wind and rain, the absence of bonnet and cloak was an advantage, so long as exertion kept her warm. Gibbie did his best to tie her shoes on with strips of her pocket handkerchief; but when at last they were of no more use, he pulled off his corduroy jacket, tore out the sleeves, and with strips from the back tied them about her feet and ankles. Her hair also was a trouble: it would keep blowing in her eyes, and in Gibbie's too, and that sometimes with quite a sharp lash. But she never lost her courage, and Gibbie, though he could not hearten her with words, was so ready with smile and laugh, was so cheerful—even merry, so fearless, so free from doubt and anxiety, while doing everything he could think of to lessen her toil and pain, that she hardly felt in his silence any lack; while often, to rest her body, and withdraw her mind from her sufferings, he made her stop and look back on the strange scene behind them. It was getting dark when they reached the only spot where he judged it possible to cross the Glashburn. He carried her over, and then it was all down-hill to the cottage. Once inside it, Ginevra threw herself into Robert's chair, and laughed, and cried, and laughed again. Gibbie blew up the peats, made a good fire, and put on water to boil; then opened Janet's drawers, and having signified to his companion to take what she could find, went to the cow house, threw himself on a heap of wet straw, worn out, and had enough to do to keep himself from falling asleep. A little rested, he rose and re-entered the cottage, when a merry laugh from both of them went ringing out into the storm: the little lady was dressed in Janet's workday garments, and making porridge. She looked very funny. Gibbie found plenty of milk in the dairy under the rock, and they ate their supper together in gladness. Then Gibbie prepared the bed in the little closet for his guest and she slept as if she had not slept for a week.

Gibbie woke with the first of the dawn. The rain still fell—descending in spoonfuls rather than drops; the wind kept shaping itself into long hopeless howls, rising to shrill yells that went drifting away over the land; and then the howling rose again. Nature seemed in despair. There must be more for Gibbie to do! He must go again to the foot of the mountain, and see if there was anybody to help. They might even be in trouble at the Mains, who could tell!

Ginevra woke, rose, made herself as tidy as she could, and left her closet. Gibbie was not in the cottage. She blew up the fire, and, finding the pot ready beside it, with clean water, set it on to boil. Gibbie did not come. The water boiled. She took it off, but being hungry, put it on again. Several times she took it off and put it on again. Gibbie never came. She made herself some porridge at last. Everything necessary was upon the table, and as she poured it into the wooden dish for the purpose, she took notice of a slate beside it, with something written upon it. The words were, "I will cum back as soon as I cann."

She was alone, then! It was dreadful; but she was too hungry to think about it. She ate her porridge, and then began to cry. It was very unkind of Gibbie to leave her, she said to herself, But then he was a sort of angel, and doubtless had to go and help somebody else. There was a little pile of books on the table, which he must have left for her. She began examining them, and soon found something to interest her, so that an hour or two passed quickly. But Gibbie did not return, and the day went wearily. She cried now and then, made great efforts to be patient, succeeded pretty well for a while, and cried again. She read and grew tired a dozen times; ate cakes and milk, cried afresh, and ate again. Still Gibbie did not come. Before the day was over, she had had a good lesson in praying. For here she was, one who had never yet acted on her own responsibility, alone on a bare mountain-side, in the heart of a storm which seemed as if it would never cease, and not a creature knew where she was but the dumb boy, and he had left her! If he should never come back, what would become of her? She could not find her way down the mountain; and if she could, where was she to go, with all Daurside under water? She would soon have eaten up all the food in the cottage, and the storm might go on for ever, who could tell? Or who could tell whether, when it was over, and she got down to the valley below, she should not find it a lifeless desert, everybody drowned, and herself the only person left alive in the world?

Then the noises were terrible. She seemed to inhabit noise. Through the general roar of wind and water and rain every now then came a sharper sound, like a report or crack, followed by a strange low thunder, as it seemed. They were the noises of stones carried down by the streams, grinding against each other, and dashed stone against stone; and of rocks falling and rolling, and bounding against their fast-rooted neighbours. When it began to grow dark, her misery seemed more than she could bear; but then, happily, she grew sleepy, and slept the darkness away.

With the new light came new promise and fresh hope. What should we poor humans do without our God's nights and mornings? Our ills are all easier to help than we know—except the one ill of a central self, which God himself finds it hard to help.—It no longer rained so fiercely; the wind had fallen; and the streams did not run so furious a race down the sides of the mountain. She ran to the burn, got some water to wash herself—she could not spare the clear water, of which there was some still left in Janet's pails—and put on her own clothes, which were now quite dry. Then she got herself some breakfast, and after that tried to say her prayers, but found it very difficult, for, do what she might to model her slippery thoughts, she could not help, as often as she turned herself towards him, seeing God like her father, the laird.

XXXV

The Whelp

Gibbie sped down the hill through a worse rain than ever. The morning was close, and the vapours that filled it were like smoke burned to the hue of the flames whence it issued. Many a man that morning believed another great deluge begun, and all measures relating to things of this world lost labour. Going down his own side of the Glashburn, the nearest path to the valley, the gamekeeper's cottage was the first dwelling on his way. It stood a little distance from the bank of the burn, opposite the bridge and gate, while such things were.

It had been with great difficulty, for even Angus did not know the mountain so well as Gibbie, that the gamekeeper reached it with the housekeeper the night before. It was within two gunshots of the house of Glashruach, yet to get to it they had to walk miles up and down Glashgar. A mountain in storm is as hard to cross as a sea. Arrived, they did not therefore feel safe. The tendency of the Glashburn was indeed away from the cottage, as the grounds of Glashruach sadly witnessed; but a torrent is double-edged, and who could tell? The yielding of one stone in its channel might send it to them. All night Angus watched, peering out ever again into the darkness, but seeing nothing save three lights that burned above the water—one of them, he thought, at the Mains. The other two went out in the darkness, but that only in the dawn. When the morning came, there was the Glashburn meeting the Lorrie in his garden. But the cottage was well built, and fit to stand a good siege, while any moment the waters might have reached their height. By breakfast time, however, they were round it from behind. There is nothing like a flood for revealing the variations of surface, the dips and swells of a country. In a few minutes they were isolated, with the current of the Glashburn on one side, and that of the Lorrie in front. When he saw the water come in at front and back doors at once, Angus ordered his family up the stair: the cottage had a large attic, with dormer windows, where they slept. He himself remained below for some time longer, in that end of the house where he kept his guns and fishing-tackle; there he sat on a table, preparing nets for the fish that would be left in the pools; and not until he found himself afloat did he take his work to the attic.

There the room was hot, and they had the window open. Mistress Mac Pholp stood at it, looking out on the awful prospect, with her youngest child, a sickly boy, in her arms. He had in his a little terrier-pup, greatly valued of the gamekeeper. In a sudden outbreak of peevish wilfulness, he threw the creature out of the window. It fell on the slooping roof, and before it could recover itself, being too young to have the full command of four legs, rolled off.

"Eh! the doggie's i' the watter!" cried Mistress Mac Pholp in dismay.

Angus threw down everything with an ugly oath, for he had given strict orders not one of the children should handle the whelp, jumped up, and got out on the roof. From there he might have managed to reach it, so high now was the water, had the little thing remained where it fell, but already it had swam a yard or two from the house. Angus, who was a fair swimmer and an angry man, threw off his coat, and plunged after it, greatly to the delight of the little one, caught the pup with his teeth by the back of the neck, and turned to make for the house. Just then a shrub, swept from the hill, caught him in the face, and so bewildered him, that, before he got rid of it, he had blundered into the edge of the current, which seized and bore him rapidly away. He dropped the pup, and struck out for home with all his strength. But he soon found the most he could do was to keep his head above water, and gave himself up for lost. His wife screamed in agony. Gibbie heard her as he came down the hill, and ran at full speed towards the cottage.

About a hundred yards from the house, the current bore Angus straight into a large elder tree. He got into the middle of it, and there remained trembling, the weak branches breaking with every motion he made, while the stream worked at the roots, and the wind laid hold of him with fierce leverage. In terror, seeming still to sink as he sat, he watched the trees dart by like battering-rams in the swiftest of the current: the least of them diverging would tear the elder tree with it. Brave enough in dealing with poachers, Angus was not the man to gaze with composure in the face of a sure slow death, against which no assault could be made. Many a man is courageous because he has not conscience enough to make a coward of him, but Angus had not quite reached that condition, and from the branches of the elder tree showed a pale, terror-stricken visage. Amidst the many objects on the face of the water, Gibbie, however, did not distinguish it, and plunging in swam round to the front of the cottage to learn what was the matter. There the wife's gesticulations directed his eyes to her drowning husband.

But what was he to do? He could swim to the tree well enough, and, he thought, back again, but how was that to be made of service to Angus? He could not save him by main force—there was not enough of that between them. If he had a line, and there must be plenty of lines in the cottage, he would carry him the end of it to haul upon—that would do. If he could send it to him that would be better still, for then he could help at the other end, and would be in the right position, up stream, to help farther, if necessary, for down the current alone was the path of communication open. He caught hold of the eaves, and scrambled on to the roof. But in the folly and faithlessness of her despair, the woman would not let him enter. With a curse caught from her husband, she struck him from the window, crying,

"Ye s' no come in here, an' my man droonin' yon'er! Gang till 'im, ye cooard!"

Never had poor Gibbie so much missed the use of speech. On the slope of the roof he could do little to force an entrance, therefore threw himself off it to seek another, and betook himself to the windows below. Through that of Angus's room, he caught sight of a floating anker cask. It was the very thing!—and there on the walls hung a quantity of nets and cordage! But how to get in? It was a sash-window, and of course swollen with the wet, therefore not to be opened; and there was not a square in it large enough to let him through. He swam to the other side, and crept softly on to the roof, and over the ridge. But a broken slate betrayed him. The woman saw him, rushed to the fire-place, caught up the poker, and darted back to defend the window.

"Ye s' no come in here, I tell ye," she screeched, "an' my man stickin' i' yon boortree buss!"

Gibbie advanced. She made a blow at him with the poker. He caught it, wrenched it from her grasp, and threw himself from the roof. The next moment they heard the poker at work, smashing the window.

"He'll be in an' murder's a'!" cried the mother, and ran to the stair, while the children screamed and danced with terror.

But the water was far too deep for her, She returned to the attic, barricaded the door, and went again to the window to watch her drowning husband.

Gibbie was inside in a moment, and seizing the cask, proceeded to attach to it a strong line. He broke a bit from a fishing-rod, secured the line round the middle of it with a notch, put the stick through the bunghole in the bilge, and corked up the hole with a net-float. Happily he had a knife in his pocket. He then joined strong lines together until he thought he had length enough, secured the last end to a bar of the grate, and knocked out both sashes of the window with an axe. A passage thus cleared, he floated out first a chair, then a creepie, and one thing after another, to learn from what point to start the barrel. Seeing and recognizing them from above, Mistress Mac Pholp raised a terrible outcry. In the very presence of her drowning husband, such a wanton dissipation of her property roused her to fiercest wrath, for she imagined Gibbie was emptying her house with leisurely revenge. Satisfied at length, he floated out his barrel, and followed with the line in his hand, to aid its direction if necessary. It struck the tree. With a yell of joy Angus laid hold of it, and hauling the line taut, and feeling it secure, committed himself at once to the water, holding by the barrel, and swimming with his legs, while Gibbie, away to the side with a hold of the rope, was swimming his hardest to draw him out of the current. But a weary man was Angus, when at length he reached the house. It was all he could do to get himself in at the window, and crawl up the stair. At the top of it he fell benumbed on the floor.

By the time that, repentant and grateful, Mistress Mac Pholp bethought herself of Gibbie, not a trace of him was to be seen; and Angus, contemplating his present experience in connection with that of Robert Grant's cottage, came to the conclusion that he must be an emissary of Satan who on two such occasions had so unexpectedly rescued him. Perhaps the idea was not quite so illogical as it must seem; for how should such a man imagine any other sort of messenger taking an interest in his life? He was confirmed in the notion when he found that a yard of the line remained attached to the grate, but the rest of it with the anker was gone—fit bark for the angel he imagined Gibbie, to ride the stormy waters withal. While they looked for him in the water and on the land, Gibbie was again in the room below, carrying out a fresh thought. With the help of the table, he emptied the cask, into which a good deal of water had got. Then he took out the stick, corked the bunghole tight, laced the cask up in a piece of net, attached the line to the net, and wound it about the cask by rolling the latter round and round, took the cask between his hands, and pushed from the window straight into the current of the Glashburn. In a moment it had swept him to the Lorrie. By the greater rapidity of the former he got easily across the heavier current of the latter, and was presently in water comparatively still, swimming quietly towards the Mains, and enjoying his trip none the less that he had to keep a sharp look-out: if he should have to dive, to avoid any drifting object, he might lose his barrel. Quickly now, had he been so minded, he could have returned to the city—changing vessel for vessel, as one after another went to pieces. Many a house-roof offered itself for the voyage; now and then a great water-wheel, horizontal and helpless, devoured of its element. Once he saw a cradle come gyrating along, and, urging all his might, intercepted it, but hardly knew whether he was more sorry or relieved to find it empty. When he was about half-way to the Mains, a whole fleet of ricks bore down upon him. He boarded one, and scrambled to the top of it, keeping fast hold of the end of his line, which unrolled from the barrel as he ascended. From its peak he surveyed the wild scene. All was running water. Not a human being was visible, and but a few house-roofs, of which for a moment it was hard to say whether or not they were of those that were afloat. Here and there were the tops of trees, showing like low bushes. Nothing was uplifted except the mountains. He drew near the Mains. All the ricks in the yard were bobbing about, as if amusing themselves with a slow contradance; but they were as yet kept in by the barn, and a huge old hedge of hawthorn. What was that cry from far away? Surely it was that of a horse in danger! It brought a lusty equine response from the farm. Where could horses be with such a depth of water about the place? Then began a great lowing of cattle. But again came the cry of the horse from afar, and Gibbie, this time recognizing the voice as Snowball's, forgot the rest. He stood up on the very top of the rick and sent his keen glance round on all sides. The cry came again and again, so that he was satisfied in what direction he must look. The rain had abated a little, but the air was so thick with vapour that he could not tell whether it was really an object he seemed to see white against the brown water, far away to the left, or a fancy of his excited hope: it might be Snowball on the turn-pike road, which thereabout ran along the top of a high embankment. He tumbled from the rick, rolled the line about the barrel, and pushed vigorously for what might be the horse.

It took him a weary hour—in so many currents was he caught, one after the other, all straining to carry him far below the object he wanted to reach: an object it plainly was before he had got half-way across, and by and by as plainly it was Snowball—testified to ears and eyes together. When at length he scrambled on the embankment beside him, the poor, shivering, perishing creature gave a low neigh of delight: he did not know Gibbie, but he was a human being. He was quite cowed and submissive, and Gibbie at once set about his rescue. He had reasoned as he came along that, if there were beasts at the Mains, there must be room for Snowball, and thither he would endeavour to take him. He tied the end of the line to the remnant of the halter on his head, the other end being still fast to the barrel, and took to the water again. Encouraged by the power upon his head, the pressure, namely, of the halter, the horse followed, and they made for the Mains. It was a long journey, and Gibbie had not breath enough to sing to Snowball, but he made what noise he could, and they got slowly along. He found the difficulties far greater now that he had to look out for the horse as well as for himself. None but one much used to the water could have succeeded in the attempt, or could indeed have stood out against its weakening influence and the strain of the continued exertion together so long. At length his barrel got water-logged, and he sent it adrift.

XXXVI

The Brander

Mistress Croale was not, after all, the last who arrived at the Mains. But that the next arrival was accounted for, scarcely rendered it less marvellous than hers.—Just after the loss of Snowball, came floating into the farmyard, over the top of the gate, with such astonishment of all who beheld that each seemed to place more confidence in his neighbour's eyes than in his own, a woman on a raft, with her four little children seated around her, holding the skirt of her gown above her head and out between her hands for a sail. She had made the raft herself, by tying some bars of a paling together, and crossing them with what other bits of wood she could find—a brander she called it, which is Scotch for a gridiron, and thence for a grating. Nobody knew her. She had come down the Lorrie. The farmer was so struck with admiration of her invention, daring, and success, that he vowed he would keep the brander as long as it would stick together; and as it could not be taken into the house, he secured it with a rope to one of the windows.

When they had the horses safe on the first floor, they brought the cattle into the lower rooms; but it became evident that if they were to have a chance, they also must be got up to the same level. Thereupon followed a greater tumult than before—such a banging of heads and hind quarters, of horns and shoulders, against walls and partitions, such a rushing and thundering, that the house seemed in more danger from within than from without; for the cattle were worse to manage than the horses, and one moment stubborn as a milestone, would the next moment start into a frantic rush. One poor wretch broke both her horns clean off against the wall, at a sharp turn of the passage; and after two or three more accidents, partly caused by over-haste in the human mortals, Donal begged that the business should be left to him and his mother. His master consented, and it was wonderful what Janet contrived to effect by gentleness, coaxing, and suggestion. When Hornie's turn came, Donal began to tie ropes to her hind hoofs. Mr. Duff objected.

"Ye dinna ken her sae weel as I dee, sir," answered Donal. "She wad caw her horns intil a man-o-war 'at angert her. An' up yon'er ye cudna get a whack at her, for hurtin' ane 'at didna deserve 't. I s' dee her no mischeef, I s' warran'. Ye jist lea' her to me, sir."

His master yielded. Donal tied a piece of rope round each hind pastern—if cows have pasterns—and made a loop at the end. The moment she was at the top of the stair, he and his mother dropped each a loop over a horn.

"Noo, she'll naither stick nor fling (gore nor kick)," said Donal: she could but bellow, and paw with her fore-feet.

The strangers were mostly in Fergus's bedroom; the horses were all in their owner's; and the cattle were in the remaining rooms. Bursts of talk amongst the women were followed by fits of silence: who could tell how long the flood might last!—or indeed whether the house might not be undermined before morning, or be struck by one of those big things of which so many floated by, and give way with one terrible crash! Mr. Duff, while preserving a tolerably calm exterior, was nearly at his wits' end. He would stand for half an hour together, with his hands in his pockets, looking motionless out of a window, murmuring now and then to himself, "This is clean ridic'lous!" But when anything had to be done he was active enough. Mistress Croale sat in a corner, very quiet, and looking not a little cowed. There was altogether more water than she liked. Now and then she lifted her lurid black eyes to Janet, who stood at one of the windows, knitting away at her master's stocking, and casting many a calm glance at the brown waters and the strange drift that covered them; but if Janet turned her head and made a remark to her, she never gave back other than curt if not rude reply. In the afternoon Jean brought the whisky bottle. At sight of it, Mistress Croale's eyes shot flame. Jean poured out a glassful, took a sip, and offered it to Janet. Janet declining it, Jean, invaded possibly by some pity of her miserable aspect, offered it to Mistress Croale. She took it with affected coolness, tossed it off at a gulp, and presented the glass—not to the hand from which she had taken it, but to Jean's other hand, in which was the bottle. Jean cast a piercing look into her greedy eyes, and taking the glass from her, filled it, and presented it to the woman who had built and navigated the brander. Mistress Croale muttered something that sounded like a curse upon scrimp measure, and drew herself farther back into the corner, where she had seated herself on Fergus's portmanteau.

"I doobt we hae an Ahchan i' the camp—a Jonah intil the ship!" said Jean to Janet, as she turned, bottle and glass in her hands, to carry them from the room.

"Na, na; naither sae guid nor sae ill," replied Janet. "Fowk 'at's been ill-guidit, no kennin' whaur their help lies, whiles taks to the boatle. But this is but a day o' punishment, no a day o' judgment yet, an' I'm thinkin' the warst's near han' ower.—Gien only Gibbie war here!"

Jean left the room, shaking her head, and Janet stood alone at the window as before. A hand was laid on her arm. She looked up. The black eyes were close to hers, and the glow that was in them gave the lie to the tone of indifference with which Mistress Croale spoke.

"Ye hae mair nor ance made mention o' ane conneckit wi' ye, by the name o' Gibbie," she said.

"Ay," answered Janet, sending for the serpent to aid the dove; "an' what may be yer wull wi' him?"

"Ow, naething," returned Mistress Croale. "I kenned ane o' the name lang syne 'at was lost sicht o'."

"There's Gibbies here an' Gibbies there," remarked Janet, probing her.

"Weel I wat!" she answered peevishly, for she had had whisky enough only to make her cross, and turned away, muttering however in an undertone, but not too low for Janet to hear, "but there's nae mony wee Sir Gibbies, or the warl' wadna be sae dooms like hell."

Janet was arrested in her turn: could the fierce, repellent, whisky-craving woman be the mother of her gracious Gibbie? Could she be, and look so lost? But the loss of him had lost her perhaps. Anyhow God was his Father, whoever was the mother of him.

"Hoo cam ye to tyne yer bairn, wuman?" she asked.

But Mistress Croale was careful also, and had her reasons.

"He ran frae the bluidy han'," she said enigmatically.

Janet recalled how Gibbie came to her, scored by the hand of cruelty. Were there always innocents in the world, who in their own persons, by the will of God, unknown to themselves, carried on the work of Christ, filling up that which was left behind of the sufferings of their Master—women, children, infants, idiots—creatures of sufferance, with souls open to the world to receive wrong, that it might pass and cease? little furnaces they, of the consuming fire, to swallow up and destroy by uncomplaining endurance—the divine destruction!

"Hoo cam he by the bonnie nickname?" she asked at length.

"Nickname!" retorted Mistress Croale fiercely; "I think I hear ye! His ain name an' teetle by law an' richt, as sure's ever there was a King Jeames 'at first pat his han' to the makin' o' baronets!—as it's aften I hae h'ard Sir George, the father o' 'im, tell the same."

She ceased abruptly, annoyed with herself, as it seemed, for having said so much.

"Ye wadna be my lady yersel', wad ye, mem?" suggested Janet in her gentlest voice.

Mistress Croale made her no answer. Perhaps she thought of the days when she alone of women did the simplest of woman's offices for Sir George. Anyhow, it was one thing to rush of herself to the verge of her secret, and quite another to be fooled over it.

"Is't lang sin' ye lost him?" asked Janet, after a bootless pause.

"Ay," she answered, gruffly and discourteously, in a tone intended to quench interrogation.

But Janet persisted.

"Wad ye ken 'im again gien ye saw 'im?"

"Ken 'im? I wad ken 'im gien he had grown a gran'father. Ken 'im, quo' she! Wha ever kenned 'im as I did, bairn 'at he was, an' wadna ken 'im gien he war deid an' an angel made o' 'im!—But weel I wat, it's little differ that wad mak!"

She rose in her excitement, and going to the other window, stood gazing vacantly out upon the rushing sea. To Janet it was plain she knew more about Gibbie than she was inclined to tell, and it gave her a momentary sting of apprehension.

"What was aboot him ye wad ken sae weel?" she asked in a tone of indifference, as if speaking only through the meshes of her work.

"I'll ken them 'at speirs afore I tell," she replied sullenly.—But the next instant she screamed aloud, "Lord God Almichty! yon's him! yon's himsel'!" and, stretching out her arms, dashed a hand through a pane, letting in an eddying swirl of wind and water, while the blood streamed unheeded from her wrist.

The same moment Jean entered the room. She heard both the cry and the sound of the breaking glass.

"Care what set the beggar-wife!" she exclaimed. "Gang frae the window, ye randy."

Mistress Croale took no heed. She stood now staring from the window still as a statue except for the panting motion of her sides. At the other window stood Janet, gazing also, with blessed face. For there, like a triton on a sea-horse, came Gibbie through the water on Snowball, swimming wearily.

He caught sight of Janet at the window, and straightway his countenance was radiant with smiles. Mistress Croale gave a shuddering sigh, drew back from her window, and betook herself again to her dark corner. Jean went to Janet's window, and there beheld the triumphal approach of her brownie, saving from the waters the lost and lamented Snowball. She shouted to her brother.

"John! John! here's yer Snawba'; here's yer Snawba'."

John ran to her call, and, beside himself with joy when he saw his favourite come swimming along, threw the window wide, and began to bawl the most unnecessary directions and encouragements, as if the exploit had been brought thus far towards a happy issue solely through him, while from all the windows Gibbie was welcomed with shouts and cheers and congratulations.

"Lord preserve 's!" cried Mr. Duff, recognizing the rider at last, "it's Rob Grant's innocent! Wha wad hae thoucht it?"

"The Lord's babes an' sucklin's are gey cawpable whiles," remarked Janet to herself.—She believed Gibbie had more faculty than any of her own, Donal included, nor did she share the prevalent prejudice of the city that heart and brains are mutually antagonistic; for in her own case she had found that her brains were never worth much to her until her heart took up the education of them. But the intellect is, so much oftener than by love, seen and felt to be sharpened by necessity and greed, that it is not surprising such a prejudice should exist.

"Tak 'im roon' to the door."—"Whaur got ye 'im?"—"Ye wad best get 'im in at the window upo' the stair."—"He'll be maist hungert."— "Ye'll be some weet, I'm thinkin'!"—"Come awa' up the stair, an' tell's a' aboot it."—A score of such conflicting shouts assailed Gibbie as he approached, and he replied to them all with the light of his countenance.

When they arrived at the door, they found a difficulty waiting them: the water was now so high that Snowball's head rose above the lintel; and, though all animals can swim, they do not all know how to dive. A tumult of suggestions immediately broke out. But Donal had already thrown himself from a window with a rope, and swum to Gibbie's assistance; the two understood each other, and heeding nothing the rest were saying, held their own communications. In a minute the rope was fastened round Snow-ball's body, and the end of it drawn between his fore-legs and through the ring of his head-stall, when Donal swam with it to his mother who stood on the stair, with the request that, as soon as she saw Snowball's head under the water, she would pull with all her might, and draw him in at the door. Donal then swam back, and threw his arms round Snowball's neck from below, while the same moment

Gibbie cast his whole weight of it from above: the horse was over head and ears in an instant, and through the door in another. With snorting nostrils and blazing eyes his head rose in the passage, and in terror he struck out for the stair. As he scrambled heavily up from the water, his master and Robert seized him, and with much petting and patting and gentling, though there was little enough difficulty in managing him now, conducted him into the bedroom to the rest of the horses. There he was welcomed by his companions, and immediately began devouring the hay upon his master's bedstead. Gibbie came close behind him, was seized by Janet at the top of the stair, embraced like one come alive from the grave, and led, all dripping as he was, into the room where the women were. The farmer followed soon after with the whisky, the universal medicine in those parts, of which he offered a glass to Gibbie, but the innocent turned from it with a curious look of mingled disgust and gratefulness: his father's life had not been all a failure; he had done what parents so rarely effect—handed the general results of his experience to his son. The sight and smell of whisky were to Gibbie a loathing flavoured with horror.

The farmer looked back from the door as he was leaving the room: Gibbie was performing a wild circular dance of which Janet was the centre, throwing his limbs about like the toy the children call a jumping Jack, which ended suddenly in a motionless ecstasy upon one leg. Having regarded for a moment the rescuer of Snowball with astonishment, John Duff turned away with the reflection, how easy it was and natural for those who had nothing, and therefore could lose nothing, to make merry in others' adversity. It did not once occur to him that it was the joy of having saved that caused Gibbie's merriment thus to overflow.

"The cratur's a born idiot!" he said afterwards to Jean; "an' it's jist a mervel what he's cawpable o'!—But, 'deed, there's little to cheese atween Janet an' him! They're baith tarred wi' the same stick." He paused a moment, then added, "They'll dee weel eneuch i' the ither warl', I doobtna, whaur naebody has to haud aff o' themsel's."

That day, however, Gibbie had proved that a man may well afford both to have nothing, and to take no care of himself, seeing he had, since he rose in the morning, rescued a friend, a foe, and a beast of the earth. Verily, he might stand on one leg!

But when he told Janet that he had been home, and had found the cottage uninjured and out of danger, she grew very sober in the midst of her gladness. She could say nothing there amongst strangers, but the dread arose in her bosom that, if indeed she had not like Peter denied her Master before men, she had like Peter yielded homage to the might of the elements in his ruling presence; and she justly saw the same faithlessness in the two failures.

"Eh!" she said to herself, "gien only I had been prayin' i'stead o' rinnin' awa', I wad hae been there whan he turnt the watter aside! I wad hae seen the mirricle! O my Maister! what think ye o' me noo?"

For all the excitement Mistress Croale had shown at first view of Gibbie, she sat still in her dusky corner, made no movement towards him, nor did anything to attract his attention, only kept her eyes fixed upon him; and Janet in her mingled joy and pain forgot her altogether. When at length it recurred to her that she was in the room, she cast a somewhat anxious glance towards the place she had occupied all day. It was empty; and Janet was perplexed to think how she had gone unseen. She had crept out after Mr. Duff, and probably Janet saw her, but as one of those who seeing see not, and immediately forget.

Just as the farmer left the room, a great noise arose among the cattle in that adjoining; he set down the bottle on a chair that happened to be in the passage, and ran to protect the partitions. Exultation would be a poor word wherewith to represent the madness of the delight that shot its fires into Mistress Croale's eyes when she saw the bottle actually abandoned within her reach. It was to her as the very key of the universe. She darted upon it, put it to her lips, and drank. Yet she took heed, thought while she drank, and did not go beyond what she could carry. Little time such an appropriation required. Noiselessly she set the bottle down, darted into a closet containing a solitary calf, and there stood looking from the open window in right innocent fashion, curiously contemplating the raft attached to it, upon which she had seen the highland woman arrive with her children.

At supper-time she was missing altogether. Nobody could with certainty say when he had last seen her. The house was searched from top to bottom, and the conclusion arrived at was, that she must have fallen from some window and been drowned—only, surely she would at least have uttered one cry! Examining certain of the windows to know whether she might not have left some sign of such an exit, the farmer discovered that the brander was gone.

"Losh!" cried the orra man, with a face bewildered to shapelessness, like that of an old moon rising in a fog, "yon'll be her I saw an hoor ago, hyne doon the water!"

"Ye muckle gowk!" said his master, "hoo cud she win sae far ohn gane to the boddom?"

"Upo' the bran'er, sir," answered the orra man. "I tuik her for a muckle dog upon a door. The wife maun be a witch!"

John Duff stared at the man with his mouth open, and for half a minute all were dumb. The thing was incredible, yet hardly to be controverted. The woman was gone, the raft was gone, and something strange that might be the two together had been observed about the time, as near as they could judge, when she ceased to be observed in the house. Had the farmer noted the change in the level of the whisky in his bottle, he might have been surer of it—except indeed the doubt had then arisen whether they might not rather find her at the foot of the stair when the water subsided.

Mr. Duff said the luck changed with the return of Snowball; his sister said, with the departure of the beggar-wife. Before dark the rain had ceased, and it became evident that the water had not risen for the last half-hour. In two hours more it had sunk a quarter of an inch.

Gibbie threw himself on the floor beside his mother's chair, she covered him with her grey cloak, and he fell fast asleep. At dawn, he woke with a start. He had dreamed that Ginevra was in trouble. He made Janet understand that he would return to guide them home as soon as the way was practicable, and set out at once.

The water fell rapidly. Almost as soon as it was morning, the people at the Mains could begin doing a little towards restoration. But from that day forth, for about a year, instead of the waters of the Daur and the Lorrie, the house was filled with the gradually subsiding flood of Jean's lamentations over her house-gear—one thing after another, and twenty things together. There was scarcely an article she did not, over and over, proclaim utterly ruined, in a tone apparently indicating ground of serious complaint against some one who did not appear, though most of the things, to other eyes than hers, remained seemingly about as useful as before. In vain her brother sought to comfort her with the assurance that there were worse losses at Culloden; she answered, that if he had not himself been specially favoured in the recovery of Snowball, he would have made a much worse complaint about him alone than she did about all her losses; whereupon, being an honest man, and not certain that she spoke other than the truth, he held his peace. But he never made the smallest acknowledgment to Gibbie for the saving of the said Snowball: what could an idiot understand about gratitude? and what use was money to a boy who did not set his life at a pin's fee? But he always spoke kindly to him thereafter, which was more to Gibbie than anything he could have given him; and when a man is content, his friends may hold their peace.

The next day Jean had her dinner strangely provided. As her brother wrote to a friend in Glasgow, she "found at the back of the house, and all lying in a heap, a handsome dish of trout, a pike, a hare, a partridge, and a turkey, with a dish of potatoes, and a dish of turnips, all brought down by the burn, and deposited there for the good of the house, except the turkey, which, alas! was one of her own favourite flock."[3]

In the afternoon, Gibbie re-appeared at the Mains, and Robert and Janet set out at once to go home with him. It was a long journey for them—he had to take them so many rounds. They rested at several houses, and saw much misery on their way. It was night before they arrived at the cottage. They found it warm and clean and tidy: Ginevra had, like a true lady, swept the house that gave her shelter: that ladies often do; and perhaps it is yet more their work in the world than they fully understand. For Ginevra, it was heavenly bliss to her to hear their approaching footsteps; and before she left them she had thoroughly learned that the poorest place where the atmosphere is love, is more homely, and by consequence more heavenly, than the most beautiful even, where law and order are elements supreme.

"Eh, gien I had only had faith an' bidden!" said Janet to herself as she entered; and to the day of her death she never ceased to bemoan her too hasty desertion of "the wee hoosie upo' the muckle rock."

As to the strange woman's evident knowledge concerning Gibbie, she could do nothing but wait—fearing rather than hoping; but she had got so far above time and chance, that nothing really troubled her, and she could wait quietly. At the same time it did not seem likely they would hear anything more of the woman herself: no one believed she could have gone very far without being whelmed, or whumled as they said, in the fierce waters.

---

3. See Sir Thomas Dick Lauder's account of the Morayshire Floods in 1829 (1st Ed., p. 181)—an enchanting book, especially to one whose earliest memories are interwoven with water-floods. For details in such kind here given, I am much indebted to it. Again and again, as I have been writing, has it rendered me miserable—my tale showing so flat and poor beside Sir Thomas's narrative. Known to me from childhood, it wakes in me far more wonder and pleasure now, than it did even in the days when the marvel of things came more to the surface.

XXXVII

Mr. Sclater

It may be remembered that, upon Gibbie's disappearance from the city, great interest was felt in his fate, and such questions started about the boy himself as moved the Rev. Clement Sclater to gather all the information at which he could arrive concerning his family and history. That done, he proceeded to attempt interesting in his unknown fortunes those relatives of his mother whose existence and residences he had discovered. In this, however, he had met with no success. At the house where she was born, there was now no one but a second cousin, to whom her brother, dying unmarried, had left the small estate of the Withrops, along with the family contempt for her husband, and for her because of him, inasmuch as, by marrying him, she had brought disgrace upon herself, and upon all her people. So said the cousin to Mr. Sclater, but seemed himself nowise humbled by the disgrace he recognized, indeed almost claimed. As to the orphan, he said, to speak honestly (as he did at least that once), the more entirely he disappeared, the better he would consider it—not that personally he was the least concerned in the matter; only if, according to the Scripture, there were two more generations yet upon which had to be visited the sins of Sir George and Lady Galbraith, the greater the obscurity in which they remained, the less would be the scandal. The brother who had taken to business, was the senior partner in a large ship-building firm at Greenock. This man, William Fuller Withrop by name—Wilful Withrop the neighbours had nicknamed him—was a bachelor, and reputed rich. Mr. Sclater did not hear of him what roused very brilliant hopes. He was one who would demand more reason than reasonable for the most reasonable of actions that involved parting with money; yet he had been known to do a liberal thing for a public object. Waste was so wicked that any other moral risk was preferable. Of the three, he would waste mind and body rather than estate. Man was made neither to rejoice nor to mourn, but to possess. To leave no stone unturned, however, Mr. Sclater wrote to Mr. Withrop. The answer he received was, that, as the sister, concerning whose child he had applied to him, had never been anything but a trouble to the family; as he had no associations with her memory save those of misery and disgrace; as, before he left home, her name had long ceased to be mentioned among them; and as her own father had deliberately and absolutely disowned her because of her obstinate disobedience and wilfulness, it could hardly be expected of him, and indeed would ill become him, to show any lively interest in her offspring. Still, although he could not honestly pretend to the smallest concern about him, he had, from pure curiosity, made inquiry of correspondents with regard to the boy; from which the resulting, knowledge was, that he was little better than an idiot, whose character, education, and manners, had been picked up in the streets. Nothing, he was satisfied, could be done for such a child, which would not make him more miserable, as well as more wicked, than he was already. Therefore, &c., &c., &c.

Thus failing, Mr. Sclater said to himself he had done all that could be required of him—and he had indeed taken trouble. Nor could anything be asserted, he said further to himself, as his duty in respect of this child, that was not equally his duty in respect of every little wanderer in the streets of his parish. That a child's ancestors had been favoured above others, and had so misused their advantages that their last representative was left in abject poverty, could hardly be a reason why that child, born, in more than probability, with the same evil propensities which had ruined them, should be made an elect object of favour. Who was he, Clement Sclater, to intrude upon the divine prerogative, and presume to act on the doctrine of election! Was a child with a Sir to his name, anything more in the eyes of God than a child without a name at all? Would any title—even that of Earl or Duke, be recognized in the kingdom of heaven? His relatives ought to do something: they failing, of whom could further requisition be made? There were vessels to honour and vessels to dishonour: to which class this one belonged, let God in his time reveal. A duty could not be passed on. It could not become the duty of the minister of a parish, just because those who ought and could, would not, to spend time and money, to the neglect of his calling, in hunting up a boy whom he would not know what to do with if he had him, a boy whose home had been with the dregs of society.

In justice to Mr. Sclater, it must be mentioned that he did not know Gibbie, even by sight. There remains room, however, for the question, whether, if Mr. Sclater had not been the man to change his course as he did afterwards, he would not have acted differently from the first.

One morning, as he sat at breakfast with his wife, late Mrs. Bonniman, and cast, as is, I fear, the rude habit of not a few husbands, not a few stolen glances, as he ate, over the morning paper, his eye fell upon a paragraph announcing the sudden death of the well-known William Fuller Withrop, of the eminent ship-building firm of Withrop and Playtell, of Greenock. Until he came to the end of the paragraph, his cup of coffee hung suspended in mid air. Then down it went untasted, he jumped from his seat, and hurried from the room. For the said paragraph ended with the remark, that the not unfrequent incapacity of the ablest of business men for looking the inevitable in the face with coolness sufficient to the making of a will, was not only a curious fact, but in the individual case a pity, where two hundred thousand pounds was concerned. Had the writer been a little more philosophical still, he might have seen that the faculty for making money by no means involves judgment in the destination of it, and that the money may do its part for good and evil without, just as well as with, a will at the back of it.

But though this was the occasion, it remains to ask what was the cause of the minister's precipitancy. Why should Clement Sclater thereupon spring from his chair in such a state of excitement that he set his cup of coffee down upon its side instead of its bottom, to the detriment of the tablecloth, and of something besides, more unquestionably the personal property of his wife? Why was it that, heedless of her questions, backed although they were both by just anger and lawful curiosity, he ran straight from the room and the house, nor stayed until, at one and the same moment, his foot was on the top step of his lawyer's door, and his hand upon its bell? No doubt it was somebody's business, and perhaps it might be Mr. Sclater's, to find the heirs of men who died intestate; but what made it so indubitably, so emphatically, so individually, so pressingly Mr. Sclater's, that he forgot breakfast, tablecloth, wife, and sermon, all together, that he might see to this boy's rights? Surely if they were rights, they could be in no such imminent danger as this haste seemed to signify. Was it only that he might be the first in the race to right him?—and if so, then again, why? Was it a certainty indisputable, that any boy, whether such an idle tramp as the minister supposed this one to be or not, would be redeemed by the heirship to the hugest of fortunes? Had it, some time before this, become at length easier for a rich boy to enter into the kingdom of heaven? Or was it that, with all his honesty, all his religion, all his churchism, all his protestantism, and his habitual appeal to the word of God, the minister was yet a most reverential worshipper of Mammon,—not the old god mentioned in the New Testament, of course, but a thoroughly respectable modern Mammon, decently dressed, perusing a subscription list! No doubt justice ought to be done, and the young man over at Roughrigs was sure to be putting in a false claim, but where were the lawyers, whose business it was? There was no need of a clergyman to remind them of their duty where the picking of such a carcase was concerned. Had Mr. Sclater ever conceived the smallest admiration or love for the boy, I would not have made these reflections; but, in his ignorance of him and indifference concerning him, he believed there would at least be trouble in proving him of approximately sound mind and decent intellect. What, then, I repeat and leave it, did all this excitement on the part of one of the iron pillars of the church indicate?

From his lawyer he would have gone at once to Mistress Croale—indeed I think he would have gone to her first, to warn her against imparting what information concerning Gibbie she might possess to any other than himself, but he had not an idea where she might even be heard of. He had cleansed his own parish, as he thought, by pulling up the tare, contrary to commandment, and throwing it into his neighbours, where it had taken root, and grown a worse tare than before; until at length, she who had been so careful over the manners and morals of her drunkards, was a drunkard herself and a wanderer, with the reputation of being a far worse woman than she really was. For some years now she had made her living, one poor enough, by hawking small household necessities; and not unfrequently where she appeared, the housewives bought of her because her eyes, and her nose, and an undefined sense of evil in her presence, made them shrink from the danger of offending her. But the real cause of the bad impression she made was, that she was sorely troubled with what is, by huge discourtesy, called a bad conscience—being in reality a conscience doing its duty so well that it makes the whole house uncomfortable.

On her next return to the Daurfoot, as the part of the city was called where now she was most at home, she heard the astounding and welcome news that Gibbie had fallen heir to a large property, and that the reward of one hundred pounds—a modest sum indeed, but where was the good of wasting money, thought Mr. Sclater—had been proclaimed by tuck of drum, to any one giving such information as should lead to the discovery of Sir Gilbert Galbraith, commonly known as wee Sir Gibbie. A description of him was added, and the stray was so kenspeckle, that Mistress Croale saw the necessity of haste to any hope of advantage. She had nothing to guide her beyond the fact of Sir George's habit, in his cups, of referring to the property on Daurside, and the assurance that with the said habit Gibbie must have been as familiar as herself. With this initiative, as she must begin somewhere, and could prosecute her business anywhere, she filled her basket and set out at once for Daurside. There, after a good deal of wandering hither and thither, and a search whose fruitlessness she probably owed to too great caution, she made the desired discovery unexpectedly and marvellously, and left behind her in the valley the reputation of having been on more familiar terms with the flood and the causes of it, than was possible to any but one who kept company worse than human.

XXXVIII

The Muckle Hoose

The next morning, Janet felt herself in duty bound to make inquiry concerning those interested in Miss Galbraith. She made, therefore, the best of her way with Gibbie to the Muckle Hoose, but, as the latter expected, found it a ruin in a wilderness. Acres of trees and shrubbery had disappeared, and a hollow waste of sand and gravel was in their place. What was left of the house stood on the edge of a red gravelly precipice of fifty feet in height, at whose foot lay the stones of the kitchen-wing, in which had been the room whence Gibbie carried Ginevra. The newer part of the house was gone from its very roots; the ancient portion, all innovation wiped from it, stood grim, desolated, marred, and defiant as of old. Not a sign of life was about the place; the very birds had fled. Angus had been there that same morning, and had locked or nailed up every possible entrance: the place looked like a ruin of centuries. With difficulty they got down into the gulf, with more difficulty crossed the burn, clambered up the rocky bank on the opposite side, and knocked at the door of the gamekeeper's cottage. But they saw only a little girl, who told them her father had gone to find the laird, that her mother was ill in bed, and Mistress Mac Farlane on her way to her own people.

It came out afterwards that when Angus and the housekeeper heard Gibbie's taps at the window, and, looking out, saw nobody there, but the burn within a few yards of the house, they took the warning for a supernatural interference to the preservation of their lives, and fled at once. Passing the foot of the stair, Mistress Mac Farlane shrieked to Ginevra to come, but ran on without waiting a reply. They told afterwards that she left the house with them, and that, suddenly missing her, they went back to look for her, but could find her nowhere, and were just able to make their second escape with their lives, hearing the house fall into the burn behind them. Mistress Mac Farlane had been severe as the law itself against lying among the maids, but now, when it came to her own defence where she knew her self wrong, she lied just like one of the wicked.

"My dear missie," said Janet, when they got home, "ye maun write to yer father, or he'll be oot o' 's wuts aboot ye."

Ginevra wrote therefore to the duke's, and to the laird's usual address in London as well; but he was on his way from the one place to the other when Angus overtook him, and received neither letter.

Now came to the girl a few such days of delight, of freedom, of life, as she had never even dreamed of. She roamed Glashgar with Gibbie, the gentlest, kindest, most interesting of companions. Wherever his sheep went, she went too, and to many places besides—some of them such strange, wild, terrible places, as would have terrified her without him. How he startled her once by darting off a rock like a seagull, straight, head-foremost, into the Death-pot! She screamed with horror, but he had done it only to amuse her; for, after what seemed to her a fearful time, he came smiling up out of the terrible darkness. What a brave, beautiful boy he was! He never hurt anything, and nothing ever seemed to hurt him. And what a number of things he knew! He showed her things on the mountain, things in the sky, things in the pools and streams wherever they went. He did better than tell her about them; he made her see them, and then the things themselves told her. She was not always certain she saw just what he wanted her to see, but she always saw something that made her glad with knowledge. He had a New Testament Janet had given him, which he carried in his pocket, and when she joined him, for he was always out with his sheep hours before she was up, she would generally find him seated on a stone, or lying in the heather, with the little book in his hand, looking solemn and sweet. But the moment he saw her, he would spring merrily up to welcome her. It were indeed an argument against religion as strong as sad, if one of the children the kingdom specially claims, could not be possessed by the life of the Son of God without losing his simplicity and joyousness. Those of my readers will be the least inclined to doubt the boy, who, by obedience, have come to know its reward. For obedience alone holds wide the door for the entrance of the spirit of wisdom. There was as little to wonder at in Gibbie as there was much to love and admire, for from the moment when, yet a mere child, he heard there was such a one claiming his obedience, he began to turn to him the hearing ear, the willing heart, the ready hand. The main thing which rendered this devotion more easy and natural to him than to others was, that, more than in most, the love of man had in him prepared the way of the Lord. He who so loved the sons of men was ready to love the Son of Man the moment he heard of him; love makes obedience a joy; and of him who obeys all heaven is the patrimony—he is fellow-heir with Christ.

On the fourth day, the rain, which had been coming and going, finally cleared off, the sun was again glorious, and the farmers began to hope a little for the drying and ripening of some portion of their crops. Then first Ginevra asked Gibbie to take her down to Glashruach; she wanted to see the ruin they had described to her. When she came near, and notions changed into visible facts, she neither wept nor wailed. She felt very miserable, it is true, but it was at finding that the evident impossibility of returning thither for a long time, woke in her pleasure and not pain. So utterly altered was the look of everything, that had she come upon it unexpectedly, she would not have recognized either place or house. They went up to a door. She seemed never to have seen it; but when they entered, she knew it as one from the hall into a passage, which, with what it led to, being gone, the inner had become an outer door. A quantity of sand was heaped up in the hall, and the wainscot was wet and swelled and bulging. They went into the dining-room. It was a miserable sight—the very picture of the soul of a drunkard. The thick carpet was sodden—spongy like a bed of moss after heavy rains; the leather chairs looked diseased; the colour was all gone from the table; the paper hung loose from the walls; and everything lay where the water, after floating it about, had let it drop as it ebbed.

She ascended the old stone stair which led to her father's rooms above, went into his study, in which not a hair was out of its place, and walked towards the window to look across to where once had been her own chamber. But as she approached it, there, behind the curtain, she saw her father, motionless, looking out. She turned pale, and stood. Even at such a time, had she known he was in the house, she would not have dared set her foot in that room. Gibbie, who had followed and entered behind her, perceived her hesitation, saw and recognized the back of the laird, knew that she was afraid of her father, and stood also waiting he know not what.

"Eh!" he said to himself, "hers is no like mine! Nae mony has had fathers sae guid's mine."

Becoming aware of a presence, the laird half turned, and seeing Gibbie, imagined he had entered in a prowling way, supposing the place deserted. With stately offence he asked him what he wanted there, and waved his dismissal. Then first he saw another, standing white-faced, with eyes fixed upon him. He turned pale also, and stood staring at her. The memory of that moment ever after disgraced him in his own eyes:

for one instant of unreasoning weakness, he imagined he saw a ghost—believed what he said he knew to be impossible. It was but one moment but it might have been more, had not Ginevra walked slowly up to him, saying in a trembling voice, as if she expected the blame of all that had happened, "I couldn't help it, papa." He took her in his arms, and, for the first time since the discovery of her atrocious familiarity with Donal, kissed her. She clung to him, trembling now with pleasure as well as apprehension. But, alas! there was no impiety in the faithlessness that pronounced such a joy too good to endure, and the end came yet sooner than she feared. For, when the father rose erect from her embrace, and was again the laird, there, to his amazement, still stood the odd-looking, outlandish intruder, smiling with the most impertinent interest! Gibbie had forgotten himself altogether, beholding what he took for a thorough reconciliation.

"Go away, boy. You have nothing to do here," said the laird, anger almost overwhelming his precious dignity.

"Oh, papa!" cried Ginevra, clasping her hands, "that's Gibbie! He saved my life. I should have been drowned but for him."

The laird was both proud and stupid, therefore more than ordinarily slow to understand what he was unprepared to hear.

"I am much obliged to him," he said haughtily; "but there is no occasion for him to wait."

At this point his sluggish mind began to recall something:—why, this was the very boy he saw in the meadow with her that morning!—He turned fiercely upon him where he lingered, either hoping for a word of adieu from Ginevra, or unwilling to go while she was uncomfortable.

"Leave the house instantly," he said, "or I will knock you down."

"O papa!" moaned Ginevra wildly—it was the braver of her that she was trembling from head to foot—"don't speak so to Gibbie. He is a good boy. It was he that Angus whipped so cruelly—long ago: I have never been able to forget it."

Her father was confounded at her presumption: how dared she expostulate with him! She had grown a bold, bad girl! Good heavens! Evil communications!

"If he does not get out of this directly," he cried, "I will have him whipped again. Angus."

He shouted the name, and its echo came back in a wild tone, altogether strange to Ginevra. She seemed struggling in the meshes of an evil dream. Involuntarily she uttered a cry of terror and distress.

Gibbie was at her side instantly, putting out his hand to comfort her. She was just laying hers on his arm, scarcely knowing what she did, when her father seized him, and dashed him to the other side of the room. He went staggering backwards, vainly trying to recover himself, and fell, his head striking against the wall. The same instant Angus entered, saw nothing of Gibbie where he lay, and approached his master. But when he caught sight of Ginevra, he gave a gasp of terror that ended in a broken yell, and stared as if he had come suddenly on the verge of the bottomless pit, while all round his head his hair stood out as if he had been electrified. Before he came to himself, Gibbie had recovered and risen. He saw now that he could be of no service to Ginevra, and that his presence only made things worse for her. But he saw also that she was unhappy about him, and that must not be. He broke into such a merry laugh—and it had need to be merry, for it had to do the work of many words of reassurance—that she could scarcely refrain from a half-hysterical response as he walked from the room. The moment he was out of the house, he began to sing; and for many minutes, as he walked up the gulf hollowed by the Glashburn, Ginevra could hear the strange, other-world voice, and knew it was meant to hold communion with her and comfort her.

"What do you know of that fellow, Angus!" asked his master.

"He's the verra deevil himsel', sir," muttered Angus, whom Gibbie's laughter had in a measure brought to his senses.

"You will see that he is sent off the property at once—and for good, Angus," said the laird. "His insolence is insufferable. The scoundrel!"

On the pretext of following Gibbie, Angus was only too glad to leave the room. Then Mr. Galbraith upon his daughter.

"So, Jenny!" he said, with, his loose lips pulled out straight, "that is the sort of companion you choose when left to yourself!—a low, beggarly, insolent scamp!—scarcely the equal of the brutes he has the charge of!"

"They're sheep, papa!" pleaded Ginevra, in a wail that rose almost to a scream.

"I do believe the girl is an idiot!" said her father, and turned from her contemptuously.

"I think I am, papa," she sobbed. "Don't mind me. Let me go away, and I will never trouble you any more." She would go to the mountain, she thought, and be a shepherdess with Gibbie.

Her father took her roughly by the arm, pushed her into a closet, locked the door, went and had his luncheon, and in the afternoon, having borrowed Snowball, took her just as she was, drove to meet the mail coach, and in the middle of the night was set down with her at the principal hotel in the city, whence the next morning he set out early to find a school where he might leave her and his responsibility with her.

When Gibbie knew himself beyond the hearing of Ginevra, his song died away, and he went home sad. The gentle girl had stepped at once from the day into the dark, and he was troubled for her. But he remembered that she had another father besides the laird, and comforted himself.

When he reached home, he found his mother in serious talk with a stranger. The tears were in her eyes, and had been running down her cheeks, but she was calm and dignified as usual.

"Here he comes!" she said as he entered. "The will o' the Lord be dene—noo an' for ever-mair! I'm at his biddin'.—An' sae's Gibbie."

It was Mr. Sclater. The witch had sailed her brander well.

XXXIX

DAUR STREET

O ne bright afternoon, towards the close of the autumn, the sun shining straight down one of the wide clean stony streets of the city, with a warmth which he had not been able to impart to the air, a company of school-girls, two and two in long file, mostly with innocent, and, for human beings, rather uninteresting faces, was walking in orderly manner, a female grenadier at its head, along the pavement, more than usually composed, from having the sun in their eyes. Amongst the faces was one very different from the rest, a countenance almost solemn and a little sad, of still, regular features, in the eyes of which by loving eyes might have been read uneasy thought patiently carried, and the lack of some essential to conscious well-being. The other girls were looking on this side and that, eager to catch sight of anything to trouble the monotony of the daily walk; but the eyes of this one were cast down, except when occasionally lifted in answer to words of the schoolmistress, the grenadier, by whose side she was walking. They were lovely brown eyes, trustful and sweet, and although, as I have said, a little sad, they never rose, even in reply to the commonest remark, without shining a little. Though younger than not a few of them, and very plainly dressed, like all the others—I have a suspicion that Scotch mothers dress their girls rather too plainly, which tends to the growth of an undue and degrading love of dress—she was not so girlish, was indeed, in some respects, more of a young woman than even the governess who walked by the side of them.

Suddenly came a rush, a confusion, a fluttering of the doves, whence or how none seemed to know, a gentle shriek from several of the girls, a general sense of question and no answer; but, as their ruffled nerves composed themselves a little, there was the vision of the schoolmistress poking the point of her parasol at a heedless face, radiant with smiles, that of an odd-looking lad, as they thought, who had got hold of one of the daintily gloved hands of her companion, laid a hand which, considered conventionally, was not that of a gentleman, upon her shoulder, and stood, without a word, gazing in rapturous delight.

"Go away, boy! What do you mean by such impertinence?" cried the outraged Miss Kimble, changing her thrust, and poking in his chest the parasol with which she had found it impossible actually to assail his smiling countenance.—Such a strange looking creature! He could not be in his sound senses, she thought. In the momentary mean time, however, she had failed to observe that, after the first start and following tremor, her companion stood quite still, and was now looking in the lad's face with roseate cheeks and tear-filled eyes, apparently forgetting to draw her hand from his, or to move her shoulder from under his caress. The next moment, up, with hasty yet dignified step, came the familiar form of their own minister, the Rev. Clement Sclater, who, with reproof in his countenance, which was red with annoyance and haste, laid his hands on the lad's shoulders to draw him from the prey on which he had pounced.

"Remember, you are not on a hill-side, but in a respectable street," said the reverend gentleman, a little foolishly.

The youth turned his head over his shoulder, not otherwise changing his attitude, and looked at him with some bewilderment. Then, not he, but the young lady spoke.

"Gibbie and I are old friends," she said, and reaching up laid her free hand in turn on his shoulder, as if to protect him—for, needlessly, with such grace and strength before her, the vision of an old horror came rushing back on the mind of Ginevra.

Gibbie had darted from his companion's side some hundred yards off. The cap which Mr. Sclater had insisted on his wearing had fallen as he ran, and he had never missed it; his hair stood out on all sides of his head, and the sun behind him shone in it like a glory, just as when first he appeared to Ginevra in the peat-moss, like an angel standing over her. Indeed, while to Miss Kimble and the girls he was "a mad-like object" in his awkward ill-fitting clothes, made by a village tailor in the height of the village fashion, to Ginevra he looked hardly less angelic now than he did then. His appearance, judged without prejudice, was rather that of a sailor boy on shore than a shepherd boy from the hills.

"Miss Galbraith!" said Miss Kimble, in the tone that indicates nostrils distended, "I am astonished at you! What an example to the school! I never knew you misbehave yourself before! Take your hand from this—this—very strange looking person's shoulder directly."

Ginevra obeyed, but Gibbie stood as before.

"Remove your hand, boy, instantly," cried Miss Kimble, growing more and more angry, and began knocking the hand on the girl's shoulder with her parasol, which apparently Gibbie took for a joke, for he laughed aloud.

"Pray do not alarm yourself, ma'am," said Mr. Sclater, slowly recovering his breath: he was not yet quite sure of Gibbie, or confident how best he was to be managed; "this young—gentleman is Sir Gilbert Galbraith, my ward.—Sir Gilbert, this lady is Miss Kimble. You must have known her father well—the Rev. Matthew Kimble of the next parish to your own?"

Gibbie smiled. He did not nod, for that would have meant that he did know him, and he did not remember having ever even heard the name of the Rev. Matthew Kimble.

"Oh!" said the lady, who had ceased her battery, and stood bewildered and embarrassed—the more that by this time the girls had all gathered round, staring and wondering.

Ginevra's eyes too had filled with wonder; she cast them down, and a strange smile began to play about her sweet strong mouth. All at once she was in the middle of a fairy tale, and had not a notion what was coming next. Her dumb shepherd boy a baronet!—and, more wonderful still, a Galbraith! She must be dreaming in the wide street! The last she had seen of him was as he was driven from the house by her father, when he had just saved her life. That was but a few weeks ago, and here he was, called Sir Gilbert Galbraith! It was a delicious bit of wonderment.

"Oh!" said Miss Kimble a second time, recovering herself a little, "I see! A relative, Miss Galbraith! I did not understand. That of course sets everything right—at least—even then—the open street, you know!— You will understand, Mr. Sclater.—I beg your pardon, Sir Gilbert. I hope I did not hurt you with my parasol!"

Gibbie again laughed aloud.

"Thank you," said Miss Kimble confused, and annoyed with herself for being so, especially before her girls. "I should be sorry to have hurt you.—Going to college, I presume, Sir Gilbert?"

Gibbie looked at Mr. Sclater.

"He is going to study with me for a while first," answered the minister.

"I am glad to hear it, He could not do better," said Miss Kimble. "Come, girls."

And with friendly farewells, she moved on, her train after her, thinking with herself what a boor the young fellow was—the young—

baronet?—Yes, he must be a baronet; he was too young to have been knighted already. But where ever could he have been brought up?

Mr. Sclater had behaved judiciously, and taken gentle pains to satisfy the old couple that they must part with Gibbie. One of the neighbouring clergy knew Mr. Sclater well, and with him paid the old people a visit, to help them to dismiss any lingering doubt that he was the boy's guardian legally appointed. To their own common sense indeed it became plain that, except some such story was true, there could be nothing to induce him to come after Gibbie, or desire to take charge of the outcast; but they did not feel thoroughly satisfied until Mr. Sclater brought Fergus Duff to the cottage, to testify to him as being what he pretended. It was a sore trial, but amongst the griefs of losing him, no fear of his forgetting them was included. Mr. Sclater's main difficulty was with Gibbie himself. At first he laughed at the absurdity of his going away from his father and mother and the sheep. They told him he was Sir Gilbert Galbraith. He answered on his slate, as well as by signs which Janet at least understood perfectly, that he had told them so, and had been so all the time, "and what differ dos that mak?" he added. Mr. Sclater told him he was—or would be, at least, he took care to add, when he came of age—a rich man as well as a baronet.

"Writch men," wrote Gibbie, "dee as they like, and Ise bide."

Mr. Sclater told him it was only poor boys who could do as they pleased, for the law looked after boys like him, so that, when it came into their hands, they might be capable of using their money properly. Almost persuaded at length that he had no choice, that he could no longer be his own master, until he was one and twenty, he turned and looked at Janet, his eyes brimful of tears. She gave him a little nod. He rose and went out, climbed the crest of Glashgar, and did not return to the cottage till midnight.

In the morning appeared on his countenance signs of unusual resolve. Amid the many thoughts he had had the night before, had come the question—what he would do with the money when he had it—first of all what he could do for Janet and Robert and everyone of their family; and naturally enough to a Scotch boy, the first thing that occurred to him was, to give Donal money to go to college like Fergus Duff. In that he know he made no mistake. It was not so easy to think of things for the rest, but that was safe. Had not Donal said twenty times he would not mind being a herd all his life, if only he could go to college first? But then he began to think what a long time it was before he would

GEORGE MACDONALD

be one and twenty, and what a number of things might come and go before then: Donal might by that time have a wife and children, and he could not leave them to go to college! Why should not Mr. Sclater manage somehow that Donal should go at once? It was now the end almost of October, and the college opened in November. Some other rich person would lend them the money, and he would pay it, with compound interest, when he got his. Before he went to bed, he got his slate, and wrote as follows:

"my dear minister, If you will teak Donal too, and lett him go to the kolledg, I will go with you as seens ye like; butt if ye will not, I will runn away."

When Mr. Sclater, who had a bed at the gamekeeper's, appeared the next morning, anxious to conclude the business, and get things in motion for their departure, Gibbie handed him the slate the moment he entered the cottage, and while he read, stood watching him.

Now Mr. Sclater was a prudent man, and always looked ahead, therefore apparently took a long time to read Gibbie's very clear, although unscholarly communication; before answering it, he must settle the probability of what Mrs. Sclater would think of the proposal to take two savages into her house together, where also doubtless the presence of this Donal would greatly interfere with the process of making a gentleman of Gibbie. Unable to satisfy himself, he raised his head at length, unconsciously shaking it as he did so. That instant Gibbie was out of the house. Mr. Sclater, perceiving the blunder he had made, hurried after him, but he was already out of sight. Returning in some dismay, he handed the slate to Janet, who, with sad, resigned countenance, was baking. She rubbed the oatmeal dough from her hands, took the slate, and read with a smile.

"Ye maunna tak Gibbie for a young cowt, Maister Sclater, an' think to brak him in," she said, after a thoughtful pause, "or ye'll hae to learn yer mistak. There's no eneuch o' himsel' in him for ye to get a grip o' 'm by that han'le. He aye kens what he wad hae, an' he'll aye get it, as sure's it'll aye be richt. As anent Donal, Donal's my ain, an' I s' say naething. Sit ye doon, sir; ye'll no see Gibbie the day again."

"Is there no means of getting at him, my good woman?" said Mr. Sclater, miserable at the prospect of a day utterly wasted.

"I cud gie ye sicht o' 'im, I daursay, but what better wad ye be for that? Gien ye hed a' the lawyers o' Embrough at yer back, ye wadna touch Gibbie upo' Glashgar."

"But you could persuade him, I am sure, Mistress Grant. You have only to call him in your own way, and he will come at once."

"What wad ye hae me perswaud him till, sir? To onything 'at's richt, Gibbie wants nae perswaudin'; an' for this 'at's atween ye, the laddies are jist verra brithers, an' I hae no richt to interfere wi' what the tane wad for the tither, the thing seemin' to me rizon eneuch."

"What sort of lad is this son of yours? The boy seems much attached to him!"

"He's a laddie 'at's been gien ower till's buik sin' ever I learnt him to read mysel'," Janet answered. "But he'll be here the nicht, I'm thinkin', to see the last o' puir Gibbie, an' ye can jeedge for yersel'."

It required but a brief examination of Donal to satisfy Mr. Sclater that he was more than prepared for the university. But I fear me greatly the time is at hand when such as Donal will no more be able to enter her courts. Unwise and unpatriotic are any who would rather have a few prime scholars sitting about the wells of learning, than see those fountains flow freely for the poor, who are yet the strength of a country. It is better to have many upon the high road of learning, than a few even at its goal, if that were possible.

As to Donal's going to Mr. Sclater's house, Janet soon relieved him.

"Na, na, sir," she said; "it wad be to learn w'ys 'at wadna be fittin' a puir lad like him."

"It would be much safer for him." said Mr. Sclater, but incidentally.

"Gien I cudna lippen my Donal till's ain company an' the hunger for better, I wad begin to doobt wha made the warl'," said his mother; and Donal's face flushed with pleasure at her confidence. "Na, he maun get a garret roomie some gait i' the toon, an' there haud till's buik; an ye'll lat Gibbie gang an' see him whiles whan he can be spared. There maun be many a dacent wuman 'at wad be pleased to tak him in."

Mr. Sclater seemed to himself to foresee no little trouble in his new responsibility, but consoled himself that he would have more money at his command, and in the end would sit, as it were, at the fountain-head of large wealth. Already, with his wife's property, he was a man of consideration; but he had a great respect for money, and much overrated its value as a means of doing even what he called good: religious people generally do—with a most unchristian dulness. We are not told that the Master made the smallest use of money for his end. When he paid the temple-rate, he did it to avoid giving offence; and he defended the woman who divinely wasted it. Ten times more grace and magnanimity would be needed, wisely and lovingly to avoid making a fortune, than it takes to spend one for what are called good objects when it is made.

When they met Miss Kimble and her "young ladies," they were on their way from the coach-office to the minister's house in Daur Street. Gibbie knew every corner, and strange was the swift variety of thoughts and sensations that went filing through his mind. Up this same street he had tended the wavering steps of a well-known if not highly respected town-councillor! that was the door, where, one cold morning of winter, the cook gave him a cup of hot coffee and a roll! What happy days they were, with their hunger and adventure! There had always been food and warmth about the city, and he had come in for his share! The Master was in its streets as certainly as on the rocks of Glashgar. Not one sheep did he lose sight of, though he could not do so much for those that would not follow, and had to have the dog sent after them!

XL

Mrs. Sclater

Gibbie was in a dream of mingled past and future delights, when his conductor stopped at a large and important-looking house, with a flight of granite steps up to the door. Gibbie had never been inside such a house in his life, but when they entered, he was not much impressed. He did look with a little surprise, it is true, but it was down, not up: he felt his feet walking soft, and wondered for a moment that there should be a field of grass in a house. Then he gave a glance round, thought it was a big place, and followed Mr. Sclater up the stair with the free mounting step of the Glashgar shepherd. Forgetful and unconscious, he walked into the drawing-room with his bonnet on his head. Mrs. Sclater rose when they entered, and he approached her with a smile of welcome to the house which he carried, always full of guests, in his bosom. He never thought of looking to her to welcome him. She shook hands with him in a doubtful kind of way.

"How do you do, Sir Gilbert?" she said. "Only ladies are allowed to wear their caps in the drawing-room, you know," she added, in a tone of courteous and half-rallying rebuke, speaking from a flowery height of conscious superiority.

What she meant by the drawing-room, Gibbie had not an idea. He looked at her head, and saw no cap; she had nothing upon it but a quantity of beautiful black hair; then suddenly remembered his bonnet; he knew well enough bonnets had to be taken off in house or cottage: he had never done so because he never had worn a bonnet. But it was with a smile of amusement only that he now took it off. He was so free from selfishness that he knew nothing of shame. Never a shadow of blush at his bad manners tinged his cheek. He put the cap in his pocket, and catching sight of a footstool by the corner of the chimney-piece, was so strongly reminded of his creepie by the cottage-hearth, which, big lad as he now was, he had still haunted, that he went at once and seated himself upon it. From this coign of vantage he looked round the room with a gentle curiosity, casting a glance of pleasure every now and then at Mrs. Sclater, to whom her husband, in a manner somewhat constrained because of his presence, was recounting some of the incidents of his journey, making choice, after the manner of many, of the most commonplace and uninteresting.

Gibbie had not been educated in the relative grandeur of things of this world, and he regarded the things he now saw just as things, without the smallest notion of any power in them to confer superiority by being possessed: can a slave knight his master? The reverend but poor Mr. Sclater was not above the foolish consciousness of importance accruing from the refined adjuncts of a more needy corporeal existence; his wife would have felt out of her proper sphere had she ceased to see them around her, and would have lost some of her aplomb; but the divine idiot Gibbie was incapable even of the notion that they mattered a straw to the life of any man. Indeed, to compare man with man was no habit of his; hence it cannot be wonderful that stone hearth and steel grate, clay floor and Brussels carpet were much the same to him. Man was the one sacred thing. Gibbie's unconscious creed was a powerful leveller, but it was a leveller up, not down. The heart that revered the beggar could afford to be incapable of homage to position. His was not one of those contemptible natures which have no reverence because they have no aspiration, which think themselves fine because they acknowledge nothing superior to their own essential baseness. To Gibbie every man was better than himself. It was for him a sudden and strange descent—from the region of poetry and closest intercourse with the strong and gracious and vital simplicities of Nature, human and other, to the rich commonplaces, amongst them not a few fashionable vulgarities, of an ordinary well-appointed house, and ordinary well-appointed people; but, however bedizened, humanity was there; and he who does not love human more than any other nature has not life in himself, does not carry his poetry in him, as Gibbie did, therefore cannot find it except where it has been shown to him. Neither was a common house like this by any means devoid of any things to please him. If there was not the lovely homeliness of the cottage which at once gave all it had, there was a certain stateliness which afforded its own reception; if there was little harmony, there were individual colours that afforded him delight—as for instance, afterwards, the crimson covering the walls of the dining-room, whose colour was of that soft deep-penetrable character which a flock paper alone can carry. Then there were pictures, bad enough most of them, no doubt, in the eyes of the critic, but endlessly suggestive, therefore endlessly delightful to Gibbie. It is not the man who knows most about Nature that is hardest to please, however he may be hardest to satisfy, with the attempt to follow her. The accomplished poet will derive pleasure from verses which are a mockery to the soul of the unhappy mortal whose business is judgment—the most thankless of all labours, and justly so. Certain fruits one is unable to like until he has eaten them in their perfection; after that, the reminder in them of the perfect will enable him to enjoy even the inferior a little, recognizing their kind—always provided he be not one given to judgment—a connoisseur, that is, one who cares less for the truth than for the knowing comparison of one embodiment of it with another. Gibbie's regard then, as it wandered round the room, lighting on this colour, and that texture, in curtain, or carpet, or worked screen, found interest and pleasure. Amidst the mere upholstery of houses and hearts, amidst the common life of the common crowd, he was, and had to be, what he had learned to be amongst the nobility and in the palace of Glashgar.

Mrs. Sclater, late Mrs. Bonniman, was the widow of a merchant who had made his money in foreign trade, and to her house Mr. Sclater had flitted when he married her. She was a well-bred woman, much the superior of her second husband in the small duties and graces of social life, and, already a sufferer in some of his not very serious *grossièretés*, regarded with no small apprehension the arrival of one in whom she expected the same kind of thing in largely exaggerated degree. She did not much care to play the mother to a bear cub, she said to her friends, with a good-humoured laugh. "Just think," she added, "with such a childhood as the poor boy had, what a mass of vulgarity must be lying in that uncultivated brain of his! It is no small mercy, as Mr. Sclater says, that our ears at least are safe. Poor boy!"—She was a woman of about forty, rather tall, of good complexion tending to the ruddy, with black smooth shining hair parted over a white forehead, black eyes, nose a little aquiline, good mouth, and fine white teeth—altogether a handsome woman—some notion of whose style may be gathered from the fact that, upon the testimony of her cheval glass, she preferred satin to the richest of silks, and almost always wore it. Now and then she would attempt a change, but was always defeated and driven back into satin. She was precise in her personal rules, but not stiff in the manners wherein she embodied them: these were indeed just a little florid and wavy, a trifle profuse in their grace. She kept an excellent table, and every appointment about the house was in good style—a favourite phrase with her. She was her own housekeeper, an exact mistress, but considerate, so that her servants had no bad time of it. She was sensible, kind, always responsive to appeal, had scarcely a thread of poetry or art in her upper texture, loved fair play, was seldom in the wrong, and never confessed it when she was. But when she saw it, she took some pains to avoid being so in a similar way again. She held hard by her own opinion; was capable of a mild admiration of truth and righteousness in another; had one or two pet commandments to which she paid more attention than to the rest; was a safe member of society, never carrying tales; was kind with condescension to the poor, and altogether a good wife for a minister of Mr. Sclater's sort. She knew how to hold her own with any who would have established superiority. A little more coldness, pride, indifference, and careless restraint, with just a touch of rudeness, would have given her the freedom of the best society, if she could have got into it. Altogether it would not have been easy to find one who could do more for Gibbie in respect for the social rapports that seemed to await him. Even some who would gladly themselves have undertaken the task, admitted that he might have fallen into much less qualified hands. Her husband was confident that, if anybody could, his wife would make a gentleman of Sir Gilbert; and he ought to know, for she had done a good deal of polishing upon him.

She was now seated on a low chair at the other side of the fire, leaning back at a large angle, slowly contemplating out of her black eyes the lad on the footstool, whose blue eyes she saw wandering about the room, in a manner neither vague nor unintelligent, but showing more of interest than of either surprise or admiration. Suddenly he turned them full upon her; they met hers, and the light rushed into them like a torrent, breaking forth after its way in a soulful smile. I hope my readers are not tired of the mention of Gibbie's smiles: I can hardly avoid it; they were all Gibbie had for the small coin of intercourse; and if my readers care to be just, they will please to remember that they have been spared many a he said and she said. Unhappily for me there is no way of giving the delicate differences of those smiles. Much of what Gibbie perhaps felt the more that he could not say it, had got into the place where the smiles are made, and, like a variety of pollens, had impregnated them with all shades and colours of expression, whose varied significance those who had known him longest, dividing and distinguishing, had gone far towards being able to interpret. In that which now shone on Mrs. Sclater, there was something, she said the next day to a friend, which no woman could resist, and which must come of his gentle blood.

If she could have seen a few of his later ancestors at least, she would have doubted if they had anything to do with that smile beyond its mere transmission from "the first stock-father of gentleness." She responded, and from that moment the lady and the shepherd lad were friends.

Now that a real introduction had taken place between them, and in her answering smile Gibbie had met the lady herself, he proceeded, in most natural sequence, without the smallest shyness or suspicion of rudeness, to make himself acquainted with the phenomena presenting her. As he would have gazed upon a rainbow, trying perhaps to distinguish the undistinguishable in the meeting and parting of its colours, only that here behind was the all-powerful love of his own, he began to examine the lady's face and form, dwelling and contemplating with eyes innocent as any baby's. This lasted; but did not last long before it began to produce in the lady a certain uncertain embarrassment, a something she did not quite understand, therefore could not account for, and did not like. Why should she mind eyes such as those making acquaintance with what a whole congregation might see any Sunday at church, or for that matter, the whole city on Monday, if it pleased to look upon her as she walked shopping in Pearl-street? Why indeed? Yet she began to grow restless, and feel as if she wanted to let down her veil. She could have risen and left the room, but she had "no notion" of being thus put to flight by her bear-cub; she was ashamed that a woman of her age and experience should be so foolish; and besides, she wanted to come to an understanding with herself as to what herself meant by it. She did not feel that the boy was rude; she was not angry with him as with one taking a liberty; yet she did wish he would not look at her like that; and presently she was relieved.

Her hands, which had been lying all the time in her lap, white upon black, had at length drawn and fixed Gibbie's attention. They were very lady-like hands, long-fingered, and with the orthodox long-oval nails, each with a quarter segment of a pale rising moon at the root—hands nearly faultless, and, I suspect, considered by their owner entirely such—but a really faultless hand, who has ever seen?—To Gibbie's eyes they were such beautiful things, that, after a moment or two spent in regarding them across the length of the hairy hearthrug, he got up, took his footstool, crossed with it to the other side of the fire, set it down by Mrs. Sclater, and reseated himself. Without moving more than her fine neck, she looked down on him curiously, wondering what would come next; and what did come next was, that he laid one of his hands on one of those that lay in the satin lap; then, struck with the contrast between them, burst out laughing. But he neither withdrew his hand, nor showed the least shame of the hard, brown, tarry-seamed, strong, though rather small prehensile member, with its worn and blackened nails, but let it calmly remain outspread, side by side with the white, shapely, spotless, gracious and graceful thing, adorned, in sign of the honour it possessed in being the hand of Mrs. Sclater,—it was her favourite hand,—with a half hoop of fine blue-green turkises, and a limpid activity of many diamonds. She laughed also—who could have helped it? that laugh would have set silver bells ringing in responsive sympathy!—and patted the lumpy thing which, odd as the fact might be, was also called a hand, with short little pecking pats; she did not altogether like touching so painful a degeneracy from the ideal. But his very evident admiration of hers, went far to reconcile her to his,—as was but right, seeing a man's admirations go farther to denote him truly, than the sort of hands or feet either he may happen to have received from this or that vanished ancestor. Still she found his presence—more than his proximity—discomposing, and was glad when Mr. Sclater, who, I forgot to mention, had left the room, returned and took Gibbie away to show him his, and instruct him what changes he must make upon his person in preparation for dinner.

When Mrs. Sclater went to bed that night she lay awake a good while thinking, and her main thought was—what could be the nature of the peculiar feeling which the stare of the boy had roused in her? Nor was it long before she began to suspect that, unlike her hand beside his, she showed to some kind of disadvantage beside the shepherd lad. Was it dissatisfaction then with herself that his look had waked? She was aware of nothing in which she had failed or been in the wrong of late. She never did anything to be called wrong—by herself, that is, or indeed by her neighbours. She had never done anything very wrong, she thought; and anything wrong she had done, was now a far away and so nearly forgotten, that it seemed to have left her almost quite innocent; yet the look of those blue eyes, searching, searching, without seeming to know it, made her feel something like the discomfort of a dream of expected visitors, with her house not quite in a condition to receive them. She must see to her hidden house. She must take dust-pan and broom and go about a little. For there are purifications in which king and cowboy must each serve himself. The things that come out of a man are they that defile him, and to get rid of them, a man must go into himself, be a convict, and scrub the floor of his cell. Mrs. Sclater's cell was very tidy and respectable for a cell, but no human consciousness can be clean, until it lies wide open to the eternal sun, and the all-potent wind; until, from a dim-lighted cellar it becomes a mountain-top.

XLI

INITIATION

Mrs. Sclater's first piece of business the following morning was to take Gibbie to the most fashionable tailor in the city, and have him measured for such clothes as she judged suitable for a gentleman's son. As they went through the streets, going and returning, the handsome lady walking with the youth in the queer country-made clothes, attracted no little attention, and most of the inhabitants who saw them, having by this time heard of the sudden importance of their old acquaintance, wee Sir Gibbie, and the search after him, were not long in divining the secret of the strange conjunction. But although Gibbie seemed as much at home with the handsome lady as if she had been his own mother, and walked by her side with a step and air as free as the wind from Glashgar, he felt anything but comfortable in his person. For here and there Tammy Breeks's seams came too close to his skin, and there are certain kinds of hardship which, though the sufferer be capable of the patience of Job, will yet fret. Gibbie could endure cold or wet or hunger, and sing like a mavis; he had borne pain upon occasion with at least complete submission; but the tight arm-holes of his jacket could hardly be such a decree of Providence as it was rebellion to interfere with; and therefore I do not relate what follows, as a pure outcome of that benevolence in him which was yet equal to the sacrifice of the best fitting of garments. As they walked along Pearl-street, the handsomest street of the city, he darted suddenly from Mrs. Sclater's side, and crossed to the opposite pavement. She stood and looked after him wondering, hitherto he had broken out in no vagaries! As he ran, worse and worse! he began tugging at his jacket, and had just succeeded in getting it off as he arrived at the other side, in time to stop a lad of about his own size, who was walking bare-footed and in his shirt sleeves—if shirt or sleeves be a term applicable to anything visible upon him. With something of the air of the tailor who had just been waiting upon himself, but with as much kindness and attention as if the boy had been Donal Grant instead of a stranger, he held the jacket for him to put on. The lad lost no time in obeying, gave him one look and nod of gratitude, and ran down a flight of steps to a street below, never doubting his benefactor an idiot, and dreading some one to whom he belonged would be after him presently to reclaim the gift. Mrs. Sclater saw the proceeding with some amusement and a little foreboding. She did not mourn the fate of the jacket; had it been the one she had just ordered, or anything like it, the loss would have been to her not insignificant: but was the boy altogether in his right mind? She in her black satin on the opposite pavement, and the lad scudding down the stair in the jacket, were of similar mind concerning the boy, who, in shirt sleeves indubitable, now came bounding back across the wide street. He took his place by her side as if nothing had happened, only that he went along swinging his arms as if he had just been delivered from manacles. Having for so many years roamed the streets with scarcely any clothes at all, he had no idea of looking peculiar, and thought nothing more of the matter.

But Mrs. Sclater soon began to find that even in regard to social externals, she could never have had a readier pupil. He watched her so closely, and with such an appreciation of the difference in things of the kind between her and her husband, that for a short period he was in danger of falling into habits of movement and manipulation too dainty for a man, a fault happily none the less objectionable in the eyes of his instructress, that she, on her own part, carried the feminine a little beyond the limits of the natural. But here also she found him so readily set right, that she imagined she was going to do anything with him she pleased, and was not a little proud of her conquest, and the power she had over the young savage. She had yet to discover that Gibbie had his own ideas too, that it was the general noble teachableness and affection of his nature that had brought about so speedy an understanding between them in everything wherein he saw she could show him the better way, but that nowhere else would he feel bound or inclined to follow her injunctions. Much and strongly as he was drawn to her by her ladyhood, and the sense she gave him of refinement and familiarity with the niceties, he had no feeling that she had authority over him. So neglected in his childhood, so absolutely trusted by the cottagers, who had never found in him the slightest occasion for the exercise of authority, he had not an idea of owing obedience to any but the One. Gifted from the first with a heart of devotion, the will of the Master set the will of the boy upon the throne of service, and what he had done from inclination he was now capable of doing against it, and would most assuredly do against it if ever occasion should arise: what other obedience was necessary to his perfection? For his father and mother and Donal he had reverence—profound and tender, and for no one else as yet among men; but at the same time something far beyond respect for every human shape and show. He would not, could not make any of the social distinctions which to Mr. and Mrs. Sclater seemed to belong to existence itself, and their recognition essential to the living of their lives; whence it naturally resulted that upon occasion he seemed to them devoid of the first rudiments of breeding, without respect or any notion of subordination.

Mr. Sclater was conscientious in his treatment of him. The very day following that of their arrival, he set to work with him. He had been a tutor, was a good scholar, and a sensible teacher, and soon discovered how to make the most of Gibbie's facility in writing. He was already possessed of a little Latin, and after having for some time accustomed him to translate from each language into the other, the minister began to think it might be of advantage to learning in general, if at least half the boys and girls at school, and three parts of every Sunday congregation, were as dumb as Sir Gilbert Galbraith. When at length he set him to Greek, he was astonished at the avidity with which he learned it! He had hardly got him over tupto, when he found him one day so intent upon the Greek Testament, that, exceptionally keen of hearing as he was, he was quite unaware that anyone had entered the room.

What Gibbie made of Mr. Sclater's prayers, either in congregational or family devotion, I am at some loss to imagine. Beside his memories of the direct fervid outpouring and appeal of Janet, in which she seemed to talk face to face with God, they must have seemed to him like the utterances of some curiously constructed wooden automaton, doing its best to pray, without any soul to be saved, any weakness to be made strong, any doubt to be cleared, any hunger to be filled. What can be less like religion than the prayers of a man whose religion is his profession, and who, if he were not "in the church," would probably never pray at all? Gibbie, however, being the reverse of critical, must, I can hardly doubt, have seen in them a good deal more than was there—a pitiful faculty to the man who cultivates that of seeing in everything less than is there.

To Mrs. Sclater, it was at first rather depressing, and for a time grew more and more painful, to have a live silence by her side. But when she came into rapport with the natural utterance of the boy, his presence grew more like a constant speech, and that which was best in her was not unfrequently able to say for the boy what he would have said could he have spoken: the nobler part of her nature was in secret alliance with the thoughts and feelings of Gibbie. But this relation between them, though perceptible, did not become at all plain to her until after she had established more definite means of communication. Gibbie, for his part, full of the holy simplicities of the cottage, had a good many things to meet which disappointed, perplexed, and shocked him. Middling good people are shocked at the wickedness of the wicked; Gibbie, who knew both so well, and what ought to be expected, was shocked only at the wickedness of the righteous. He never came quite to understand Mr. Sclater: the inconsistent never can be understood. That only which has absolute reason in it can be understood of man. There is a bewilderment about the very nature of evil which only he who made us capable of evil that we might be good, can comprehend.

XLII

Donal's Lodging

Donal had not accompanied Mr. Sclater and his ward, as he generally styled him, to the city, but continued at the Mains until another herd-boy should be found to take his place. All were sorry to part with him, but no one desired to stand in the way of his good fortune by claiming his service to the end of his half-year. It was about a fortnight after Gibbie's departure when he found himself free. His last night he spent with his parents on Glashgar, and the next morning set out in the moonlight to join the coach, with some cakes and a bit of fresh butter tied up in a cotton handkerchief. He wept at leaving them, nor was too much excited with the prospect before him to lay up his mother's parting words in his heart. For it is not every son that will not learn of his mother. He who will not goes to the school of Gideon. Those last words of Janet to her Donal were, "Noo, min' yer no a win'le strae (a straw dried on its root), but a growin' stalk 'at maun luik till 'ts corn."

When he reached the spot appointed, there already was the cart from the Mains, with his kist containing all his earthly possessions. They did not half fill it, and would have tumbled about in the great chest, had not the bounty of Mistress Jean complemented its space with provision—a cheese, a bag of oatmeal, some oatcakes, and a pound or two of the best butter in the world; for now that he was leaving them, a herd-boy no more, but a colliginer, and going to be a gentleman, it was right to be liberal. The box, whose ponderosity was unintelligible to its owner, having been hoisted, amid the smiles of the passengers, to the mid region of the roof of the coach, Donal clambered after it, and took, for the first time in his life, his place behind four horses—to go softly rushing through the air towards endless liberty. It was to the young poet an hour of glorious birth—in which there seemed nothing too strange, nothing but what should have come. I fancy, when they die, many will find themselves more at home than ever they were in this world. But Donal is not the subject of my story, and I must not spend upon him. I will only say that his feelings on this grand occasion were the less satisfactory to himself, that, not being poet merely, but philosopher as well, he sought to understand them: the mere poet, the man-bird, would have been content with them in themselves. But if he who is both does not rise above both by learning obedience, he will have a fine time of it between them.

The streets of the city at length received them with noise and echo. At the coach-office Mr. Sclater stood waiting, welcomed him with dignity rather than kindness, hired a porter with his truck whom he told where to take the chest, said Sir Gilbert would doubtless call on him the next day, and left him with the porter.

It was a cold afternoon, the air half mist, half twilight. Donal followed the rattling, bumping truck over the stones, walking close behind it, almost in the gutter. They made one turning, went a long way through the narrow, sometimes crowded, Widdiehill, and stopped. The man opened a door, returned to the truck, and began to pull the box from it. Donal gave him effective assistance, and they entered with it between them. There was just light enough from a tallow candle with a wick like a red-hot mushroom, to see that they were in what appeared to Donal a house in most appalling disorder, but was in fact a furniture shop. The porter led the way up a dark stair, and Donal followed with his end of the trunk. At the top was a large room, into which the last of the day glimmered through windows covered with the smoke and dust of years, showing this also full of furniture, chiefly old. A lane through the furniture led along the room to a door at the other end. To Donal's eyes it looked a dreary place; but when the porter opened the other door, he saw a neat little room with a curtained bed, a carpeted floor, a fire burning in the grate, a kettle on the hob, and the table laid for tea: this was like a bit of a palace, for he had never in his life even looked into such a chamber. The porter set down his end of the chest, said "Guid nicht to ye," and walked out, leaving the door open.

Knowing nothing about towns and the ways of them, Donal was yet a little surprised that there was nobody to receive him. He approached the fire, and sat down to warm himself, taking care not to set his hobnailed shoes on the grandeur of the little hearthrug. A few moments and he was startled by a slight noise, as of suppressed laughter. He jumped up. One of the curtains of his bed was strangely agitated. Out leaped Gibbie from behind it, and threw his arms about him.

"Eh, cratur! ye gae me sic a fleg!" said Donal. "But, losh! they hae made a gentleman o' ye a'ready!" he added, holding him at arms length, and regarding him with wonder and admiration.

A notable change had indeed passed upon Gibbie, mere externals considered, in that fortnight. He was certainly not so picturesque as before, yet the alteration was entirely delightful to Donal. Perhaps he felt it gave a good hope for the future of his own person. Mrs. Sclater had had his hair cut; his shirt was of the whitest of linen, his necktie of the richest of black silk, his clothes were of the newest cut and best possible fit, and his boots perfect: the result was altogether even to her satisfaction. In one thing only was she foiled: she could not get him to wear gloves. He had put on a pair, but found them so miserably uncomfortable that, in merry wrath, he pulled them off on the way home, and threw them—"The best kid!" exclaimed Mrs. Sclater—over the Pearl Bridge. Prudently fearful of over-straining her influence, she yielded for the present, and let him go without.

Mr. Sclater also had hitherto exercised prudence in his demands upon Gibbie—not that he desired anything less than unlimited authority with him, but, knowing it would be hard to enforce, he sought to establish it by a gradual tightening of the rein, a slow encroachment of law upon the realms of disordered license. He had never yet refused to do anything he required of him, had executed entirely the tasks he set him, was more than respectful, and always ready; yet somehow Mr. Sclater could never feel that the lad was exactly obeying him. He thought it over, but could not understand it, and did not like it, for he was fond of authority. Gibbie in fact did whatever was required of him from his own delight in meeting the wish expressed, not from any sense of duty or of obligation to obedience. The minister had no perception of what the boy was, and but a very small capacity for appreciating what was best in him, and had a foreboding suspicion that the time would come when they would differ.

He had not told him that he was going to meet the coach, but Gibbie was glad to learn from Mrs. Sclater that such was his intention, for he preferred meeting Donal at his lodging. He had recognized the place at once from the minister's mention of it to his wife, having known the shop and its owner since ever he could remember himself. He loitered near until he saw Donal arrive, then crept after him and the porter up the stair, and when Donal sat down by the fire, got into the room and behind the curtain.

The boys had then a jolly time of it. They made their tea, for which everything was present, and ate as boys know how, Donal enjoying the rarity of the white bread of the city, Gibbie, who had not tasted oatmeal since he came, devouring "mother's cakes." When they had done, Gibbie, who had learned much since he came, looked about the room till he found a bell-rope, and pulled it, whereupon the oddest-looking old woman, not a hair altered from what Gibbie remembered her, entered, and, with friendly chatter, proceeded to remove the tray. Suddenly something arrested her, and she began to regard Gibbie with curious looks; in a moment she was sure of him, and a torrent of exclamations and reminiscences and appeals followed, which lasted, the two lads now laughing, now all but crying for nearly an hour, while, all the time, the old woman kept doing and undoing about the hearth and the tea table. Donal asked many questions about his friend, and she answered freely, except as often as one approached his family, when she would fall silent, and bustle about as if she had not heard. Then Gibbie would look thoughtful and strange and a little sad, and a far-away gaze would come into his eyes, as if he were searching for his father in the other world.

When the good woman at length left them, they uncorded Donal's kist, discovered the cause of its portentous weight, took out everything, put the provisions in a cupboard, arranged the few books, and then sat down by the fire for "a read" together.

The hours slipped away; it was night; and still they sat and read. It must have been after ten o' clock when they heard footsteps coming through the adjoining room; the door opened swiftly; in walked Mr. Sclater, and closed it behind him. His look was angry—severe enough for boys caught card-playing, or drinking, or reading something that was not divinity on a Sunday. Gibbie had absented himself without permission, had stayed away for hours, had not returned even when the hour of worship arrived; and these were sins against the respectability of his house which no minister like Mr. Sclater could pass by. It mattered nothing what they were doing! it was all one when it got to midnight! then it became revelling, and was sinful and dangerous, vulgar and ungentlemanly, giving the worst possible example to those beneath them! What could their landlady think?—the very first night?—and a lodger whom he had recommended? Such was the sort of thing with which Mr. Sclater overwhelmed the two boys. Donal would have pleaded in justification, or at least excuse, but he silenced him peremptorily. I suspect there had been some difference between Mrs. Sclater and him just before he left: how otherwise could he have so entirely forgotten his wise resolves anent Gibbie's gradual subjugation?

When first he entered, Gibbie rose with his usual smile of greeting, and got him a chair. But he waved aside the attention with indignant indifference, and went on with his foolish reproof—unworthy of record except for Gibbie's following behaviour. Beaten down by the suddenness of the storm, Donal had never risen from his chair, but sat glowering into the fire. He was annoyed, vexed, half-ashamed; with that readiness of the poetic nature to fit itself to any position, especially one suggested by an unjust judgment, he felt, with the worthy parson thus storming at him, almost as if guilty in everything laid to their joint charge. Gibbie on his feet looked the minister straight in the face. His smile of welcome, which had suddenly mingled itself with bewilderment, gradually faded into one of concern, then of pity, and by degrees died away altogether, leaving in its place a look of question. More and more settled his countenance grew, while all the time he never took his eyes off Mr. Sclater's, until its expression at length was that of pitiful unconscious reproof, mingled with sympathetic shame. He had never met anything like this before. Nothing low like this—for all injustice, and especially all that sort of thing which Janet called "dingin' the motes wi' the beam," is eternally low—had Gibbie seen in the holy temple of Glashgar! He had no way of understanding or interpreting it save by calling to his aid the sad knowledge of evil, gathered in his earliest years. Except in the laird and Fergus and the gamekeeper, he had not, since fleeing from Lucky Croale's houff, seen a trace of unreasonable anger in any one he knew. Robert or Janet had never scolded him. He might go and come as he pleased. The night was sacred as the day in that dear house. His father, even when most overcome by the wicked thing, had never scolded him!

The boys remaining absolutely silent, the minister had it all his own way. But before he had begun to draw to a close, across the blinding mists of his fog-breeding wrath he began to be aware of the shining of two heavenly lights, the eyes, namely, of the dumb boy fixed upon him. They jarred him a little in his onward course; they shook him as if with a doubt; the feeling undefined slowly grew to a notion, first obscure, then plain: they were eyes of reproof that were fastened upon his! At the first suspicion, his anger flared up more fierce than ever; but it was a flare of a doomed flame; slowly the rebuke told, was telling; the self-satisfied in-the-rightness—a very different thing from righteousness—of the man was sinking before the innocent difference of the boy; he began to feel awkward, he hesitated, he ceased: for the moment Gibbie, unconsciously, had conquered; without knowing it, he was the superior of the two, and Mr. Sclater had begun to learn that he could never exercise authority over him. But the wordly-wise man will not seem to be defeated even where he knows he is. If he do give in, he will make it look as if it came of the proper motion of his own goodness. After a slight pause, the minister spoke again, but with the changed tone of one who has had an apology made to him, whose anger is appeased, and who therefore acts the Neptune over the billows of his own sea. That was the way he would slide out of it.

"Donal Grant," he said, "you had better go to bed at once, and get fit for your work to-morrow. I will go with you to call upon the principal. Take care you are not out of the way when I come for you.—Get your cap, Sir Gilbert, and come. Mrs. Sclater was already very uneasy about you when I left her."

Gibbie took from his pocket the little ivory tablets Mrs. Sclater had given him, wrote the following words, and handed them to the minister:

"Dear sir, I am going to slepe this night with Donal. The bed is bigg enuf for 2. Good night, sir."

For a moment the minister's wrath seethed again. Like a volcano, however, that has sent out a puff of steam, but holds back its lava, he thought better of it: here was a chance of retiring with grace—in well-conducted retreat, instead of headlong rout.

"Then be sure you are home by lesson-time," he said. "Donal can come with you. Good night. Mind you don't keep each other awake."

Donal said "Good night, sir," and Gibbie gave him a serious and respectful nod. He left the room, and the boys turned and looked at each other. Donal's countenance expressed an indignant sense of wrong, but Gibbie's revealed a more profound concern. He stood motionless, intent on the receding steps of the minister. The moment the sound of them ceased, he darted soundless after him. Donal, who from Mr. Sclater's reply had understood what Gibbie had written, was astonished, and starting to his feet followed him. By the time he reached the door, Gibbie was past the second lamp, his shadow describing a huge half-circle around him, as he stole from lamp to lamp after the minister, keeping always a lamp-post still between them. When the minister turned a corner, Gibbie made a soundless dart to it, and peeped round, lingered a moment looking, then followed again. On and on went Mr. Sclater, and on and on went Gibbie, careful constantly not to be seen by him; and on and on went Donal, careful to be seen of neither. They went a long way as he thought, for to the country boy distance between houses seemed much greater than between dykes or hedges. At last the minister went up the steps of a handsome house, took a key from his pocket, and opened the door. From some impulse or other, as he stepped in, he turned sharp round, and saw Gibbie.

"Come in," he said, in a loud authoritative tone, probably taking the boy's appearance for the effect of repentance and a desire to return to his own bed.

Gibbie lifted his cap, and walked quietly on towards the other end of Daur-street. Donal dared not follow, for Mr. Sclater stood between, looking out. Presently however the door shut with a great bang, and Donal was after Gibbie like a hound. But Gibbie had turned a corner, and was gone from his sight. Donal turned a corner too, but it was a wrong corner. Concluding that Gibbie had turned another corner ahead of him, he ran on and on, in the vanishing hope of catching sight of him again; but he was soon satisfied he had lost him,—nor him only, but himself as well, for he had not the smallest idea how to return, even as far as the minister's house. It rendered the matter considerably worse that, having never heard the name of the street where he lodged but once—when the minister gave direction to the porter, he had utterly forgotten it. So there he was, out in the night, astray in the streets of a city of many tens of thousands, in which he had never till that day set foot—never before having been in any larger abode of men than a scattered village of thatched roofs. But he was not tired, and so long as a man is not tired, he can do well, even in pain. But a city is a dreary place at night, even to one who knows his way in it—much drearier to one lost—in some respects drearier than a heath—except there be old mine-shafts in it.

"It's as gien a' the birds o' a country had creepit intil their bit eggs again, an' the day was left bare o' sang!" said the poet to himself as he walked. Night amongst houses was a new thing to him. Night on the hillsides and in the fields he knew well; but this was like a place of tombs—what else, when all were dead for the night? The night is the world's graveyard, and the cities are its catacombs. He repeated to himself all his own few ballads, then repeated them aloud as he walked, indulging the fancy that he had a long audience on each side of him; but he dropped into silence the moment any night-wanderer appeared. Presently he found himself on the shore of the river, and tried to get to the edge of the water; but it was low tide, the lamps did not throw much light so far, the moon was clouded, he got among logs and mud, and regained the street bemired, and beginning to feel weary. He was saying to himself what ever was he to do all the night long, when round a corner a little way off came a woman. It was no use asking counsel of her, however, or of anyone, he thought, so long as he did not know even the name of the street he wanted—a street which as he walked along it had seemed interminable. The woman drew near. She was rather tall, erect in the back, but bowed in the shoulders, with fierce black eyes, which were all that he could see of her face, for she had a little tartan shawl over her head, which she held together with one hand, while in the other she carried a basket. But those eyes were enough to make him fancy he must have seen her before. They were just passing each other, under a lamp, when she looked hard at him, and stopped.

"Man," she said, "I hae set e'en upo' your face afore!"

"Gien that be the case," answered Donal, "ye set e'en upo' 't again."

"Whaur come ye frae?" she asked.

"That's what I wad fain speir mysel'," he replied. "But, wuman," he went on, "I fancy I hae set e'en upo' your e'en afore—I canna weel say for yer face. Whaur come ye frae?"

"Ken ye a place they ca'—Daurside?" she rejoined.

"Daurside's a gey lang place," answered Donal; "an' this maun be aboot the tae en' o' 't, I'm thinkin'."

"Ye're no far wrang there," she returned; "an' ye hae a gey gleg tongue i' yer heid for a laad frae Daurside."

"I never h'ard 'at tongues war cuttit shorter there nor ither gaits," said Donal; "but I didna mean ye ony offence."

"There's nane ta'en, nor like to be," answered the woman.—"Ken ye a place they ca' Mains o' Glashruach?"

As she spoke she let go her shawl, and it opened from her face like two curtains.

"Lord! it's the witch-wife!" cried Donal, retreating a pace in his astonishment.

The woman burst into a great laugh, a hard, unmusical, but not unmirthful laugh.

"Ay!" she said, "was that hoo the fowk wad hae't o' me?"

"It wasna muckle won'er, efter ye cam wydin' throu' watter yairds deep, an' syne gaed doon the spate on a bran'er."

"Weel, it was the maddest thing!" she returned, with another laugh which stopped abruptly. "—I wadna dee the like again to save my life.

But the Michty cairried me throu'.—An' hoo's wee Sir Gibbie?—Come in—I dinna ken yer name—but we're jist at the door o' my bit garret. Come quaiet up the stair, an' tell me a' aboot it."

"Weel, I wadna be sorry to rist a bit, for I hae tint mysel a'thegither, an' I'm some tiret," answered Donal. "I but left the Mains thestreen."

"Come in an' walcome; an whan ye're ristit, an' I'm rid o' my basket, I'll sune pit ye i' the gait o' hame."

Donal was too tired, and too glad to be once more in the company of a human being, to pursue further explanation at present. He followed her, as quietly as he could, up the dark stair. When she struck a light, he saw a little garret-room—better than decently furnished, it seemed to the youth from the hills, though his mother would have thought it far from tidy. The moment the woman got a candle lighted, she went to a cupboard, and brought thence a bottle and a glass. When Donal declined the whisky she poured out, she seemed disappointed, and setting down the glass, let it stand. But when she had seated herself, and begun to relate her adventures in quest of Gibbie, she drew it towards her, and sipped as she talked. Some day she would tell him, she said, the whole story of her voyage on the brander, which would make him laugh; it made her laugh, even now, when it came back to her in her bed at night, though she was far enough from laughing at the time. Then she told him a great deal about Gibbie and his father.

"An' noo," remarked Donal, "he'll be thinkin' 't a' ower again, as he rins aboot the toon this verra meenute, luikin' for me!"

"Dinna ye trible yersel' aboot him," said the woman. "He kens the toon as weel's ony rottan kens the drains o' 't.—But whaur div ye pit up?" she added, "for it's time dacent fowk was gauin' to their beds."

Donal explained that he knew neither the name of the street nor of the people where he was lodging.

"Tell me this or that—something—onything aboot the hoose or the fowk, or what they're like, an' it may be 'at I'll ken them," she said.

But scarcely had he begun his description of the house when she cried,

"Hoot, man! it's at Lucky Murkison's ye are, i' the Wuddiehill. Come awa', an' I s' tak ye hame in a jiffey."

So saying, she rose, took the candle, showed him down the stair, and followed.

It was past midnight, and the moon was down, but the street-lamps were not yet extinguished, and they walked along without anything to interrupt their conversation—chiefly about Sir Gibbie and Sir George. But perhaps if Donal had known the cause of Gibbie's escape from the city, and that the dread thing had taken place in this woman's house, he would not have walked quite so close to her.

Poor Mistress Croale, however, had been nowise to blame for that, and the shock it gave her had even done something to check the rate of her downhill progress. It let her see, with a lightning flash from the pit, how wide the rent now yawned between her and her former respectability. She continued, as we know, to drink whisky, and was not unfrequently overcome by it; but in her following life as peddler, she measured her madness more; and, much in the open air and walking a great deal, with a basket sometimes heavy, her indulgence did her less physical harm; her temper recovered a little, she regained a portion of her self-command; and at the close of those years of wandering, she was less of a ruin, both mentally and spiritually, than at their commencement.

When she received her hundred pounds for the finding of Sir Gibbie, she rented a little shop in the gallery of the market, where she sold such things as she had carried about the country, adding to her stock, upon the likelihood of demand, without respect to unity either conventional or real, in the character of the wares she associated. The interest and respectability of this new start in life, made a little fresh opposition to the inroads of her besetting sin; so that now she did not consume as much whisky in three days as she did in one when she had her houff on the shore. Some people seem to have been drinking all their lives, of necessity getting more and more into the power of the enemy, but without succumbing at a rapid rate, having even their times of uplifting and betterment. Mistress Croale's complexion was a little clearer; her eyes were less fierce; her expression was more composed; some of the women who like her had shops in the market, had grown a little friendly with her; and, which was of more valuable significance, she had come to be not a little regarded by the poor women of the lower parts behind the market, who were in the way of dealing with her. For the moment a customer of this class, and she had but few of any other, appeared at her shop, or covered stall, rather, she seemed in spirit to go outside the counter and buy with her, giving her the best counsel she had, now advising the cheaper, now the dearer of two articles; while now and then one could tell of having been sent by her to another shop, where, in the particular case, she could do better. A love of affairs, no doubt, bore a part in this peculiarity, but there is all the difference between the two ways of embodying activity—to one's own advantage only, and—to the advantage of one's neighbour as well. For my part, if I knew a woman behaved to her neighbours as Mistress Croale did to hers, were she the worst of drunkards in between, I could not help both respecting and loving her. Alas that such virtue is so portentously scarce! There are so many that are sober for one that is honest! Deep are the depths of social degradation to which the clean, purifying light yet reaches, and lofty are the heights of social honour where yet the light is nothing but darkness. Any thoughtful person who knew Mistress Croale's history, would have feared much for her, and hoped a little: her so-called fate was still undecided. In the mean time she made a living, did not get into debt, spent an inordinate portion of her profits in drink, but had regained and was keeping up a kind and measure of respectability.

Before they reached the Widdiehill, Donal, with the open heart of the poet, was full of friendliness to her, and rejoiced in the mischance that had led him to make her acquaintance.

"Ye ken, of coorse," he happened to say, "'at Gibbie's wi' Maister Sclater?"

"Weel eneuch," she answered. "I hae seen him tee; but he's a gran' gentleman grown, an' I wadna like to be affrontit layin' claim till's acquaintance,—walcome as he ance was to my hoose!"

She had more reason for the doubt and hesitation she thus expressed than Donal knew. But his answer was none the less the true one as regarded his friend.

"Ye little ken Gibbie," he said "gien ye think that gait o' 'im! Gang ye to the minister's door and speir for 'im! He'll be doon the stair like a shot.—But 'deed maybe he's come back, an' 's i' my chaumer the noo! Ye'll come up the stair an' see?"

"Na, I wunna dee that," said Mistress Croale, who did not wish to face Mistress Murkison, well known to her in the days of her comparative prosperity.

She pointed out the door to him, but herself stood on the other side of the way till she saw it opened by her old friend in her night-cap, and heard her make jubilee over his return.

Gibbie had come home and gone out again to look for him, she said.

"Weel," remarked Donal, "there wad be sma' guid in my gaein' to luik for him. It wad be but the sheep gaein' to luik for the shepherd."

"Ye're richt there," said his landlady. "A tint bairn sud aye sit doon an' sit still."

"Weel, ye gang till yer bed, mem," returned Donal. "Lat me see hoo yer door works, an' I'll lat him in whan he comes."

Gibbie came within an hour, and all was well. They made their communication, of which Donal's was far the more interesting, had their laugh over the affair, and went to bed.

XLIII

The Minister's Defeat

The minister's wrath, when he found he had been followed home by Gibbie who yet would not enter the house, instantly rose in redoubled strength. He was ashamed to report the affair to Mrs. Sclater just as it had passed. He was but a married old bachelor, and fancied he must keep up his dignity in the eyes of his wife, not having yet learned that, if a man be true, his friends and lovers will see to his dignity. So his anger went on smouldering all night long, and all through his sleep, without a touch of cool assuagement, and in the morning he rose with his temper very feverish. During breakfast he was gloomy, but would confess to no inward annoyance. What added to his unrest was, that, although he felt insulted, he did not know what precisely the nature of the insult was. Even in his wrath he could scarcely set down Gibbie's following of him to a glorying mockery of his defeat. Doubtless, for a man accustomed to deal with affairs, to rule over a parish—for one who generally had his way in the kirk-session, and to whom his wife showed becoming respect, it was scarcely fitting that the rude behaviour of an ignorant country dummy should affect him so much: he ought to have been above such injury. But the lad whom he so regarded, had first with his mere looks lowered him in his own eyes, then showed himself beyond the reach of his reproof by calmly refusing to obey him, and then become unintelligible by following him like a creature over whom surveillance was needful! The more he thought of this last, the more inexplicable it seemed to become, except on the notion of deliberate insult. And the worst was, that henceforth he could expect to have no power at all over the boy! If it was like this already, how would it be in the time to come? If, on the other hand, he were to re-establish his authority at the cost of making the boy hate him, then, the moment he was of age, his behaviour would be that of a liberated enemy: he would go straight to the dogs, and his money with him!—The man of influence and scheme did well to be annoyed.

Gibbie made his appearance at ten o'clock, and went straight to the study, where at that hour the minister was always waiting him. He entered with his own smile, bending his head in morning salutation.

The minister said "Good morning," but gruffly, and without raising his eyes from the last publication of the Spalding Club. Gibbie seated himself in his usual place, arranged his book and slate, and was ready to commence—when the minister, having now summoned resolution, lifted his head, fixed his eyes on him, and said sternly—

"Sir Gilbert, what was your meaning in following me, after refusing to accompany me?"

Gibbie's face flushed. Mr. Sclater believed he saw him for the first time ashamed of himself; his hope rose; his courage grew; he augured victory and a re-established throne: he gathered himself up in dignity, prepared to overwhelm him. But Gibbie showed no hesitation; he took his slate instantly, found his pencil, wrote, and handed the slate to the minister. There stood these words:

"I thought you was drunnk."

Mr. Sclater started to his feet, the hand which held the offending document uplifted, his eyes flaming, his checks white with passion, and with the flat of the slate came down a great blow on the top of Gibbie's head. Happily the latter was the harder of the two, and the former broke, flying mostly out of the frame. It took Gibbie terribly by surprise. Half-stunned, he started to his feet, and for one moment the wild beast which was in him, as it is in everybody, rushed to the front of its cage. It would have gone ill then with the minister, had not as sudden a change followed; the very same instant, it was as if an invisible veil, woven of gracious air and odour and dew, had descended upon him; the flame of his wrath went out, quenched utterly; a smile of benignest compassion overspread his countenance; in his offender he saw only a brother. But Mr. Sclater saw no brother before him, for when Gibbie rose he drew back to better his position, and so doing made it an awkard one indeed. For it happened occasionally that, the study being a warm room, Mrs. Sclater, on a winter evening, sat there with her husband, whence it came that on the floor squatted a low foot-stool, subject to not unfrequent clerical imprecation: when he stepped back, he trod on the edge of it, stumbled, and fell. Gibbie darted forward. A part of the minister's body rested upon the stool, and its elevation, made the first movement necessary to rising rather difficult, so that he could not at once get off his back.

What followed was the strangest act for a Scotch boy, but it must be kept in mind how limited were his means of expression. He jumped over the prostrate minister, who the next moment seeing his face bent

GEORGE MACDONALD

over him from behind, and seized, like the gamekeeper, with suspicion born of his violence, raised his hands to defend himself, and made a blow at him. Gibbie avoided it, laid hold of his arms inside each elbow, clamped them to the floor, kissed him on forehead and cheek, and began to help him up like a child.

Having regained his legs, the minister stood for a moment, confused and half-blinded. The first thing he saw was a drop of blood stealing down Gibbie's forehead. He was shocked at what he had done. In truth he had been frightfully provoked, but it was not for a clergyman so to avenge an insult, and as mere chastisement it was brutal. What would Mrs. Sclater say to it? The rascal was sure to make his complaint to her! And there too was his friend, the herd-lad, in the drawing-room with her!

"Go and wash your face," he said, "and come back again directly."

Gibbie put his hand to his face, and feeling something wet, looked, and burst into a merry laugh.

"I am sorry I have hurt you," said the minister, not a little relieved at the sound; "but how dared you write such a—such an insolence? A clergyman never gets drunk."

Gibbie picked up the frame which the minister had dropped in his fall: a piece of the slate was still sticking in one side, and he wrote upon it:

I will kno better the next time. I thout it was alwais whisky that made peeple like that. I begg your pardon, sir.

He handed him the fragment, ran to his own room, returned presently, looking all right, and when Mr. Sclater would have attended to his wound, would not let him even look at it, laughing at the idea. Still further relieved to find there was nothing to attract observation to the injury, and yet more ashamed of himself, the minister made haste to the refuge of their work; but it did not require the gleam of the paper substituted for the slate, to keep him that morning in remembrance of what he had done; indeed it hovered about him long after the gray of the new slate had passed into a dark blue.

From that time, after luncheon, which followed immediately upon lessons, Gibbie went and came as he pleased. Mrs. Sclater begged he would never be out after ten o'clock without having let them know that he meant to stay all night with his friend: not once did he neglect this request, and they soon came to have perfect confidence not only in any individual promise he might make, but in his general punctuality. Mrs. Sclater never came to know anything of his wounded head, and it gave the minister a sharp sting of compunction, as well as increased his sense of moral inferiority, when he saw that for a fortnight or so he never took his favourite place at her feet, evidently that she should not look down on his head.

The same evening they had friends to dinner. Already Gibbie was so far civilized, as they called it, that he might have sat at any dining-table without attracting the least attention, but that evening he attracted a great deal. For he could scarcely eat his own dinner for watching the needs of those at the table with him, ready to spring from his chair and supply the least lack. This behaviour naturally harassed the hostess, and at last, upon one of those occasions, the servants happening to be out of the room, she called him to her side, and said,

"You were quite right to do that now, Gilbert, but please never do such a thing when the servants are in the room. It confuses them, and makes us all uncomfortable."

Gibbie heard with obedient ear, but took the words as containing express permission to wait upon the company in the absence of other ministration. When therefore the servants finally disappeared, as was the custom there in small households, immediately after placing the dessert, Gibbie got up, and, much to the amusement of the guests, waited on them as quite a matter of course. But they would have wondered could they have looked into the heart of the boy, and beheld the spirit in which the thing was done, the soil in which was hid the root of the service; for to him the whole thing was sacred as an altar-rite to the priest who ministers. Round and round the table, deft and noiseless, he went, altogether aware of the pleasure of the thing, not at all of its oddity—which, however, had he understood it perfectly, he would not in the least have minded.

All this may, both in Gibbie and the narrative, seem trifling, but I more than doubt whether, until our small services are sweet with divine affection, our great ones, if such we are capable of, will ever have the true Christian flavour about them. And then such eagerness to pounce upon every smallest opportunity of doing the will of the Master, could not fail to further proficiency in the service throughout.

Presently the ladies rose, and when they had left the room, the host asked Gibbie to ring the bell. He obeyed with alacrity, and a servant appeared. She placed the utensils for making and drinking toddy, after Scotch custom, upon the table. A shadow fell upon the soul of Gibbie: for the first time since he ran from the city, he saw the well-known appointments of midnight orgy, associated in his mind with all the horrors from which he had fled. The memory of old nights in the street, as he watched for his father, and then helped him home; of his father's last prayer, drinking and imploring; of his white, motionless face the next morning; of the row at Lucky Croale's, and poor black Sambo's gaping throat—all these terrible things came back upon him, as he stood staring at the tumblers and the wine glasses and the steaming kettle.

"What is the girl thinking of!" exclaimed the minister, who had been talking to his next neighbour, when he heard the door close behind the servant. "She has actually forgotten the whisky!—Sir Gilbert," he went on, with a glance at the boy, "as you are so good, will you oblige me by bringing the bottle from the sideboard?"

Gibbie started at the sound of his name, but did not move from the place. After a moment, the minister, who had resumed the conversation, thinking he had not heard him, looked up. There, between the foot of the table and the sideboard, stood Gibbie as if fixed to the floor gazing out of his blue eyes at the minister—those eyes filmy with gathering tears, the smile utterly faded from his countenance.—Would the Master have drunk out of that bottle? he was thinking with himself. Imagining some chance remark had hurt the boy's pride, and not altogether sorry—it gave hope of the gentleman he wanted to make him—Mr. Sclater spoke again:

"It's just behind you, Sir Gilbert—the whisky bottle—that purple one with the silver top."

Gibbie never moved, but his eyes began to run over. A fearful remembrance of the blow he had given him on the head rushed back on Mr. Sclater: could it be the consequence of that? Was the boy paralyzed? He was on the point of hurrying to him, but restrained himself, and rising with deliberation, approached the sideboard. A nearer sight of the boy's face reassured him.

"I beg your pardon, Sir Gilbert," he said; "I thought you would not mind waiting on us as well as on the ladies. It is your own fault, you know.—There," he added, pointing to the table; "take your place, and have a little toddy. It won't hurt you."

The eyes of all the guests were by this time fixed on Gibbie. What could be the matter with the curious creature? they wondered. His gentle merriment and quiet delight in waiting upon them, had given a pleasant concussion to the spirits of the party, which had at first threatened to be rather a stiff and dull one; and there now was the boy all at once looking as if he had received a blow, or some cutting insult which he did not know how to resent!

Between the agony of refusing to serve, and the impossibility of putting his hand to unclean ministration, Gibbie had stood as if spell-bound. He would have thought little of such horrors in Lucky Croale's houff, but the sight of the things here terrified him. He felt as a Corinthian Christian must, catching a sight of one of the elders of the church feasting in a temple. But the last words of the minister broke the painful charm. He burst into tears, and darting from the room, not a little to his guardian's relief, hurried to his own.

The guests stared bewildered.

"He'll be gone to the ladies," said their host. "He's an odd creature. Mrs. Sclater understands him better than I do. He's more at home with her."

Therewith he proceeded to tell them his history, and whence the interest he had in him, not bringing down his narrative beyond the afternoon of the preceding day.

The next morning, Mrs. Sclater had a talk with him concerning his whim of waiting at table, telling him he must not do so again; it was not the custom for gentlemen to do the things that servants were paid to do; it was not fair to the servants, and so on—happening to end with an utterance of mild wonder at his fancy for such a peculiarity. This exclamation Gibbie took for a question, or at least the expression of a desire to understand the reason of the thing. He went to a side-table, and having stood there a moment or two, returned with a New Testament, in which he pointed out the words, "But I am among you as he that serveth." Giving her just time to read them, he took the book again, and in addition presented the words, "The disciple is not above his master, but every one that is perfect shall be as his master."

Mrs. Sclater was as much put out as if he had been guilty of another and worse indiscretion. The idea of anybody ordering his common doings, not to say his oddities, by principles drawn from a source far too sacred to be practically regarded, was too preposterous to have ever become even a notion to her. Henceforth, however, it was a mote to trouble her mind's eye, a mote she did not get rid of until it began to turn to a glimmer of light. I need hardly add that Gibbie waited at her dinner-table no more.

XLIV

The Sinner

No man can order his life, for it comes flowing over him from behind. But if it lay before us, and we could watch its current approaching from a long distance, what could we do with it before it had reached the now? In like wise a man thinks foolishly who imagines he could have done this and that with his own character and development, if he had but known this and that in time. Were he as good as he thinks himself wise he could but at best have produced a fine cameo in very low relief: with a work in the round, which he is meant to be, he could have done nothing. The one secret of life and development, is not to devise and plan, but to fall in with the forces at work—to do every moment's duty aright—that being the part in the process allotted to us; and let come— not what will, for there is no such thing—but what the eternal Thought wills for each of us, has intended in each of us from the first. If men would but believe that they are in process of creation, and consent to be made—let the maker handle them as the potter his clay, yielding themselves in respondent motion and submissive hopeful action with the turning of his wheel, they would ere long find themselves able to welcome every pressure of that hand upon them, even when it was felt in pain, and sometimes not only to believe but to recognize the divine end in view, the bringing of a son into glory; whereas, behaving like children who struggle and scream while their mother washes and dresses them, they find they have to be washed and dressed, notwithstanding, and with the more discomfort: they may even have to find themselves set half naked and but half dried in a corner, to come to their right minds, and ask to be finished.

At this time neither Gibbie nor Donal strove against his creation— what the wise of this world call their fate. In truth Gibbie never did; and for Donal, the process was at present in a stage much too agreeable to rouse any inclination to resist. He enjoyed his new phase of life immensely. If he did not distinguish himself as a scholar, it was not because he neglected his work, but because he was at the same time doing that by which alone the water could ever rise in the well he was digging: he was himself growing. Far too eager after knowledge to indulge in emulation, he gained no prizes: what had he to do with how much or how little those around him could eat as compared with himself? No work noble or lastingly good can come of emulation any more than of greed: I think the motives are spiritually the same. To excite it is worthy only of the commonplace vulgar schoolmaster, whose ambition is to show what fine scholars he can turn out, that he may get the more pupils. Emulation is the devil-shadow of aspiration. The set of the current in the schools is at present towards a boundless swamp, but the wise among the scholars see it, and wisdom is the tortoise which shall win the race. In the mean time how many, with the legs and the brain of the hare, will think they are gaining it, while they are losing things whose loss will make any prize unprized! The result of Donal's work appeared but very partially in his examinations, which were honest and honourable to him; it was hidden in his thoughts, his aspirations, his growth, and his verse—all which may be seen should I one day tell Donal's story. For Gibbie, the minister had not been long teaching him, before he began to desire to make a scholar of him. Partly from being compelled to spend some labour upon it, the boy was gradually developing an unusual facility in expression. His teacher, compact of conventionalities, would have modelled the result upon some writer imagined by him a master of style; but the hurtful folly never got any hold of Gibbie: all he ever cared about was to say what he meant, and avoid saying something else; to know when he had not said what he meant, and to set the words right. It resulted that, when people did not understand what he meant, the cause generally lay with them not with him; and that, if they sometimes smiled over his mode, it was because it lay closer to nature than theirs: they would have found it a hard task to improve it.

What the fault with his organs of speech was, I cannot tell. His guardian lost no time in having them examined by a surgeon in high repute, a professor of the university, but Dr. Skinner's opinion put an end to question and hope together. Gibbie was not in the least disappointed. He had got on very well as yet without speech. It was not like sight or hearing. The only voice he could not hear was his own, and that was just the one he had neither occasion nor desire to hear. As to his friends, those who had known him the longest minded his dumbness the least. But the moment the defect was understood to be irreparable, Mrs. Sclater very wisely proceeded to learn the finger-speech; and as she learned it, she taught it to Gibbie.

As to his manners, which had been and continued to be her chief care, a certain disappointment followed her first rapid success: she never could get them to take on the case-hardening needful for what she counted the final polish. They always retained a certain simplicity which she called childishness. It came in fact of childlikeness, but the lady was not child enough to distinguish the difference—as great as that between the back and the front of a head. As, then, the minister found him incapable of forming a style, though time soon proved him capable of producing one, so the minister's wife found him as incapable of putting on company manners of any sort, as most people are incapable of putting them off—without being rude. It was disappointing to Mrs. Sclater, but Gibbie was just as content to appear what he was, as he was unwilling to remain what he was. Being dumb, she would say to herself he would pass in any society; but if he had had his speech, she never could have succeeded in making him a thorough gentleman: he would have always been saying the right thing in the wrong place. By the wrong place she meant the place where alone the thing could have any pertinence. In after years, however, Gibbie's manners were, whether pronounced such or not, almost universally felt to be charming. But Gibbie knew nothing of his manners any more than of the style in which he wrote.

One night on their way home from an evening party, the minister and his wife had a small difference, probably about something of as little real consequence to them as the knowledge of it is to us, but by the time they reached home, they had got to the very summit of politeness with each other. Gibbie was in the drawing-room, as it happened, waiting their return. At the first sound of their voices, he knew, before a syllable reached him that something was wrong. When they entered, they were too much engrossed in difference to heed his presence, and went on disputing—with the utmost external propriety of words and demeanour, but with both injury and a sense of injury in every tone. Had they looked at Gibbie, I cannot think they would have been silenced; but while neither of them dared turn eyes the way of him, neither had moral strength sufficient to check the words that rose to the lips. A discreet, socially wise boy would have left the room, but how could Gibbie abandon his friends to the fiery darts of the wicked one! He ran to the side-table before mentioned. With a vague presentiment of what was coming, Mrs. Sclater, feeling rather than seeing him move across the room like a shadow, sat in dread expectation; and presently her fear arrived, in the shape of a large New Testament, and a face of loving sadness, and keen discomfort, such as she had never before seen Gibbie wear. He held out the book to her, pointing with a finger to the words—she could not refuse to let her eyes fall upon them—"Have salt in yourselves, and have peace one with another." What Gibbie made of the salt, I do not know; and whether he understood it or not was of little consequence, seeing he had it; but the rest of the sentence he understood so well that he would fain have the writhing yoke-fellows think of it.

The lady's cheeks had been red before, but now they were redder. She rose, cast an angry look at the dumb prophet, a look which seemed to say "How dare you suggest such a thing?" and left the room.

"What have you got there?" asked the minister, turning sharply upon him. Gibbie showed him the passage.

"What have you got to do with it?" he retorted, throwing the book on the table. "Go to bed."

"A detestable prig!" you say, reader?—That is just what Mr. and Mrs. Sclater thought him that night, but they never quarrelled again before him. In truth, they were not given to quarrelling. Many couples who love each other more, quarrel more, and with less politeness. For Gibbie, he went to bed—puzzled, and afraid there must be a beam in his eye.

The very first time Donal and he could manage it, they set out together to find Mistress Croale. Donal thought he had nothing to do but walk straight from Mistress Murkison's door to hers, but, to his own annoyance, and the disappointment of both, he soon found he had not a notion left as to how the place lay, except that it was by the river. So, as it was already rather late, they put off their visit to another time, and took a walk instead.

But Mistress Croale, haunted by old memories, most of them far from pleasant, grew more and more desirous of looking upon the object of perhaps the least disagreeable amongst them: she summoned resolution at last, went to the market a little better dressed than usual, and when business there was over, and she had shut up her little box of a shop, walked to Daur-street to the minister's house.

"He's aften eneuch crossed my door," she said to herself, speaking of Mr. Sclater; "an' though, weel I wat, the sicht o' 'im never bodit me onything but ill, I never loot him ken he was less nor walcome; an' gien bein' a minister gies the freedom o' puir fowk's hooses, it oucht in the niffer (exchange) to gie them the freedom o' his."

Therewith encouraging herself, she walked up the steps and rang the bell. It was a cold, frosty winter evening and as she stood waiting for the door to be opened, much the poor woman longed for her own fireside and a dram. Her period of expectation was drawn out not a little through the fact that the servant whose duty it was to answer the bell was just then waiting at table: because of a public engagement, the minister had to dine earlier than usual. They were in the middle of their soup—cockie-leekie, nice and hot, when the maid informed her master that a woman was at the door, wanting to see Sir Gilbert.

Gibbie looked up, put down his spoon, and was rising to go, when the minister, laying his hand on his arm, pressed him gently back to his chair, and Gibbie yielded, waiting.

"What sort of a woman?" he asked the girl.

"A decent-lookin' workin'-like body," she answered. "I couldna see her verra weel, it's sae foggy the nicht aboot the door."

"Tell her we're at dinner; she may call again in an hour. Or if she likes to leave a message—Stay: tell her to come again to-morrow morning.—I wonder who she is," he added, turning, he thought, to Gibbie.

But Gibbie was gone. He had passed behind his chair, and all he saw of him was his back as he followed the girl from the room. In his eagerness he left the door open, and they saw him dart to the visitor, shake hands with her in evident delight, and begin pulling her towards the room.

Now Mistress Croale, though nowise inclined to quail before the minister, would not willingly have intruded herself upon him, especially while he sat at dinner with his rather formidable lady; but she fancied, for she stood where she could not see into the dining-room, that Gibbie was taking her where they might have a quiet news together, and, occupied with her bonnet or some other source of feminine disquiet, remained thus mistaken until she stood on the threshold, when, looking up, she started, stopped, made an obedience to the minister, and another to the minister's lady, and stood doubtful, if not a little abashed.

"Not here! my good woman," said Mr. Sclater, rising. "—Oh, it's you, Mistress Croale!—I will speak to you in the hall."

Mrs. Croale's face flushed, and she drew back a step. But Gibbie still held her, and with a look to Mr. Sclater that should have sent straight to his heart the fact that she was dear to his soul, kept drawing her into the room; he wanted her to take his chair at the table. It passed swiftly through her mind that one who had been so intimate both with

Sir George and Sir Gibbie in the old time, and had given the latter his tea every Sunday night for so long, might surely, even in such changed circumstances, be allowed to enter the same room with him, however grand it might be; and involuntarily almost she yielded half a doubtful step, while Mr. Sclater, afraid of offending Sir Gilbert, hesitated on the advance to prevent her. How friendly the warm air felt! how consoling the crimson walls with the soft flicker of the great fire upon them! how delicious the odour of the cockie-leekie! She could give up whisky a good deal more easily, she thought, if she had the comforts of a minister to fall back upon! And this was the same minister who had once told her that her soul was as precious to him as that of any other in his parish—and then driven her from respectable Jink Lane to the disreputable Daurfoot! It all passed through her mind in a flash, while yet Gibbie pulled and she resisted.

"Gilbert, come here," called Mrs. Sclater.

He went to her side, obedient and trusting as a child.

"Really, Gilbert, you must not," she said, rather loud for a whisper. "It won't do to turn things upside down this way. If you are to be a gentleman, and an inmate of my house, you must behave like other people. I cannot have a woman like that sitting at my table.—Do you know what sort of a person she is?"

Gibbie's face shone up. He raised his hands. He was already able to talk a little.

"Is she a sinner?" he asked on his fingers.

Mrs. Sclater nodded.

Gibbie wheeled round, and sprang back to the hall, whither the minister had, coming down upon her, bows on, like a sea-shouldering whale, in a manner ejected Mistress Croale, and where he was now talking to her with an air of confidential condescension, willing to wipe out any feeling of injury she might perhaps be inclined to cherish at not being made more welcome: to his consternation, Gibbie threw his arms round her neck, and gave her a great hug.

"Sir Gilbert!" he exclaimed, very angry, and the more angry that he knew he was in the right, "leave Mistress Croale alone, and go back to your dinner immediately.—Jane, open the door."

Jane opened the door, Gibbie let her go, and Mrs. Croale went. But on the threshold she turned.

"Weel, sir," she said, with more severity than pique, and a certain sad injury not unmingled with dignity, "ye hae stappit ower my door-

sill mony's the time, an' that wi' sairer words i' yer moo' nor I ever
mintit at peyin' ye back; an' I never said to ye gang. Sae first ye turnt
me oot o' my ain hoose, an' noo ye turn me oot o' yours; an' what's
left ye to turn me oot o' but the hoose o' the Lord? An', 'deed, sir, ye
need never won'er gien the likes o' me disna care aboot gangin' to hear
a preacht gospel: we wad fain see a practeesed ane! Gien ye had said
to me noo the nicht, 'Come awa' ben, Mistress Croale, an' tak a plet
o' cockie-leekie wi' 's; it's a cauld nicht;' it's mysel' wad hae been sae
upliftit wi' yer kin'ness, 'at I wad hae gane hame an' ta'en—I dinna
ken—aiblins a read at my Bible, an' been to be seen at the kirk upo'
Sunday I wad—o' that ye may be sure; for it's a heap easier to gang
to the kirk nor to read the buik yer lane, whaur ye canna help thinkin'
upo' what it says to ye. But noo, as 'tis, I'm awa' hame to the whusky
boatle, an' the sin o' 't, gien there be ony in sic a nicht o' cauld an' fog,
'ill jist lie at your door."

"You shall have a plate of soup, and welcome, Mistress Croale!" said
the minister, in a rather stagey tone of hospitality "—Jane, take Mistress
Croale to the kitchen with you, and—"

"The deil's tail i' yer soup!—'At I sud say 't!" cried Mistress Croale,
drawing herself up suddenly, with a snort of anger: "whan turnt I
beggar? I wad fain be informt! Was't yer soup or yer grace I soucht till,
sir? The Lord be atween you an' me! There's first 'at 'll be last, an' last 'at
'll be first. But the tane's no me, an' the tither's no you, sir."

With that she turned and walked down the steps, holding her head
high.

"Really, Sir Gilbert," said the minister, going back into the dining-
room—but no Gibbie was there!—nobody but his wife, sitting in
solitary discomposure at the head of her dinner-table. The same instant,
he heard a clatter of feet down the steps, and turned quickly into the
hall again, where Jane was in the act of shutting the door.

"Sir Gilbert's run oot efter the wuman, sir!" she said.

"Hoot!" grunted the minister, greatly displeased, and went back to
his wife.

"Take Sir Gilbert's plate away," said Mrs. Sclater to the servant.

"That's his New Testament again!" she went on, when the girl had
left the room.

"My dear! my dear! take care," said her husband. He had not much
notion of obedience to God, but he had some idea of respect to religion.
He was just an idolater of a Christian shade.

"Really, Mr. Sclater," his wife continued, "I had no idea what I was undertaking. But you gave me no choice. The creature is incorrigible. But of course he must prefer the society of women like that. They are the sort he was accustomed to when he received his first impressions, and how could it be otherwise? You knew how he had been brought up, and what you had to expect!"

"Brought up!" cried the minister, and caused his spoonful of cockie-leekie to rush into his mouth with the noise of the German schlürfen, then burst into a loud laugh. "You should have seen him about the streets!—with his trowsers—"

"Mister Sclater! Then you ought to have known better!" said his wife, and laying down her spoon, sat back into the embrace of her chair.

But in reality she was not the least sorry he had undertaken the charge. She could not help loving the boy, and her words were merely the foam of vexation, mingled with not a little jealousy, that he had left her, and his nice hot dinner, to go with the woman. Had she been a fine lady like herself, I doubt if she would have liked it much better; but she specially recoiled from coming into rivalry with one in whose house a horrible murder had been committed, and who had been before the magistrates in consequence.

Nothing further was said until the second course was on the table. Then the lady spoke again:

"You really must, Mr. Sclater, teach him the absurdity of attempting to fit every point of his behaviour to—to—words which were of course quite suitable to the time when they were spoken, but which it is impossible to take literally now-a-days—as impossible as to go about the streets with a great horn on your head and a veil hanging across it.—Why!"—Here she laughed—a laugh the less lady-like that, although it was both low and musical, it was scornful, and a little shaken by doubt.—"You saw him throw his arms round the horrid creature's neck!—Well, he had just asked me if she was a sinner. I made no doubt she was. Off with the word goes my gentleman to embrace her!"

Here they laughed together.

Dinner over, they went to a missionary meeting, where the one stood and made a speech and the other sat and listened, while Gibbie was having tea with Mistress Croale.

From that day Gibbie's mind was much exercised as to what he could do for Mistress Croale, and now first he began to wish he had his money. As fast as he learned the finger-alphabet he had taught it to

Donal, and, as already they had a good many symbols in use between them, so many indeed that Donal would often instead of speaking make use of signs, they had now the means of intercourse almost as free as if they had had between them two tongues instead of one. It was easy therefore for Gibbie to impart to Donal his anxiety concerning her, and his strong desire to help her, and doing so, he lamented in a gentle way his present inability. This communication Donal judged it wise to impart in his turn to Mistress Croale.

"Ye see, mem," he said in conclusion, "he's some w'y or anither gotten 't intil's heid 'at ye're jist a wheen ower free wi' the boatle. I kenna. Ye'll be the best jeedge o' that yersel'!"

Mistress Croale was silent for a whole minute by the clock. From the moment when Gibbie forsook his dinner and his grand new friends to go with her, the woman's heart had begun to grow to the boy, and her old memories fed the new crop of affection.

"Weel," she replied at length, with no little honesty, "—I mayna be sae ill 's he thinks me, for he had aye his puir father afore 's e'en; but the bairn's richt i' the main, an' we maun luik till't, an' see what can be dune; for eh! I wad be laith to disappint the bonnie laad!—Maister Grant, gien ever there wis a Christi-an sowl upo' the face o' this wickit warl', that Christi-an sowl's wee Sir Gibbie!—an' wha cud hae thoucht it! But it's the Lord's doin', an' mervellous in oor eyes!—Ow! ye needna luik like that; I ken my Bible no that ill!" she added, catching a glimmer of surprise on Donal's countenance. "But for that Maister Scletter—dod! I wadna be sair upon 'im—but gien he be fit to caw a nail here an' a nail there, an fix a sklet or twa, creepin' upo' the riggin' o' the kirk, I'm weel sure he's nae wise maister-builder fit to lay ony fundation.—Ay! I tellt ye I kent my beuk no that ill!" she added with some triumph; then resumed: "What the waur wad he or she or Sir Gibbie hae been though they hed inveetit me, as I was there, to sit me doon, an' tak' a plet o' their cockie-leekie wi' them? There was ane 'at thoucht them 'at was far waur nor me, guid eneuch company for him; an' maybe I may sit doon wi' him efter a', wi' the help o' my bonnie wee Sir Gibbie.—I canna help ca'in' him wee Sir Gibbie—a' the toon ca'd 'im that, though haith! he'll be a big man or he behaud. An' for 's teetle, I was aye ane to gie honour whaur honour was due, an' never ance, weel as I kenned him, did I ca' his honest father, for gien ever there was an honest man yon was him!—never did I ca' him onything but Sir George, naither mair nor less, an' that though he vroucht at the hardest at the cobblin' a' the ook, an' upo' Setterdays was pleased to hae a guid wash i' my ain bedroom, an' pit on a clean sark o' my deid man's, rist his sowl!—no 'at I'm a papist, Maister Grant, an' aye kent better nor think it was ony eese prayin' for them 'at's gane; for wha is there to pey ony heed to sic haithenish prayers as that wad be? Na! we maun pray for the livin' 'at it may dee some guid till, an' no for them 'at its a' ower wi'—the Lord hae mercy upo' them!"

My readers may suspect, one for one reason another for another, that she had already, before Donal came that evening been holding communion with the idol in the three-cornered temple of her cupboard; and I confess that it was so. But it is equally true that before the next year was gone, she was a shade better—and that not without considerable struggle, and more failures than successes.

Upon one occasion—let those who analyze the workings of the human mind as they would the entrails of an eight-day clock, explain the phenomenon I am about to relate, or decline to believe it, as they choose—she became suddenly aware that she was getting perilously near the brink of actual drunkenness.

"I'll tak but this ae mou'fu' mair," she said to herself; "it's but a mou'fu', an' it's the last i' the boatle, an' it wad be a peety naebody to get the guid o' 't."

She poured it out. It was nearly half a glass. She took it in one large mouthful. But while she held it in her mouth to make the most of it, even while it was between her teeth, something smote her with the sudden sense that this very moment was the crisis of her fate, that now the axe was laid to the root of her tree. She dropped on her knees—not to pray like poor Sir George—but to spout the mouthful of whisky into the fire. In roaring flame it rushed up the chimney. She started back.

"Eh!" she cried; "guid God! sic a deevil's I maun be, to cairry the like o' that i' my inside!—Lord! I'm a perfec' byke o' deevils! My name it maun be Legion. What is to become o' my puir sowl!"

It was a week before she drank another drop—and then she took her devils with circumspection, and the firm resolve to let no more of them enter into her than she could manage to keep in order.

Mr. and Mrs. Sclater got over their annoyance as well as they could, and agreed that in this case no notice should be taken of Gibbie's conduct.

XLV

SHOALS AHEAD

It had come to be the custom that Gibbie should go to Donal every Friday afternoon about four o'clock, and remain with him till the same time on Saturday, which was a holiday with both. One Friday, just after he was gone, the temptation seized Mrs. Sclater to follow him, and, paying the lads an unexpected visit, see what they were about.

It was a bright cold afternoon; and in fur tippet and muff, amidst the snow that lay everywhere on roofs and window-sills and pavements, and the wind that blew cold as it blows in few places besides, she looked, with her bright colour and shining eyes, like life itself laughing at death. But not many of those she met carried the like victory in their countenances, for the cold was bitter. As she approached the Widdiehill, she reflected that she had followed Gibbie so quickly, and walked so fast, that the boys could hardly have had time to settle to anything, and resolved therefore to make a little round and spend a few more minutes upon the way. But as, through a neighbouring street, she was again approaching the Widdiehill, she caught sight of something which, as she was passing a certain shop, that of a baker known to her as one of her husband's parishioners, made her stop and look in through the glass which formed the upper half of the door. There she saw Gibbie, seated on the counter, dangling his legs, eating a penny loaf, and looking as comfortable as possible.—"So soon after luncheon, too!" said Mrs. Sclater to herself with indignation, reading through the spectacles of her anger a reflection on her housekeeping. But a second look revealed, as she had dreaded, far weightier cause for displeasure: a very pretty girl stood behind the counter, with whose company Gibbie was evidently much pleased. She was fair of hue, with eyes of gray and green, and red lips whose smile showed teeth whiter than the whitest of flour. At the moment she was laughing merrily, and talking gaily to Gibbie. Clearly they were on the best of terms, and the boy's bright countenance, laughter, and eager motions, were making full response to the girl's words.

Gibbie had been in the shop two or three times before, but this was the first time he had seen his old friend, Mysie, of the amethyst ear-ring.

And now one of them had reminded the other of that episode in which their histories had run together; from that Mysie had gone on to other reminiscences of her childhood in which wee Gibbie bore a part, and he had, as well as he could, replied with others, of his, in which she was concerned. Mysie was a simple, well-behaved girl, and the entrance of neither father nor mother would have made the least difference in her behaviour to Sir Gilbert, though doubtless she was more pleased to have a chat with him than with her father's apprentice, who could speak indeed, but looked dull as the dough he worked in, whereas Gibbie, although dumb, was radiant. But the faces of people talking often look more meaningful to one outside the talk-circle than they really are, and Mrs. Sclater, gazing through the glass, found, she imagined, large justification of displeasure. She opened the door sharply, and stepped in. Gibbie jumped from his seat on the counter, and, with a smile of playful roguery, offered it to her; a vivid blush overspread Mysie's fair countenance.

"I thought you had gone to see Donal," said Mrs. Sclater, in the tone of one deceived, and took no notice of the girl.

Gibbie gave her to understand that Donal would arrive presently, and they were then going to the point of the pier, that Donal might learn what the sea was like in a nor'-easter.

"But why did you make your appointment here?" asked the lady.

"Because Mysie and I are old friends," answered the boy on his fingers.

Then first Mrs. Sclater turned to the girl: having got over her first indignation, she spoke gently and with a frankness natural to her.

"Sir Gilbert tells me you are old friends," she said.

Thereupon Mysie told her the story of the ear-ring, which had introduced their present conversation, and added several other little recollections, in one of which she was drawn into a description, half pathetic, half humorous, of the forlorn appearance of wee Gibbie, as he ran about in his truncated trousers. Mrs. Slater was more annoyed, however, than interested, for, in view of the young baronet's future, she would have had all such things forgotten; but Gibbie was full of delight in the vivid recollections thus brought him of some of the less painful portions of his past, and appreciated every graphic word that fell from the girl's pretty lips.

Mrs. Sclater took good care not to leave until Donal came. Then the boys, having asked her if she would not go with them, which invitation she declined with smiling thanks, took their departure and went to pay their visit to the German Ocean, leaving her with Mysie—which they certainly would not have done, could they have foreseen how the well-meaning lady—nine-tenths of the mischiefs in the world are well-meant—would hurt the feelings of the gentle-conditioned girl. For a long time after, as often as Gibbie entered the shop, Mysie left it and her mother came—a result altogether as Mrs. Sclater would have had it. But hardly anybody was ever in less danger of falling in love than Gibbie; and the thing would not have been worth recording, but for the new direction it caused in Mrs. Sclater's thoughts: measures, she judged, must be taken.

Gladly as she would have centred Gibbie's boyish affections in herself, she was too conscientious and experienced not to regard the danger of any special effort in that direction, and began therefore to cast about in her mind what could be done to protect him from one at least of the natural consequences of his early familiarity with things unseemly—exposure, namely, to the risk of forming low alliances—the more imminent that it was much too late to attempt any restriction of his liberty, so as to keep him from roaming the city at his pleasure. Recalling what her husband had told her of the odd meeting between the boy and a young lady at Miss Kimble's school—some relation, she thought he had said—also the desire to see her again which Gibbie, on more than one occasion, had shown, she thought whether she could turn the acquaintance to account. She did not much like Miss Kimble, chiefly because of her affectations—which, by the way, were caricatures of her own; but she knew her very well, and there was no reason why she should not ask her to come and spend the evening, and bring two or three of the elder girls with her: a little familiarity with the looks, manners, and dress of refined girls of his own age, would be the best antidote to his taste for low society, from that of bakers' daughters downwards.

It was Mrs. Sclater's own doing that Gibbie had not again spoken to Ginevra. Nowise abashed at the thought of the grenadier or her array of doves, he would have gone, the very next day after meeting them in the street, to call upon her: it was some good, he thought, of being a rich instead of a poor boy, that, having lost thereby those whom he loved best, he had come where he could at least see Miss Galbraith; but Mrs. Sclater had pretended not to understand where he wanted to go, and used other artifices besides—well-meant, of course—to keep him to herself until she should better understand him. After that he had seen Ginevra more than once at church, but had had no chance of speaking to her. For, in the sudden dispersion of its agglomerate particles, a Scotch congregation is—or was in Gibbie's time—very like the well-known vitreous drop called a Prince Rupert's tear, in which the mutually repellent particles are held together by a strongly contracted homogeneous layer—to separate with explosion the instant the tough skin is broken and vibration introduced; and as Mrs. Sclater generally sat in her dignity to the last, and Gibbie sat with her, only once was he out in time to catch a glimpse of the ultimate rank of the retreating girls. He was just starting to pursue them, when Mrs. Sclater, perceiving his intention, detained him by requesting the support of his arm—a way she had, pretending to be weary, or to have given her ankle a twist, when she wanted to keep him by her side. Another time he had followed them close enough to see which turn they took out of Daur-street; but that was all he had learned, and when the severity of the winter arrived, and the snow lay deep, sometimes for weeks together, the chances of meeting them were few. The first time the boys went out together, that when they failed to find Mistress Croale's garret, they made an excursion in search of the girls' school, but had been equally unsuccessful in that; and although they never after went for a walk without contriving to pass through some part of the region in which they thought it must lie, they had never yet even discovered a house upon which they could agree as presenting probabilities.

Mr. Galbraith did not take Miss Kimble into his confidence with respect to his reasons for so hurriedly placing his daughter under her care: he was far too reticent, too proud, and too much hurt for that. Hence, when Mrs. Sclater's invitation arrived, the schoolmistress was aware of no reason why Miss Galbraith should not be one of the girls to go with her, especially as there was her cousin, Sir Gilbert, whom she herself would like to meet again, in the hope of removing the bad impression which, in the discharge of her duty, she feared she must have made upon him.

One day, then, at luncheon, Mrs. Sclater told Gibbie that some ladies were coming to tea, and they were going to have supper instead of dinner. He must put on his best clothes, she said. He did as she desired, was duly inspected, approved on the whole, and finished off by a few deft fingers at his necktie, and a gentle push or two from the loveliest of hands against his hair-thatch, and was seated in the drawing-room with Mrs. Sclater when the ladies arrived. Ginevra and he shook hands, she with the sweetest of rose-flushes, he with the radiance of delighted surprise. But, a moment after, when Mrs. Sclater and her guests had seated themselves, Gibbie, their only gentleman, for Mr. Sclater had not yet made his appearance, had vanished from the room. Tea was not brought until some time after, when Mr. Sclater came home, and then Mrs. Sclater sent Jane to find Sir Gilbert; but she returned to say he was not in the house. The lady's heart sank, her countenance fell, and all was gloom: her project had miscarried! he was gone! who could tell whither?—perhaps to the baker's daughter, or to the horrid woman Croale!

The case was however very much otherwise. The moment Gibbie ended his greetings, he had darted off to tell Donal: it was not his custom to enjoy alone anything sharable.

The news that Ginevra was at that moment seated in Mrs. Sclater's house, at that moment, as his eagerness had misunderstood Gibbie's, expecting his arrival, raised such a commotion in Donal's atmosphere, that for a time it was but a huddle of small whirlwinds. His heart was beating like the trample of a trotting horse. He never thought of inquiring whether Gibbie had been commissioned by Mrs. Sclater to invite him, or reflected that his studies were not half over for the night. An instant before the arrival of the blessed fact, he had been absorbed in a rather abstruse metaphysico-mathematical question; now not the metaphysics of the universe would have appeared to him worth a moment's meditation. He went pacing up and down the room, and seemed lost to everything. Gibbie shook him at length, and told him, by two signs, that he must put on his Sunday clothes. Then first shyness, like the shroud of northern myth that lies in wait in a man's path, leaped up, and wrapped itself around him. It was very well to receive ladies in a meadow, quite another thing to walk into their company in a grand room, such as, before entering Mrs. Sclater's, he had never beheld even in Fairyland or the Arabian Nights. He knew the ways of the one, and not the ways of the other. Chairs ornate were doubtless poor things to daisied banks, yet the other day he had hardly brought himself to sit on one of Mrs. Sclater's! It was a moment of awful seeming. But what would he not face to see once more the lovely lady-girl! He bethought himself that he was no longer a cowherd but a student, and that such feelings were unworthy of one who would walk level with his fellows. He rushed to the labours of his toilette, performed severe ablutions, endued his best shirt—coarse, but sweet from the fresh breezes of Glashgar, a pair of trousers of buff-coloured fustian stamped over with a black pattern, an olive-green waistcoat, a blue tailcoat with lappets behind, and a pair of well-polished shoes, the soles of which in honour of Sunday were studded with small instead of large knobs of iron, set a tall beaver hat, which no brushing would make smooth, on the back of his head, stuffed a silk hankerchief, crimson and yellow, in his pocket, and declared himself ready.

Now Gibbie, although he would not have looked so well in his woolly coat in Mrs. Sclater's drawing-room as on the rocks of Glashgar, would have looked better in almost any other than the evening dress, now, alas! nearly European. Mr. Sclater, on the other hand, would have looked worse in any other because being less commonplace, it would have been less like himself; and so long as the commonplace conventional so greatly outnumber the simply individual, it is perhaps well the present fashion should hold. But Donal could hardly have put on any clothes that would have made him look worse, either in respect of himself or of the surroundings of social life, than those he now wore. Neither of the boys, however, had begun to think about dress in relation either to custom or to fitness, and it was with complete satisfaction that Gibbie carried off Donal to present to the guest of his guardians.

Donal's preparations had taken a long time, and before they reached the house, tea was over and gone. They had had some music; and Mrs. Sclater was now talking kindly to two of the school-girls, who, seated erect on the sofa, were looking upon her elegance with awe and envy. Ginevra, was looking at the pictures of an annual. Mr. Sclater was making Miss Kimble agreeable to herself. He had a certain gift of talk—depending in a great measure on the assurance of being listened to, an assurance which is, alas! nowise the less hurtful to many a clergyman out of the pulpit, that he may be equally aware no one heeds him in it.

XLVI

THE GIRLS

T he door was opened. Donal spent fully a minute rubbing his shoes on the mat, as diligently as if he had just come out of the cattle-yard, and then Gibbie led him in triumph up the stair to the drawing-room. Donal entered in that loose-jointed way which comes of the brains being as yet all in the head, and stood, resisting Gibbie's pull on his arm, his keen hazel eyes looking gently round upon the company, until he caught sight of the face he sought, when, with the stride of a sower of corn, he walked across the room to Ginevra. Mrs. Sclater rose; Mr. Sclater threw himself back and stared; the latter astounded at the presumption of the youths, the former uneasy at the possible results of their ignorance. To the astonishment of the company, Ginevra rose, respect and modesty in every feature, as the youth, clownish rather than awkward, approached her, and almost timidly held out her hand to him. He took it in his horny palm, shook it hither and thither sideways, like a leaf in a doubtful air, then held it like a precious thing he was at once afraid of crushing by too tight a grasp, and of dropping from too loose a hold, until Ginevra took charge of it herself again. Gibbie danced about behind him, all but standing on one leg, but, for Mrs. Sclater's sake, restraining himself. Ginevra sat down, and Donal, feeling very large and clumsy, and wanting to "be naught a while," looked about him for a chair, and then first espying Mrs. Sclater, went up to her with the same rolling, clamping stride, but without embarrassment, and said, holding out his hand,

"Hoo are ye the nicht, mem? I sawna yer bonnie face whan I cam in. A gran' hoose, like this o' yours—an' I'm sure, mem, it cudna be ower gran' to fit yersel', but it's jist some perplexin' to plain fowk like me, 'at's been used to mair room, an' less intill't."

Donal was thinking of the meadow on the Lorrie bank.

"I was sure of it!" remarked Mrs. Sclater to herself. "One of nature's gentlemen! He would soon be taught."

She was right; but he was more than a gentleman, and could have taught her what she could have taught nobody in turn.

"You will soon get accustomed to our town ways, Mr. Grant. But many of the things we gather about us are far more trouble than use," she replied, in her sweetest tones, and with a gentle pressure of the hand, which went a long way to set him at his ease. "I am glad to see you have friends here," she added.

"Only ane, mem. Gibbie an' me—"

"Excuse me, Mr. Grant, but would you oblige me—of course with me it is of no consequence, but just for habit's sake, would you oblige me by calling Gilbert by his own name—Sir Gilbert, please. I wish him to get used to it."

"Yer wull be't, mem.—Weel, as I was sayin', Sir Gibbie—Sir Gilbert, that is, mem—an mysel', we hae kenned Miss Galbraith this lang time, bein' o' the laird's ain fowk, as I may say."

"Will you take a seat beside her, then," said Mrs. Sclater, and rising, herself placed a chair for him near Ginevra, wondering how any Scotch laird, the father of such a little lady as she, could have allowed her such an acquaintance.

To most of the company he must have looked very queer. Gibbie, indeed, was the only one who saw the real Donal. Miss Kimble and her pupils stared at the distorted reflexion of him in the spoon-bowl of their own elongated narrowness; Mrs. Sclater saw the possible gentleman through the loop-hole of a compliment he had paid her; and Mr. Sclater beheld only the minimum which the reversed telescope of his own enlarged importance, he having himself come of sufficiently humble origin, made of him; while Ginevra looked up to him more as one who marvelled at the grandly unintelligible, than one who understood the relations and proportions of what she beheld. Nor was it possible she could help feeling that he was a more harmonious object to the eye both of body and mind when dressed in his corduroys and blue bonnet, walking the green fields, with cattle about him, his club under his arm, and a book in his hand. So seen, his natural dignity was evident; now he looked undeniably odd. A poet needs a fine house rather than a fine dress to set him off, and Mrs. Sclater's drawing-room was neither large nor beautiful enough to frame this one, especially with his Sunday clothes to get the better of. To the school ladies, mistress and pupils, he was simply a clodhopper, and from their report became a treasure of poverty-stricken amusement to the school. Often did Ginevra's cheek burn with indignation at the small insolences of her fellow-pupils. At first she attempted to make them understand something of what Donal really was, but finding them unworthy of the confidence, was driven to betake herself to such a silence as put a stop to their offensive remarks in her presence.

"I thank ye, mem," said Donal, as he took the chair; "ye're verra condescendin'." Then turning to Ginevra, and trying to cross one knee over the other, but failing from the tightness of certain garments, which, like David with Saul's not similarly faulty armour, he had not hitherto proved, "Weel, mem," he said, "ye haena forgotten Hornie, I houp."

The other girls must be pardoned for tittering, offensive as is the habit so common to their class, for the only being they knew by that name was one to whom the merest reference sets pit and gallery in a roar. Miss Kimble was shocked—disgusted, she said afterwards; and until she learned that the clown was there uninvited, cherished a grudge against Mrs. Sclater.

Ginevra smiled him a satisfactory negative.

"I never read the ballant aboot the worm lingelt roun' the tree," said Donal, making rather a long link in the chain of association, "ohn thoucht upo' that day, mem, whan first ye cam doon the brae wi' my sister Nicie, an' I cam ower the burn till ye, an' ye garred me lauch aboot weetin' o' my feet! Eh, mem! wi' you afore me there, I see the blew lift again, an' the gerse jist lowin' (flaming) green, an' the nowt at their busiest, the win' asleep, an' the burn sayin', 'Ye need nane o' ye speyk: I'm here, an' it's my business.' Eh, mem! whan I think upo' 't a', it seems to me 'at the human hert closed i' the mids o' sic a coffer o' cunnin' workmanship, maun be a terrible precious-like thing."

Gibbie, behind Donal's chair, seemed pulsing light at every pore, but the rest of the company, understanding his words perfectly, yet not comprehending a single sentence he uttered, began to wonder whether he was out of his mind, and were perplexed to see Ginevra listening to him with such respect. They saw a human offence where she knew a poet. A word is a word, but its interpretations are many, and the understanding of a man's words depends both on what the hearer is, and on what is his idea of the speaker. As to the pure all things are pure, because only purity can enter, so to the vulgar all things are vulgar, because only the vulgar can enter. Wherein then is the commonplace man to be blamed, for as he is, so must he think? In this, that he consents to be commonplace, willing to live after his own idea of himself, and not after God's idea of him—the real idea, which, every now and then stirring in him, makes him uneasy with silent rebuke.

Ginevra said little in reply. She had not much to say. In her world the streams were still, not vocal. But Donal meant to hold a little communication with her which none of them, except indeed Gibbie—he did not mind Gibbie—should understand.

"I hed sic a queer dream the ither nicht, mem," he said, "an' I'll jist tell ye't.—I thoucht I was doon in an awfu' kin' o' a weet bog, wi' dry graively-like hills a' aboot it, an' naething upo' them but a wheen short hunger-like gerse. An' oot o' the mids o' the bog there grew jist ae tree—a saugh, I think it was, but unco auld—'maist past kennin' wi' age;—an' roun' the rouch gnerlet trunk o' 't was twistit three faulds o' the oogliest, ill-fauredest cratur o' a serpent 'at ever was seen. It was jist laithly to luik upo'. I cud describe it till ye, mem, but it wad only gar ye runkle yer bonny broo, an' luik as I wadna hae ye luik, mem, 'cause ye wadna luik freely sae bonny as ye div noo whan ye luik jist yersel'. But ae queer thing was, 'at atween hit an' the tree it grippit a buik, an' I kent it for the buik o' ballants. An' I gaed nearer, luikin' an' luikin', an' some frichtit. But I wadna stan' for that, for that wad be to be caitiff vile, an' no true man: I gaed nearer an' nearer, till I had gotten within a yaird o' the tree, whan a' at ance, wi' a swing an' a swirl, I was three-fauld aboot the tree, an' the laithly worm was me mesel'; an' I was the laithly worm. The verra hert gaed frae me for hoarible dreid, an' scunner at mysel'! Sae there I was! But I wasna lang there i' my meesery, afore I saw, oot o' my ain serpent e'en, maist blin't wi' greitin', ower the tap o' the brae afore me, 'atween me an' the lift, as gien it reacht up to the verra stars, for it wasna day but nicht by this time aboot me, as weel it micht be,—I saw the bonny sicht come up o' a knicht in airmour, helmet an' shield an' iron sheen an' a'; but somehoo I kent by the gang an' the stan' an' the sway o' the bonny boady o' the knicht, 'at it was nae man, but a wuman.—Ye see, mem, sin I cam frae Daurside, I hae been able to get a grip o' buiks 'at I cudna get up there; an' I hed been readin' Spenser's Fairy Queen the nicht afore, a' yon aboot the lady 'at pat on the airmour o' a man, an' foucht like a guid ane for the richt an' the trowth—an' that hed putten 't i' my heid maybe; only whan I saw her, I kent her, an' her name wasna Britomart. She had a twistit brainch o' blew berries aboot her helmet, an' they ca'd her Juniper: wasna that queer, noo? An' she cam doon the hill wi' bonny big strides, no ower big for a stately wuman, but eh, sae different frae the nipperty mincin' stippety-stap o' the leddies ye see upo' the streets here! An' sae she cam doon the brae. An' I soucht sair to cry oot—first o' a' to tell her gien she didna luik till her feet, she wad he lairt i' the bog, an' syne to beg o' her for mercy's sake to draw her swoord, an' caw the oogly heid aff o' me, an' lat me dee. Noo I maun confess 'at the ballant o' Kemp Owen was rinnin' i' the worm-heid o' me, an' I cudna help thinkin' what, notwithstan'in' the cheenge o' han's i' the story, lay still to the pairt o' the knicht; but hoo was ony man, no to say a mere ugsome serpent, to mint at sic a thing till a leddy, whether she was in steel beets an' spurs or in lang train an' silver slippers? An' haith! I sune fan' 'at I cudna hae spoken the word, gien I had daured ever sae stoot. For whan I opened my moo' to cry till her, I cud dee naething but shot oot a forkit tongue, an' cry sss. Mem, it was dreidfu'! Sae I had jist to tak in my tongue again, an' say naething, for fear o' fleggin' awa' my bonny leddy i' the steel claes. An' she cam an' cam, doon an' doon, an' on to the bog; an' for a' the weicht o' her airmour she sankna a fit intill 't. An' she cam, an' she stude, an' she luikit at me; an' I hed seen her afore, an' kenned her weel. An' she luikit at me, an' aye luikit; an' I winna say what was i' the puir worm's hert. But at the last she gae a gret sich, an' a sab, like, an' stude jist as gien she was tryin' sair, but could not mak up her bonny min' to yon 'at was i' the ballant. An' eh! hoo I grippit the buik atween me an' the tree—for there it was—a' as I saw 't afore! An' sae at last she gae a kin' o' a cry, an' turnt an' gaed awa', wi' her heid hingin' doon, an' her swoord trailin', an' never turnt to luik ahint her, but up the brae, an' ower the tap o' the hill, an' doon an' awa'; an' the brainch wi' the blew berries was the last I saw o' her gaein' doon like the meen ahint the hill. An' jist wi' the fell greitin' I cam to mysel', an' my hert was gaein' like a pump 'at wad fain pit oot a fire.—Noo wasna that a queer-like dream?—I'll no say, mem, but I hae curriet an' kaimbt it up a wee, to gar 't tell better."

Ginevra had from the first been absorbed in listening, and her brown eyes seemed to keep growing larger and larger as he went on. Even the girls listened and were silent, looking as if they saw a peacock's feather in a turkey's tail. When he ended, the tears rushed from Ginevra's eyes—for bare sympathy—she had no perception of personal intent in the parable; it was long before she saw into the name of the lady-knight, for she had never been told the English of Ginevra; she was the simplest, sweetest of girls, and too young to suspect anything in the heart of a man.

"O Donal!" she said, "I am very sorry for the poor worm; but it was naughty of you to dream such a dream."

"Hoo's that, mem?" returned Donal, a little frightened.

"It was not fair of you," she replied, "to dream a knight of a lady, and then dream her doing such an unknightly thing. I am sure if ladies went out in that way, they would do quite as well, on the whole, as gentlemen."

"I mak nae doobt o' 't, mem: h'aven forbid!" cried Donal; "but ye see dreams is sic senseless things 'at they winna be helpit;—an' that was hoo I dreemt it."

"Well, well, Donal!" broke in the harsh pompous voice of Mr. Sclater, who, unknown to the poet, had been standing behind him almost the whole time, "you have given the ladies quite enough of your romancing. That sort of thing, you know, my man, may do very well round the fire in the farm kitchen, but it's not the sort of thing for a drawing-room. Besides, the ladies don't understand your word of mouth; they don't understand such broad Scotch.—Come with me, and I'll show you something you would like to see."

He thought Donal was boring his guests, and at the same time preventing Gibbie from having the pleasure in their society for the sake of which they had been invited.

Donal rose, replying,

"Think ye sae, sir? I thoucht I was in auld Scotlan' still—here as weel's upo' Glashgar. But may be my jography buik's some auld-fashioned.—Didna ye un'erstan' me, mem?" he added, turning to Ginevra.

"Every word, Donal," she answered.

Donal followed his host contented.

Gibbie took his place, and began to teach Ginevra the finger alphabet. The other girls found him far more amusing than Donal—first of all because he could not speak, which was much less objectionable than speaking like Donal—and funny too, though not so funny as Donal's clothes. And then he had such a romantic history! and was a baronet!

In a few minutes Ginevra knew the letters, and presently she and Gibbie were having a little continuous talk together, a thing they had never had before. It was so slow, however, as to be rather tiring. It was mainly about Donal. But Mrs. Sclater opened the piano, and made a diversion. She played something brilliant, and then sang an Italian song in strillaceous style, revealing to Donal's clownish ignorance a thorough mastery of caterwauling. Then she asked Miss Kimble to play something, who declined, without mentioning that she had neither voice nor ear nor love of music, but said Miss Galbraith should sing—"for once in a way, as a treat.—That little Scotch song you sing now and then, my dear," she added.

Ginevra rose timidly, but without hesitation, and going to the piano, sang, to a simple old Scotch air, to which they had been written, the following verses. Before she ended, the minister, the late herd-boy, and the dumb baronet were grouped crescent-wise behind the music-stool.

I dinna ken what's come ower me!
There's a how whaur ance was a hert; (hollow)
I never luik oot afore me,
An' a cry winna gar me stert;
There's naething nae mair to come ower me,
Blaw the win' frae ony airt. (quarter)

For i' yon kirkyaird there's a hillock,
A hert whaur ance was a how;
An' o' joy there's no left a mealock—(crumb)
Deid aiss whaur ance was a low; (ashes)(flame)
For i' you kirkyaird, i' the hillock,
Lies a seed 'at winna grow.

It's my hert 'at hauds up the wee hillie—
That's hoo there's a how i' my breist;
It's awa' doon there wi' my Willie,
Gaed wi' him whan he was release't;
It's doon i' the green-grown hillie,
But I s' be efter it neist.

Come awa', nichts and mornin's,
Come ooks, years, a' time's clan;
Ye're walcome ayont a' scornin':
Tak me till him as fest as ye can.
Come awa', nichts an' mornin's,
Ye are wings o' a michty span!

For I ken he's luikin' an' waitin',
Luikin' aye doon as I clim':
Wad I hae him see me sit greitin',
I'stead o' gaein' to him?
I'll step oot like ane sure o' a meetin',
I'll traivel an' rin to him.

Three of them knew that the verses were Donal's. If the poet went home feeling more like a fellow in blue coat and fustian trowsers, or a winged genius of the tomb, I leave my reader to judge. Anyhow, he felt he had had enough for one evening, and was able to encounter his work again. Perhaps also, when supper was announced, he reflected that his reception had hardly been such as to justify him in partaking of their food, and that his mother's hospitality to Mr. Sclater had not been in expectation of return. As they went down the stair, he came last and alone, behind the two whispering school-girls; and when they passed on into the dining-room, he spilt out of the house, and ran home to the furniture-shop and his books.

When the ladies took their leave, Gibbie walked with them. And now at last he learned where to find Ginevra.

XLVII

A Lesson of Wisdom

In obedience to the suggestion of his wife, Mr. Sclater did what he could to show Sir Gilbert how mistaken he was in imagining he could fit his actions to the words of our Lord. Shocked as even he would probably have been at such a characterization of his attempt, it amounted practically to this: Do not waste your powers in the endeavour to keep the commandments of our Lord, for it cannot be done, and he knew it could not be done, and never meant it should be done. He pointed out to him, not altogether unfairly, the difficulties, and the causes of mistake, with regard to his words; but said nothing to reveal the spirit and the life of them. Showing more of them to be figures than at first appeared, he made out the meanings of them to be less, not more than the figures, his pictures to be greater than their subjects, his parables larger and more lovely than the truths they represented. In the whole of his lecture, through which ran from beginning to end a tone of reproof, there was not one flash of enthusiasm for our Lord, not a sign that, to his so-called minister, he was a refuge, or a delight—that he who is the joy of his Father's heart, the essential bliss of the universe, was anything to the soul of his creature, who besides had taken upon him to preach his good news, more than a name to call himself by—that the story of the Son of God was to him anything better than the soap and water wherewith to blow theological bubbles with the tobacco-pipe of his speculative understanding. The tendency of it was simply to the quelling of all true effort after the knowing of him through obedience, the quenching of all devotion to the central good. Doubtless Gibbie, as well as many a wiser man, might now and then make a mistake in the embodiment of his obedience, but even where the action misses the command, it may yet be obedience to him who gave the command, and by obeying one learns how to obey. I hardly know, however, where Gibbie blundered, except it was in failing to recognize the animals before whom he ought not to cast his pearls—in taking it for granted that, because his guardian was a minister, and his wife a minister's wife, they must therefore be the disciples of the Jewish carpenter, the eternal Son of the Father of us all. Had he had more of the wisdom of the serpent, he would not have carried them the New Testament as an ending of strife, the words of the Lord as an enlightening law; he would perhaps have known that to try too hard to make people good, is one way to make them worse; that the only way to make them good is to be good—remembering well the beam and the mote; that the time for speaking comes rarely, the time for being never departs.

But in talking thus to Gibbie, the minister but rippled the air: Gibbie was all the time pondering with himself where he had met the same kind of thing, the same sort of person before. Nothing he said had the slightest effect upon him. He was too familiar with truth to take the yeasty bunghole of a working barrel for a fountain of its waters. The unseen Lord and his reported words were to Gibbie realities, compared with which the very visible Mr. Sclater and his assured utterance were as the merest seemings of a phantom mood. He had never resolved to keep the words of the Lord: he just kept them; but he knew amongst the rest the Lord's words about the keeping of his words, and about being ashamed of him before men, and it was with a pitiful indignation he heard the minister's wisdom drivel past his ears. What he would have said, and withheld himself from saying, had he been able to speak, I cannot tell; I only know that in such circumstances the less said the better, for what can be more unprofitable than a discussion where but one of the disputants understands the question, and the other has all the knowledge? It would have been the eloquence of the wise and the prudent against the perfected praise of the suckling.

The effect of it all upon Gibbie was to send him to his room to his prayers, more eager than ever to keep the commandments of him who had said, If ye love me. Comforted then and strengthened, he came down to go to Donal—not to tell him, for to none but Janet could he have made such a communication. But in the middle of his descent he remembered suddenly of what and whom Mr. Sclater had all along been reminding him, and turned aside to Mrs. Sclater to ask her to lend him the Pilgrim's Progress. This, as a matter almost of course, was one of the few books in the cottage on Glashgar—a book beloved of Janet's soul—and he had read it again and again. Mrs. Sclater told him where in her room to find a copy, and presently he had satisfied himself that it was indeed Mr. Worldly Wiseman whom his imagination had, in cloudy fashion, been placing side by side with the talking minister.

Finding his return delayed, Mrs. Sclater went after him, fearing he might be indulging his curiosity amongst her personal possessions.

GEORGE MACDONALD

Peeping in, she saw him seated on the floor beside her little bookcase, lost in reading: she stole behind, and found that what so absorbed him was the conversation between Christian and Worldly—I beg his pardon, he is nothing without his Mr.—between Christian and Mr. Worldly Wiseman.

In the evening, when her husband was telling her what he had said to "the young Pharisee" in the morning, the picture of Gibbie on the floor, with the Pilgrim's Progress and Mr. Worldly Wiseman, flashed back on her mind, and she told him the thing. It stung him, not that Gibbie should perhaps have so paralleled him, but that his wife should so interpret Gibbie. To her, however, he said nothing. Had he been a better man, he would have been convinced by the lesson; as it was, he was only convicted, and instead of repenting was offended grievously. For several days he kept expecting the religious gadfly to come buzzing about him with his sting, that is, his forefinger, stuck in the Pilgrim's Progress, and had a swashing blow ready for him; but Gibbie was beginning to learn a lesson or two, and if he was not yet so wise as some serpents, he had always been more harmless than some doves.

That he had gained nothing for the world was pretty evident to the minister the following Sunday—from the lofty watchtower of the pulpit where he sat throned, while the first psalm was being sung. His own pew was near one of the side doors, and at that door some who were late kept coming in. Amongst them were a stranger or two, who were at once shown to seats. Before the psalm ended, an old man came in and stood by the door—a poor man in mean garments, with the air of a beggar who had contrived to give himself a Sunday look. Perhaps he had come hoping to find it warmer in church than at home. There he stood, motionless as the leech-gatherer, leaning on his stick, disregarded of men—it may have been only by innocent accident, I do not know. But just ere the minister must rise for the first prayer, he saw Gibbie, who had heard a feeble cough, cast a glance round, rise as swiftly as noiselessly, open the door of the pew, get out into the passage, take the old man by the hand, and lead him to his place beside the satin-robed and sable-muffed ministerial consort. Obedient to Gibbie's will, the old man took the seat, with an air both of humility and respect, while happily for Mrs. Sclater's remnant of ruffled composure, there was plenty of room in the pew, so that she could move higher up. The old man, it is true, followed, to make a place for Gibbie, but there was still an interval between them sufficient to afford space to the hope that none of the evils she dreaded would fall upon her to devour her. Flushed, angry, uncomfortable, notwithstanding, her face glowed like a bale-fire to the eyes of her husband, and, I fear, spoiled the prayer—but that did not matter much.

While the two thus involuntarily signalled each other, the boy who had brought discomposure into both pulpit and pew, sat peaceful as a summer morning, with the old man beside him quiet in the reverence of being himself revered. And the minister, while he preached from the words, Let him that thinketh he standeth take heed lest he fall, for the first time in his life began to feel doubtful whether he might not himself be a humbug. There was not much fear of his falling, however, for he had not yet stood on his feet.

Not a word was said to Gibbie concerning the liberty he had taken: the minister and his wife were in too much dread—not of St. James and the "poor man in vile raiment," for they were harmless enough in themselves, but of Gibbie's pointing finger to back them. Three distinct precautions, however, they took; the pew-opener on that side was spoken to; Mrs. Sclater made Gibbie henceforth go into the pew before her; and she removed the New Testament from the drawing-room.

XLVIII

Needfull Odds and Ends

It will be plain from what I have told, that Donal's imagination was full of Ginevra, and his was not an economy whose imagination could enjoy itself without calling the heart to share. At the same time, his being in love, if already I may use concerning him that most general and most indefinite of phrases, so far from obstructing his study, was in reality an aid to his thinking and a spur to excellence—not excellence over others, but over himself. There were moments, doubtless, long moments too, in which he forgot Homer and Cicero and differential calculus and chemistry, for "the bonnie lady-lassie,"—that was what he called her to himself; but it was only, on emerging from the reverie, to attack his work with fresh vigour. She was so young, so plainly girlish, that as yet there was no room for dread or jealousy; the feeling in his heart was a kind of gentle angel-worship; and he would have turned from the idea of marrying her, if indeed it had ever presented itself, as an irreverent thought, which he dared not for a moment be guilty of entertaining. It was besides, an idea too absurd to be indulged in by one who, in his wildest imaginations, always, through every Protean embodiment, sought and loved and clung to the real. His chief thought was simply to find favour in the eyes of the girl. His ideas hovered about her image, but it was continually to burn themselves in incense to her sweet ladyhood. As often as a song came fluttering its wings at his casement, the next thought was Ginevra—and there would be something to give her! I wonder how many loves of the poets have received their offerings in correspondent fervour. I doubt if Ginevra, though she read them with marvel, was capable of appreciating the worth of Donal's. She was hardly yet woman enough to do them justice; for the heart of a girl, in its very sweetness and vagueness, is ready to admire alike the good and the indifferent, if their outer qualities be similar. It would cause a collapse in many a swelling of poet's heart if, while he heard lovely lips commending his verses, a voice were to whisper in his ear what certain other verses the lady commended also.

On Saturday evenings, after Gibbie left him, Donal kept his own private holiday, which consisted in making verses, or rather in setting himself in the position for doing so, when sometimes verses would be the result, sometimes not. When the moon was shining in at the windows of the large room adjoining, he would put out his lamp, open his door, and look from the little chamber, glowing with fire-light, into the strange, eerie, silent waste, crowded with the chaos of dis-created homes. There scores on scores of things, many of them unco, that is uncouth, the first meaning of which is unknown, to his eyes, stood huddled together in the dim light. The light looked weary and faint, as if with having forced its way through the dust of years on the windows; and Donal felt as if gazing from a clear conscious present out into a faded dream. Sometimes he would leave his nest, and walk up and down among spider-legged tables, tall cabinets, secret-looking bureaus, worked chairs—yielding himself to his fancies. He was one who needed no opium, or such-like demon-help, to set him dreaming; he could dream at his will—only his dreams were brief and of rapid change—probably not more so, after the clock, than those other artificial ones, in which, to speculate on the testimony, the feeling of their length appears to be produced by an infinite and continuous subdivision of the subjective time. Now he was a ghost come back to flit, hovering and gliding about sad old scenes, that had gathered a new and a worse sadness from the drying up of the sorrow which was the heart of them—his doom, to live thus over again the life he had made so little of in the body; his punishment, to haunt the world and pace its streets, unable to influence by the turn of a hair the goings on of its life,—so to learn what a useless being he had been, and repent of his self-embraced insignificance. Now he was a prisoner, pining and longing for life and air and human companionship; that was the sun outside, whose rays shone thus feebly into his dungeon by repeated reflections. Now he was a prince in disguise, meditating how to appear again and defeat the machinations of his foes, especially of the enchanter who made him seem to the eyes of his subjects that which he was not. But ever his thoughts would turn again to Ginevra, and ever the poems he devised were devised as in her presence and for her hearing. Sometimes a dread would seize him—as if the strange things were all looking at him, and something was about to happen; then he would stride hastily back to his own room, close the door hurriedly, and sit down by the fire. Once or twice he was startled by the soft entrance of his landlady's grand-daughter, come to search for something in one of the cabinets they had made a repository for small odds and ends of things. Once he told Gibbie that something had looked at him, but he could not tell what or whence or how, and laughed at himself, but persisted in his statement.

He had not yet begun to read his New Testament in the way Gibbie did, but he thought in the direction of light and freedom, and looked towards some goal dimly seen in vague grandeur of betterness. His condition was rather that of eyeless hunger after growth, than of any conscious aspiration towards less undefined good. He had a large and increasing delight in all forms of the generous, and shrunk instinctively from the base, but had not yet concentrated his efforts towards becoming that which he acknowledged the best, so that he was hardly yet on the straight path to the goal of such oneness with good as alone is a man's peace. I mention these things not with the intent of here developing the character of Donal, but with the desire that my readers should know him such as he then was.

Gibbie and he seldom talked about Ginevra. She was generally understood between them—only referred to upon needful occasion: they had no right to talk about her, any more than to intrude on her presence unseasonably.

Donal went to Mr. Sclater's church because Mr. Sclater required it, in virtue of the position he assumed as his benefactor. Mr. Sclater in the pulpit was a trial to Donal, but it consoled him to be near Gibbie, also that he had found a seat in the opposite gallery, whence he could see Ginevra when her place happened to be not far from the door of one of the school-pews. He did not get much benefit from Mr. Sclater's sermons: I confess he did not attend very closely to his preaching—often directed against doctrinal errors of which, except from himself, not one of his congregation had ever heard, or was likely ever to hear. But I cannot say he would have been better employed in listening, for there was generally something going on in his mind that had to go on, and make way for more. I have said generally, for I must except the times when his thoughts turned upon the preacher himself, and took forms such as the following. But it might be a lesson to some preachers to know that a decent lad like Donal may be making some such verses about one of them while he is preaching. I have known not a few humble men in the pulpit of whom rather than write such a thing Donal would have lost the writing hand.

> 'Twas a sair sair day 'twas my hap till
> Come under yer soon', Mr. Sclater;
> But things maun he putten a tap till,
> An' sae maun ye, seener or later!

For to hear ye rowtin' an' scornin',
Is no to hark to the river;
An' to sit here till brak trowth's mornin',
Wad be to be lost for ever.

I confess I have taken a liberty, and changed one word for another in the last line. He did not show these verses to Gibbie; or indeed ever find much fault with the preacher in his hearing; for he knew that while he was himself more open-minded to the nonsense of the professional gentleman, Gibbie was more open-hearted towards the merits of the man, with whom he was far too closely associated on week-days not to feel affection for him; while, on the other hand, Gibbie made neither head nor tail of his sermons, not having been instructed in the theological mess that goes with so many for a theriac of the very essentials of religion; and therefore, for anything he knew, they might be very wise and good. At first he took refuge from the sermon in his New Testament; but when, for the third time, the beautiful hand of the ministerial spouse appeared between him and the book, and gently withdrew it, he saw that his reading was an offence in her eyes, and contented himself thereafter with thinking: listening to the absolutely unintelligible he found impossible. What a delight it would have been to the boy to hear Christ preached such as he showed himself, such as in no small measure he had learned him—instead of such as Mr. Sclater saw him reflected from the tenth or twentieth distorting mirror! They who speak against the Son of Man oppose mere distortions and mistakes of him, having never beheld, neither being now capable of beholding, him; but those who have transmitted to them these false impressions, those, namely, who preach him without being themselves devoted to him, and those who preach him having derived their notions of him from other scources than himself, have to bear the blame that they have such excuses for not seeking to know him. He submits to be mis-preached, as he submitted to be lied against while visibly walking the world, but his truth will appear at length to all: until then until he is known as he is, our salvation tarrieth.

Mrs. Sclater showed herself sincere, after her kind, to Donal as well as to Gibbie. She had by no means ceased to grow, and already was slowly bettering under the influences of the New Testament in Gibbie, notwithstanding she had removed the letter of it from her public table. She told Gibbie that he must talk to Donal about his dress and his speech.

That he was a lad of no common gifts was plain, she said, but were he ever so "talented" he could do little in the world, certainly would never raise himself, so long as he dressed and spoke ridiculously. The wisest and best of men would be utterly disregarded, she said, if he did not look and speak like other people. Gibbie thought with himself this could hardly hold, for there was John the Baptist; he answered her, however, that Donal could speak very good English if he chose, but that the affected tone and would-be-fine pronunciation of Fergus Duff had given him the notion that to speak anything but his mother-tongue would be unmanly and false. As to his dress, Donal was poor, Gibbie said, and could not give up wearing any clothes so long as there was any wear in them. "If you had seen me once!" he added, with a merry laugh to finish for his fingers.

Mrs. Sclater spoke to her husband, who said to Gibbie that, if he chose to provide Donal with suitable garments, he would advance him the money:—that was the way he took credit for every little sum he handed his ward, but in his accounts was correct to a farthing.

Gibbie would thereupon have dragged Donal at once to the tailor; but Donal was obstinate.

"Na, na," he said; "the claes is guid eneuch for him 'at weirs them. Ye dee eneuch for me, Sir Gilbert, a'ready; an' though I wad be obleeged to you as I wad to my mither hersel', to cleed me gien I warna dacent, I winna tak your siller nor naebody ither's to gang fine. Na, na; I'll weir the claes oot, an' we s' dee better wi' the neist. An' for that bonnie wuman, Mistress Scletter, ye can tell her, 'at by the time I hae onything to say to the warl', it winna be my claes 'at'll haud fowk ohn hearkent; an' gien she considers them 'at I hae noo, ower sair a disgrace till her gran' rooms, she maun jist no inveet me, an' I'll no come; for I canna presently help them. But the neist session, whan I hae better, for I'm sure to get wark eneuch in atween, I'll come an' shaw mysel', an' syne she can dee as she likes."

This high tone of liberty, so free from offence either given or taken, was thoroughly appreciated by both Mr. and Mrs. Sclater, and they did not cease to invite him. A little talk with the latter soon convinced him that there was neither assumption nor lack of patriotism in speaking the language of the people among whom he found himself; and as he made her his model in the pursuit of the accomplishment, he very soon spoke a good deal better English than Mr. Sclater. But with Gibbie, and even with the dainty Ginevra, he could not yet bring himself to talk anything but his mother-tongue.

"I cannot mak my moo'," he would say, "to speyk onything but the nat'ral tongue o' poetry till sic a bonnie cratur as Miss Galbraith; an' for yersel', Gibbie—man! I wad be ill willin' to bigg a stane wa' atween me an' the bonnie days whan Angus Mac Pholp was the deil we did fear, an' Hornie the deil we didna.—Losh, man! what wad come o' me gien I hed to say my prayers in English! I doobt gien 't wad come oot prayin' at a'!"

I am well aware that most Scotch people of that date tried to say their prayers in English, but not so Janet or Robert, and not so had they taught their children. I fancy not a little unreality was thus in their case avoided.

"What will you do when you are a minister?" asked Gibbie on his fingers.

"Me a minnister?" echoed Donal. "Me a minnister!" he repeated. "Losh, man! gien I can save my ain sowl, it'll be a' 'at I'm fit for, ohn lo'dent it wi' a haill congregation o' ither fowk's. Na, na; gien I can be a schuilmaister, an' help the bairnies to be guid, as my mither taucht mysel', an' hae time to read, an' a feow shillin's to buy buiks aboot Aigypt an' the Holy Lan', an' a full an' complete edition o' Plato, an' a Greek Lexicon—a guid ane, an' a Jamieson's Dictionar', haith, I'll be a hawpy man! An' gien I dinna like the schuilmaisterin', I can jist tak to the wark again, whilk I cudna dee sae weel gien I had tried the preachin': fowk wad ca' me a stickit minister! Or maybe they'll gie me the sheep to luik efter upo' Glashgar, whan they're ower muckle for my father, an' that wad weel content me. Only I wad hae to bigg a bit mair to the hoosie, to haud my buiks: I maun hae buiks. I wad get the newspapers whiles, but no aften, for they're a sair loss o' precious time. Ye see they tell ye things afore they're sure, an' ye hae to spen' yer time the day readin' what ye'll hae to spen' yer time the morn readin' oot again; an' ye may as weel bide till the thing's sattled a wee. I wad jist lat them fecht things oot 'at thoucht they saw hoo they oucht to gang; an' I wad gie them guid mutton to haud them up to their dreary wark, an' maybe a sangy noo an' than 'at wad help them to drap it a'thegither."

"But wouldn't you like to have a wife, Donal, and children, like your father and mother?" spelt Gibbie.

"Na, na; nae wife for me, Gibbie!" answered the philosopher. "Wha wad hae aither a pure schuilmaister or a shepherd?—'cep' it was maybe some lass like my sister Nicie, 'at wadna ken Euclid frae her hose, or Burns frae a mill-dam, or conic sections frae the hole i' the great peeramid."

"I don't like to hear you talk like that, Donal," said Gibbie. "What do you say to mother?"

"The mither's no to be said aboot," answerd Donal. "She's ane by hersel', no ane like ither fowk. Ye wadna think waur o' the angel Gabriel 'at he hedna jist read Homer clean throu', wad ye?"

"If I did," answered Gibbie, "he would only tell me there was time enough for that."

When they met on a Friday evening, and it was fine, they would rove the streets, Gibbie taking Donal to the places he knew so well in his childhood, and enjoying it the more that he could now tell him so much better what he remembered. The only place he did not take him to was Jink Lane, with the house that had been Mistress Croale's. He did take him to the court in the Widdiehill, and show him the Auld Hoose o' Galbraith, and the place under the stair where his father had worked. The shed was now gone; the neighbours had by degrees carried it away for firewood. The house was occupied still as then by a number of poor people, and the door was never locked, day or night, any more than when Gibbie used to bring his father home. He took Donal to the garret where they had slept—one could hardly say lived, and where his father died. The door stood open, and the place was just as they had left it. A year or two after, Gibbie learned how it came to be thus untenanted: it was said to be haunted. Every Sunday Sir George was heard at work, making boots for his wee Gibbie from morning to night; after which, when it was dark, came dreadful sounds of supplication, as of a soul praying in hell-fire. For a while the house was almost deserted in consequence.

"Gien I was you, Sir Gilbert," said Donal, who now and then remembered Mrs. Sclater's request—they had come down, and looking at the outside of the house, had espied a half-obliterated stone-carving of the Galbraith arms—"Gien I was you, Sir Gilbert, I wad gar Maister Scletter keep a sherp luik oot for the first chance o' buyin' back this hoose. It wad be a great peety it sud gang to waur afore ye get it. Eh! sic tales as this hoose cud tell!"

"How am I to do that, Donal? Mr. Sclater would not mind me. The money's not mine yet, you know," said Gibbie.

"The siller is yours, Gibbie," answered Donal; "it's yours as the kingdom o' h'aven's yours; it's only 'at ye canna jist lay yer han's upo' 't yet. The seener ye lat that Maister Scletter ken 'at ye ken what ye're aboot, the better. An' believe me, whan he comes to un'erstan' 'at ye want that hoose koft, he'll no be a day ohn gane to somebody or anither aboot it."

Donal was right, for within a month the house was bought, and certain necessary repairs commenced.

Sometimes on those evenings they took tea with Mistress Croale, and it was a proud time with her when they went. That night at least the whisky bottle did not make its appearance.

Mrs. Sclater continued to invite young ladies to the house for Gibbie's sake, and when she gave a party, she took care there should be a proportion of young people in it; but Gibbie, although of course kind and polite to all, did not much enjoy these gatherings. It began to trouble him a little that he seemed to care less for his kind than before; but it was only a seeming, and the cause of it was this: he was now capable of perceiving facts in nature and character which prevented real contact, and must make advances towards it appear as offensive as they were useless. But he did not love the less that he had to content himself, until the kingdom should come nearer, with loving at a more conscious distance; by loving kindness and truth he continued doing all he could to bring the kingdom whose end is unity. Hence he had come to restrain his manner—nothing could have constrained his manners, which now from the conventional point of view were irreproachable; but if he did not so often execute a wild dance, or stand upon one leg, the glow in his eyes had deepened, and his response to any advance was as ready and thorough, as frank and sweet as ever; his eagerness was replaced by a stillness from which his eyes took all coldness, and his smile was as the sun breaking out in a gray day of summer, and turning all from doves to peacocks. In this matter there was one thing worthy of note common to Donal and him, who had had the same divine teaching from Janet: their manners to all classes were the same, they showed the same respect to the poor, the same ease with the rich.

I must confess, however, that before the session was over, Donal found it required all his strength of mind to continue to go to Mrs. Sclater's little parties—from kindness she never asked him to her larger ones; and the more to his praise it was that he did not refuse one of her invitations. The cause was this: one bright Sunday morning in February, coming out of his room to go to church, and walking down the path through the furniture in a dreamy mood, he suddenly saw a person meeting him straight in the face. "Sic a queer-like chield!" he remarked inwardly, stepped on one side to let him pass—and perceived it was himself reflected from head to foot in a large mirror, which had been placed while he was out the night before. The courage with which he persisted, after such a painful enlightenment, in going into company in those same garments, was right admirable and enviable; but no one knew of it until its exercise was long over.

The little pocket-money Mr. Sclater allowed Gibbie, was chiefly spent at the shop of a certain secondhand bookseller, nearly opposite Mistress Murkison's. The books they bought were carried to Donal's room, there to be considered by Gibbie Donal's, and by Donal Gibbie's. Among the rest was a reprint of Marlow's Faust, the daring in the one grand passage of which both awed and delighted them; there were also some of the Ettrick Shepherd's eerie stories, alone in their kind; and above all there was a miniature copy of Shelley, whose verse did much for the music of Donal's, while yet he could not quite appreciate the truth for the iridescence of it: he said it seemed to him to have been all composed in a balloon. I have mentioned only works of imagination, but it must not be supposed they had not a relish for stronger food: the books more severe came afterwards, when they had liberty to choose their own labours; now they had plenty of the harder work provided for them.

Somewhere about this time Fergus Duff received his license to preach, and set himself to acquire what his soul thirsted after—a reputation, namely, for eloquence. This was all the flood-mark that remained of the waters of verse with which he had at one time so plentifully inundated his soul. He was the same as man he had been as youth—handsome, plausible, occupied with himself, determined to succeed, not determined to labour. Praise was the very necessity of his existence, but he had the instinct not to display his beggarly hunger—which reached even to the approbation of such to whom he held himself vastly superior. He seemed generous, and was niggardly, by turns; cultivated suavity; indulged in floridity both of manners and speech; and signed his name so as nobody could read it, though his handwriting was plain enough.

In the spring, summer, and autumn, Donal laboured all day with his body, and in the evening as much as he could with his mind. Lover of Nature as he was, however, more alive indeed than before to the delights of the country, and the genial companionship of terrene sights and sounds, scents and motions, he could not help longing for the winter and the city, that his soul might be freer to follow its paths. And yet what a season some of the labours of the field afforded him for thought! To the student who cannot think without books, the easiest of such labours are a dull burden, or a distress; but for the man in whom the wells have been unsealed, in whom the waters are flowing, the labour mingles gently and genially with the thought, and the plough he holds with his hands lays open to the sun and the air more soils than one. Mr. Sclater without his books would speedily have sunk into the mere shrewd farmer; Donal, never opening a book, would have followed theories and made verses to the end of his days.

Every Saturday, as before, he went to see his father and mother. Janet kept fresh and lively, although age told on her, she said, more rapidly since Gibbie went away.

"But gien the Lord lat auld age wither me up," she said, "he'll luik efter the cracks himsel'."

Six weeks of every summer between Donal's sessions, while the minister and his wife took their holiday, Gibbie spent with Robert and Janet. It was a blessed time for them all. He led then just the life of the former days, with Robert and Oscar and the sheep, and Janet and her cow and the New Testament—only he had a good many more things to think about now, and more ways of thinking about them. With his own hands he built a neat little porch to the cottage door, with close sides and a second door to keep the wind off: Donal and he carried up the timber and the mortar. But although he tried hard to make Janet say what he could do for her more, he could not bring her to reveal any desire that belonged to this world—except, indeed, for two or three trifles for her husband's warmth and convenience.

"The sicht o' my Lord's face," she said once, when he was pressing her, "is a' 'at I want, Sir Gibbie. For this life it jist blecks me to think o' onything I wad hae or wad lowse. This boady o' mine's growin' some heavy-like, I maun confess, but I wadna hae't ta'en aff o' me afore the time. It wad be an ill thing for the seed to be shal't ower sune."

They almost always called him Sir Gibbie, and he never objected, or seemed either annoyed or amused at it; he took it just as the name that was his, the same way as his hair or his hands were his; he had been called wee Sir Gibbie for so long.

XLIX

The Houseless

The minister kept Gibbie hard at work, and by the time Donal's last winter came, Gibbie was ready for college also. To please Mr. Sclater he competed for a bursary, and gained a tolerably good one, but declined accepting it. His guardian was annoyed, he could not see why he should refuse what he had "earned." Gibbie asked him whether it was the design of the founder of those bursaries that rich boys should have them. Were they not for the like of Donal? Whereupon Mr. Sclater could not help remembering what a difference it would have made to him in his early struggles, if some rich bursar above him had yielded a place—and held his peace.

Daur-street being too far from Elphinstone College for a student to live there, Mr. Sclater consented to Gibbie's lodging with Donal, but would have insisted on their taking rooms in some part of the town—more suitable to the young baronet's position, he said; but as there was another room to be had at Mistress Murkison's, Gibbie insisted that one who had shown them so much kindness must not be forsaken; and by this time he seldom found difficulty in having his way with his guardian. Both he and his wife had come to understand him better, and nobody could understand Gibbie better without also understanding better all that was good and true and right: although they hardly knew the fact themselves, the standard of both of them had been heightened by not a few degrees since Gibbie came to them; and although he soon ceased to take direct notice of what in their conduct distressed him, I cannot help thinking it was not amiss that he uttered himself as he did at the first; knowing a little his ways of thinking they came to feel his judgment unexpressed. For Mrs. Sclater, when she bethought herself that she had said or done something he must count worldly, the very silence of the dumb boy was a reproof to her.

One night the youths had been out for a long walk and came back to the city late, after the shops were shut. Only here and there a light glimmered in some low-browed little place, probably used in part by the family. Not a soul was visible in the dingy region through which they now approached their lodging, when round a corner, moving like a shadow, came, soft-pacing, a ghostly woman in rags, with a white, worn face, and the largest black eyes, it seemed to the youths that they had ever seen—an apparition of awe and grief and wonder. To compare a great thing to a small, she was to their eyes as a ruined, desecrated shrine to the eyes of the saint's own peculiar worshipper. I may compare her to what I please, great or small—to a sapphire set in tin, to an angel with draggled feathers; for far beyond all comparison is that temple of the holy ghost in the desert—a woman in wretchedness and rags. She carried her puny baby rolled hard in the corner of her scrap of black shawl. To the youths a sea of trouble looked out of those wild eyes. As she drew near them, she hesitated, half-stopped, and put out a hand from under the shawl—stretched out no arm, held out only a hand from the wrist, white against the night. Donal had no money. Gibbie had a shilling. The hand closed upon it, a gleam crossed the sad face, and a murmur of thanks fluttered from the thin lips as she walked on her way. The youths breathed deep, and felt a little relieved, but only a little. The thought of the woman wandering in the dark and the fog and the night, was a sickness at their hearts. Was it impossible to gather such under the wings of any night-brooding hen? That Gibbie had gone through so much of the same kind of thing himself, and had found it endurable enough, did not make her case a whit the less pitiful in his eyes, and indeed it was widely, sadly different from his. Along the deserted street, which looked to Donal like a waterless canal banked by mounds of death, and lighted by phosphorescent grave-damps, they followed her with their eyes, the one living thing, fading away from lamp to lamp; and when they could see her no farther, followed her with their feet; they could not bear to lose sight of her. But they kept just on the verge of vision, for they did not want her to know the espial of their love. Suddenly she disappeared, and keeping their eyes on the spot as well as they could, they found when they reached it a little shop, with a red curtain, half torn down, across the glass door of it. A dim oil lamp was burning within. It looked like a rag-shop, dirty and dreadful. There she stood, while a woman with a bloated face, looking to Donal like a feeder of hell-swine, took from some secret hole underneath, a bottle which seemed to Gibbie the very one his father used to drink from. He would have rushed in and dashed it from her hand, but Donal withheld him.

"Hoots!" he said, "we canna follow her a' nicht; an' gien we did, what better wad she be i' the mornin'? Lat her be, puir thing!"

She received the whisky in a broken tea-cup, swallowed some of it eagerly, then, to the horror of the youths, put some of it into the mouth of her child from her own. Draining the last drops from the cup, she set it quietly down, turned, and without a word spoken, for she had paid beforehand, came out, her face looking just as white and thin as before, but having another expression in the eyes of it. At the sight Donal's wisdom forsook him.

"Eh, wuman," he cried, "yon wasna what ye hed the shillin' for!"

"Ye said naething," answered the poor creature, humbly, and walked on, hanging her head, and pressing her baby to her bosom.

The boys looked at each other.

"That wasna the gait yer shillin' sud hae gane, Gibbie," said Donal. "It's clear it winna dee to gie shillin's to sic like as her. Wha kens but the hunger an' the caul', an' the want o' whisky may be the wuman's evil things here, 'at she may 'scape the hellfire o' the Rich Man hereafter?"

He stopped, for Gibbie was weeping. The woman and her child he would have taken to his very heart, and could do nothing for them. Love seemed helpless, for money was useless. It set him thinking much, and the result appeared. From that hour the case of the homeless haunted his heart and brain and imagination; and as his natural affections found themselves repelled and chilled in what is called Society, they took refuge more and more with the houseless and hungry and shivering. Through them, also, he now, for the first time, began to find grave and troublous questions mingling with his faith and hope; so that already he began to be rewarded for his love: to the true heart every doubt is a door. I will not follow and describe the opening of these doors to Gibbie, but, as what he discovered found always its first utterance in action, wait until I can show the result.

For the time the youths were again a little relieved about the woman: following her still, to a yet more wretched part of the city, they saw her knock at a door, pay something, and be admitted. It looked a dreadful refuge, but she was at least under cover, and shelter, in such a climate as ours in winter, must be the first rudimentary notion of salvation. No longer haunted with the idea of her wandering all night about the comfortless streets, "like a ghost awake in Memphis," Donal said, they went home. But it was long before they got to sleep, and in the morning their first words were about the woman.

"Gien only we hed my mither here!" said Donal.

"Mightn't you try Mr. Sclater?" suggested Gibbie.

Donal answered with a great roar of laughter.

"He wad tell her she oucht to tak shame till hersel'," he said, "an' I'm thinkin' she's lang brunt a' her stock o' that firin'. He wud tell her she sud work for her livin', an' maybe there isna ae turn the puir thing can dee 'at onybody wad gie her a bawbee for a day o'!—But what say ye to takin' advice o' Miss Galbraith?"

It was strange how, with the marked distinctions between them, Donal and Gibbie would every now and then, like the daughters of the Vicar of Wakefield, seem to change places and parts.

"God can make praise-pipes of babes and sucklings," answered Gibbie; "but it does not follow that they can give advice. Don't you remember your mother saying that the stripling David was enough to kill a braggart giant, but a sore-tried man was wanted to rule the people?"

It ended in their going to Mistress Croale. They did not lay bare to her their perplexities, but they asked her to find out who the woman was, and see if anything could be done for her. They said to themselves she would know the condition of such a woman, and what would be moving in her mind, after the experience she had herself had, better at least than the minister or his lady-wife. Nor were they disappointed. To be thus taken into counsel revived for Mistress Croale the time of her dignity while yet she shepherded her little flock of drunkards. She undertook the task with hearty good will, and carried it out with some success. Its reaction on herself to her own good was remarkable. There can be no better auxiliary against our own sins than to help our neighbour in the encounter with his. Merely to contemplate our neighbour will recoil upon us in quite another way: we shall see his faults so black, that we will not consent to believe ours so bad, and will immediately begin to excuse, which is the same as to cherish them, instead of casting them from us with abhorrence.

One day early in the session, as the youths were approaching the gate of Miss Kimble's school, a thin, care-worn man, in shabby clothes, came out, and walked along meeting them. Every now and then he bowed his shoulders, as if something invisible had leaped upon them from behind, and as often seemed to throw it off and with effort walk erect. It was the laird. They lifted their caps, but in return he only stared, or rather tried to stare, for his eyes seemed able to fix themselves on nothing. He was now at length a thoroughly ruined man, and had come to the city to end his days in a cottage belonging to his daughter.

Already Mr. Sclater, who was unweariedly on the watch over the material interests of his ward, had, through his lawyer, and without permitting his name to appear, purchased the whole of the Glashruach property. For the present, however, he kept Sir Gilbert in ignorance of the fact.

L

A Walk

The cottage to which Mr. Galbraith had taken Ginevra, stood in a suburban street—one of those small, well-built stone houses common, I fancy, throughout Scotland, with three rooms and a kitchen on its one floor, and a large attic with dormer windows. It was low and wide-roofed, and had a tiny garden between it and the quiet street. This garden was full of flowers in summer and autumn, but the tops of a few gaunt stems of hollyhocks, and the wiry straggling creepers of the honeysuckle about the eaves, was all that now showed from the pavement. It had a dwarf wall of granite, with an iron railing on the top, through which, in the season, its glorious colours used to attract many eyes, but Mr. Galbraith had had the railing and the gate lined to the very spikes with boards: the first day of his abode he had discovered that the passers-by—not to say those who stood to stare admiringly at the flowers, came much too near his faded but none the less conscious dignity. He had also put a lock on the gate, and so made of the garden a sort of propylon to the house. For he had of late developed a tendency towards taking to earth, like the creatures that seem to have been created ashamed of themselves, and are always burrowing. But it was not that the late laird was ashamed of himself in any proper sense. Of the dishonesty of his doings he was as yet scarcely half conscious, for the proud man shrinks from repentance, regarding it as disgrace. To wash is to acknowledge the need of washing. He avoided the eyes of men for the mean reason that he could no longer appear in dignity as laird of Glashruach and chairman of a grand company; while he felt as if something must have gone wrong with the laws of nature that it had become possible for Thomas Galbraith, of Glashruach, Esq., to live in a dumpy cottage. He had thought seriously of resuming his patronymic of Durrant, but reflected that he was too well known to don that cloak of transparent darkness without giving currency to the idea that he had soiled the other past longer wearing. It would be imagined, he said, picking out one dishonesty of which he had not been guilty, that he had settled money on his wife, and retired to enjoy it.

His condition was far more pitiful than his situation. Having no faculty for mental occupation except with affairs, finding nothing to do but cleave, like a spent sailor, with hands and feet to the slippery rock of what was once his rectitude, such as it was, trying to hold it still his own, he would sit for hours without moving—a perfect creature, temple, god, and worshipper, all in one—only that the worshipper was hardly content with his god, and that a worm was gnawing on at the foundation of the temple. Nearly as motionless, her hands excepted, would Ginevra sit opposite to him, not quieter but more peaceful than when a girl, partly because now she was less afraid of him. He called her, in his thoughts as he sat there, heartless and cold, but not only was she not so, but it was his fault that she appeared to him such. In his moral stupidity he would rather have seen her manifest concern at the poverty to which he had reduced her, than show the stillness of a contented mind. She was not much given to books, but what she read was worth reading, and such as turned into thought while she sat. They are not the best students who are most dependent on books. What can be got out of them is at best only material: a man must build his house for himself. She would have read more, but with her father beside her doing nothing, she felt that to take a book would be like going into a warm house, and leaving him out in the cold. It was very sad to her to see him thus shrunk and withered, and lost in thought that plainly was not thinking. Nothing interested him; he never looked at the papers, never cared to hear a word of news. His eyes more unsteady, his lips looser, his neck thinner and longer, he looked more than ever like a puppet whose strings hung slack. How often would Ginevra have cast herself on his bosom if she could have even hoped he would not repel her! Now and then his eyes did wander to her in a dazed sort of animal-like appeal, but the moment she attempted response, he turned into a corpse. Still, when it came, that look was a comfort, for it seemed to witness some bond between them after all. And another comfort was, that now, in his misery, she was able, if not to forget those painful thoughts about him which had all these years haunted her, at least to dismiss them when they came, in the hope that, as already such a change had passed upon him, further and better change might follow.

She was still the same brown bird as of old—a bird of the twilight, or rather a twilight itself, with a whole night of stars behind it, of whose existence she scarcely knew, having but just started on the voyage of discovery which life is. She had the sweetest, rarest smile—not frequent and flashing like Gibbie's, but stealing up from below, like the shadowy reflection of a greater light, gently deepening, permeating her countenance until it reached her eyes, thence issuing in soft flame. Always however, an soon as her eyes began to glow duskily, down went their lids, and down dropt her head like the frond of a sensitive plant. Her atmosphere was an embodied stillness; she made a quiet wherever she entered; she was not beautiful, but she was lovely; and her presence at once made a place such as one would desire to be in.

The most pleasant of her thoughts were of necessity those with which the two youths were associated. How dreary but for them and theirs would the retrospect of her life have been! Several times every winter they had met at the minister's, and every summer she had again and again seen Gibbie with Mrs. Sclater, and once or twice had had a walk with them, and every time Gibbie had something of Donal's to give her. Twice Gibbie had gone to see her at the school, but the second time she asked him not to come again, as Miss Kimble did not like it. He gave a big stare of wonder, and thought of Angus and the laird; but followed the stare with a swift smile, for he saw she was troubled, and asked no question, but waited for the understanding of all things that must come. But now, when or where was she ever to see them more? Gibbie was no longer at the minister's, and perhaps she would never be invited to meet them there again. She dared not ask Donal to call: her father would be indignant; and for her father's sake she would not ask Gibbie; it might give him pain; while the thought that he would of a certainty behave so differently to him now that he was well-dressed, and mannered like a gentleman, was almost more unendurable to her than the memory of his past treatment of him.

Mr. and Mrs. Sclater had called upon them the moment they were settled in the cottage; but Mr. Galbraith would see nobody. When the gate-bell rang, he always looked out, and if a visitor appeared, withdrew to his bedroom.

One brilliant Saturday morning, the second in the session, the ground hard with an early frost, the filmy ice making fairy caverns and grottos in the cart-ruts, and the air so condensed with cold that every breath, to those who ate and slept well, had the life of two, Mrs. Sclater rang the said bell. Mr. Galbraith peeping from the window, saw a lady's bonnet, and went. She walked in, followed by Gibbie, and would have Ginevra go with them for a long walk. Pleased enough with the proposal, for the outsides of life had been dull as well as painful of late, she went and asked her father. If she did not tell him that Sir Gilbert was with Mrs. Sclater, perhaps she ought to have told him; but I am not sure, and therefore am not going to blame her. When parents are not fathers and mothers, but something that has no name in the kingdom of heaven, they place the purest and most honest of daughters in the midst of perplexities.

"Why do you ask me?" returned her father. "My wishes are nothing to any one now; to you they never were anything."

"I will stay at home, if you wish it, papa,—with pleasure," she replied, as cheerfully as she could after such a reproach.

"By no means. If you do, I shall go and dine at the Red Hart," he answered—not having money enough in his possession to pay for a dinner there.

I fancy he meant to be kind, but, like not a few, alas! took no pains to look as kind as he was. There are many, however, who seem to delight in planting a sting where conscience or heart will not let them deny. It made her miserable for a while of course, but she had got so used to his way of breaking a gift as he handed it, that she answered only with a sigh. When she was a child, his ungraciousness had power to darken the sunlight, but by repetition it had lost force. In haste she put on her little brown-ribboned bonnet, took the moth-eaten muff that had been her mother's, and rejoined Mrs. Sclater and Gibbie, beaming with troubled pleasure. Life in her was strong, and their society soon enabled her to forget, not her father's sadness, but his treatment of her.

At the end of the street, they found Donal waiting them—without greatcoat or muffler, the picture of such health as suffices to its own warmth, not a mark of the midnight student about him, and looking very different, in town-made clothes, from the Donal of the mirror. He approached and saluted her with such an air of homely grace as one might imagine that of the Red Cross Knight, when, having just put on the armour of a Christian man, from a clownish fellow he straightway appeared the goodliest knight in the company. Away they walked together westward, then turned southward. Mrs. Sclater and Gibbie led, and Ginevra followed with Donal. And they had not walked far, before something of the delight of old times on Glashruach began to revive in the bosom of the too sober girl. In vain she reminded herself that her father sat miserable at home, thinking of her probably as the most heartless of girls; the sun, and the bright air like wine in her veins, were too much for her, Donal had soon made her cheerful, and now and then she answered his talk with even a little flash of merriment. They crossed the bridge, high-hung over the Daur, by which on that black morning Gibbie fled; and here for the first time, with his three friends about him, he told on his fingers the dire deed of the night, and heard from Mrs. Sclater that the murderers had been hanged. Ginevra grew white and faint as she read his fingers and gestures, but it was more at the thought of what the child had come through, than from the horror of his narrative. They then turned eastward to the sea, and came to the top of the rock-border of the coast, with its cliffs rent into gullies, eerie places to look down into, ending in caverns into which the waves rushed with bellow and boom. Although so nigh the city, this was always a solitary place, yet, rounding a rock, they came upon a young man, who hurried a book into his pocket, and would have gone by the other side, but perceiving himself recognized, came to meet them, and saluted Mrs. Sclater, who presented him to Ginevra as the Rev. Mr. Duff.

"I have not had the pleasure of seeing you since you were quite a little girl, Miss Galbraith," said Fergus.

Ginevra said coldly she did not remember him. The youths greeted him in careless student fashion: they had met now and then for a moment about the college; and a little meaningless talk followed.

He was to preach the next day—and for several Sundays following—at a certain large church in the city, at the time without a minister; and when they came upon him he was studying his sermon—I do not mean the truths he intended to press upon his audience—those he had mastered long ago—but his manuscript, studying it in the sense in which actors use the word, learning it, that is, by heart laboriously, that the words might come from his lips as much like an extemporaneous utterance as possible, consistently with not being mistaken for one, which, were it true as the Bible, would have no merit in the ears of those who counted themselves judges of the craft. The kind of thing suited Fergus, whose highest idea of life was seeming. Naturally capable, he had already made of himself rather a dull fellow; for when a man spends his energy on appearing to have, he is all the time destroying what he has, and therein the very means of becoming what he desires to seem. If he gains his end his success is his punishment.

Fergus never forgot that he was a clergyman, always carrying himself according to his idea of the calling; therefore when the interchange of commonplaces flagged, he began to look about him for some remark sufficiently tinged with his profession to be suitable for him to make, and for the ladies to hear as his. The wind was a thoroughly wintry one from the north-east, and had been blowing all night, so that the waves were shouldering the rocks with huge assault. Now Fergus's sermon, which he meant to use as a spade for the casting of the first turf of the first parallel in the siege of the pulpit of the North parish, was upon the vanity of human ambition, his text being the grand verse—And so I saw the wicked buried, who had come and gone from the place of the holy; there was no small amount of fine writing in the manuscript he had thrust into his pocket; and his sermon was in his head when he remarked, with the wafture of a neatly-gloved hand seawards—

"I was watching these waves when you found me: they seem to me such a picture of the vanity of human endeavour! But just as little as those waves would mind me, if I told them they were wasting their labour on these rocks, will men mind me, when I tell them to-morrow of the emptiness of their ambitions."

"A present enstance o' the vainity o' human endeevour!" said Donal. "What for sud ye, in that case, gang on preachin', sae settin' them an ill exemple?"

Duff gave him a high-lidded glance, vouchsafing no reply.

"Just as those waves," he continued, "waste themselves in effort, as often foiled as renewed, to tear down these rocks, so do the men of this world go on and on, spending their strength for nought."

"Hoots, Fergus!" said Donal again, in broadest speech, as if with its bray he would rebuke not the madness but the silliness of the prophet, "ye dinna mean to tell me yon jaws (billows) disna ken their business better nor imaigine they hae to caw doon the rocks?"

Duff cast a second glance of scorn at what he took for the prosaic stupidity or poverty-stricken logomachy of Donal, while Ginevra opened on him big brown eyes, as much as to say, "Donal, who was it set me down for saying a man couldn't be a burn?" But Gibbie's face was expectant: he knew Donal. Mrs. Sclater also looked interested: she did not much like Duff, and by this time she suspected Donal of genius. Donal turned to Ginevra with a smile, and said, in the best English he could command—

"Bear with me a moment, Miss Galbraith. If Mr. Duff will oblige me by answering my question, I trust I shall satisfy you I am no turncoat."

Fergus stared. What did his father's herd-boy mean by talking such English to the ladies, and such vulgar Scotch to him? Although now a

magistrand—that is, one about to take his degree of Master of Arts—
Donal was still to Fergus the cleaner-out of his father's byres—an upstart,
whose former position was his real one—towards him at least, who knew
him. And did the fellow challenge him to a discussion? Or did he presume
on the familiarity of their boyhood, and wish to sport his acquaintance
with the popular preacher? On either supposition, he was impertinent.

"I spoke poetically," he said, with cold dignity.

"Ye'll excuse me, Fergus," replied Donal, "—for the sake o' auld
langsyne, whan I was, as I ever will be, sair obligatit till ye—but i' that
ye say noo, ye're sair wrang: ye wasna speykin' poetically, though I ken
weel ye think it, or ye wadna say 't; an' that's what garred me tak ye
up. For the verra essence o' poetry is trowth, an' as sune's a word's no
true, it's no poetry, though it may hae on the cast claes o' 't. It's nane
but them 'at kens na what poetry is, 'at blethers aboot poetic license, an'
that kin' o' hen-scraich, as gien a poet was sic a gowk 'at naebody eedit
hoo he lee'd, or whether he gaed wi' 's cwite (coat) hin' side afore or no."

"I am at a loss to understand you—Donal?—yes, Donal Grant. I
remember you very well; and from the trouble I used to take with you
to make you distinguish between the work of the poet and that of the
rhymester, I should have thought by this time you would have known
a little more about the nature of poetry. Personification is a figure of
speech in constant use by all poets."

"Ow ay! but there's true and there's fause personification; an' it's no
ilka poet 'at kens the differ. Ow, I ken! ye'll be doon upo' me wi' yer
Byron,"—Fergus shook his head as at a false impeachment, but Donal
went on—"but even a poet canna mak lees poetry. An' a man 'at in ane
o' his gran'est verses cud haiver aboot the birth o' a yoong airthquack!—
losh! to think o' 't growin' an auld airthquack!—haith, to me it's no
up till a deuk-quack!—sic a poet micht weel, I grant ye, be he ever sic
a guid poet whan he tuik heed to what he said, he micht weel, I say,
blether nonsense aboot the sea warrin' again' the rocks, an' sic stuff."

"But don't you see them?" said Fergus, pointing to a great billow that
fell back at the moment, and lay churning in the gulf beneath them.
"Are they not in fact wasting the rocks away by slow degrees?"

"What comes o' yer seemile than, anent the vainity o' their endeevour?
But that's no what I'm carin' aboot. What I mainteen is, 'at though they
div weir awa' the rocks, that's nae mair their design nor it's the design
o' a yewky owse to kill the tree whan he rubs hit's skin an' his ain aff
thegither."

"Tut! nobody ever means, when he personifies the powers of nature, that they know what they are about."

"The mair necessar' till attreebute till them naething but their rale design."

"If they don't know what they are about, how can you be so foolish as talk of their design?"

"Ilka thing has a design,—an' gien it dinna ken't itsel', that's jist whaur yer true an' lawfu' personification comes in. There's no rizon 'at a poet sudna attreebute till a thing as a conscious design that which lies at the verra heart o' 'ts bein', the design for which it's there. That an' no ither sud determine the personification ye gie a thing—for that's the trowth o' the thing. Eh, man, Fergus! the jaws is fechtin' wi' nae rocks. They're jist at their pairt in a gran' cleansin' hermony. They're at their hoosemaid's wark, day an' nicht, to haud the warl' clean, an' gran' an' bonnie they sing at it. Gien I was you, I wadna tell fowk any sic nonsense as yon; I wad tell them 'at ilk ane 'at disna dee his wark i' the warl', an' dee 't the richt gait, 's no the worth o' a minnin, no to say a whaul, for ilk ane o' thae wee craturs dis the wull o' him 'at made 'im wi' ilka whisk o' his bit tailie, fa'in' in wi' a' the jabble o' the jaws again' the rocks, for it's a' ae thing—an' a' to haud the muckle sea clean. An' sae whan I lie i' my bed, an' a' at ance there comes a wee soughie o' win' i' my face, an' I luik up an' see it was naething but the wings o' a flittin' flee, I think wi' mysel' hoo a' the curses are but blessin's 'at ye dinna see intill, an' hoo ilka midge, an' flee, an' muckle dronin' thing 'at gangs aboot singin' bass, no to mention the doos an' the mairtins an' the craws an' the kites an' the oolets an' the muckle aigles an' the butterflees, is a' jist haudin' the air gauin' 'at ilka defilin' thing may be weel turnt ower, an' brunt clean. That's the best I got oot o' my cheemistry last session. An' fain wad I haud air an' watter in motion aboot me, an' sae serve my en'—whether by waggin' wi' my wings or whiskin' wi' my tail. Eh! it's jist won'erfu'. Its a' ae gran' consortit confusion o' hermony an' order; an' what maks the confusion is only jist 'at a' thing's workin' an' naething sits idle. But awa! wi' the nonsense o' ae thing worryin' an' fechtin' at anither!—no till ye come to beasts an' fowk, an' syne ye hae eneuch o' 't."

All the time Fergus had been poking the point of his stick into the ground, a smile of superiority curling his lip.

"I hope, ladies, our wits are not quite swept away in this flood of Doric," he said.

"You have a poor opinion of the stability of our brains, Mr. Duff," said Mrs. Sclater.

"I was only judging by myself," he replied, a little put out. "I can't say I understood our friend here. Did you?"

"Perfectly," answered Mrs. Sclater.

At that moment came a thunderous wave with a great bowff into the hollow at the end of the gully on whose edge they stood.

"There's your housemaid's broom, Donal!" said Ginevra.

They all laughed.

"Everything depends on how you look at a thing," said Fergus, and said no more—inwardly resolving, however, to omit from his sermon a certain sentence about the idle waves dashing themselves to ruin on the rocks they would destroy, and to work in something instead about the winds of the winter tossing the snow. A pause followed.

"Well, this is Saturday, and tomorrow is my work-day, you know, ladies," he said. "If you would oblige me with your address, Miss Galbraith, I should do myself the honour of calling on Mr. Galbraith."

Ginevra told him where they lived, but added she was afraid he must not expect to see her father, for he had been out of health lately, and would see nobody.

"At all events I shall give myself the chance," he rejoined, and bidding the ladies good-bye, and nodding to the youths, turned and walked away.

For some time there was silence. At length Donal spoke.

"Poor Fergus!" he said with a little sigh. "He's a good-natured creature, and was a great help to me; but when I think of him a preacher, I seem to see an Egyptian priest standing on the threshold of the great door at Ipsambul, blowing with all his might to keep out the Libyan desert; and the four great stone gods, sitting behind the altar, far back in the gloom, laughing at him."

Then Ginevra asked him something which led to a good deal of talk about the true and false in poetry, and made Mrs. Sclater feel it was not for nothing she had befriended the lad from the hills in the strange garments. And she began to think whether her husband might not be brought to take a higher view of his calling.

On Monday Fergus went to pay his visit to Mr. Galbraith. As Ginevra had said, her father did not appear, but Fergus was far from disappointed. He had taken it into his head that Miss Galbraith sided with him when that ill-bred fellow made his rude, not to say ungrateful, attack upon him, and was much pleased to have a talk with her. Ginevra thought it would not be right to cherish against him the memory of the one sin of his youth in her eyes, but she could not like him. She did not know why, but the truth was, she felt, without being able to identify, his unreality: she thought it was because, both in manners and in dress, so far as the custom of his calling would permit, he was that unpleasant phenomenon, a fine gentleman. She had never heard him preach, or she would have liked him still less; for he was an orator wilful and prepense, choice of long words, fond of climaxes, and always aware of the points at which he must wave his arm, throw forward his hands, wipe his eyes with the finest of large cambric handkerchiefs. As it was, she was heartily tired of him before he went, and when he was gone, found, as she sat with her father, that she could not recall a word he had said. As to what had made the fellow stay so long, she was therefore positively unable to give her father an answer; the consequence of which was, that, the next time he called, Mr. Galbraith, much to her relief, stood the brunt of his approach, and received him. The ice thus broken, his ingratiating manners, and the full-blown respect he showed Mr. Galbraith, enabling the weak man to feel himself, as of old, every inch a laird, so won upon him that, when he took his leave, he gave him a cordial invitation to repeat his visit.

He did so, in the evening this time, and remembering a predilection of the laird's, begged for a game of backgammon. The result of his policy was, that, of many weeks that followed, every Monday evening at least he spent with the laird. Ginevra was so grateful to him for his attention to her father, and his efforts to draw him out of his gloom, that she came gradually to let a little light of favour shine upon him. And if the heart of Fergus Duff was drawn to her, that is not to be counted to him a fault—neither that, his heart thus drawn, he should wish to marry her. Had she been still heiress of Glashruach, he dared not have dreamed of such a thing, but, noting the humble condition to which they were reduced, the growing familiarity of the father, and the friendliness of the daughter, he grew very hopeful, and more anxious than ever to secure the presentation to the North church, which was in the gift of the city. He could easily have got a rich wife, but he was more greedy of distinction than of money, and to marry the daughter of the man to whom he had been accustomed in childhood to look up as the greatest in the known world, was in his eyes like a patent of nobility, would be a ratification of his fitness to mingle with the choice of the land.

LI

The North Church

It was a cold night in March, cloudy and blowing. Every human body was turned into a fortress for bare defence of life. There was no snow on the ground, but it seemed as if there must be snow everywhere else. There was snow in the clouds overhead, and there was snow in the mind of man beneath. The very air felt like the quarry out of which the snow had been dug which was being ground above. The wind felt black, the sky was black, and the lamps were blowing about as if they wanted to escape for the darkness was after them. It was the Sunday following the induction of Fergus, and this was the meteoric condition through which Donal and Gibbie passed on their way to the North church, to hear him preach in the pulpit that was now his own.

The people had been gathering since long before the hour, and the youths could find only standing room near the door. Cold as was the weather, and keen as blew the wind into the church every time a door was opened, the instant it was shut again it was warm, for the place was crowded from the very height of the great steep-sloping galleries, at the back of which the people were standing on the window sills, down to the double swing-doors, which were constantly cracking open as if the house was literally too full to hold the congregation. The aisles also were crowded with people standing, all eager yet solemn, with granite faces and live eyes. One who did not know better might well have imagined them gathered in hunger after good tidings from the kingdom of truth and hope, whereby they might hasten the coming of that kingdom in their souls and the souls they loved. But it was hardly that; it was indeed a long way from it, and no such thing: the eagerness was, in the mass, doubtless with exceptions, to hear the new preacher, the pyrotechnist of human logic and eloquence, who was about to burn his halfpenny blue lights over the abyss of truth, and throw his yelping crackers into it.

The eyes of the young men went wandering over the crowd, looking for any of their few acquaintants, but below they mostly fell of course on the backs of heads. There was, however, no mistaking either Ginevra's bonnet or the occiput perched like a capital on the long neck of her father. They sat a good way in front, about the middle of the great church. At the sight of them Gibbie's face brightened, Donal's turned pale as death. For, only the last week but one, he had heard of the frequent visits of the young preacher to the cottage, and of the favour in which he was held by both father and daughter; and his state of mind since, had not, with all his philosophy to rectify and support it, been an enviable one. That he could not for a moment regard himself as a fit husband for the lady-lass, or dream of exposing himself or her to the insult which the offer of himself as a son-in-law would bring on them both from the laird, was not a reflection to render the thought of such a bag of wind as Fergus Duff marrying her, one whit the less horribly unendurable. Had the laird been in the same social position as before, Donal would have had no fear of his accepting Fergus; but misfortune alters many relations. Fergus's father was a man of considerable property, Fergus himself almost a man of influence, and already in possession of a comfortable income: it was possible to imagine that the impoverished Thomas Galbraith, late of Glashruach, Esq., might contrive to swallow what annoyance there could not but in any case be in wedding his daughter to the son of John Duff, late his own tenant of the Mains. Altogether Donal's thoughts were not of the kind to put him in fit mood—I do not say to gather benefit from the prophesying of Fergus, but to give fair play to the peddler who now rose to display his loaded calico and beggarly shoddy over the book-board of the pulpit. But the congregation listened rapt. I dare not say there was no divine reality concerned in his utterance, for Gibbie saw many a glimmer through the rents in his logic, and the thin-worn patches of his philosophy; but it was not such glimmers that fettered the regards of the audience, but the noisy flow and false eloquence of the preacher. In proportion to the falsehood in us are we exposed to the falsehood in others. The false plays upon the false without discord; comes to the false, and is welcomed as the true; there is no jar, for the false to the false look the true; darkness takes darkness for light, and great is the darkness. I will not attempt an account of the sermon; even admirably rendered, it would be worthless as the best of copies of a bad wall-paper. There was in it, to be sure, such a glowing description of the city of God as might have served to attract thither all the diamond-merchants of Amsterdam; but why a Christian should care to go to such a place, let him tell who knows; while, on the other hand, the audience appeared equally interested in his equiponderating description of the place of misery. Not once did he even attempt to give, or indeed could have given, the feeblest idea, to a single soul present, of the one terror of the universe—the peril of being cast from the arms of essential Love and Life into the bosom of living Death. For this teacher of men knew nothing whatever but by hearsay, had not in himself experienced one of the joys or one of the horrors he endeavoured to embody.

Gibbie was not at home listening to such a sermon; he was distressed, and said afterwards to Donal he would far rather be subjected to Mr. Sclater's isms than Fergus's ations. It caused him pain too to see Donal look so scornful, so contemptuous even; while it added to Donal's unrest, and swelled his evil mood, to see Mr. Galbraith absorbed. For Ginevra's bonnet, it did not once move—but then it was not set at an angle to indicate either eyes upturned in listening, or cast down in emotion. Donal would have sacrificed not a few songs, the only wealth he possessed, for one peep round the corner of that bonnet. He had become painfully aware, that, much as he had seen of Ginevra, he knew scarcely anything of her thoughts; he had always talked so much more to her than she to him, that now, when he longed to know, he could not even guess what she might be thinking, or what effect such "an arrangement" of red and yellow would have upon her imagination and judgment. She could not think or receive what was not true, he felt sure, but she might easily enough attribute truth where it did not exist.

At length the rockets, Roman candles, and squibs were all burnt out, the would-be "eternal blazon" was over, and the preacher sunk back exhausted in his seat. The people sang; a prayer, fit pendent to such a sermon, followed, and the congregation was dismissed—it could not be with much additional strength to meet the sorrows, temptations, sophisms, commonplaces, disappointments, dulnesses, stupidities, and general devilries of the week, although not a few paid the preacher welcome compliments on his "gran' discoorse."

The young men were out among the first, and going round to another door, in the church-yard, by which they judged Ginevra and her father must issue, there stood waiting. The night was utterly changed. The wind had gone about, and the vapours were high in heaven, broken all into cloud-masses of sombre grandeur. Now from behind, now upon their sides, they were made glorious by the full moon, while through their rents appeared the sky and the ever marvellous stars. Gibbie's eyes went climbing up the spire that shot skyward over their heads. Around its point the clouds and the moon seemed to gather, grouping themselves in grand carelessness; and he thought of the Son of Man coming in the clouds of heaven; to us mere heaps of watery vapour, ever ready to fall, drowning the earth in rain, or burying it in snow, to angel-feet they might be solid masses whereon to tread attendant upon him, who, although with his word he ruled winds and seas, loved to be waited on by the multitude of his own! He was yet gazing, forgetful of the human tide about him, watching the glory dominant over storm, when his companion pinched his arm: he looked, and was aware that Fergus, muffled to the eyes, was standing beside them. He seemed not to see them, and they were nowise inclined to attract his attention, but gazed motionless on the church door, an unsealed fountain of souls. What a curious thing it is to watch an issuing crowd of faces for one loved one— all so unattractive, provoking, blamable, as they come rolling round corners, dividing, and flowing away—not one of them the right one! But at last out she did come—Ginevra, like a daisy among mown grass! It was really she!—but with her father. She saw Donal, glanced from him to Gibbie, cast down her sweet eyes, and made no sign. Fergus had already advanced and addressed the laird.

"Ah, Mr. Duff!" said Mr. Galbraith; "excuse me, but would you oblige me by giving your arm to my daughter? I see a friend waiting to speak to me. I shall overtake you in a moment."

Fergus murmured his pleasure, and Ginevra and he moved away together. The youths for a moment watched the father. He dawdled— evidently wanted to speak to no one. They then followed the two, walking some yards behind them. Every other moment Fergus would bend his head towards Ginevra; once or twice they saw the little bonnet turn upwards in response or question. Poor Donal was burning with lawless and foolish indignation: why should the minister muffle himself up like an old woman in the crowd, and take off the great handkerchief when talking with the lady? When the youths reached the street where the cottage stood, they turned the corner after them, and walked quickly up to them where they stood at the gate waiting for it to be opened.

"Sic a gran' nicht!" said Donal, after the usual greetings. "Sir Gibbie an' me's haein' a dauner wi' the mune. Ye wad think she had licht eneuch to haud the cloods aff o' her, wad ye no, mem? But na! they'll be upon her, an' I'm feart there's ae unco black ane yon'er—dinna ye see't—wi' a straik o' white, aboot the thrapple o' 't?—There—dinna ye see 't?" he went on pointing to the clouds about the moon, "—that ane, I'm doobtin', 'ill hae the better o' her or lang—tak her intill 'ts airms, an' bray a' the licht oot o' her. Guid nicht, mem.—Guid nicht, Fergus. You ministers sudna mak yersels sae like cloods. Ye sud be cled in white an' gowd, an' a' colours o' stanes, like the new Jerooslem ye tell sic tales aboot, an' syne naebody wad mistak the news ye bring."

Therewith Donal walked on, doubtless for the moment a little relieved. But before they had walked far, he broke down altogether.

"Gibbie," he said, "yon rascal's gauin' to merry the leddy-lass! an' it drives me mad to think it. Gien I cud but ance see an' speyk till her—ance—jist ance! Lord! what 'll come o' a' the gowans upo' the Mains, an' the heather upo' Glashgar!"

He burst out crying, but instantly dashed away his tears with indignation at his weakness.

"I maun dree my weird," (undergo my doom), he said, and said no more.

Gibbie's face had grown white in the moon-gleams, and his lips trembled. He put his arm through Donal's and clung to him, and in silence they went home. When they reached Donal's room, Donal entering shut the door behind him and shut out Gibbie. He stood for a moment like one dazed, then suddenly coming to himself, turned away, left the house, and ran straight to Daur-street.

When the minister's door was opened to him, he went to that of the dining-room, knowing Mr. and Mrs. Sclater would then be at supper. Happily for his intent, the minister was at the moment having his tumbler of toddy after the labours of the day, an indulgence which, so long as Gibbie was in the house, he had, ever since that first dinner-party, taken in private, out of regard, as he pretended to himself, for the boy's painful associations with it, but in reality, to his credit be it told if it may, from a little shame of the thing itself; and his wife therefore, when she saw Gibbie, rose, and, meeting him, took him with her to her own little sitting-room, where they had a long talk, of which the result appeared the next night in a note from Mrs. Sclater to Gibbie, asking him and Donal to spend the evening of Tuesday with her.

LII

THE QUARRY

Donal threw everything aside, careless of possible disgrace in the class the next morning, and, trembling with hope, accompanied Gibbie: she would be there—surely! It was one of those clear nights in which a gleam of straw-colour in the west, with light-thinned gray-green deepening into blue above it, is like the very edge of the axe of the cold—the edge that reaches the soul. But the youths were warm enough: they had health and hope. The hospitable crimson room, with its round table set out for a Scotch tea, and its fire blazing hugely, received them. And there sat Ginevra by the fire! with her pretty feet on a footstool before it: in those days ladies wore open shoes, and showed dainty stockings. Her face looked rosy, but it was from the firelight, for when she turned it towards them, it showed pale as usual. She received them, as always, with the same simple sincerity that had been hers on the bank of the Lorrie burn. But Gibbie read some trouble in her eyes, for his soul was all touch, and, like a delicate spiritual seismograph, responded at once to the least tremble of a neighbouring soul. The minister was not present, and Mrs. Sclater had both to be the blazing coal, and keep blowing herself, else, however hot it might be at the smouldering hearth, the little company would have sent up no flame of talk.

When tea was over, Gibbie went to the window, got within the red curtains, and peeped out. Returning presently, he spelled with fingers and signed with hands to Ginevra that it was a glorious night: would she not come for a walk? Ginevra looked to Mrs. Sclater.

"Gibbie wants me to go for a walk," she said.

"Certainly, my dear—if you are well enough to go with him," replied her friend.

"I am always well," answered Ginevra.

"I can't go with you," said Mrs. Sclater, "for I expect my husband every moment; but what occasion is there, with two such knights to protect you?"

She was straining hard on the bit of propriety; but she knew them all so well? she said to herself. Then first perceiving Gibbie's design,

Donal cast him a grateful glance, while Ginevra rose hastily, and ran to put on her outer garments. Plainly to Donal, she was pleased to go.

When they stood on the pavement, there was the moon, the very cream of light, ladying it in a blue heaven. It was not all her own, but the clouds about her were white and attendant, and ever when they came near her took on her livery—the poor paled-rainbow colours, which are all her reflected light can divide into: that strange brown we see so often on her cloudy people must, I suppose, be what the red or the orange fades to. There was a majesty and peace about her airy domination, which Donal himself would have found difficult, had he known her state, to bring into harmony with her aeonian death. Strange that the light of lovers should be the coldest of all cold things within human ken—dead with cold, millions of years before our first father and mother appeared each to the other on the earth! The air was keen but dry. Nothing could fall but snow; and of anything like it there was nothing but those few frozen vapours that came softly out of the deeps to wait on the moon. Between them and behind them lay depth absolute, expressed in the perfection of nocturnal blues, deep as gentle, the very home of the dwelling stars. The steps of the youths rang on the pavements, and Donal's voice seemed to him so loud and clear that he muffled it all in gentler meaning. He spoke low, and Ginevra answered him softly. They walked close together, and Gibbie flitted to and fro, now on this side, now on that, now in front of them, now behind.

"Hoo likit ye the sermon, mem?" asked Donal.

"Papa thought it a grand sermon," answered Ginevra.

"An' yersel'?" persisted Donal.

"Papa tells me I am no judge," she replied.

"That's as muckle as to say ye didna like it sae weel as he did!" returned Donal, in a tone expressing some relief.

"Mr. Duff is very good to my father, Donal," she rejoined, "and I don't like to say anything against his sermon; but all the time I could not help thinking whether your mother would like this and that; for you know, Donal, any good there is in me I have got from her, and from Gibbie—and from you, Donal."

The youth's heart beat with a pleasure that rose to physical pain. Had he been a winged creature he would have flown straight up; but being a sober wingless animal, he stumped on with his two happy legs. Gladly would he have shown her the unreality of Fergus—that he was a poor shallow creature, with only substance enough to carry show and seeming, but he felt, just because he had reason to fear him, that it would be unmanly to speak the truth of him behind his back, except in the absolute necessity of rectitude. He felt also that, if Ginevra owed her father's friend such delicacy, he owed him at least a little silence; for was he not under more obligation to this same shallow-pated orator, than to all eternity he could wipe out, even if eternity carried in it the possibility of wiping out an obligation? Few men understand, but Donal did, that he who would cancel an obligation is a dishonest man. I cannot help it that many a good man—good, that is, because he is growing better—must then be reckoned in the list of the dishonest: he is in their number until he leaves it.

Donal remaining silent, Ginevra presently returned him his own question:

"How did you like the sermon, Donal?"

"Div ye want me to say, mem?" he asked.

"I do, Donal," she answered.

"Weel, I wad jist say, in a general w'y, 'at I canna think muckle o' ony sermon 'at micht gar a body think mair o' the precher nor o' him 'at he comes to prech aboot. I mean, 'at I dinna see hoo onybody was to lo'e God or his neebour ae jot the mair for hearin' yon sermon last nicht."

"But might not some be frightened by it, and brought to repentance, Donal?" suggested the girl.

"Ou ay; I daur say; I dinna ken. But I canna help thinkin' 'at what disna gie God onything like fair play, canna dee muckle guid to men, an' may, I doobt, dee a heap o' ill. It's a pagan kin' o' a thing yon."

"That's just what I was feeling—I don't say thinking, you know—for you say we must not say think when we have taken no trouble about it. I am sorry for Mr. Duff, if he has taken to teaching where he does not understand."

They had left the city behind them, and were walking a wide open road, with a great sky above it. On its borders were small fenced fields, and a house here and there with a garden. It was a plain-featured, slightly undulating country, with hardly any trees—not at all beautiful, except as every place under the heaven which man has not defiled is beautiful to him who can see what is there. But this night the earth was nothing: what was in them and over them was all. Donal felt—as so many will feel, before the earth, like a hen set to hatch the eggs of a soaring bird, shall have done rearing broods for heaven—that, with this essential love and wonder by his side, to be doomed to go on walking to all eternity would be a blissful fate, were the landscape turned to a brick-field, and the sky to persistent gray.

"Wad ye no tak my airm, mem?" he said at length, summoning courage. "I jist fin' mysel' like a horse wi' a reyn brocken, gaein' by mysel' throu' the air this gait."

Before he had finished the sentence Ginevra had accepted the offer. It was the first time. His arm trembled. He thought it was her hand.

"Ye're no cauld, are ye, mem?" he said.

"Not the least," she answered.

"Eh, mem! gien fowk was but a' made oot o' the same clay, like, 'at ane micht say till anither—'Ye hae me as ye hae yersel'!'"

"Yes, Donal," rejoined Ginevra; "I wish we were all made of the poet-clay like you! What it would be to have a well inside, out of which to draw songs and ballads as I pleased! That's what you have, Donal—or, rather, you're just a draw-well of music yourself."

Donal laughed merrily. A moment more and he broke out singing:

> *My thoughts are like fireflies, pulsing in moonlight;*
> *My heart is a silver cup, full of red wine;*
> *My soul a pale gleaming horizon, whence soon light*
> *Will flood the gold earth with a torrent divine.*

"What's that, Donal?" cried Ginevra.

"Ow, naething," answered Donal. "It was only my hert lauchin'."

"Say the words," said Ginevra.

"I canna—I dinna ken them noo," replied Donal.

"Oh, Donal! are those lovely words gone—altogether—for ever? Shall I not hear them again?"

"I'll try to min' upo' them whan I gang hame," he said. "I canna the noo. I can think o' naething but ae thing."

"And what is that, Donal?"

"Yersel'," answered Donal.

Ginevra's hand lifted just a half of its weight from Donal's arm, like a bird that had thought of flying, then settled again.

"It is very pleasant to be together once more as in the old time, Donal—though there are no daisies and green fields.—But what place is that, Donal?"

Instinctively, almost unconsciously, she wanted to turn the conversation. The place she pointed to was an opening immediately on the roadside, through a high bank—narrow and dark, with one side half lighted by the moon. She had often passed it, walking with her school-fellows, but had never thought of asking what it was. In the shining dusk it looked strange and a little dreadful.

"It's the muckle quarry, mem," answered Donal: "div ye no ken that? That's whaur maist the haill toon cam oot o'. It's a some eerie kin' o' a place to luik at i' this licht. I won'er at ye never saw't."

"I have seen the opening there, but never took much notice of it before," said Ginevra.

"Come an' I'll lat ye see't," rejoined Donal. "It's weel worth luikin' intill. Ye hae nae notion sic a place as 'tis. It micht be amo' the grenite muntains o' Aigypt, though they takna freely sic fine blocks oot o' this ane as they tuik oot o' that at Syene. Ye wadna be fleyt to come an' see what the meen maks o' 't, wad ye, mem?"

"No, Donal. I would not be frightened to go anywhere with you. But—"

"Eh, mem! it maks me richt prood to hear ye say that. Come awa' than."

So saying, he turned aside, and led her into the narrow passage, cut through a friable sort of granite. Gibbie, thinking they had gone to have but a peep and return, stood in the road, looking at the clouds and the moon, and crooning to himself. By and by, when he found they did not return, he followed them.

When they reached the end of the cutting, Ginevra started at sight of the vast gulf, the moon showing the one wall a ghastly gray, and from the other throwing a shadow half across the bottom. But a winding road went down into it, and Donal led her on. She shrunk at first, drawing back from the profound, mysterious-looking abyss, so awfully still; but when Donal looked at her, she was ashamed to refuse to go farther, and indeed almost afraid to take her hand from his arm; so he led her down the terrace road. The side of the quarry was on one hand, and on the other she could see only into the gulf.

"Oh, Donal!" she said at length, almost in a whisper, "this is like a dream I once had, of going down and down a long roundabout road, inside the earth, down and down, to the heart of a place full of the dead—the ground black with death, and between horrible walls."

Donal looked at her; his face was in the light reflected from the opposite gray precipice: she thought it looked white and strange, and grew more frightened, but dared not speak. Presently Donal again began to sing, and this is something like what he sang:—

"Death! whaur do ye bide, auld Death?"
"I bide in ilka breath,"
Quo' Death.
"No i' the pyramids,
An' no the worms amids,
'Neth coffin-lids;
I bidena whaur life has been,
An' whaur's nae mair to be dune."

"Death! whaur do ye bide, auld Death?"
"Wi' the leevin', to dee 'at's laith,"
Quo' Death.
"Wi' the man an' the wife
'At lo'e like life,
But strife; (without)
Wi' the bairns 'at hing to their mither,
An' a' 'at lo'e ane anither."

"Death! whaur do ye bide, auld Death?"
"Abune an' aboot an' aneath,"
Quo' Death.
"But o' a' the airts,
An' o' a' the pairts,
In herts,
Whan the tane to the tither says na,
An' the north win' begins to blaw."

"What a terrible song, Donal!" said Ginevra.

He made no reply, but went on, leading her down into the pit: he had been afraid she was going to draw back, and sang the first words her words suggested, knowing she would not interrupt him. The aspect of the place grew frightful to her.

"Are you sure there are no holes—full of water, down there?" she faltered.

"Ay, there's ane or twa," replied Donal, "but we'll haud oot o' them."

Ginevra shuddered, but was determined to show no fear: Donal should not reproach her with lack of faith! They stepped at last on the level below, covered with granite chips and stones and great blocks. In the middle rose a confused heap of all sorts. To this, and round to the other side of it, Donal led her. There shone the moon on the corner of a pool, the rest of which crept away in blackness under an overhanging mass. She caught his arm with both hands. He told her to look up. Steep granite rock was above them all round, on one side dark, on the other mottled with the moon and the thousand shadows of its own roughness; over the gulf hung vaulted the blue, cloud-blotted sky, whence the moon seemed to look straight down upon her, asking what they were about, away from their kind, in such a place of terror.

Suddenly Donal caught her hand. She looked in his face. It was not the moon that could make it so white.

"Ginevra!" he said, with trembling voice.

"Yes, Donal," she answered.

"Ye're no angry at me for ca'in ye by yer name? I never did it afore."

"I always call you Donal," she answered.

"That's nait'ral. Ye're a gran' leddy, an' I'm naething abune a herd-laddie."

"You're a great poet, Donal, and that's much more than being a lady or a gentleman."

"Ay, maybe," answered Donal listlessly, as if he were thinking of something far away; "but it winna mak up for the tither; they're no upo' the same side o' the watter, like. A puir lad like me daurna lift an ee till a gran' leddy like you, mem. A' the warl' wad but scorn him, an' lauch at the verra notion. My time's near ower at the college, an' I see naething for 't but gang hame an' fee (hire myself). I'll be better workin' wi' my han's nor wi' my heid whan I hae nae houp left o' ever seein' yer face again. I winna lowse a day aboot it. Gien I lowse time I may lowse my rizon. Hae patience wi' me ae meenute, mem; I'm jist driven to tell ye the trowth. It's mony a lang sin' I hae kent mysel' wantin' you. Ye're the boady, an' I'm the shaidow. I dinna mean nae hyperbolics—that's the w'y the thing luiks to me i' my ain thouchts. Eh, mem, but ye're bonnie! Ye dinna ken yersel' hoo bonnie ye are, nor what a subversion you mak i' my hert an' my heid. I cud jist cut my heid aff, an' lay 't aneth yer feet to haud them aff o' the cauld flure."

Still she looked him in the eyes, like one bewildered, unable to withdraw her eyes from his. Her face too had grown white.

"Tell me to haud my tongue, mem, an' I'll haud it," he said.

Her lips moved, but no sound came.

"I ken weel," he went on, "ye can never luik upo' me as onything mair nor a kin' o' a human bird, 'at ye wad hing in a cage, an' gie seeds an' bits o' sugar till, an' hearken till whan he sang. I'll never trouble ye nae mair, an' whether ye grant me my prayer or no, ye'll never see me again. The only differ 'ill be 'at I'll aither hing my heid or haud it up for the rest o' my days. I wad fain ken 'at I wasna despised, an' 'at maybe gien things had been different,—but na, I dinna mean that; I mean naething 'at wad fricht ye frae what I wad hae. It sudna mean a hair mair nor lies in itsel'."

"What is it, Donal?" said Ginevra, half inaudibly, and with effort: she could scarcely speak for a fluttering in her throat.

"I cud beseech ye upo' my k-nees," he went on, as if she had not spoken, "to lat me kiss yer bonnie fut; but that ye micht grant for bare peety, an' that wad dee me little guid; sae for ance an' for a', till maybe efter we're a' ayont the muckle sea, I beseech at the fauvour o' yer sweet sowl, to lay upo' me, as upo' the lips o' the sowl 'at sang ye the sangs ye likit sae weel to hear whan ye was but a leddy-lassie—ae solitary kiss. It shall be holy to me as the licht; an' I sweir by the Trowth I'll think o' 't but as ye think, an' man nor wuman nor bairn, no even Gibbie himsel', sall ken—"

The last word broke the spell upon Ginevra.

"But, Donal," she said, as quietly as when years ago they talked by the Lorrie side, "would it be right?—a secret with you I could not tell to any one?—not even if afterwards—"

Donal's face grew so ghastly with utter despair that absolute terror seized her; she turned from him and fled, calling "Gibbie! Gibbie!"

He was not many yards off, approaching the mound as she came from behind it. He ran to meet her. She darted to him like a dove pursued by a hawk, threw herself into his arms, laid her head on his shoulder, and wept. Gibbie held her fast, and with all the ways in his poor power sought to comfort her. She raised her face at length. It was all wet with tears which glistened in the moonlight. Hurriedly Gibbie asked on his fingers:

"Was Donal not good to you?"

"He's beautiful," she sobbed; "but I couldn't, you know, Gibbie, I couldn't. I don't care a straw about position and all that—who would with a poet?—but I couldn't, you know, Gibbie. I couldn't let him think I might have married him—in any case: could I now, Gibbie?"

She laid her head again on his shoulder and sobbed. Gibbie did not well understand her. Donal, where he had thrown himself on a heap of granite chips, heard and understood, felt and knew and resolved all in

GEORGE MACDONALD

one. The moon shone, and the clouds went flitting like ice-floe about the sky, now gray in distance, now near the moon and white, now in her very presence and adorned with her favour on their bosoms, now drifting again into the gray; and still the two, Ginevra and Gibbie, stood motionless—Gibbie with the tears in his eyes, and Ginevra weeping as if her heart would break; and behind the granite blocks lay Donal.

Again Ginevra raised her head.

"Gibbie, you must go and look after poor Donal," she said.

Gibbie went, but Donal was nowhere to be seen. To escape the two he loved so well, and be alone as he felt, he had crept away softly into one of the many recesses of the place. Again and again Gibbie made the noise with which he was accustomed to call him, but he gave back no answer, and they understood that wherever he was he wanted to be left to himself. They climbed again the winding way out of the gulf, and left him the heart of its desolation.

"Take me home, Gibbie," said Ginevra, when they reached the high road.

As they went, not a word more passed between them. Ginevra was as dumb as Gibbie, and Gibbie was sadder than he had ever been in his life—not only for Donal's sake, but because, in his inexperienced heart, he feared that Ginevra would not listen to Donal because she could not—because she had already promised herself to Fergus Duff; and with all his love to his kind, he could not think it well that Fergus should be made happy at such a price. He left her at her own door, and went home, hoping to find Donal there before him.

He was not there. Hour after hour passed, and he did not appear. At eleven o'clock, Gibbie set out to look for him, but with little hope of finding him. He went all the way back to the quarry, thinking it possible he might be waiting there, expecting him to return without Ginevra. The moon was now low, and her light reached but a little way into it, so that the look of the place was quite altered, and the bottom of it almost dark. But Gibbie had no fear. He went down to the spot, almost feeling his way, where they had stood, got upon the heap, and called and whistled many times. But no answer came. Donal was away, he did not himself know where, wandering wherever the feet in his spirit led him. Gibbie went home again, and sat up all night, keeping the kettle boiling, ready to make tea for him the moment he should come in. But even in the morning Donal did not appear. Gibbie was anxious—for Donal was unhappy.

He might hear of him at the college, he thought, and went at the usual hour. Sure enough, as he entered the quadrangle, there was Donal going in at the door leading to the moral philosophy class-room. For hours, neglecting his own class, he watched about the court, but Donal never showed himself. Gibbie concluded he had watched to avoid him, and had gone home by Crown-street, and himself returned the usual and shorter way, sure almost of now finding him in his room—although probably with the door locked. The room was empty, and Mistress Murkison had not seen him.

Donal's final examination, upon which alone his degree now depended, came on the next day: Gibbie watched at a certain corner, and unseen saw him pass—with a face pale but strong, eyes that seemed not to have slept, and lips that looked the inexorable warders of many sighs. After that he did not see him once till the last day of the session arrived. Then in the public room he saw him go up to receive his degree. Never before had he seen him look grand; and Gibbie knew that there was not any evil in the world, except wrong. But it had been the dreariest week he had ever passed. As they came from the public room, he lay in wait for him once more, but again in vain: he must have gone through the sacristan's garden behind.

When he reached his lodging, he found a note from Donal waiting him, in which he bade him good-bye, said he was gone to his mother, and asked him to pack up his things for him: he would write to Mistress Murkison and tell her what to do with the chest.

LIII

A Night-Watch

A sense of loneliness, such as in all his forsaken times he had never felt, overshadowed Gibbie when he read this letter. He was altogether perplexed by Donal's persistent avoidance of him. He had done nothing to hurt him, and knew himself his friend in his sorrow as well as in his joy. He sat down in the room that had been his, and wrote to him. As often as he raised his eyes—for he had not shut the door—he saw the dusty sunshine on the old furniture. It was a bright day, one of the poursuivants of the yet distant summer, but how dreary everything looked! how miserable and heartless now Donal was gone, and would never regard those things any more! When he had ended his letter, almost for the first time in his life, he sat thinking what he should do next. It was as if he were suddenly becalmed on the high seas; one wind had ceased to blow, and another had not begun. It troubled him a little that he must now return to Mr. Sclater, and once more feel the pressure of a nature not homogeneous with his own. But it would not be for long.

Mr. Sclater had thought of making a movement towards gaining an extension of his tutelage beyond the ordinary legal period, on the ground of unfitness in his ward for the management of his property; but Gibbie's character and scholarship, and the opinion of the world which would follow failure, had deterred him from the attempt. In the month of May, therefore, when, according to the registry of his birth in the parish book, he would be of age, he would also be, as he expected, his own master, so far as other mortals were concerned. As to what he would then do, he had thought much, and had plans, but no one knew anything of them except Donal—who had forsaken him.

He was in no haste to return to Daur-street. He packed Donal's things, with all the books they had bought together, and committed the chest to Mistress Murkison. He then told her he would rather not give up his room just yet, but would like to keep it on for a while, and come and go as he pleased; to which the old woman replied,

"As ye wull, Sir Gibbie. Come an' gang as free as the win'. Mak o' my hoose as gien it war yer ain."

He told her he would sleep there that night, and she got him his dinner as usual; after which, putting a Greek book in his pocket, he went out, thinking to go to the end of the pier and sit there a while. He would gladly have gone to Ginevra, but she had prevented him when she was at school, and had never asked him since she left it. But Gibbie was not *ennuyé*: the pleasure of his life came from the very roots of his being, and would therefore run into any channel of his consciousness; neither was he greatly troubled; nothing could "put rancours in the vessel of" his "peace;" he was only very hungry after the real presence of the human; and scarcely had he set his foot on the pavement, when he resolved to go and see Mistress Croale. The sun, still bright, was sinking towards the west, and a cold wind was blowing. He walked to the market, up to the gallery of it, and on to the farther end, greeting one and another of the keepers of the little shops, until he reached that of Mistress Croale. She was overjoyed at sight of him, and proud the neighbours saw the terms they were on. She understood his signs and finger-speech tolerably, and held her part of the conversation in audible utterance. She told him that for the week past Donal had occupied her garret—she did not know why, she said, and hoped nothing had gone wrong between them. Gibbie signed that he could not tell her about it there, but would go and take tea with her in the evening.

"I'm sorry I canna be hame sae ear'," she replied. "I promised to tak my dish o' tay wi' auld Mistress Green—the kail-wife, ye ken, Sir Gibbie."—Gibbie nodded and she resumed:—"But gien ye wad tak a lug o' a Fin'on haddie wi' me at nine o'clock, I wad be prood."

Gibbie nodded again, and left her.

All this time he had not happened to discover that the lady who stood at the next counter, not more than a couple of yards from him, was Miss Kimble—which was the less surprising in that the lady took some trouble to hide the fact. She extended her purchasing when she saw who was shaking hands with the next stall-keeper, but kept her face turned from him, heard all Mrs. Croale said to him, and went away asking herself what possible relations except objectionable ones could exist between such a pair. She knew little or nothing of Gibbie's early history, for she had not been a dweller in the city when Gibbie was known as well as the town-cross to almost every man, woman, and child in it, else perhaps she might, but I doubt it, have modified her conclusion. Her instinct was in the right, she said, with self-gratulation; he was a lad of low character and tastes, just what she had taken him for the first moment she saw him: his friends could not know what he was; she was bound to acquaint them with his conduct; and first of all, in duty to her old pupil, she must let Mr. Galbraith know what sort of friendships this Sir Gilbert, his nephew, cultivated. She went therefore straight to the cottage.

Fergus was there when she rang the bell. Mr. Galbraith looked out, and seeing who it was, retreated—the more hurriedly that he owed her money, and imagined she had come to dun him. But when she found to her disappointment that she could not see him, Miss Kimble did not therefore attempt to restrain a little longer the pent-up waters of her secret. Mr. Duff was a minister, and the intimate friend of the family: she would say what she had seen and heard. Having then first abjured all love of gossip, she told her tale, appealing to the minister whether she had not been right in desiring to let Sir Gilbert's uncle know how he was going on.

"I was not aware that Sir Gilbert was a cousin of yours, Miss Galbraith," said Fergus.

Ginevra's face was rosy red, but it was now dusk, and the fire-light had friendly retainer-shadows about it.

"He is not my cousin," she answered.

"Why, Ginevra! you told me he was your cousin," said Miss Kimble, with keen moral reproach.

"I beg your pardon; I never did," said Ginevra.

"I must see your father instantly," cried Miss Kimble, rising in anger. "He must be informed at once how much he is mistaken in the young gentleman he permits to be on such friendly terms with his daughter."

"My father does not know him," rejoined Ginevra; "and I should prefer they were not brought together just at present."

Her words sounded strange even in her own ears, but she knew no way but the straight one.

"You quite shock me, Ginevra!" said the school-mistress, resuming her seat: "you cannot mean to say you cherish acquaintance with a young man of whom your father knows nothing, and whom you dare not introduce to him?"

To explain would have been to expose her father to blame.

"I have known Sir Gilbert from my childhood," she said.

"Is it possible your duplicity reaches so far?" cried Miss Kimble, assured in her own mind that Ginevra had said he was her cousin.

Fergus thought it was time to interfere.

"I know something of the circumstances that led to the acquaintance of Miss Galbraith with Sir Gilbert," he said, "and I am sure it would only annoy her father to have any allusion made to it by one—excuse me, Miss Kimble—who is comparatively a stranger. I beg you will leave the matter to me."

Fergus regarded Gibbie as a half witted fellow, and had no fear of him. He knew nothing of the commencement of his acquaintance with Ginevra, but imagined it had come about through Donal; for, studiously as Mr. Galbraith had avoided mention of his quarrel with Ginevra because of the lads, something of it had crept out, and reached the Mains; and in now venturing allusion to that old story, Fergus was feeling after a nerve whose vibration, he thought, might afford him some influence over Ginevra.

He spoke authoritatively, and Miss Kimble, though convinced it was a mere pretence of her graceless pupil that her father would not see her, had to yield, and rose. Mr. Duff rose also, saying he would walk with her. He returned to the cottage, dined with them, and left about eight o'clock.

Already well enough acquainted in the city to learn without difficulty where Mistress Croale lived, and having nothing very particular to do, he strolled in the direction of her lodging, and saw Gibbie go into the house. Having seen him in, he was next seized with the desire to see him out again; having lain in wait for him as a beneficent brownie, he must now watch him as a profligate baronet forsooth! To haunt the low street until he should issue was a dreary prospect—in the east wind of a March night, which some giant up above seemed sowing with great handfuls of rain-seed; but having made up his mind, he stood his ground. For two hours he walked, vaguely cherishing an idea that he was fulfilling a duty of his calling, as a moral policeman.

When at length Gibbie appeared, he had some difficulty in keeping him in sight, for the sky was dark, the moon was not yet up, and Gibbie walked like a swift shadow before him. Suddenly, as if some old association had waked the old habit, he started off at a quick trot. Fergus did his best to follow. As he ran, Gibbie caught sight of a woman seated on a doorstep, almost under a lamp, a few paces up a narrow passage, stopped, stepped within the passage, and stood in a shadow watching her. She had turned the pocket of her dress inside out, and seemed unable to satisfy herself that there was nothing there but the hole, which she examined again and again, as if for the last news of her last coin. Too thoroughly satisfied at length, she put back the pocket, and laid her head on her hands. Gibbie had not a farthing. Oh, how cold it was! and there sat his own flesh and blood shivering in it! He went up to her. The same moment Fergus passed the end of the court. Gibbie took her by the hand. She started in terror, but his smile reassured her. He drew her, and she rose. He laid her hand on his arm, and she went with him. He had not yet begun to think about prudence, and perhaps, if some of us thought more about right, we should have less occasion to cultivate the inferior virtue. Perhaps also we should have more belief that there is One to care that things do not go wrong.

Fergus had given up the chase, and having met a policeman, was talking to him, when Gibbie came up with the woman on his arm, and passed them. Fergus again followed, sure of him now. Had not fear of being recognized prevented him from passing them and looking, he would have seen only a poor old thing, somewhere about sixty; but if she had been beautiful as the morning, of course Gibbie would have taken her all the same. He was the Gibbie that used to see the drunk people home. Gibbies like him do not change; they grow.

After following them through several streets, Fergus saw them stop at a door. Gibbie opened it with a key which his spy imagined the woman gave him. They entered, and shut it almost in Fergus's face, as he hurried up determined to speak. Gibbie led the poor shivering creature up the stair, across the chaos of furniture, and into his room, in the other corner next to Donal's. To his joy he found the fire was not out. He set her in the easiest chair he had, put the kettle on, blew the fire to a blaze, made coffee, cut bread and butter, got out a pot of marmalade, and ate and drank with his guest. She seemed quite bewildered and altogether unsure. I believe she took him at last, finding he never spoke, for half-crazy, as not a few had done, and as many would yet do. She smelt of drink, but was sober, and ready enough to eat. When she had taken as much as she would, Gibbie turned down the bed-clothes, made a sign to her she was to sleep there, took the key from the outside of the door, and put it in the lock on the inside, nodded a good-night, and left her, closing the door softly, which he heard her lock behind him, and going to Donal's room, where he slept.

In the morning he knocked at her door, but there was no answer, and opening it, he found she was gone.

When he told Mistress Murkison what he had done, he was considerably astonished at the wrath and indignation which instantly developed themselves in the good creature's atmosphere. That her respectable house should be made a hiding-place from the wind and a covert from the tempest, was infuriating. Without a moment's delay, she began a sweeping and scrubbing, and general cleansing of the room, as if all the devils had spent the night in it. And then for the first time Gibbie reflected, that, when he ran about the streets, he had never been taken home—except once, to be put under the rod and staff of the old woman. If Janet had been like the rest of them, he would have died upon Glashgar, or be now wandering about the country, doing odd jobs for half-pence! He must not do like other people—would not, could not, dared not be like them! He had had such a thorough schooling in humanity as nobody else had had! He had been to school in the streets, in dark places of revelry and crime, and in the very house of light!

When Mistress Murkison told him that if ever he did the like again, she would give him notice to quit, he looked in her face: she stared a moment in return, then threw her arms round his neck, and kissed him.

"Ye're the bonniest cratur o' a muckle idiot 'at ever man saw!" she cried; "an' gien ye dinna tak the better care, ye'll be soopit aff to haiven afore ye ken whaur ye are or what ye're aboot."

Her feelings, if not her sentiments, experienced a relapse when she discovered that one of her few silver tea-spoons was gone—which, beyond a doubt, the woman had taken: she abused her, and again scolded Gibbie, with much vigour. But Gibbie said to himself, "The woman is not bad, for there were two more silver spoons on the table." Even in the matter of stealing we must think of our own beam before our neighbour's mote. It is not easy to be honest. There is many a thief who is less of a thief than many a respectable member of society. The thief must be punished, and assuredly the other shall not come out until he has paid the uttermost farthing. Gibbie, who would have died rather than cast a shadow of injustice, was not shocked at the woman's depravity like Mistress Murkison. I am afraid he smiled. He took no notice either of her scoldings or her lamentations; but the first week after he came of age, he carried her a present of a dozen spoons.

Fergus could not tell Ginevra what he had seen; and if he told her father, she would learn that he had been playing the spy. To go to Mr. Sclater would have compromised him similarly. And what great occasion was there? He was not the fellow's keeper!

That same day Gibbie went back to his guardians. At his request Mrs. Sclater asked Ginevra to spend the following evening with them: he wanted to tell her about Donal. She accepted the invitation. But in a village near the foot of Glashgar, Donal had that morning done what was destined to prevent her from keeping her engagement: he had posted a letter to her. In an interval of comparative quiet, he had recalled the verses he sang to her as they walked that evening, and now sent them—completed in a very different tone. Not a word accompanied them.

> *My thoughts are like fire-flies pulsing in moonlight;*
> *My heart like a silver cup full of red wine;*
> *My soul a pale gleaming horizon, whence soon light*
> *Will flood the gold earth with a torrent divine.*

> *My thouchts are like worms in a starless gloamin';*
> *My hert like a sponge that's fillit wi' gall;*
> *My sowl like a bodiless ghaist sent a roamin',*
> *To bide i' the mirk till the great trumpet call.*

> *But peace be upo' ye, as deep as ye're lo'esome!*
> *Brak na an hoor o' yer fair-dreamy slap,*
> *To think o' the lad wi' a weicht in his bosom,*
> *'At ance sent a cry till ye oot o' the deep.*

> *Some sharp rocky heicht, to catch a far mornin'*
> *Ayont a' the nichts o' this warld, he'll clim';*
> *For nane shall say, Luik! he sank doon at her scornin',*
> *Wha rase by the han' she hield frank oot to him.*

The letter was handed, with one or two more, to Mr. Galbraith, at the breakfast table. He did not receive many letters now, and could afford time to one that was for his daughter. He laid it with the rest by his side, and after breakfast took it to his room and read it. He could no more understand it than Fergus could the Epistle to the Romans, and therefore the little he did understand of it was too much. But he had begun to be afraid of his daughter: her still dignity had begun to tell upon him in his humiliation. He laid the letter aside, said nothing, and waited, inwardly angry and contemptuous. After a while he began to flatter himself with the hope that perhaps it was but a sort of impertinent valentine, the writer of which was unknown to Ginevra. From the moment of its arrival, however, he kept a stricter watch upon her, and that night prevented her from going to Mrs. Sclater's. Gibbie, aware that Fergus continued his visits, doubted less and less that she had given herself to "The Bledder," as Donal called the popular preacher.

LIV

Of Age

There were no rejoicings upon Gibbie's attainment of his twenty-first year. His guardian, believing he alone had acquainted himself with the date, and desiring in his wisdom to avoid giving him a feeling of importance, made no allusion to the fact, as would have been most natural, when they met at breakfast on the morning of the day. But, urged thereto by Donal, Gibbie had learned the date for himself, and finding nothing was said, fingered to Mrs. Sclater, "This is my birthday."

"I wish you many happy returns," she answered, with kind empressement. "How old are you to-day?"

"Twenty-one," he answered—by holding up all his fingers twice and then a forefinger.

She looked struck, and glanced at her husband, who thereupon, in his turn, gave utterance to the usual formula of goodwill, and said no more. Seeing he was about to leave the table, Gibbie, claiming his attention, spelled on his fingers, very slowly, for Mr. Sclater was slow at following this mode of communication:

"If you please, sir, I want to be put in possession of my property as soon as possible."

"All in good time, Sir Gilbert," answered the minister, with a superior smile, for he clung with hard reluctance to the last vestige of his power.

"But what is good time?" spelled Gibbie with a smile, which, none the less that it was of genuine friendliness, indicated there might be difference of opinion on the point.

"Oh! we shall see," returned the minister coolly. "These are not things to be done in a hurry," he added, as if he had been guardian to twenty wards in chancery before, "We'll see in a few days what Mr. Torrie proposes."

"But I want my money at once," insisted Gibbie. "I have been waiting for it, and now it is time, and why should I wait still?"

"To learn patience, if for no other reason, Sir Gilbert," answered the minister, with a hard laugh, meant to be jocular. "But indeed such affairs cannot be managed in a moment. You will have plenty of time to make a good use of your money, if you should have to wait another year or two."

So saying he pushed back his plate and cup, a trick he had, and rose from the table.

"When will you see Mr. Torrie?" asked Gibbie, rising too, and working his telegraph with greater rapidity than before.

"By and by," answered Mr. Sclater, and walked towards the door. But Gibbie got between him and it.

"Will you go with me to Mr. Torrie to-day?" he asked.

The minister shook his head. Gibbie withdrew, seeming a little disappointed. Mr. Sclater left the room.

"You don't understand business, Gilbert," said Mrs. Sclater.

Gibbie smiled, got his writing-case, and sitting down at the table, wrote as follows:—

"Dear Mr. Sclater,—As you have never failed in your part, how can you wish me to fail in mine? I am now the one accountable for this money, which surely has been idle long enough, and if I leave it still unused, I shall be doing wrong, and there are things I have to do with it which ought to be set about immediately. I am sorry to seem importunate, but if by twelve o'clock you have not gone with me to Mr. Torrie, I will go to Messrs. Hope & Waver, who will tell me what I ought to do next, in order to be put in possession. It makes me unhappy to write like this, but I am not a child any longer, and having a man's work to do, I cannot consent to be treated as a child. I will do as I say. I am, dear Mr. Sclater, your affectionate ward, Gilbert Galbraith."

He took the letter to the study, and having given it to Mr. Sclater, withdrew. The minister might have known by this time with what sort of a youth he had to deal! He came down instantly, put the best face on it he could, said that if Sir Gilbert was so eager to take up the burden, he was ready enough to cast it off, and they would go at once to Mr. Torrie.

With the lawyer, Gibbie insisted on understanding everything, and that all should be legally arranged as speedily as possible. Mr. Torrie saw that, if he did not make things plain, or gave the least cause for doubt, the youth would most likely apply elsewhere for advice, and therefore took trouble to set the various points, both as to the property and the proceedings necessary, before him in the clearest manner.

"Thank you," said Gibbie, through Mr. Sclater. "Please remember I am more accountable for this money than you, and am compelled to understand."—Janet's repeated exhortations on the necessity of sending for the serpent to take care of the dove, had not been lost upon him.

The lawyer being then quite ready to make him an advance of money, they went with him to the bank, where he wrote his name, and received a cheque book. As they left the bank, he asked the minister whether he would allow him to keep his place in his house till the next session, and was almost startled at finding how his manner to him was changed. He assured Sir Gilbert, with a deference and respect both painful and amusing, that he hoped he would always regard his house as one home, however many besides he might now choose to have.

So now at last Gibbie was free to set about realizing a long-cherished scheme.

The repairs upon the Auld Hoose o' Galbraith were now nearly finished. In consequence of them, some of the tenants had had to leave, and Gibbie now gave them all notice to quit at their earliest convenience, taking care, however, to see them provided with fresh quarters, towards which he could himself do not a little, for several of the houses in the neighbourhood had been bought for him at the same time with the old mansion. As soon as it was empty, he set more men to work, and as its internal arrangements had never been altered, speedily, out of squalid neglect, caused not a little of old stateliness to reappear. He next proceeded to furnish at his leisure certain of the rooms, chiefly from the accumulations of his friend Mistress Murkison. By the time he had finished, his usual day for going home had arrived: while Janet lived, the cottage on Glashgar was home. Just as he was leaving, the minister told him that Glashruach was his. Mrs. Sclater was present, and read in his eyes what induced her instantly to make the remark: "How could that man deprive his daughter of the property he had to take her mother's name to get!"

"He had misfortunes," indicated Gibbie, "and could not help it, I suppose."

"Yes indeed!" she returned, "—misfortunes so great that they amounted to little less than swindling. I wonder how many he has brought to grief besides himself! If he had Glashruach once more he would begin it all over again."

"Then I'll give it to Ginevra," said Gibbie.

"And let her father coax her out of it, and do another world of mischief with it!" she rejoined.

Gibbie was silent. Mrs. Sclater was right! To give is not always to bless. He must think of some way. With plenty to occupy his powers of devising he set out.

He would gladly have seen Ginevra before he left, but had no chance. He had gone to the North church every Sunday for a long time now, neither for love of Fergus, nor dislike to Mr. Sclater, but for the sake of seeing his lost friend: had he not lost her when she turned from Donal to Fergus? Did she not forsake him too when she forsook his Donal? His heart would rise into his throat at the thought, but only for a moment: he never pitied himself. Now and then he had from her a sweet sad smile, but no sign that he might go and see her. Whether he was to see Donal when he reached Daurside, he could not tell; he had heard nothing of him since he went; his mother never wrote letters.

"Na, na; I canna," she would say. "It wad tak a' the pith oot o' me to vreet letters. A' 'at I hae to say I sen' the up-road; it's sure to win hame ear' or late."

Notwithstanding his new power, it was hardly, therefore, with his usual elation, that he took his seat on the coach. But his reception was the same as ever. At his mother's persuasion, Donal, he found, instead of betaking himself again to bodily labours as he had purposed, had accepted a situation as tutor offered him by one of the professors. He had told his mother all his trouble.

"He'll be a' the better for 't i' the en'," she said, with a smile of the deepest sympathy, "though, bein' my ain, I canna help bein' wae for 'im. But the Lord was i' the airthquak, an' the fire, an' the win' that rave the rocks, though the prophet couldna see 'im. Donal 'ill come oot o' this wi' mair room in's hert an' mair licht in's speerit."

Gibbie took his slate from the crap o' the wa' and wrote. "If money could do anything for him, I have plenty now."

"I ken yer hert, my bairn," replied Janet; "but na; siller's but a deid horse for onything 'at smacks o' salvation. Na; the puir fallow maun warstle oot o' the thicket o' deid roses as best he can—sair scrattit, nae doobt. Eh! it's a fearfu' an' won'erfu' thing that drawin' o' hert to hert, an' syne a great snap, an' a stert back, an' there's miles atween them! The Lord alane kens the boddom o' 't; but I'm thinkin' there's mair intill't, an' a heap mair to come oot o' 't ere a' be dune, than we hae ony guiss at."

Gibbie told her that Glashruach was his. Then first the extent of his wealth seemed to strike his old mother.

"Eh! ye'll be the laird, wull ye, than? Eh, sirs! To think o' this hoose an' a' bein' wee Gibbie's! Weel, it dings a'. The w'ys o' the Lord are to be thoucht upon! He made Dawvid a king, an' Gibbie he's made the laird! Blest be his name."

"They tell me the mountain is mine," Gibbie wrote: "your husband shall be laird of Glashgar if he likes."

"Na, na," said Janet, with a loving look. "He's ower auld for that. He micht na dee sae easy for't.—Eh! please the Lord, I wad fain gang wi' him.—An' what better wad Robert be to be laird? We pey nae rent as 'tis, an' he has as mony sheep to lo'e as he can weel ken ane frae the ither, noo 'at he's growin' auld, I ken naething 'at he lacks, but Gibbie to gang wi' 'im aboot the hill. A neebour's laddie comes an' gangs, to help him, but, eh, says Robert, he's no Gibbie!—But gien Glashruach be yer ain, my bonnie man, ye maun gang doon there this verra nicht, and gie a luik to the burn; for the last time I was there, I thoucht it was creepin' in aneth the bank some fearsome like for what's left o' the auld hoose, an' the suner it's luikit efter maybe the better. Eh, Sir Gibbie, but ye sud merry the bonnie leddy, an' tak her back till her ain hoose."

Gibbie gave a great sigh to think of the girl that loved the hill and the heather and the burns, shut up in the city, and every Sunday going to the great church—with which in Gibbie's mind was associated no sound of glad tidings. To him Glashgar was full of God; the North church or Mr. Sclater's church—well, he had tried hard, but had not succeeded in discovering temple-signs about either.

The next day he sent to the city for an architect; and within a week masons and quarrymen were at work, some on the hill blasting blue boulders and red granite, others roughly shaping the stones, and others laying the foundation of a huge facing and buttressing wall, which was to slope up from the bed of the Glashburn fifty feet to the foot of the castle, there to culminate in a narrow terrace with a parapet. Others again were clearing away what of the ruins stuck to the old house, in order to leave it, as much as might be, in its original form. There was no space left for rebuilding, neither was there any between the two burns for adding afresh. The channel of the second remained dry, the landslip continuing to choke it, and the stream to fall into the Glashburn. But Gibbie would not consent that the burn Ginevra had loved should sing no more as she had heard it sing. Her chamber was gone, and could not be restored, but another chamber should be built for her, beneath whose window it should again run: when she was married to Fergus, and her father could not touch it, the place should be hers. More masons were gathered, and foundations blasted in the steep rock that formed the other bank of the burn. The main point in the building was to be a room for Ginevra. He planned it himself—with a windowed turret projecting from the wall, making a recess in the room, and overhanging the stream. The turret he carried a story higher than the wall, and in the wall placed a stair leading to its top, whence, over the roof of the ancient part of the house, might be seen the great Glashgar, and its streams coming down from heaven, and singing as they came. Then from the middle of the first stair in the old house, the wall, a yard and a half thick, having been cut through, a solid stone bridge, with a pointed arch, was to lead across the burn to a like landing in the new house—a close passage, with an oriel window on each side, looking up and down the stream, and a steep roof. And while these works were going on below, two masons, high on the mountain, were adding to the cottage a warm bedroom for Janet and Robert.

The architect was an honest man, and kept Gibbie's secret, so that, although he was constantly about the place, nothing disturbed the general belief that Glashruach had been bought, and was being made habitable, by a certain magnate of the county adjoining.

LV

Ten Auld Hoose O' Galbraith

One cold afternoon in the end of October, when Mistress Croale was shutting up her shop in the market, and a tumbler of something hot was haunting her imagination, Gibbie came walking up the long gallery with the light hill-step which he never lost, and startled her with a hand on her shoulder, making signs that she must come with him. She made haste to lock her door, and they walked side by side to the Widdiehill. As they crossed the end of it she cast a look down Jink Lane, and thought of her altered condition with a sigh. Then the memory of the awful time amongst the sailors, in which poor Sambo's frightful death was ever prominent, came back like a fog from hell. But so far gone were those times now, that, seeing their events more as they really were, she looked upon them with incredulous horror, as things in which she could hardly have had any part or lot. Then returned her wanderings and homeless miseries, when often a haystack or a heap of straw in a shed was her only joy—whisky always excepted. Last of all came the dread perils, the hairbreadth escapes of her too adventurous voyage on the brander;—and after all these things, here she was, walking in peace by the side of wee Sir Gibbie, a friend as strong now as he had always been true! She asked herself, or some power within asked her, whence came the troubles that had haunted her life. Why had she been marked out for such misfortunes? Her conscience answered—from her persistence in living by the sale of drink after she had begun to feel it was wrong. Thence it was that she had learned to drink, and that she was even now liable, if not to be found drunk in the streets, yet to go to bed drunk as any of her former customers. The cold crept into her bones; the air seemed full of blue points and clear edges of cold, that stung and cut her. She was a wretched, a low creature! What would her late aunt think to see her now? What if this cold in her bones were the cold of coming death? To lie for ages in her coffin, with her mouth full of earth, longing for whisky! A verse from the end of the New Testament with "nor drunkards" in it, came to her mind. She had always had faith, she said to herself; but let them preach what they liked about salvation by faith, she knew there was nothing but hell for her if she were to die that night. There was Mistress Murkison looking out of her shop-door! She was respected as much as ever! Would Mistress Murkison be saved if she died that night? At least nobody would want her damned; whereas not a few, and Mr. Sclater in particular, would think it no fair play if Mistress Croale were not damned!

They turned into the close of the Auld Hoose o' Galbraith.

"Wee Gibbie's plottin' to lead me to repentance!" she said to herself. "He's gaein' to shaw me whaur his father dee'd, an' whaur they leevit in sic meesery—a' throu' the drink I gae 'im, an' the respectable hoose I keepit to 'tice him till't! He wad hae me persuaudit to lea' aff the drink! Weel, I'm a heap better nor ance I was, an' gie't up I wull a'thegither—afore it comes to the last wi' me."

By this time Gibbie was leading her up the dark stair. At the top, on a wide hall-like landing, he opened a door. She drew back with shy amaze. Her first thought was—"That prood madam, the minister's wife, 'ill be there!" Was affront lying in wait for her again? She looked round angrily at her conductor. But his smile re-assured her, and she stepped in.

It was almost a grand room, rich and sombre in colour, old-fashioned in its somewhat stately furniture. A glorious fire was blazing and candles were burning. The table was covered with a white cloth, and laid for two. Gibbie shut the door, placed a chair for Mistress Croale by the fire, seated himself, took out his tablets, wrote "Will you be my housekeeper? I will give you £100 a year," and handed them to her.

"Lord, Sir Gibbie!" she cried, jumping to her feet, "hae ye tint yer wuts? Hoo wad an auld wife like me luik in sic a place—an' in sic duds as this? It wad gar Sawtan lauch, an' that he can but seldom."

Gibbie rose, and taking her by the hand, led her to the door of an adjoining room. It was a bedroom, as grand as the room they had left, and if Mistress Croale was surprised before, she was astonished now. A fire was burning here too, candles were alight on the dressing-table, a hot bath stood ready, on the bed lay a dress of rich black satin, with linen and everything down, or up, to collars, cuffs, mittens, cap, and shoes. All these things Gibbie had bought himself, using the knowledge he had gathered in shopping with Mrs. Sclater, and the advice of her dressmaker, whom he had taken into his confidence, and who had entered heartily into his plan. He made signs to Mistress Croale that everything there was at her service, and left her.

Like one in a dream she yielded to the rush of events, not too much bewildered to dress with care, and neither too old nor too wicked nor too ugly to find pleasure in it. She might have been a born lady just restored to the habits of her youth, to judge by her delight over the ivory brushes and tortoise-shell comb, and great mirror. In an hour or so she made her appearance—I can hardly say reappeared, she was so altered. She entered the room neither blushing nor smiling, but wiping the tears from her eyes like a too blessed child. What Mrs. Sclater would have felt, I dare hardly think; for there was "the horrid woman" arrayed as nearly after her fashion as Gibbie had been able to get her up! A very good "get-up" nevertheless it was, and satisfactory to both concerned. Mistress Croale went out a decent-looking poor body, and entered a not uncomely matron of the housekeeper class, rather agreeable to look upon, who had just stood a nerve-shaking but not unpleasant surprise, and was recovering. Gibbie was so satisfied with her appearance that, come of age as he was, and vagrant no more, he first danced round her several times with a candle in his hand, much to the danger but nowise to the detriment of her finery, then set it down, and executed his old lavolta of delight, which, as always, he finished by standing on one leg.

Then they sat down to a nice nondescript meal, also of Gibbie's own providing.

When their meal was ended, he went to a bureau, and brought thence a paper, plainly written to this effect:

"I agree to do whatever Sir Gilbert Galbraith may require of me, so long as it shall not be against my conscience; and consent that, if I taste whisky once, he shall send me away immediately, without further reason given."

He handed it to Mistress Croale; she read, and instantly looked about for pen and ink: she dreaded seeming for a moment to hesitate. He brought them to her, she signed, and they shook hands.

He then conducted her all over the house—first to the rooms prepared for his study and bedroom, and next to the room in the garret, which he had left just as it was when his father died in it. There he gave her a look by which he meant to say, "See what whisky brings people to!" but which her conscience interpreted, "See what you brought my father to!" Next, on the floor between, he showed her a number of bedrooms, all newly repaired and fresh-painted,—with double windows, the inside ones filled with frosted glass. These rooms, he gave her to understand, he wished her to furnish, getting as many things as she could from Mistress Murkison. Going back then to the sitting-room, he proceeded to explain his plans, telling her he had furnished the house that he might not any longer be himself such a stranger as to have no place to take a stranger to. Then he got a Bible there was in the room, and showed her those words in the book of Exodus—"Also, thou shalt not oppress a stranger; for ye know the heart of a stranger, seeing ye were strangers in the land of Egypt;" and while she thought again of her wanderings through the country, and her nights in the open air, made her understand that whomsoever he should at any time bring home she was to treat as his guest. She might get a servant to wait upon herself, he said, but she must herself help him to wait upon his guests, in the name of the Son of Man.

She expressed hearty acquiescence, but would not hear of a servant: the more work the better for her! she said. She would to-morrow arrange for giving up her shop and disposing of her stock and the furniture in her garret. But Gibbie requested the keys of both those places. Next, he insisted that she should never utter a word as to the use he intended making of his house; if the thing came out, it would ruin his plans, and he must give them up altogether—and thereupon he took her to the ground floor and showed her a door in communication with a poor little house behind, by which he intended to introduce and dismiss his guests, that they should not know where they had spent the night. Then he made her read to him the hundred and seventh Psalm; after which he left her, saying he would come to the house as soon as the session began, which would be in a week; until then he should be at Mr. Sclater's.

Left alone in the great house—like one with whom the most beneficent of fairies had been busy, the first thing Mistress Croale did was to go and have a good look at herself—from head to foot—in the same mirror that had enlightened Donal as to his outermost man. Very different was the re-reflection it caused in Mistress Croale: she was satisfied with everything she saw there, except her complexion, and that she resolved should improve. She was almost painfully happy. Out there was the Widdiehill, dark and dismal and cold, through which she had come, sad and shivering and haunted with miserable thoughts, into warmth and splendour and luxury and bliss! Wee Sir Gibbie had made a lady of her! If only poor Sir George were alive to see and share!— There was but one thing wanted to make it Paradise indeed—a good tumbler of toddy by the fire before she went to bed!

Then first she thought of the vow she had made as she signed the paper, and shuddered—not at the thought of breaking it, but at the thought of having to keep it, and no help.—No help! it was the easiest thing in the world to get a bottle of whisky. She had but to run to Jink Lane at the farthest, to her own old house, which, for all Mr. Sclater, was a whisky shop yet! She had emptied her till, and had money in her pocket. Who was there to tell? She would not have a chance when Sir Gibbie came home to her. She must make use of what time was left her. She was safe now from going too far, because she must give it up; and why not then have one farewell night of pleasure, to bid a last good-bye to her old friend Whisky? what should she have done without him, lying in the cold wind by a dykeside, or going down the Daur like a shot on her brander?—Thus the tempting passion; thus, for aught I know, a tempting devil at the ear of her mind as well.—But with that came the face of Gibbie; she thought how troubled that face would look if she failed him. What a lost, irredeemable wretch was she about to make of herself after all he had done for her! No; if whisky was heaven, and the want of it was hell, she would not do it! She ran to the door, locked it, brought away the key, and laid it under the Bible from which she had been reading to Sir Gibbie. Perhaps she might have done better than betake herself again to her finery, but it did help her through the rest of the evening, and she went to her grand bed not only sober, but undefiled of the enemy. When Gibbie came to her a week after, he came to a true woman, one who had kept faith with him.

LVI

The Laird and the Preacher

S ince he came to town, Gibbie had seen Ginevra but once—that was in the North church. She looked so sad and white that his heart was very heavy for her. Could it be that she repented?—She must have done it to please her father! If she would marry Donal, he would engage to give her Glashruach. She should have Glashruach all the same whatever she did, only it might influence her father. He paced up and down before the cottage once for a whole night, but no good came of that. He paced before it from dusk to bedtime again and again, in the poor hope of a chance of speaking to Ginevra, but he never saw even her shadow on the white blind. He went up to the door once, but in the dread of displeasing her lost his courage, and paced the street the whole morning instead, but saw no one come out.

Fergus had gradually become essential to the small remaining happiness of which the laird was capable. He had gained his favour chiefly through the respect and kindly attention he showed him. The young preacher knew little of the laird's career, and looked upon him as an unfortunate man, towards whom loyalty now required even a greater show of respect than while he owned his father's farm. The impulse transmitted to him from the devotion of ancestors to the patriarchal head of the clan, had found blind vent in the direction of the mere feudal superior, and both the impulse and its object remained. He felt honoured, even now that he had reached the goal of his lofty desires and was a popular preacher, in being permitted to play backgammon with the great man, or to carve a chicken, when the now trembling hands, enfeebled far more through anxiety and disappointment than from age, found themselves unequal to the task: the laird had begun to tell long stories, and drank twice as much as he did a year ago; he was sinking in more ways than one.

Fergus at length summoned courage to ask him if he might pay his addresses to Miss Galbraith. The old man started, cast on him a withering look, murmured "The heiress of Glashruach!" remembered, threw himself back in his chair, and closed his eyes. Fergus, on the other side of the table, sat erect, a dice-box in his hand, waiting a reply. The father reflected that if he declined what he could not call an honour, he must lose what was unquestionably a comfort: how was he to pass all the evenings of the week without the preacher? On the other hand, if he accepted him, he might leave the miserable cottage, and go to the manse: from a moral point of view—that was, from the point of other people's judgment of him—it would be of consequence to have a clergyman for a son-in-law. Slowly he raised himself in his chair, opened his unsteady eyes, which rolled and pitched like boats on a choppy sea, and said solemnly,

"You have my permission, Mr. Duff."

The young preacher hastened to find Ginevra, but only to meet a refusal, gentle and sorrowful. He pleaded for permission to repeat his request after an interval, but she distinctly refused. She did not, however, succeed in making a man with such a large opinion of himself hopeless. Disappointed and annoyed he was, but he sought and fancied he found reasons for her decision which were not unfavourable to himself, and continued to visit her father as before, saying to him he had not quite succeeded in drawing from her a favourable answer, but hoped to prevail. He nowise acted the despairing lover, but made grander sermons than ever, and, as he came to feel at home in his pulpit, delivered them with growing force. But delay wrought desire in the laird; and at length, one evening, having by cross-questioning satisfied himself that Fergus made no progress, he rose, and going to his desk, handed him Donal's verses. Fergus read them, and remarked he had read better, but the first stanza had a slight flavour of Shelley.

"I don't care a straw about their merit or demerit," said Mr. Galbraith; "poetry is nothing but spoilt prose. What I want to know is, whether they do not suggest a reason for your want of success with Jenny. Do you know the writing?"

"I cannot say I do. But I think it is very likely that of Donal Grant; he sets up for the Burns of Daurside."

"Insolent scoundrel!" cried the laird, bringing down his fist on the table, and fluttering the wine glasses. "Next to superstition I hate romance—with my whole heart I do!" And something like a flash of cold moonlight on wintred water gleamed over, rather than shot from, his poor focusless eyes.

"But, my dear sir," said Fergus, "if I am to understand these lines—"

"Yes! if you are to understand where there is no sense whatever!"

"I think I understand them—if you will excuse me for venturing to say so; and what I read in them is, that, whoever the writer may be, the lady, whoever she may be, had refused him."

"You cannot believe that the wretch had the impudence to make my daughter—the heiress of—at least—What! make my daughter an offer! She would at once have acquainted me with the fact, that he might receive suitable chastisement. Let me look at the stuff again."

"It is quite possible," said Fergus, "it may be only a poem some friend has copied for her from a newspaper."

While he spoke, the laird was reading the lines, and persuading himself he understood them. With sudden resolve, the paper held torch-like in front of him, he strode into the next room, where Ginevra sat.

"Do you tell me," he said fiercely, "that you have so far forgotten all dignity and propriety as to give a dirty cow-boy the encouragement to make you an offer of marriage? The very notion sets my blood boiling. You will make me hate you, you—you—unworthy creature!"

Ginevra had turned white, but looking him straight in the face, she answered,

"If that is a letter for me, you know I have not read it."

"There! see for yourself.—Poetry!" He uttered the word with contempt inexpressible.

She took the verses from his hand and read them. Even with her father standing there, watching her like an inquisitor, she could not help the tears coming in her eyes as she read.

"There is no such thing here, papa," she said. "They are only verses—bidding me good-bye."

"And what right has any such fellow to bid my daughter good-bye? Explain that to me, if you please. Of course I have been for many years aware of your love of low company, but I had hoped as you grew older you would learn manners: modesty would have been too much to look for.—If you had nothing to be ashamed of, why did you not tell me of the unpleasant affair? Is not your father your best friend?"

"Why should I make both him and you uncomfortable, papa—when there was not going to be anything more of it?"

"Why then do you go hankering after him still, and refusing Mr. Duff? It is true he is not exactly a gentleman by birth, but he is such by education, by manners, by position, by influence."

"Papa, I have already told Mr. Duff, as plainly as I could without being rude, that I would never let him talk to me so. What lady would refuse Donal Grant and listen to him!"

"You are a bold, insolent hussey!" cried her father in fresh rage and leaving the room, rejoined Fergus.

They sat silent both for a while—then the preacher spoke.

"Other communications may have since reached her from the same quarter," he said.

"That is impossible," rejoined the laird.

"I don't know that," insisted Fergus. "There is a foolish—a half-silly companion of his about the town. They call him Sir Gibbie Galbraith."

"Jenny knows no such person."

"Indeed she does. I have seen them together."

"Oh! you mean the lad the minister adopted! the urchin he took off the streets!—Sir Gibbie Galbraith!" he repeated sneeringly, but as one reflecting. "—I do vaguely recall a slanderous rumour in which a certain female connection of the family was hinted at.—Yes! that's where the nickname comes from.—And you think she keeps up a communication with the clown through him?"

"I don't say that, sir. I merely think it possible she may see this Gibbie occasionally; and I know he worships the cow-boy: it is a positive feature of his foolishness, and I wish it were the worst."

Therewith he told what he heard from Miss Kimble, and what he had seen for himself on the night when he watched Gibbie.

"Her very blood must be tainted!" said her father to himself, but added, "—from her mother's side;" and his attacks upon her after this were at least diurnal. It was a relief to his feeling of having wronged her, to abuse her with justice. For a while she tried hard to convince him now that this now that that notion of her conduct, or of Gibbie's or Donal's, was mistaken: he would listen to nothing she said, continually insisting that the only amends for her past was to marry according to his wishes; to give up superstition, and poetry, and cow-boys, and dumb rascals, and settle down into a respectable matron, a comfort to the gray hairs she was now bringing with sorrow to the grave. Then Ginevra became absolutely silent; he had taught her that any reply was but a new start for his objurgation, a knife wherewith to puncture a fresh gall-bladder of abuse. He stormed at her for her sullenness, but she persisted in her silence, sorely distressed to find how dead her heart seemed growing under his treatment of her: what would at one time have made her utterly miserable, now passed over her as one of the billows of a trouble that had to be borne, as one of the throbs of a headache, drawing from her scarcely a sigh. She did not understand that, her heaven being dark, she could see no individual cloud against it, that, her emotional nature untuned, discord itself had ceased to jar.

LVII

A Hiding-Place from the Wind

G ibbie found everything at the Auld Hoose in complete order for his reception: Mistress Croale had been very diligent, and promised well for a housekeeper—looked well, too, in her black satin and lace, with her complexion, she justly flattered herself, not a little improved. She had a good meal ready for him, with every adjunct in proper style, during the preparation of which she had revelled in the thought that some day, when she had quite established her fitness for her new position, Sir Gibbie would certainly invite the minister and his lady to dine with him, when she, whom they were too proud to ask to partake of their cockie-leekie, would show them she knew both what a dinner ought to be, and how to preside at it; and the soup it should be cockie-leekie.

Everything went comfortably. Gibbie was so well up in mathematics, thanks to Mr. Sclater, that, doing all requisite for honourable studentship, but having no desire to distinguish himself, he had plenty of time for more important duty. Now that he was by himself, as if old habit had returned in the shape of new passion, he roamed the streets every night. His custom was this: after dinner, which he had when he came from college, about half-past four, he lay down, fell asleep in a moment, as he always did, and slept till half-past six; then he had tea, and after that, studied—not dawdled over his books, till ten o'clock, when he took his Greek Testament. At eleven he went out, seldom finally returning before half-past one, sometimes not for an hour longer—during which time Mistress Croale was in readiness to receive any guest he might bring home.

The history of the special endeavour he had now commenced does not belong to my narrative. Some nights, many nights together, he would not meet a single wanderer; occasionally he would meet two or three in the same night. When he found one, he would stand regarding him until he spoke. If the man was drunk he would leave him: such were not those for whom he could now do most. If he was sober, he made him signs of invitation. If he would not go with him, he left him, but kept him in view, and tried him again. If still he would not, he gave him a piece of bread, and left him. If he called, he stopped, and by circuitous ways brought him to the little house at the back. It was purposely quite dark. If the man was too apprehensive to enter, he left him; if he followed, he led him to Mistress Croale. If anything suggested the possibility of helping farther, a possibility turning entirely on the person's self, the attempt was set on foot; but in general, after a good breakfast, Gibbie led him through a dark passage into the darkened house, and dismissed him from the door by which he had entered. He never gave money, and never sought such guest except in the winter. Indeed, he was never in the city in the summer. Before the session was over, they had one woman and one girl in a fair way of honest livelihood, and one small child, whose mother had an infant besides, and was evidently dying, he had sent "in a present" to Janet, by the hand of Mistress Murkison. Altogether it was a tolerable beginning, and during the time not a word reached him indicating knowledge of his proceedings, although within a week or two a rumour was rife in the lower parts of the city, of a mysterious being who went about doing this and that for poor folk, but, notwithstanding his gifts, was far from canny.

Mr. and Mrs. Sclater could not fail to be much annoyed when they found he was no longer lodging with Mistress Murkison, but occupying the Auld Hoose, with "that horrible woman" for a housekeeper; they knew, however, that expostulation with one possessed by such a headstrong sense of duty was utterly useless, and contented themselves with predicting to each other some terrible check, the result of his ridiculous theory concerning what was required of a Christian—namely, that the disciple should be as his Master. At the same time Mrs. Sclater had a sacred suspicion that no real ill would ever befall God's innocent, Gilbert Galbraith.

Fergus had now with his father's help established himself in the manse of the North Church, and thither he invited Mr. and Miss Galbraith to dine with him on a certain evening. Her father's absolute desire compelled Ginevra's assent; she could not, while with him, rebel absolutely. Fergus did his best to make the evening a pleasant one, and had special satisfaction in showing the laird that he could provide both a good dinner and a good bottle of port. Two of his congregation, a young lawyer and his wife, were the only other guests. The laird found the lawyer an agreeable companion, chiefly from his readiness to listen to his old law stories, and Fergus laid himself out to please the two ladies:

secure of the admiration of one, he hoped it might help to draw the favour of the other. He had conceived the notion that Ginevra probably disliked his profession, and took pains therefore to show how much he was a man of the world—talked about Shakspere, and flaunted rags of quotation in elocutionary style; got books from his study, and read passages from Byron, Shelley, and Moore—chiefly from "The Loves of the Angels" of the last, ecstasizing the lawyer's lady, and interesting Ginevra, though all he read taken together seemed to her unworthy of comparison with one of poor Donal's songs.

It grew late. The dinner had been at a fashionable hour; they had stayed an unfashionable time: it was nearly twelve o'clock when guests and host left the house in company. The lawyer and his wife went one way, and Fergus went the other with the laird and Ginevra.

Hearing the pitiful wailing of a child and the cough of a woman, as they went along a street bridge, they peeped over the parapet, and saw, upon the stair leading to the lower street, a woman, with a child asleep in her lap, trying to eat a piece of bread, and coughing as if in the last stage of consumption. On the next step below sat a man hushing in his bosom the baby whose cry they had heard. They stood for a moment, the minister pondering whether his profession required of him action, and Ginevra's gaze fixed on the head and shoulders of the foreshortened figure of the man, who vainly as patiently sought to soothe the child by gently rocking it to and fro. But when he began a strange humming song to it, which brought all Glashgar before her eyes, Ginevra knew beyond a doubt that it was Gibbie. At the sound the child ceased to wail, and presently the woman with difficulty rose, laying a hand for help on Gibbie's shoulder. Then Gibbie rose also, cradling the infant on his left arm, and making signs to the mother to place the child on his right. She did so, and turning, went feebly up the stair. Gibbie followed with the two children, one lying on his arm, the other with his head on his shoulder, both wretched and pining, with gray cheeks, and dark hollows under their eyes. From the top of the stair they went slowly up the street, the poor woman coughing, and Gibbie crooning to the baby, who cried no more, but now and then moaned. Then Fergus said to the laird:

"Did you see that young man, sir? That is the so-called Sir Gilbert Galbraith we were talking of the other night. They say he has come into a good property, but you may judge for yourself whether he seems fit to manage it!"

Ginevra withdrew her hand from his arm.

"Good God, Jenny!" exclaimed the laird, "you do not mean to tell me you have ever spoken to a young man like that?"

"I know him very well, papa," replied Ginevra, collectedly.

"You are incomprehensible, Jenny! If you know him, why do I not know him? If you had not known good reason to be ashamed of him, you would, one time or other, have mentioned his name in my hearing.—I ask you, and I demand an answer,"—here he stopped, and fronted her—"why have you concealed from me your acquaintance with this—this—person?"

"Because I thought it might be painful to you, papa," she answered, looking in his face.

"Painful to me! Why should it be painful to me—except indeed that it breaks my heart as often as I see you betray your invincible fondness for low company?"

"Do you desire me to tell you, papa, why I thought it might be painful to you to make that young man's acquaintance?"

"I do distinctly. I command you."

"Then I will: that young man, Sir Gilbert Galbraith,—"

"Nonsense, girl! there is no such Galbraith. It is the merest of scoffs."

Ginevra did not care to argue with him this point. In truth she knew little more about it than he.

"Many years ago," she recommenced, "when I was a child,—Excuse me, Mr. Duff, but it is quite time I told my father what has been weighing upon my mind for so many years."

"Sir Gilbert!" muttered her father contemptuously.

"One day," again she began, "Mr. Fergus Duff brought a ragged little boy to Glashruach—the most innocent and loving of creatures, who had committed no crime but that of doing good in secret. I saw Mr. Duff box his ears on the bridge; and you, papa, gave him over to that wretch, Angus Mac Pholp, to whip him—so at least Angus told me, after he had whipped him till he dropped senseless. I can hardly keep from screaming now when I think of it."

"All this, Jenny, is nothing less than cursed folly. Do you mean to tell me you have all these years been cherishing resentment against your own father, for the sake of a little thieving rascal, whom it was a good deed to fright from the error of his ways? I have no doubt Angus gave him merely what he deserved."

"You must remember, Miss Galbraith, we did not know he was dumb," said Fergus, humbly.

"If you had had any heart," said Ginevra, "you would have seen in his face that he was a perfect angelic child. He ran to the mountain, without a rag to cover his bleeding body, and would have died of cold and hunger, had not the Grants, the parents of your father's herd-boy, Mr. Duff, taken him to their hearts, and been father and mother to him."—Ginevra's mouth was opened at last.—"After that," she went on, "Angus, that bad man, shot him like a wild beast, when he was quietly herding Robert Grant's sheep. In return Sir Gilbert saved his life in the flood. And just before the house of Glashruach fell—the part in which my room was, he caught me up, because he could not speak, and carried me out of it; and when I told you that he had saved my life, you ordered him out of the house, and when he was afraid to leave me alone with you, dashed him against the wall, and sent for Angus to whip him again. But I should have liked to see Angus try it then!"

"I do remember an insolent fellow taking advantage of the ruinous state the house was in to make his way into my study," said the laird.

"And now," Ginevra continued, "Mr. Duff makes question of his wits because he finds him carrying a poor woman's children, going to get them a bed somewhere! If Mr. Duff had run about the streets when he was a child, like Sir Gilbert, he might not, perhaps, think it so strange he should care about a houseless woman and her brats!"

Therewith Ginevra burst into tears.

"Abominably disagreeable!" muttered the laird. "I always thought she was an idiot!—Hold your tongue, Jenny! you will wake the street. All you say may or may not be quite true; I do not say you are telling lies, or even exaggerating; but I see nothing in it to prove the lad a fit companion for a young lady. Very much to the contrary. I suppose he told you he was your injured, neglected, ill-used cousin? He may be your cousin: you may have any number of such cousins, if half the low tales concerning your mother's family be true."

Ginevra did not answer him—did not speak another word. When Fergus left them at their own door, she neither shook hands with him nor bade him good night.

"Jenny," said her father, the moment he was gone, "if I hear of your once speaking again to that low vagabond,—and now I think of it," he cried, interrupting himself with a sudden recollection, "there was a cobbler-fellow in the town here they used to call Sir Somebody Galbraith!—that must be his father! Whether the Sir was title or nickname, I neither know nor care. A title without money is as bad as a saintship without grace. But this I tell you, that if I hear of your speaking one word, good or bad, to the fellow again, I will, I swear to Almighty God, I will turn you out of the house."

To Ginevra's accumulated misery, she carried with her to her room a feeling of contempt for her father, with which she lay struggling in vain half the night.

LVIII

The Confession

Although Gibbie had taken no notice of the laird's party, he had recognized each of the three as he came up the stair, and in Ginevra's face read an appeal for deliverance. It seemed to say, "You help everybody but me! Why do you not come and help me too? Am I to have no pity because I am neither hungry nor cold?" He did not, however, lie awake the most of the night, or indeed a single hour of it, thinking what he should do; long before the poor woman and her children were in bed, he had made up his mind.

As soon as he came home from college the next day and had hastily eaten his dinner, going upon his vague knowledge of law business lately acquired, he bought a stamped paper, wrote upon it, and put it in his pocket; then he took a card and wrote on it: Sir Gilbert Galbraith, Baronet, of Glashruach, and put that in his pocket also. Thus provided, and having said to Mistress Croale that he should not be home that night—for he expected to set off almost immediately in search of Donal, and had bespoken horses, he walked deliberately along Pearl-street out into the suburb, and turning to the right, rang the bell at the garden gate of the laird's cottage. When the girl came, he gave her his card, and followed her into the house. She carried it into the room where, dinner over, the laird and the preacher were sitting, with a bottle of the same port which had pleased the laird at the manse between them. Giving time, as he judged, and no more, to read the card, Gibbie entered the room: he would not risk a refusal to see him.

It was a small room with a round table. The laird sat sideways to the door; the preacher sat between the table and the fire.

"What the devil does this mean? A vengeance take him!" cried the laird.

His big tumbling eyes had required more time than Gibbie had allowed, so that, when with this exclamation he lifted them from the card, they fell upon the object of his imprecation standing in the middle of the room between him and the open door. The preacher, snug behind the table, scarcely endeavoured to conceal the smile with which he took no notice of Sir Gilbert. The laird rose in the perturbation of mingled anger and unpreparedness.

"Ah!" he said, but it was only a sound, not a word, "to what—may I ask—have I—I have not the honour of your acquaintance, Mr.—Mr.—" Here he looked again at the card he held, fumbled for and opened a double eyeglass, then with deliberation examined the name upon it, thus gaining time by rudeness, and gathering his force for more, while Gibbie remained as unembarrassed as if he had been standing to his tailor for his measure. "Mr.—ah, I see! Galbraith, you say.—To what, Mr., Mr."—another look at the card—"Galbraith, do I owe the honour of this unexpected—and—and—I must say—un—looked-for visit— and at such an unusual hour for making a business call—for business, I presume, it must be that brings you, seeing I have not the honour of the slightest acquaintance with you?"

He dropped his eyeglass with a clatter against his waistcoat, threw the card into his finger-glass, raised his pale eyes, and stared at Sir Gilbert with all the fixedness they were capable of. He had already drunk a good deal of wine, and it was plain he had, although he was far from being overcome by it. Gibbie answered by drawing from the breast-pocket of his coat the paper he had written, and presenting it like a petition. Mr. Galbraith sneered, and would not have touched it had not his eye caught the stamp, which from old habit at once drew his hand. From similar habit, or perhaps to get it nearer the light, he sat down. Gibbie stood, and Fergus stared at him with insolent composure. The laird read, but not aloud: I, Gilbert Galbraith, Baronet, hereby promise and undertake to transfer to Miss Galbraith, only daughter of Thomas Galbraith, Esq., on the day when she shall be married to Donal Grant, Master of Arts, the whole of the title deeds of the house and lands of Glashruach, to have and to hold as hers, with absolute power to dispose of the same as she may see fit. Gilbert Galbraith, Old House of Galbraith, Widdiehill, March, etc., etc.

The laird stretched his neck like a turkeycock, and gobbled inarticulately, threw the paper to Fergus, and turning on his chair, glowered at Gibbie. Then suddenly starting to his feet, he cried,

"What do you mean, you rascal, by daring to insult me in my own house? Damn your insolent foolery!"

"A trick! a most palpable trick! and an exceedingly silly one!" pronounced Fergus, who had now read the paper; "quite as foolish as unjustifiable! Everybody knows Glashruach is the property of Major

Culsalmon!"—Here the laird sought the relief of another oath or two.—
"I entreat you to moderate your anger, my dear sir," Fergus resumed.
"The thing is hardly worth so much indignation. Some animal has been
playing the poor fellow an ill-natured trick—putting him up to it for
the sake of a vile practical joke. It is exceedingly provoking, but you
must forgive him. He is hardly to blame, scarcely accountable, under
the natural circumstances.—Get away with you," he added, addressing
Gibbie across the table. "Make haste before worse comes of it. You have
been made a fool of."

When Fergus began to speak, the laird turned, and while he spoke
stared at him with lack-lustre yet gleaming eyes, until he addressed
Gibbie, when he turned on him again as fiercely as before. Poor Gibbie
stood shaking his head, smiling, and making eager signs with hands
and arms; but in the laird's condition of both heart and brain he might
well forget and fail to be reminded that Gibbie was dumb.

"Why don't you speak, you fool?" he cried. "Get out and don't stand
making faces there. Be off with you, or I will knock you down with a
decanter."

Gibbie pointed to the paper, which lay before Fergus, and placed a
hand first on his lips, then on his heart.

"Damn your mummery!" said the laird, choking with rage. "Go away,
or, by God! I will break your head."

Fergus at this rose and came round the table to get between them.
But the laird caught up a pair of nutcrackers, and threw it at Gibbie. It
struck him on the forehead, and the blood spirted from the wound. He
staggered backwards. Fergus seized the laird's arm, and sought to pacify
him.

Her father's loud tones had reached Ginevra in her room; she ran
down, and that instant entered: Gibbie all but fell into her arms. The
moment's support she gave him, and the look of loving terror she cast
in his face, restored him; and he was again firm on his feet, pressing her
handkerchief to his forehead, when Fergus, leaving the laird, advanced
with the pacific intention of getting him safe from the house. Ginevra
stepped between them. Her father's rage thereupon broke loose quite,
and was madness. He seized hold of her with violence, and dragged her
from the room. Fergus laid hands upon Gibbie more gently, and half
would have forced, half persuaded him to go. A cry came from Ginevra:
refusing to be sent to her room before Gibbie was in safety, her father
struck her. Gibbie would have darted to her help. Fergus held him fast,

but knew nothing of Gibbie's strength, and the next moment found himself on his back upon the table, amidst the crash of wineglasses and china. Having locked the door, Gibbie sprung to the laird, who was trying to drag his daughter, now hardly resisting, up the first steps of the stair, took him round the waist from behind, swept him to the other room, and there locked him up also. He then returned to Ginevra where she lay motionless on the stair, lifted her in his arms, and carried her out of the house, nor stopped until, having reached the farther end of the street, he turned the corner of it into another equally quiet.

The laird and Fergus, when they were released by the girl from their respective prisons and found that the enemy was gone, imagined that Ginevra had retired again to her room; and what they did after is not interesting.

Under a dull smoky oil-lamp Gibbie stopped. He knew by the tightening of her arms that Ginevra was coming to herself.

"Let me down," she said feebly.

He did so, but kept his arm round her. She gave a deep sigh, and gazed bewildered. When she saw him, she smiled.

"With you, Gibbie!" she murmured. "—But they will be after us!"

"They shall not touch you," signified Gibbie.

"What was it all about?" she asked.

Gibbie spelled on his fingers,

"Because I offered to give you Glashruach, if your father would let you marry Donal."

"Gibbie! how could you?" she cried almost in a scream, and pushing away his arm, turned from him and tried to run, but after two steps, tottered to the lamp-post, and leaned against it—with such a scared look!

"Then come with me and be my sister, Ginevra, and I will take care of you," spelled Gibbie. "I can do nothing to take care of you while I can't get near you."

"Oh, Gibbie! nobody does like that," returned Ginevra, "—else I should be so glad!"

"There is no other way then that I know. You won't marry anybody, you see."

"Won't I, Gibbie? What makes you think that?"

"Because of course you would never refuse Donal and marry anybody else; that is not possible."

"Oh! don't tease me, Gibbie."

"Ginevra, you don't mean you would?"

In the dull light, and with the imperfect means of Gibbie for the embodiment of his thoughts, Ginevra misunderstood him.

"Yea, Gibbie," she said, "I would. I thought it was understood between us, ever since that day you found me on Glashgar. In my thoughts I have been yours all the time."

She turned her face to the lamp-post. But Gibbie made her look.

"You do not mean," he spelled very hurriedly, "that you would marry me?—Me? I never dreamed of such a thing!"

"You didn't mean it then!" said Ginevra, with a cry—bitter but feeble with despair and ending in a stifled shriek. "What have I been saying then! I thought I belonged to you! I thought you meant to take me all the time!" She burst into an agony of sobbing. "Oh me! me! I have been alone all the time, and did not know it!"

She sank on the pavement at the foot of the lamp-post, weeping sorely, and shaken with her sobs. Gibbie was in sad perplexity. Heaven had opened before his gaze; its colours filled his eyes; its sounds filled his ears and heart and brain; but the portress was busy crying and would not open the door. Neither could he get at her to comfort her, for, her eyes being wanted to cry with, his poor signs were of no use. Dumbness is a drawback to the gift of consolation.

It was a calm night early in March, clear overhead, and the heaven full of stars. The first faint think-odour of spring was in the air. A crescent moon hung half-way between the zenith and the horizon, clear as silver in firelight, and peaceful in the consciousness that not much was required of her yet. Both bareheaded, the one stood under the lamp, the other had fallen in a heap at its foot; the one was in the seventh paradise, and knew it; the other was weeping her heart out, yet was in the same paradise, if she would but have opened her eyes. Gibbie held one of her hands and stroked it. Then he pulled off his coat and laid it softly upon her. She grew a little quieter.

"Take me home, Gibbie," she said, in a gentle voice. All was over; there was no use in crying or even in thinking any more.

Gibbie put his arms round her, and helped her to her feet. She looked at him, and saw a face glorious with bliss. Never, not even on Glashgar, in the skin-coat of the beast-boy, had she seen him so like an angel. And in his eyes was that which triumphed, not over dumbness, but over speech. It brought the rose-fire rushing into her wan cheeks; she hid her face on his bosom; and, under the dingy red flame of the lamp in the stony street, they held each other, as blessed as if they had been under an orange tree haunted with fire-flies. For they knew each the heart of the other, and God is infinite.

How long they stood thus, neither of them knew. The lady would not have spoken if she could, and the youth could not if he would. But the lady shivered, and because she shivered, she would have the youth take his coat. He mocked at cold; made her put her arms in the sleeves, and buttoned it round her: both laughed to see how wide it was. Then he took her by the hand, and led her away, obedient as when first he found her and her heart upon Glashgar. Like two children, holding each other fast, they hurried along, in dread of pursuit. He brought her to Daur-street, and gave her into Mrs. Sclater's arms. Ginevra told her everything except that her father had struck her, and Gibbie begged her to keep his wife for him till they could be married. Mrs. Sclater behaved like a mother to them, sent Gibbie away, and Ginevra to a hot bath and to bed.

LIX

CATASTROPHE

G ibbie went home as if Pearl-street had been the stairs of Glashgar, and the Auld Hoose a mansion in the heavens. He seemed to float along the way as one floats in a happy dream, where motion is born at once of the will, without the intermediating mechanics of nerve, muscle, and fulcrum. Love had been gathering and ever storing itself in his heart so many years for this brown dove! now at last the rock was smitten, and its treasure rushed forth to her service. In nothing was it changed as it issued, save as the dark, silent, motionless water of the cavern changes into the sparkling, singing, dancing rivulet. Gibbie's was love simple, unselfish, undemanding—not merely asking for no return, but asking for no recognition, requiring not even that its existence should be known. He was a rare one, who did not make the common miserable blunder of taking the shadow cast by love—the desire, namely, to be loved—for love itself; his love was a vertical sun, and his own shadow was under his feet. Silly youths and maidens count themselves martyrs of love, when they are but the pining witnesses to a delicious and entrancing selfishness. But do not mistake me through confounding, on the other hand, the desire to be loved—which is neither wrong nor noble, any more than hunger is either wrong or noble—and the delight in being loved, to be devoid of which a man must be lost in an immeasurably deeper, in an evil, ruinous, yea, a fiendish selfishness. Not to care for love is the still worse reaction from the self-foiled and outworn greed of love. Gibbie's love was a diamond among gem-loves. There are men whose love to a friend is less selfish than their love to the dearest woman; but Gibbie's was not a love to be less divine towards a woman than towards a man. One man's love is as different from another's as the one is himself different from the other. The love that dwells in one man is an angel, the love in another is a bird, that in another a hog. Some would count worthless the love of a man who loved everybody. There would be no distinction in being loved by such a man!—and distinction, as a guarantee of their own great worth, is what such seek. There are women who desire to be the sole object of a man's affection, and are all their lives devoured by unlawful jealousies.

A love that had never gone forth upon human being but themselves, would be to them the treasure to sell all that they might buy. And the man who brought such a love might in truth be all-absorbed therein himself: the poorest of creatures may well be absorbed in the poorest of loves. A heart has to be taught to love, and its first lesson, however well learnt, no more makes it perfect in love, than the A B C makes a savant. The man who loves most will love best. The man who throughly loves God and his neighbour is the only man who will love a woman ideally—who can love her with the love God thought of between them when he made man male and female. The man, I repeat, who loves God with his very life, and his neighbour as Christ loves him, is the man who alone is capable of grand, perfect, glorious love to any woman. Because Gibbie's love was towards everything human, he was able to love Ginevra as Donal, poet and prophet, was not yet grown able to love her. To that of the most passionate of unbelieving lovers, Gibbie's love was as the fire of a sun to that of a forest. The fulness of a world of love-ways and love-thoughts was Gibbie's. In sweet affairs of loving-kindness, he was in his own kingdom, and sat upon its throne. And it was this essential love, acknowledging and embracing, as a necessity of its being, everything that could be loved, which now concentrated its rays on the individual's individual. His love to Ginevra stood like a growing thicket of aromatic shrubs, until her confession set the fire of heaven to it, and the flame that consumes not, but gives life, arose and shot homeward. He had never imagined, never hoped, never desired she should love him like that. She had refused his friend, the strong, the noble, the beautiful, Donal the poet, and it never could but from her own lips have found way to his belief that she had turned her regard upon wee Sir Gibbie, a nobody, who to himself was a mere burning heart running about in tattered garments. His devotion to her had forestalled every pain with its antidote of perfect love, had negatived every lack, had precluded every desire, had shut all avenues of entrance against self. Even if "a little thought unsound" should have chanced upon an entrance, it would have found no soil to root and grow in: the soil for the harvest of pain is that brought down from the peaks of pride by the torrents of desire. Immeasurably the greater therefore was his delight, when the warmth and odour of the love that had been from time to him immemorial passing out from him in virtue of consolation and healing, came back upon him in the softest and sweetest of flower-waking spring-winds. Then indeed was his heart a bliss worth God's making. The sum of happiness in the city, if gathered that night into one wave, could not have reached half-way to the crest of the mighty billow tossing itself heavenward as it rushed along the ocean of Gibbie's spirit.

He entered the close of the Auld Hoose. But the excess of his joy had not yet turned to light, was not yet passing from him in physical flame: whence then the glow that illumined the court? He looked up. The windows of Mistress Croale's bedroom were glaring with light! He opened the door hurriedly and darted up. On the stair he was met by the smell of burning, which grew stronger as he ascended. He opened Mistress Croale's door. The chintz curtains of her bed were flaming to the ceiling. He darted to it. Mistress Croale was not in it. He jumped upon it, and tore down the curtains and tester, trampling them under his feet upon the blankets. He had almost finished, and, at the bottom of the bed, was reaching up and pulling at the last of the flaming rags, when a groan came to his ears. He looked down: there, at the foot of the bed, on her back upon the floor, lay Mistress Croale in her satin gown, with red swollen face, wide-open mouth, and half-open eyes, dead drunk, a heap of ruin. A bit of glowing tinder fell on her forehead. She opened her eyes, looked up, uttered a terrified cry, closed them, and was again motionless, except for her breathing. On one side of her lay a bottle, on the other a chamber-candlestick upset, with the candle guttered into a mass.

With the help of the water-jugs, and the bath which stood ready in his room, he succeeded at last in putting out the fire, and then turned his attention to Mistress Croale. Her breathing had grown so stertorous that he was alarmed, and getting more water, bathed her head, and laid a wet handkerchief on it, after which he sat down and watched her. It would have made a strange picture: the middle of the night, the fire-blasted bed, the painful, ugly carcase on the floor, and the sad yet—I had almost said radiant youth, watching near. The slow night passed.

The gray of the morning came, chill and cheerless. Mistress Croale stirred, moved, crept up rather than rose to a sitting position, and stretched herself yawning. Gibbie had risen and stood over her. She caught sight of him; absolute terror distorted her sodden face; she stared at him, then stared about her, like one who had suddenly waked in hell. He took her by the arm. She obeyed, rose, and stood, fear conquering the remnants of drunkenness, with her whisky-scorched eyes following his every movement, as he got her cloak and bonnet. He put them on her. She submitted like a child caught in wickedness, and cowed by the capture. He led her from the house, out into the dark morning, made her take his arm, and away they walked together, down to the riverside. She gave a reel now and then, and sometimes her knees would double under her; but Gibbie was no novice at the task, and brought her safe to the door of her lodging—of which, in view of such a possibility, he had been paying the rent all the time. He opened the door with her pass-key, led her up the stair, unlocked the door of her garret, placed her in a chair, and left her, closing the doors gently behind him. Instinctively she sought her bed, fell upon it, and slept again.

When she woke, her dim mind was haunted by a terrible vision of resurrection and damnation, of which the only point she could plainly recall, was an angel, as like Sir Gibbie as he could look, hanging in the air above her, and sending out flames on all sides of him, which burned her up, inside and out, shrivelling soul and body together. As she lay thinking over it, with her eyes closed, suddenly she remembered, with a pang of dismay, that she had got drunk and broken her vow—that was the origin of the bad dream, and the dreadful headache, and the burning at her heart! She must have water! Painfully lifting herself upon one elbow, she opened her eyes. Then what a bewilderment, and what a discovery, slow unfolding itself, were hers! Like her first parents she had fallen; her paradise was gone; she lay outside among the thorns and thistles before the gate. From being the virtual mistress of a great house, she was back in her dreary lonely garret! Re-exiled in shame from her briefly regained respectability, from friendship and honourable life and the holding forth of help to the world, she lay there a sow that had been washed, and washed in vain! What a sight of disgrace was her grand satin gown—wet, and scorched, and smeared with candle! and ugh! how it smelt of smoke and burning and the dregs of whisky! And her lace!—She gazed at her finery as an angel might on his feathers which the enemy had burned while he slept on his watch.

She must have water! She got out of bed with difficulty, then for a whole hour sat on the edge of it motionless, unsure that she was not in hell. At last she wept—acrid tears, for very misery. She rose, took off her satin and lace, put on a cotton gown, and was once more a decent-looking poor body—except as to her glowing face and burning eyes, which to bathe she had nothing but tears. Again she sat down, and for a space did nothing, only suffered in ignominy. At last life began to revive a little. She rose and moved about the room, staring at the things in it as a ghost might stare at the grave-clothes on its abandoned body. There on the table lay her keys; and what was that under them?—A letter addressed to her. She opened it, and found five pound-notes, with these words: "I promise to pay to Mrs. Croale five pounds monthly, for nine months to come. Gilbert Galbraith." She wept again. He would never speak to her more! She had lost him at last—her only friend!—her sole link to God and goodness and the kingdom of heaven!—lost him for ever!

The day went on, cold and foggy without, colder and drearier within. Sick and faint and disgusted, the poor heart had no atmosphere to beat in save an infinite sense of failure and lost opportunity. She had fuel enough in the room to make a little fire, and at length had summoned resolve sufficient for the fetching of water from the street-pump. She went to the cupboard to get a jug: she could not carry a pailful. There in the corner stood her demon-friend! her own old familiar, the black bottle! as if he had been patiently waiting for her all the long dreary time she had been away! With a flash of fierce joy she remembered she had left it half-full. She caught it up, and held it between her and the fading light of the misty window: it was half-full still!—One glass—a hair of the dog—would set her free from faintness and sickness, disgust and misery! There was no one to find fault with her now! She could do as she liked—there was no one to care!—nothing to take fire!—She set the bottle on the table, because her hand shook, and went again to the cupboard to get a glass. On the way—borne upward on some heavenly current from the deeps of her soul, the face of Gibbie, sorrowful because loving, like the face of the Son of Man, met her. She turned, seized the bottle, and would have dashed it on the hearthstone, but that a sudden resolve arrested her lifted arm: Gibbie should see! She would be strong! That bottle should stand on that shelf until the hour when she could show it him and say, "See the proof of my victory!" She drove the cork fiercely in. When its top was level with the neck, she set the bottle back in its place, and from that hour it stood there, a temptation, a ceaseless warning, the monument of a broken but reparable vow, a pledge of hope. It may not have been a prudent measure. To a weak nature it would have involved certain ruin. But there are natures that do better under difficulty; there are many such. And with that fiend-like shape in her cupboard the one ambition of Mistress Croale's life was henceforth inextricably bound up: she would turn that bottle into a witness for her

GEORGE MACDONALD

against the judgment she had deserved. Close by the cupboard door, like a kite or an owl nailed up against a barn, she hung her soiled and dishonoured satin gown; and the dusk having now gathered, took the jug, and fetched herself water. Then, having set her kettle on the fire, she went out with her basket, and bought bread, and butter. After a good cup of tea and some nice toast, she went to bed again, much easier both in mind and body, and slept.

In the morning she went to the market, opened her shop, and waited for customers. Pleasure and surprise at her reappearance brought the old ones quickly back. She was friendly and helpful to them as before; but the slightest approach to inquiry as to where she had been or what she had been doing, she met with simple obstinate silence. Gibbie's bounty and her faithful abstinence enabled her to add to her stock and extend her trade. By and by she had the command of a little money; and when in the late autumn there came a time of scarcity and disease, she went about among the poor like a disciple of Sir Gibbie. Some said that, from her knowledge of their ways, from her judgment, and by her personal ministration of what, for her means, she gave more bountifully than any, she did more to hearten their endurance, than all the ladies together who administered money subscribed. It came to Sir Gibbie's ears, and rejoiced his heart: his old friend was on the King's highway still! In the mean time she saw nothing of him. Not once did he pass her shop, where often her mental, and not unfrequently her bodily, attitude was that of a watching lover. The second day, indeed, she saw him at a little distance, and sorely her heart smote her, for one of his hands was in a sling; but he crossed to the other side, plainly to avoid her. She was none the less sure, however, that when she asked him he would forgive her; and ask him she would, as soon as she had satisfactory proof of repentance to show him.

LX

Arrangement and Preparation

The next morning, the first thing after breakfast, Mr. Sclater, having reflected that Ginevra was under age and they must be careful, resumed for the nonce, with considerable satisfaction, his office of guardian, and holding no previous consultation with Gibbie, walked to the cottage, and sought an interview with Mr. Galbraith, which the latter accorded with a formality suitable to his idea of his own inborn grandeur. But his assumption had no effect on nut-headed Mr. Sclater, who, in this matter at all events, was at peace with his conscience.

"I have to inform you, Mr. Galbraith," he began, "that Miss Galbraith—"

"Oh!" said the laird, "I beg your pardon; I was not aware it was my daughter you wished to see."

He rose and rang the bell. Mr. Sclater, annoyed at his manner, held his peace.

"Tell your mistress," said the laird, "that the Rev. Mr. Sclater wishes to see her."

The girl returned with a scared face, and the news that her mistress was not in her room. The laird's loose mouth dropped looser.

"Miss Galbraith did us the honour to sleep at our house last night," said Mr. Sclater deliberately.

"The devil!" cried the laird, relieved. "Why!—What!—Are you aware of what you are saying, sir?"

"Perfectly; and of what I saw too. A blow looks bad on a lady's face."

"Good heavens! the little hussey dared to say I struck her?"

"She did not say so; but no one could fail to see some one had. If you do not know who did it, I do."

"Send her home instantly, or I will come and fetch her," cried the laird.

"Come and dine with us if you want to see her. For the present she remains where she is. You want her to marry Fergus Duff; she prefers my ward, Gilbert Galbraith, and I shall do my best for them."

"She is under age," said the laird.

"That fault will rectify itself as fast in my house as in yours," returned the minister. "If you invite the publicity of a legal action, I will employ counsel, and wait the result."

Mr. Sclater was not at all anxious to hasten the marriage; he would much rather, in fact, have it put off, at least until Gibbie should have taken his degree. The laird started up in a rage, but the room was so small that he sat down again. The minister leaned back in his chair. He was too much displeased with the laird's behaviour to lighten the matter for him by setting forth the advantages of having Sir Gibbie for a son-in-law.

"Mr. Sclater," said the laird at length, "I am shocked, unspeakably shocked, at my daughter's conduct. To leave the shelter of her father's roof, in the middle of the night, and—"

"About seven o'clock in the evening," interjected Mr. Sclater.

"—and take refuge with strangers!" continued the laird.

"By no means strangers, Mr. Galbraith!" said the minister. "You drive your daughter from your house, and are then shocked to find she has taken refuge with friends!"

"She is an unnatural child. She knows well enough what I think of her, and what reason she has given me so to think."

"When a man happens to be alone in any opinion," remarked the minister, "even if the opinion should be of his own daughter, the probabilities are he is wrong. Every one but yourself has the deepest regard for Miss Galbraith."

"She has always cultivated strangely objectionable friendships," said the laird.

"For my own part," said the minister, as if heedless of the laird's last remark, "although I believe she has no dowry, and there are reasons besides why the connection should not be desirable, I do not know a lady I should prefer for a wife to my ward."

The minister's plain speaking was not without effect upon the laird. It made him uncomfortable. It is only when the conscience is wide awake and regnant that it can be appealed to without giving a cry for response. Again he sat silent a while. Then gathering all the pomp and stiffness at his command,

"Oblige me by informing my daughter," he said, "that I request her, for the sake of avoiding scandal, to return to her father's house until she is of age."

"And in the mean time you undertake—"

"I undertake nothing," shouted the laird, in his feeble, woolly, yet harsh voice.

"Then I refuse to carry your message. I will be no bearer of that from which, as soon as delivered, I should dissuade."

"Allow me to ask, are you a minister of the gospel, and stir up a child against her own father?"

"I am not here to bandy words with you, Mr. Galbraith. It is nothing to me what you think of me. If you will engage not to urge your choice upon Miss Galbraith, I think it probable she will at once return to you. If not—"

"I will not force her inclinations," said the laird. "She knows my wish, and she ought to know the duty of a daughter."

"I will tell her what you say," answered the minister, and took his departure.

When Gibbie heard, he was not at all satisfied with Mr. Sclater's interference to such result. He wished to marry Ginevra at once, in order to take her from under the tyranny of her father. But he was readily convinced it would be better, now things were understood, that she should go back to him, and try once more to gain him. The same day she did go back, and Gibbie took up his quarters at the minister's.

Ginevra soon found that her father had not yielded the idea of having his own way with her, but her spirits and courage were now so good, that she was able not only to endure with less suffering, but to carry herself quite differently. Much less afraid of him, she was the more watchful to minister to his wants, dared a loving liberty now and then in spite of his coldness, took his objurgations with something of the gaiety of one who did not or would not believe he meant them, and when he abused Gibbie, did not answer a word, knowing events alone could set him right in his idea of him. Rejoiced that he had not laid hold of the fact that Glashruach was Gibbie's, she never mentioned the place to him; for she shrunk with sharpest recoil from the humiliation of seeing him, upon conviction, turn from Fergus to Gibbie: the kindest thing they could do for him would be to marry against his will, and save him from open tergiversation; for no one could then blame him, he would be thoroughly pleased, and not having the opportunity of self-degradation, would be saved the cause for self-contempt.

For some time Fergus kept on hoping. The laird, blinded by his own wishes, and expecting Gibbie would soon do something to bring public disgrace upon himself, did not tell him of his daughter's determination and self-engagement, while, for her part, Ginevra believed she fulfilled her duty towards him in the endeavour to convince him by her conduct that nothing could ever induce her to marry him. So the remainder of the session passed—the laird urging his objections against Gibbie, and growing extravagant in his praises of Fergus, while Ginevra kept taking fresh courage, and being of good cheer. Gibbie went to the cottage once or twice, but the laird made it so uncomfortable for them, and Fergus was so rude, that they agreed it would be better to content themselves with meeting when they had the chance.

At the end of the month Gibbie went home as usual, telling Ginevra he must be present to superintend what was going on at Glashruach to get the house ready for her, but saying nothing of what he was building there. By the beginning of the winter, they had got the buttress-wall finished and the coping on it, also the shell of the new house roofed in, so that the carpenters had been at work all through the frost and snow, and things had made great progress without any hurry; and now, since the first day the weather had permitted, the masons were at work again. The bridge was built, the wall of the old house broken through, the turret carried aloft. The channel of the little burn they had found completely blocked by a great stone at the farther edge of the landslip; up to this stone they opened the channel, protecting it by masonry against further slip, and by Gibbie's directions left it so—after boring the stone, which still turned every drop of the water aside into the Glashburn, for a good charge of gunpowder. All the hollow where the latter burn had carried away pine-wood and shrubbery, gravel drive and lawn, had been planted, mostly with fir trees; and a weir of strong masonry, a little way below the house, kept the water back, so that it rose and spread, and formed a still pool just under the house, reflecting it far beneath. If Ginevra pleased, Gibbie meant to raise the weir, and have quite a little lake in the hollow. A new approach had been contrived, and was nearly finished before Gibbie returned to college.

LXI

The Wedding

In the mean time Fergus, dull as he was to doubt his own importance and success—for did not the public acknowledge both?—yet by degrees lost heart and hope so far as concerned Ginevra, and at length told the laird that, much as he valued his society, and was indebted for his kindness, he must deny himself the pleasure of visiting any more at the cottage—so plainly was his presence unacceptable to Miss Galbraith. The laird blustered against his daughter, and expostulated with the preacher, not forgetting to hint at the ingratitude of forsaking him, after all he had done and borne in the furthering of his interests: Jenny must at length come to see what reason and good sense required of her! But Fergus had at last learned his lesson, and was no longer to be blinded. Besides, there had lately come to his church a certain shopkeeper, retired rich, with one daughter; and as his hope of the dignity of being married to Ginevra faded, he had come to feel the enticement of Miss Lapraik's money and good looks—which gained in force considerably when he began to understand the serious off-sets there were to the honour of being son-in-law to Mr. Galbraith: a nobody as was old Lapraik in himself and his position, he was at least looked upon with respect, argued Fergus; and indeed the man was as honest as it is possible for any worshipper of Mammon to be. Fergus therefore received the laird's expostulations and encouragements with composure, but when at length, in his growing acidity, Mr. Galbraith reflected on his birth, and his own condescension in showing him friendship, Fergus left the house, never to go near it again. Within three months, for a second protracted courtship was not to be thought of, he married Miss Lapraik, and lived respectable ever after—took to writing hymns, became popular afresh through his poetry, and exercised a double influence for the humiliation of Christianity. But what matter, while he counted himself fortunate, and thought himself happy! his fame spread; he had good health; his wife worshipped him; and if he had had a valet, I have no doubt he would have been a hero to him, thus climbing the topmost untrodden peak of the world's greatness.

GEORGE MACDONALD

When the next evening came, and Fergus did not appear, the laird fidgeted, then stormed, then sank into a moody silence. When the second night came, and Fergus did not come, the sequence was the same, with exasperated symptoms. Night after night passed thus, and Ginevra began to fear for her father's reason. She challenged him to play backgammon with her, but he scorned the proposal. She begged him to teach her chess, but he scouted the notion of her having wit enough to learn. She offered to read to him, entreated him to let her do something with him, but he repelled her every advance with contempt and surliness, which now and then broke into rage and vituperation.

As soon as Gibbie returned, Ginevra let him know how badly things were going with her father. They met, consulted, agreed that the best thing was to be married at once, made their preparations, and confident that, if asked, he would refuse his permission, proceeded, for his sake, as if they had had it.

One morning, as he sat at breakfast, Mr. Galbraith received from Mr. Torrie, whom he knew as the agent in the purchase of Glashruach, and whom he supposed to have bought it for Major Culsalmon, a letter, more than respectful, stating that matters had come to light regarding the property which rendered his presence on the spot indispensable for their solution, especially as there might be papers of consequence in view of the points in question, in some drawer or cabinet of those he had left locked behind him. The present owner, therefore, through Mr. Torrie, begged most respectfully that Mr. Galbraith would sacrifice two days of his valuable time, and visit Glashruach. The result, he did not doubt, would be to the advantage of both parties. If Mr. Galbraith would kindly signify to Mr. Torrie his assent, a carriage and four, with postilions, that he might make the journey in all possible comfort, should be at his house the next morning, at ten o'clock, if that hour would be convenient.

For weeks the laird had been an unmitigated bore to himself, and the invitation laid hold upon him by the most projecting handle of his being, namely, his self-importance. He wrote at once to signify his gracious assent; and in the evening told his daughter he was going to Glashruach on business, and had arranged for Miss Kimble to come and stay with her till his return.

At nine o'clock the schoolmistress came to breakfast, and at ten a travelling-carriage with four horses drew up at the door, looking nearly as big as the cottage. With monstrous stateliness, and a fur-coat on his arm, the laird descended to his garden gate, and got into the carriage, which instantly dashed away for the western road, restoring Mr. Galbraith to the full consciousness of his inherent grandeur: if he was not exactly laird of Glashruach again, he was something quite as important. His carriage was just out of the street, when a second, also with four horses, drew up, to the astonishment of Miss Kimble, at the garden gate. Out of it stepped Mr. and Mrs. Sclater! then a young gentleman, whom she thought very graceful until she discovered it was that low-lived Sir Gilbert! and Mr. Torrie, the lawyer! They came trooping into the little drawing-room, shook hands with them both, and sat down, Sir Gilbert beside Ginevra—but nobody spoke. What could it mean! A morning call? It was too early. And four horses to a morning call! A pastoral visitation? Four horses and a lawyer to a pastoral visitation! A business call? There was Mrs. Sclater! and that Sir Gilbert!—It must after all be a pastoral visitation, for there was the minister commencing a religious service!—during which however it suddenly revealed itself to the horrified spinster that she was part and parcel of a clandestine wedding! An anxious father had placed her in charge of his daughter, and this was how she was fulfilling her trust! There was Ginevra being married in a brown dress! and to that horrid lad, who called himself a baronet, and hobnobbed with a low market-woman! But, alas! just as she was recovering her presence of mind, Mr. Sclater pronounced them husband and wife! She gave a shriek, and cried out, "I forbid the banns," at which the company, bride and bridegroom included, broke into "a loud smile." The ceremony over, Ginevra glided from the room, and returned almost immediately in her little brown bonnet. Sir Gilbert caught up his hat, and Ginevra held out her hand to Miss Kimble. Then at length the abashed and aggrieved lady found words of her own.

"Ginevra!" she cried, "you are never going to leave me alone in the house!—after inviting me to stay with you till your father returned!"

But the minister answered her.

"It was her father who invited you, I believe, not Lady Galbraith," he said; "and you understood perfectly that the invitation was not meant to give her pleasure. You would doubtless have her postpone her wedding-journey on your account, but my lady is under no obligation to think of you."—He had heard of her tattle against Sir Gilbert, and thus rudely showed his resentment.

Miss Kimble burst into tears. Ginevra kissed her, and said,

"Never mind, dear Miss Kimble. You could not help it. The whole thing was arranged. We are going after my father, and we have the best horses."

Mr. Torrie laughed outright.

"A new kind of runaway marriage!" he cried. "The happy couple pursuing the obstinate parent with four horses! Ha! ha! ha!"

"But after the ceremony!" said Mr. Sclater.

Here the servant ran down the steps with a carpet-bag, and opened the gate for her mistress. Lady Galbraith got into the carriage; Sir Gilbert followed; there was kissing and tears at the door of it; Mrs. Sclater drew back; the postilions spurred their horses; off went the second carriage faster than the first; and the minister's party walked quietly away, leaving Miss Kimble to declaim to the maid of all work, who cried so that she did not hear a word she said. The schoolmistress put on her bonnet, and full of indignation carried her news of the treatment to which she had been subjected to the Rev. Fergus Duff, who remarked to himself that it was sad to see youth and beauty turn away from genius and influence to wed money and idiocy, gave a sigh, and went to see Miss Lapraik.

Between the second stage and the third, Gibbie and Ginevra came in sight of their father's carriage. Having arranged with the postilions that the two carriages should not change horses at the same places, they easily passed unseen by him, while, thinking of nothing so little as their proximity, he sat in state before the door of a village inn.

Just as Mr. Galbraith was beginning to hope the major had contrived a new approach to the place, the carriage took an unexpected turn, and he found presently they were climbing, by a zig-zag road, the height over the Lorrie burn; but the place was no longer his, and to avoid a sense of humiliation, he avoided taking any interest in the change.

A young woman—it was Donal's eldest sister, but he knew nothing of her—opened the door to him, and showed him up the stair to his old study. There a great fire was burning; but, beyond that, everything, even to the trifles on his writing table, was just as when last he left the house. His chair stood in its usual position by the fire, and wine and biscuits were on a little table near.

"Very considerate!" he said to himself. "I trust the major does not mean to keep me waiting, though. Deuced hard to have to leave a place like this!"

Weary with his journey he fell into a doze, dreamed of his dead wife, woke suddenly, and heard the door of the room open. There was Major

Culsalmon entering with outstretched hand! and there was a lady—his wife doubtless! But how young the major was! he had imagined him a man in middle age at least!—Bless his soul! was he never to get rid of this impostor fellow! it was not the major! it was the rascal calling himself Sir Gilbert Galbraith!—the half-witted wretch his fool of a daughter insisted on marrying! Here he was, ubiquitous as Satan! And—bless his soul again! there was the minx, Jenny! looking as if the place was her own! The silly tears in her eyes too!—It was all too absurd! He had just been dreaming of his dead wife, and clearly that was it! he was not awake yet!

He tried hard to wake, but the dream mastered him.

"Jenny!" he said, as the two stood for a moment regarding him, a little doubtfully, but with smiles of welcome, "what is the meaning of this? I did not know Major Culsalmon had invited you! And what is this person doing here?"

"Papa," replied Ginevra, with a curious smile, half merry, half tearful, "this person is my husband, Sir Gilbert Galbraith of Glashruach; and you are at home in your own study again."

"Will you never have done masquerading, Jenny?" he returned. "Inform Major Culsalmon that I request to see him immediately."

He turned towards the fire, and took up a newspaper. They thought it better to leave him. As he sat, by degrees the truth grew plain to him. But not one other word on the matter did the man utter to the day of his death. When dinner was announced, he walked straight from the dining-room door to his former place at the foot of the table. But Robina Grant was equal to the occasion. She caught up the dish before him, and set it at the side. There Gibbie seated himself; and, after a moment's hesitation, Ginevra placed herself opposite her husband.

The next day Gibbie provided him with something to do. He had the chest of papers found in the Auld Hoose o' Galbraith carried into his study, and the lawyer found both employment and interest for weeks in deciphering and arranging them. Amongst many others concerning the property, its tenures, and boundaries, appeared some papers which, associated and compared, threw considerable doubt on the way in which portions of it had changed hands, and passed from those of Gibbie's ancestors into those of Ginevra's—who were lawyers as well as Galbraiths; and the laird was keen of scent as any nose-hound after dishonesty in other people. In the course of a fortnight he found himself so much at home in his old quarters, and so much interested in those papers and his books, that when Sir Gilbert informed him Ginevra and he were going back to the city, he pronounced it decidedly the better plan, seeing he was there himself to look after affairs.

For the rest of the winter, therefore, Mr. Galbraith played the grand seigneur as before among the tenants of Glashruach.

LXII

The Burn

The moment they were settled in the Auld Hoose, Gibbie resumed the habits of the former winter, which Mistress Croale's failure had interrupted. And what a change it was to Ginevra—from imprisonment to ministration! She found difficulties at first, as may readily be believed. But presently came help. As soon as Mistress Croale heard of their return, she went immediately to Lady Galbraith, one morning while Sir Gibbie was at college, literally knelt at her feet, and with tears told her the whole tale, beseeching her intercession with Sir Gibbie.

"I want naething," she insisted, "but his fawvour, an' the licht o' his bonnie coontenance."

The end of course was that she was gladly received again into the house, where once more she attended to all the principal at least of her former duties. Before she died, there was a great change and growth in her: she was none of those before whom pearls must not be cast.

Every winter, for many years, Sir Gilbert and Lady Galbraith occupied the Auld Hoose; which by degrees came at length to be known as the refuge of all that were in honest distress, the salvation of all in themselves such as could be helped, and a covert for the night to all the houseless, of whatever sort, except those drunk at the time. Caution had to be exercised, and judgment used; the caution was tender and the judgment stern. The next year they built a house in a sheltered spot on Glashgar, and thither from the city they brought many invalids, to spend the summer months under the care of Janet and her daughter Robina, whereby not a few were restored sufficiently to earn their bread for a time thereafter.

The very day the session was over, they returned to Glashruach, where they were received by the laird, as he was still called, as if they had been guests. They found Joseph, the old butler, reinstated, and Angus again acting as gamekeeper. Ginevra welcomed Joseph, but took the first opportunity of telling Angus that for her father's sake Sir Gilbert allowed him to remain, but on the first act of violence he should at once be dismissed, and probably prosecuted as well. Donal's eldest brother was made bailiff. Before long Gibbie got the other two also about him, and as soon as, with justice, he was able, settled them together upon one of his farms. Every Saturday, so long as Janet lived, they met, as in the old times, at the cottage—only with Ginevra in the place of the absent Donal. More to her own satisfaction, after all, than Robert's, Janet went home first,—"to be at han'," she said, "to open the door till him whan he chaps." Then Robert went to his sons below on their farm, where he was well taken care of; but happily he did not remain long behind his wife. That first summer, Nicie returned to Glashruach to wait on Lady Galbraith, was more her friend than her servant, and when she married, was settled on the estate.

For some little time Ginevra was fully occupied in getting her house in order, and furnishing the new part of it. When that was done, Sir Gilbert gave an entertainment to his tenants. The laird preferred a trip to the city, "on business," to the humiliation of being present as other than the greatest; though perhaps he would have minded it less had he ever himself given a dinner to his tenants.

Robert and Janet declined the invitation.

"We're ower auld for makin' merry 'cep' in oor ain herts," said Janet. "But bide ye, my bonny Sir Gibbie, till we're a' up yon'er, an' syne we'll see."

The place of honour was therefore given to Jean Mavor, who was beside herself with joy to see her broonie lord of the land, and be seated beside him in respect and friendship. But her brother said it was "clean ridic'lous;" and not to the last would consent to regard the new laird as other than half-witted, insisting that everything was done by his wife, and that the talk on his fingers was a mere pretence.

When the main part of the dinner was over, Sir Gilbert and his lady stood at the head of the table, and, he speaking by signs and she interpreting, made a little speech together. In the course of it Sir Gibbie took occasion to apologize for having once disturbed the peace of the country-side by acting the supposed part of a broonie, and in relating his adventures of the time, accompanied his wife's text with such graphic illustration of gesture, that his audience laughed at the merry tale till the tears ran down their cheeks. Then with a few allusions to his strange childhood, he thanked the God who led him through thorny ways into the very arms of love and peace in the cottage of Robert and Janet Grant, whence, and not from the fortune he had since inherited, came all his peace.

"He desires me to tell you," said Lady Galbraith, "that he was a stranger, and you folk of Daurside took him in, and if ever he can do a kindness to you or yours, he will.—He desires me also to say, that you ought not to be left ignorant that you have a poet of your own, born and bred among you—Donal Grant, the son of Robert and Janet, the friend of Sir Gilbert's heart, and one of the noblest of men. And he begs you to allow me to read you a poem he had from him this very morning—probably just written. It is called The Laverock. I will read it as well as I can. If any of you do not like poetry, he says—I mean Sir Gilbert says—you can go to the kitchen and light your pipes, and he will send your wine there to you."

She ceased. Not one stirred, and she read the verses—which, for the sake of having Donal in at the last of my book, I will print. Those who do not care for verse, may—metaphorically, I would not be rude—go and smoke their pipes in the kitchen.

The Laverock. (lark)

The Man Says:

Laverock i' the lift, (sky)
Hae ye nae sang-thrift,
'At ye scatter't sae heigh, an' lat it a' drift?
Wasterfu' laverock!

Dinna ye ken
'At ye hing ower men
Wha haena a sang or a penny to spen'?
Hertless laverock!

But up there, you,
I' the bow o' the blue,
Haud skirlin' on as gien a' war new! (keep shrilling)
Toom-heidit laverock! (empty-headed)

Haith! ye're ower blythe:
I see a great scythe
Swing whaur yer nestie lies, doon i' the lythe, (shelter)
Liltin' laverock!

Eh, sic a soon'!
Birdie, come doon—

Ye're fey to sing sic a merry tune, (death-doomed)
Gowkit laverock! (silly)

Come to yer nest;
Yer wife's sair prest;
She's clean worn oot wi' duin' her best,
Rovin' laverock!

Winna ye haud?
Ye're surely mad!
Is there naebody there to gie ye a daud? (blow)
Menseless laverock!

Come doon an' conform;
Pyke an honest worm,
An' hap yer bairns frae the muckle sturm,
Spendrife laverock!

The Bird Sings:

My nestie it lieth
I' the how o' a han'; (hollow)
The swing o' the scythe
'Ill miss 't by a span.

The lift it's sae cheerie!
The win' it's sae free!
I hing ower my dearie,
An' sing 'cause I see.

My wifie's wee breistie
Grows warm wi' my sang,
An' ilk crumpled-up beastie
Kens no to think lang.

Up here the sun sings, but
He only shines there!
Ye haena nae wings, but
Come up on a prayer.

The Man Sings:

Ye wee daurin' cratur,
Ye rant an' ye sing
Like an oye o' auld Natur' (grandchild)
Ta'en hame by the King!

Ye wee feathert priestie,
Yer bells i' yer thro't.
Yer altar yer breistie
Yer mitre forgot—

Offerin' an' Aaron,
Ye burn hert an' brain
An' dertin' an' daurin
Flee back to yer ain

Ye wee minor prophet,
It's 'maist my belief
'At I'm doon i' Tophet,
An' you abune grief!

Ye've deavt me an' daudit, (deafened) (buffeted)
An' ca'd me a fule:
I'm nearhan' persuaudit
To gang to your schule!

For, birdie, I'm thinkin'
Ye ken mair nor me—
Gien ye haena been drinkin',
An' sing as ye see.

Ye maun hae a sicht 'at
Sees geyan far ben; (considerably) (inwards)
An' a hert for the micht o' 't
Wad sair for nine men! (serve)

Somebody's been till
Roun to ye wha (whisper)

Said birdies war seen till
E'en whan they fa'!

After the reading of the poem, Sir Gilbert and Lady Galbraith withdrew, and went towards the new part of the house, where they had their rooms. On the bridge, over which Ginevra scarcely ever passed without stopping to look both up and down the dry channel in the rock, she lingered as usual, and gazed from its windows. Below, the waterless bed of the burn opened out on the great valley of the Daur; above was the landslip, and beyond it the stream rushing down the mountain. Gibbie pointed up to it. She gazed a while, and gave a great sigh. He asked her—their communication was now more like that between two spirits: even signs had become almost unnecessary—what she wanted or missed. She looked in his face and said, "Naething but the sang o' my burnie, Gibbie." He took a small pistol from his pocket, and put it in her hand; then, opening the window, signed to her to fire it. She had never fired a pistol, and was a little frightened, but would have been utterly ashamed to shrink from anything Gibbie would have her do. She held it out. Her hand trembled. He laid his upon it, and it grew steady. She pulled the trigger, and dropped the pistol with a little cry. He signed to her to listen. A moment passed, and then, like a hugely magnified echo, came a roar that rolled from mountain to mountain, like a thunder drum. The next instant, the landslip seemed to come hurrying down the channel, roaring and leaping: it was the mud-brown waters of the burn, careering along as if mad with joy at having regained their ancient course. Ginevra stared with parted lips, delight growing to apprehension as the live thing momently neared the bridge. With tossing mane of foam, the brown courser came rushing on, and shot thundering under. They turned, and from the other window saw it tumbling headlong down the steep descent to the Lorrie. By quick gradations, even as they gazed, the mud melted away; the water grew clearer and clearer, and in a few minutes a small mountain-river, of a lovely lucid brown, transparent as a smoke-crystal, was dancing along under the bridge. It had ceased its roar and was sweetly singing.

"Let us see it from my room, Gibbie," said Ginevra.

They went up, and from the turret window looked down upon the water. They gazed until, like the live germ of the gathered twilight, it was scarce to be distinguished but by abstract motion.

"It's my ain burnie," said Ginevra, "an' it's ain auld sang! I'll warran' it hasna forgotten a note o''t! Eh, Gibbie, ye gie me a' thing!"

"Gien I was a burnie, wadna I rin!" sang Gibbie, and Ginevra heard the words, though Gibbie could utter only the air he had found for them so long ago. She threw herself into his arms, and hiding her face on his shoulder, clung silent to her silent husband. Over her lovely bowed head, he gazed into the cool spring night, sparkling with stars, and shadowy with mountains. His eyes climbed the stairs of Glashgar to the lonely peak dwelling among the lights of God; and if upon their way up the rocks they met no visible sentinels of heaven, he needed neither ascending stairs nor descending angels, for a better than the angels was with them.

bookfinity™

Discover more of your favorite classics with Bookfinity™.

- Track your reading with custom book lists.
- Get great book recommendations for your personalized Reader Type.
- Add reviews for your favorite books.
- AND MUCH MORE!

Visit **bookfinity.com** and take the fun Reader Type quiz to get started.

Enjoy our classic and modern companion pairings!

Classic & Modern

9 781513 272283